LAST DITCH

Caught Dead in Wyoming
Book 4

Patricia McLinn

✧ ✧ ✧ ✧

Copyright © Patricia McLinn
ISBN: 978-1-939215-62-8
Second Print Edition
www.PatriciaMcLinn.com

Dear Readers: If you encounter typos or errors in this book, please send them to me
at Patricia@patriciamclinn.com. Even with many layers of editing, mistakes can slip
through, alas. But, together, we can eradicate the nasty nuisances. Thank you!
– Patricia McLinn

DAY ONE

MONDAY

Chapter One

THE STIR IN the KWMT-TV newsroom occurred at four-twenty-six p.m.

Newsroom stirs come in many varieties.

There are those rare history-making events that everyone—journalist or not—remembers. How they heard the news, where they were, what they were doing. Those moments when, at least during that initial jolt, you forget you're a journalist.

Then there are journalist-first major news stories that are so good they rouse an entire newsroom, whether you're working on the story or not.

More frequent are the exciting-person-is-visiting stirs. Presidents, certain prime ministers, a rare Supreme Court Justice, an even rarer Nobel Peace Prize winner. And, of course, movie stars. Movie stars are always good for a stir.

This stir didn't have the gravitas of a major event. Besides, there were no bulletins on the wire, which I'd been idly checking while waiting for someone to answer the call I'd just made.

And if there was any reason a president, prime minister, Supreme Court justice, Nobel Peace Prize winner, or movie star happened to be in Sherman, Wyoming, it was beyond my imagination.

For that matter, the reason *I* was in Sherman, Wyoming was often beyond my imagination.

My chair only turned to the right, so to see the cause of the newsroom stir ninety degrees to my left I pivoted three-quarters of the way around.

Thomas David Burrell.

Tom was a rancher in Cottonwood County, and well thought of by most of its citizens. And, yes, he had a certain something that draws a fair number of people to his rough-hewn face and tall, lanky body. But I wouldn't have predicted that his arrival would produce an exciting-person stir.

Except his purposeful stride and tight jaw added a potential layer of Big Story, especially since he was headed straight for the closed office door of News Director Les Haeburn.

I stood, disconnecting the phone as my source answered, and went after Tom.

His knock was somewhere between perfunctory and nonexistent. He'd swung open the door and strode up to Haeburn's desk as I reached the room.

"Haeburn. I'm Tom Burrell. We—"

I spoke over Haeburn's flustered half-syllables as I came up beside the newsroom-stirrer. "Tom?"

He didn't look at or answer me. We'd had our issues, but never to that extent. "—need your help to put out a call for volunteers for a search. Immediately."

I swallowed the *Oh God* that tried to come first, and demanded, "Tamantha?"

His daughter was formidable, yet there were dangers that could find any living soul. Even formidable third-graders.

Tom still didn't look at me, but he reached out and rested a large hand on my shoulder. "She's fine, Elizabeth."

"Hey, I heard—Tom? What's going on?" We'd been joined by KWMT-TV's sports anchor, Mike Paycik. Actually, as a hometown sports hero who'd made it to the National Football League for a respectable career, then returned here to serve his apprenticeship in TV, he provided the station more than simply a sports anchor.

What he was to me—if anything more than a respected colleague and sometimes fellow ad hoc investigator—remained to be seen.

Whether part of the reason it was unseen was Thomas David Burrell also remained to be seen.

"It's Brian Walterston, Connie's husband. He's missing," Tom said.

"I thought he was in a wheelchair," Mike said.

"He is. But he has a special wheelchair so he can get around some outside. Connie got back from Cody and he's gone and so is the wheelchair."

"He must be in one of the ranch buildings—"

"She's looked. Connie wouldn't yell fire unless there's a fire. He's gone. Somewhere beyond the home ranch."

"That's too bad," Haeburn said woodenly. "But what—"

"He can die out there. Sun'll set before long and a man in his condition might not last the night. Even if it is warm for October. We need to find him. Fast. To do that we need as many pairs of eyes as we can get. Break into your show and—"

"Break into—We can't!" Haeburn gasped.

"Ask the Heathertons. Or I'll talk to them."

So, Tom knew the nearly mythical owners of the station. Knew them and was confident he could persuade them to his way of thinking.

"We can't interrupt programming," Haeburn repeated. "We've never—"

"Doesn't mean you can't," Mike snapped.

Faced with these two men, I could see Haeburn drawing back into the stubborn certainty of the weak, like a turtle into its shell.

"Possibly it can be mentioned during the five o'clock—"

"We need searchers now. This minute. Waiting could—"

"A crawl," I said. "We can put up a crawl."

"What's a crawl?" Now Tom did look at me, and there was something deep in his dark eyes that flicked at a nerve developed over years of journalism. There was something below the surface. Something he didn't intend to reveal.

"It's a moving message across the bottom of the screen. A ticker."

"Great idea," Mike said. "We'll get with graphics while Tom checks with the Heathertons about a special report."

"Special report?" Les squeaked. "A special report for a guy who's gone for a walk? That's out of—"

"He can't walk." Tom's flat tone stopped Haeburn.

I'd have to try that on Haeburn. My pointed remarks didn't always get through that turtle shell. Though it probably helped that Tom was half a foot taller, and significantly more muscled than KWMT-TV's news director.

"Where do you want people to report to, Tom? Okay to say who's missing? Tell them to bring supplies for a night search?"

"Red Sail Ranch. Yes and yes."

Tom already had his phone out. Figuring he had Haeburn in hand, Mike and I exited past a knot of staffers by the door.

Then Mike turned back toward the room. "I'll join the search as soon as we have this going. Won't take long," he told Tom.

"You can't. You're on air for the five." Haeburn was referring to the five o'clock broadcast, though Mike wouldn't be on until toward the end.

"I'll get Pauly in," Mike said of a stringer he used for sports coverage. "He can handle it."

"You're the one paid to handle it. You better be here, Paycik."

"I'm going to help with this search." He turned away.

"Me, too," I said to Mike.

He gave me a look. "It's going to be tough going over rough ground."

"I'm coming. There'll be something I can do."

Chapter Two

WHAT I'D DONE so far was keep Connie Walterston supplied with coffee and water as she sat outside her low-slung ranch house. Other people came by, saying a few words, touching her hand or shoulder, then moving on and letting the next in.

Red Sail Ranch was east and some south of Sherman in the area of Cottonwood County known as "low side." Here the soil wasn't as fertile, the land not as valuable as the "high side," which climbed toward the mountains and benefited from more generous moisture. Since it took more acres to support the same number of cattle, low side ranches tended to be larger. Which did not help the search efforts.

Beyond the Walterston house and main outbuildings, land stretched flat to the south with cattle visible in the distance. In every other direction was what Mike called broken ground. Not a bad term, considering the way gullies, creeks, and fissures slashed the landscape, exposing bands and ribs of red rock.

A search command center occupied an open area in front of the solid house. Weeds warred with wilted perennials in a front flowerbed, dust dimmed the windows, and dried mud trailed up the steps to a wide porch. I suspected Brian's long illness explained these signs of recent inattention.

Tables stretched across a three-sided tent's open fourth side. Several people—including Tom Burrell—worked from behind the tables.

Deputies gathered inside the tent, each holding a coffee cup. I recognized Deputy Wayne Shelton's short, stocky frame and Richard Alvaro's slim build among a half dozen others, some wearing uniforms from a neighboring county.

People signed in on sheets on clipboards and were given paper maps along with GPS coordinates for devices. These would be the next batch of searchers dispatched, following earlier groups Mike had pointed out departing as we'd arrived.

Connie exuded determined calm, but clutched the chair arms when I didn't keep a cup in her hands.

I'd met Connie this past summer at the house of Mike's Aunt Gee.

What had first impressed me was that Connie's three sons had put a serious dent in Aunt Gee's Sunday dinner spread—quite an accomplishment.

Then Connie had come over and said "Thank you." I'd had no idea what I might have done that warranted thanks from this pleasant stranger.

She told me she ran the office for the road construction outfit Tom Burrell operated in addition to ranching. Business had dried up when he'd become prime suspect in a disappearance, leaving her feeling she wasn't earning her pay. But—according to her—business quickly picked up after Tom was cleared as a result of digging Mike and I did.

She hadn't given details, but I'd picked up that her job was vital because there'd been an issue with insurance and medical coverage for her husband's illness.

Now, a gray-haired woman came up to Connie. I rose, gestured her to my chair, and moved away.

I scanned the crowd, noting familiar faces.

Caswell Newton stood amid a knot of six teenage boys. He was the nephew of Linda Caswell, one of the county's leading citizens. He was also the son of my former landlord Stan Newton. A very mixed bag.

A ranch foreman Mike had worked for as a boy was alone, appearing half asleep and watching everything. I'd wager he'd be good in a search party.

I was less enthusiastic to see Hiram Poppinger, who owned a ranch in the northeast part of the county. He had a short fuse combined with a penchant for taking matters into his own hands.

Diana Stendahl, my favorite cameraperson, was there, though not on behalf of KWMT-TV. Each group of volunteers included at least one law enforcement person and a civilian leader. Diana was one of the civilian leaders.

She was a widow, raising two good kids, working full-time, leasing out her land to keep the ranch intact for the next generation. She'd also become my landlady recently, and she was my friend.

More and more people kept coming. It was hard to keep track. I did a second pan.

"What're you looking for?" Mike asked from beside me, having finished signing up. He didn't wait for an answer. "The sons? Oldest's at college. Jaden."

I almost made the mistake of asking how he knew that's who I'd been looking for. Bad enough to have him read my mind, no sense giving him the all-clear to celebrate it.

"UW," he added. "Tom's got someone driving him home. Second son, that's Kade, is in the official tent with Shelton. Haven't seen Austin, but—"

"Mike Paycik. Haven't seen you since you returned from the bright lights and big city." A cowboy-hatted man about Mike's age had come up on his other side.

Mike's bright lights and big cities had been during his NFL career, playing for the Chicago Bears. The majority of Cottonwood County treated him like a demi-god. It was to his credit that he didn't take it too seriously.

"Ted. How are you?"

They shook with enthusiasm. I had the impression their voices were subdued only because of the circumstances.

My attention had been drawn in another direction.

You know that test where you have to find one item that isn't like the others?

I'd just spotted the unlike item in this crowd.

Even without being surrounded by cowboy hats and ball caps, the pork pie hat this guy wore would have looked wrong. It sat too high on his big round head, emphasizing a flat, round face, making him look as if he'd borrowed his father's hat. Maybe his black leather coat was also borrowed, because it covered his round middle only under the protest of straining buttons.

Another reason he looked so out of place was the to-the-knees length of his coat. Every other man and most of the women wore jackets to their waists, their hips at most. The better to ride a horse, I suspected. Not this guy.

A stir rippled through the gathering and shifted my attention.

I recognized the youngest Walterston brother from that meal at Aunt Gee's. He hurried toward his mother, apparently having just arrived.

Kade came out of the tent and intercepted him near Connie. There were low, intense words, then Connie rose, gripping each son by the upper arm and saying something low and sharp.

Kade broke away and strode back toward the tables. Connie sat and at her nod, Austin took the chair beside her, his head down. She patted his leg, then stroked his shirt sleeve. In contrast to his older brother's work clothes, his jeans were clean and new, his yellow shirt neatly pressed.

From the corner of my eye I spotted Mr. Pork Pie Hat on the move.

He'd reached the sheriff's department tent when he was stopped by a deputy. When Shelton emerged, he tried to attach himself. Shelton stiff-armed him—sending the guy stumbling—and kept going.

Shelton didn't even treat me that badly. So Pork Pie Hat must really be persona non grata.

"Listen up." Deputy Shelton had stepped onto a chair, unabashedly using its height to make up for his lack. "As you know, each of you has been assigned to a team led by a deputy." He gestured to deputies now taking spots around the rim of the group. "When we break, go to your deputy and form up your assigned teams. Don't stray. Your leader knows the area you're covering. We sent a few early groups out and we don't want you covering the same territory. Most all of you are experienced, but it can't hurt to remind you—take no chances. The first order is to not get yourself lost or hurt. Because we'll be pissed if you slow us the hell down."

A low murmur conveyed appreciation for his priorities.

Shelton gave brief, direct instructions about never losing connection with the group. To be sure their assigned territory was covered before moving on to the next. To check in when they finished each assigned area—if there was no cell service, send someone back to report.

"Brian was in the house and okay when Connie left the house at eleven this morning. He wasn't in the house when Kade returned at two forty-five. Connie—"

"I thought he was with Mom," Kade said.

Shelton didn't talk over him, but didn't let the interruption detour him, either. "—called in the report at three fifty-five when she got home. That means at least an hour and possibly five hours he's been gone.

"We're working on the theory Brian was in his all-terrain chair. So he could get farther than walking, but it's still limited on what ground it can get over. We're searching on foot, looking for signs. Best we can tell, Brian was wearing a pale blue shirt, khaki colored pants. But don't get hung up on that. Don't ignore other colors because we can't be sure he didn't have a jacket or some such.

"We're short on daylight, so work fast, but even more important, work careful and work sure. You all know Connie and Brian. You know they'd be the first in line to help you in any kind of trouble. Enough said. Go."

Mike and I made eye contact. He nodded, then headed to his assigned group.

Connie's mug was full and with the groups heading out, room opened near the tables. I moved closer, yet staying well to the side so I didn't get in the way. I also was staying away from a knot of women heading into the house. I didn't want to get swept inside.

My maneuvering put me close to the official tent. A happy coincidence. That's all.

One word snagged my attention: "candidates."

The county had been short a sheriff and a county attorney for months. One had resigned. The other hadn't. I'd been involved in both events.

County attorney and sheriff were elected positions, unlike judge— yes, Cottonwood County was short one of those, too—who was appointed, then subject to a pass-fail retention election. The replacement judge had been named quickly amid general approval.

The county attorney and sheriff jobs each had more than three years left on their elected terms, which meant the replacements were essentially incumbents for the next election and incumbents are notoriously difficult to dislodge.

The only known candidate for either job was the acting sheriff.

A good journalist would have leads on more candidates, but KWMT-TV anchor Thurston Fine insisted he alone covered local politics, so viewers didn't even know the acting sheriff was interested. I knew that—and that the acting county attorney was not interested in the job—from reading coverage in the *Independence* by editor and publisher Needham Bender.

The political party of the elected-but-now-departed officeholder selects three candidates and the Cottonwood County commissioners choose which will fill the term. I also learned that from the *Independence*.

I'd have to corner Needham over coffee—or maybe dinner, along with his wife Thelma—to pump him.

The breeze shifted and I heard Deputy Lloyd Sampson say, "...out of towners. Both of them. The guy they want for county attorney has someone he wants to bring in as sheriff. They go way back and he's making it a two-fer."

Interesting.

A voice—young and harsh—rose, pulling me away from contemplation of Cottonwood County politics.

"I'm going," the voice said. "Dammit, I'm going. I don't care what you say."

"We're both going."

It was Connie's two sons, Austin had joined his older brother at the tables, standing shoulder to shoulder and daring Tom to say otherwise. They didn't even look at Shelton.

Tom said something low, though I caught the words "stay," "mother" and "need"—plenty to guess what he was saying.

"Others can. I'm going."

"*We're* going," corrected Austin for a second time.

"We'll handle this first." This time Tom's voice was full of command. At his gesture, the boys stepped aside, looking stubborn and unhappy, but no longer blocking two people coming to the table, writing their names, taking the information, then catching up with departing search groups.

Tom wrote down a couple more names of stragglers, then looked up to see me approaching the tables.

"Elizabeth? You're not—"

"No, I'm not volunteering for search duty. I know my limitations. But I can stay here with Connie so perhaps—" I tipped my head in the direction of the two boys.

He shot a look—not toward them, but toward Connie. "You sure?"

"Yes."

"Okay. Thanks." He turned to Deputy Shelton. "Wayne?"

"I've got to stay. You go ahead, Tom. Looks like we've got more coming in."

I turned to see that the newcomers were in three pickups. That was no surprise. Most of the vehicles now lining the ranch road were pickups. But a sense of instant chill as the trucks' occupants emerged was both surprising and in contrast to the quiet connection among the other searchers.

A young couple climbed out of the first pickup, the woman with awkward movements explained by her very pregnant belly.

The driver of the next truck had gray stubble, worn but clean clothes, and scowl lines dug into his face.

His scowl deepened as the third driver, a solid young man, started to pass him, apparently heading for the couple. The older man grasped his arm and said something. The third driver jerked away, but slowed his gait to stay beside the older man.

The two from the first pickup quickly decoupled, with the woman heading toward the house without stopping by where Connie sat and the man coming toward the sign-in table.

Shelton shot a look at the newcomers and called out to the last group of searchers, the one led by Deputy Richard Alvaro, which had only made it a few yards away, "Hold up."

The older man and the driver of the third pickup reached the table.

"What the hell you doing bringing her out here?" Driver 3 demanded of Driver 1.

"Wasn't going to leave her on her own in her condition. I don't desert—"

That's enough," Shelton snapped. "Terry, Kade, Austin, you hustle up and get with Richard Alvaro's group. Go on now."

Driver 1—by process of elimination, Terry—glared around at all and sundry, but obeyed the order.

"Three for you, Alvaro," Shelton shouted. "Send back the Baranski boys and Newton."

Clearly, he was juggling the groups to separate Terry and Driver 3.

The deputy nodded. As soon as Terry and the Walterston boys had joined his group, they resumed moving away.

In a few more minutes, Tom departed with a smaller group consisting of Driver 3, the older man I thought of as Driver 2, two cowboy-looking men I hadn't recognized but guessed were the "Baranski boys," and young Cas Newton.

I looked toward the sun sliding closer to the horizon.

In June, being this far north created long days and leisurely twilights, but now the Wyoming skies made up for those generous summer days by chopping them ever shorter. Sunset would come by seven with maybe another half hour of twilight.

As I turned toward the coffee maker, the back door of the house squeaked open, releasing the sound of female voices and what sounded like thin, high-pitched crying, then slapped closed.

A woman came out, hips swaying despite her speed. She shot a look toward Connie, now seated alone by a camp table, then altered her route, her new path bringing her toward me.

"You're smart to be out here." She poured herself a cup of coffee.

"I could not take one more minute of it in there."

She leaned her hips against the table. She was dark-haired, small, and attractive.

"You'd think she's the first person to ever be pregnant the way they're all over her. And before you blast me for being an unnatural female who doesn't like babies, it's not that. It's all the tears. I swear someone could say hello to her and she'd start crying."

Her gaze narrowed at the sound of a distant pickup, then relaxed with what might have been disappointment when it passed the turnoff to the Walterstons' ranch.

"At least half of them are all over her," she amended. "The other half are busy tutting themselves into a frenzy over her morals." Her long nose twitched slightly. In some people that might have indicated outrage, but I didn't get that sense with her.

"You know the story, don't you?" she asked.

She didn't wait for my answer.

"You wouldn't think it to look at her, but Hannah Chaney was having an affair. Worse, she got caught. And then she compounded all that by getting pregnant. Word is she doesn't know which one is the father. Husband gets in a miff and kicks her out, though any idiot can see he's not over her. Of course she goes to the boyfriend. Who happens to live practically next door. Then she's all dewy-eyed—well, I was going to say innocence, but that doesn't fit the situation, now does it? Make it dewy-eyed ignorance. Anyway, she genuinely seemed surprised they're about ready to kill each other. And that makes her cry even more."

Ah. This could explain the atmosphere and dialogue among the occupants of those three late-arriving trucks. I pegged Driver 3 as the outraged but still ensnared husband and Terry/Driver 1 as the sheltering boyfriend. Driver 2, apparently, was a concerned onlooker.

The woman shook her head.

"It must be the male instinct to go for good breeding stock, because it's sure not brains they're seeing in that girl. Even Do— Speaking of not brains," she said quickly, trying to mask the broken reference, "I sure haven't displayed mine, have I? I just realized—

you're that reporter on TV, aren't you? I should have declared this was all on background or something before I opened my mouth. You won't do an exposé on me gossiping about my neighbors, will you?"

I gave a perfunctory smile. "Not unless it has to do with consumer affairs. I'm Elizabeth Margaret Danniher. I do the 'Helping Out' segment."

I extended a hand. She met it. Not a full-fledged shake as I would have expected, but one of those fingertips-only gestures. It surprised me. She didn't seem the type. That kind of handshake always gives me an uneasy feeling that the handshaker—and it's mostly women who default to this style—might expect her hand to be kissed.

"Loriana. We're neighbors of the Walterstons. Me for only the past couple of years, but Don—that's Don Hazen—for longer. We have the next spread over." She tipped her head to the north. "Such a shame about Brian. You know he's had terminal liver cancer?"

I shook my head. I'd known he was very ill, but no one had given specifics and, for once, I hadn't asked.

"Not that he was a drinker or a needle-using druggie or anything like that. The doctors think he got Hepatitis C from a blood transfusion when he was a teenager—that was back before they knew to screen for Hepatitis C. It damaged his liver and that led to the cancer. He'd smoked for a number of years, drank—not to excess—but with Hep C that makes it a lot worse. Even taking over the counter meds for aches and pains all ranchers get probably made it worse. It was the perfect storm. Never showed symptoms until too late. Apparently what he was most concerned about was Connie and the boys. But they've all tested clean, so he didn't have that worry." She sighed. "I guess it's understandable."

I met her gaze, indicating interest.

"His doing this. With the liver cancer so advanced, I mean. Wouldn't have been long. You know that's where Connie was today— talking to hospice services, picking a few to come out and meet him."

Another pickup made itself heard and she focused on the entry again.

"Waiting for someone?" I asked.

"He said he was going to join the search, so I assumed— Unless…" Her gaze darted toward the house. I could almost swear I heard crying. "But maybe he went out on his own. That must be what happened. He went out on his own." Her mouth formed a perfect smile. Her eyes didn't join the fun. "Don's an independent cuss. Probably approached the search from where our property meets the Walterstons'."

Why did I have the feeling she was trying to persuade herself?

"That's not the best for coordinating what's been searched and what hasn't, is it?" I asked mildly.

She shrugged. "As I said, he's independent. Doesn't like taking orders from, uh, anybody. Besides, he knows that area well, so he could cover it faster on his own than waiting for somebody else. Then again, it's not a real likely spot for Brian to be, so Don probably figures he can do his neighborly duty without much risk of actually seeing Brian."

This time her smile not only didn't reach her eyes, but her lips seemed to receive a mixed signal.

"Oh?" I asked neutrally.

She hitched a shoulder as she settled back to sit on the table. "They've had run-ins—Don and Brian. Some folks might be surprised Don stirred himself at all to search, but he really does care about the area. You know how it is. People both caring passionately about the same thing but with different ideas about how it should be done, letting their tempers get the better of them. Anyway, that's another reason he wouldn't want to join the main search. He wouldn't want to hear anybody else's opinion about his showing up."

I had no response ready, so I was glad to see another pickup arriving. "More searchers, I hope," I said.

"Mmm," she responded.

When the driver emerged, I recognized Needham Bender, editor and publisher of the *Independence*, and the best journalist I'd encountered here, short of Penny Czylinski. But since Penny only disseminated her work by telling those who passed through her checkout lane at the Sherman Supermarket, I don't know if she officially qualified.

As Needham neared, he raised a hand in greeting, which both Loriana and I returned silently, then he headed for Connie. He sat, resting one hand on her shoulder.

The door of the house opened again and Pork Pie Hat emerged, holding a plate of food.

Loriana grunted. "Think I'll brave going back inside now."

The timing left the impression that Pork Pie Hat's emergence prompted that decision.

"Who is that?" I asked as he headed toward Connie and Needham.

"Rich Taylorman. An insurance broker."

"What kind of insurance?"

"Any kind that will make him money. Crops to start. But then he added medical, life." Her tone dropped on the last word and her gaze went to Connie.

Abruptly, she stood. "You want to come in with me? The human water fountain has to dry up some time. Even if it hasn't it's preferable to him."

"No thanks. I'll take my chances."

Once she'd departed, I poured two mugs of coffee and headed toward Connie and the two men.

"...you must have some idea of where he went, and if you don't tell me, if you don't cooperate with me fully, that can be fraud," Rich Taylorman was saying to Connie.

Needham rose quickly. Before he could do anything that might get him in trouble, I stepped between the two men and extended a mug toward Connie.

Damned if Taylorman didn't shift his plate to one hand and reach for the mug.

I avoided his reach by turning away from him, saying over my shoulder. "This is for Connie."

She took it without any sign of recognizing what she held or what was going on around her.

"Fine. Give me the other one."

I turned to him, both hands encircling the mug. "No. It's mine.

The coffee pot's over there."

He curled his lips back in what might have been meant as a snarl. It lost impact because of a kernel of corn between his front teeth.

Needham clapped a hand on my shoulder. I saw that the danger of his doing something rash was past.

"Stay here with Connie, will you, Elizabeth? I'm going to go talk to Wayne."

In other circumstances I might have ribbed him about trying to get ahead of me on a story. Not now.

"I'm coming with," Taylorman said, starting after him, plate still in hand.

Needham gave me a rueful look over his shoulder and I was sure he'd sacrificed himself to draw the insurance broker away from Connie.

A good journalist and a good man.

Chapter Three

"**More coffee. Black.**"

Connie didn't look up at my announcement, just took the mug from my hands. Again.

I'd lost count of how many times we'd done this now.

She'd gone inside briefly once—probably a result of the coffee I kept plying her with. Other than that, we sat together in silence. Waiting.

I shivered out of nowhere. Perhaps from the abrupt departure of the cup's warmth. Perhaps not.

The sun had set, twilight had given up, requiring electric lights on tall poles to illuminate the open area. The light poles were supplemented by fires burning in barrels.

"Winter's coming on," Connie said.

It was the first thing she'd said to me other than mumbled thanks for a mug delivery.

"Winter? It's barely fall." Weather—as long as it was theoretical and not the specific conditions her wheelchair-bound husband might be facing—seemed a safe topic.

"Uh-huh," she said.

So much for the weather.

But she surprised me by turning her head toward me as I sat beside her again. For the first time I thought she truly knew I was there.

"I was sorry to hear about your house burning down and destroying your car, Elizabeth. But so relieved you and your dog are okay. I should have written a note or called to see if you needed help—"

"No, you shouldn't have." I put my hand on hers. It felt rough and bony. "We're fine. Diana Stendahl took us both in and I can't say the hovel is much of a loss."

The hovel had been my less-than-fond name for the furnished rental house I'd lived in from my arrival in Sherman last spring until it burned down. Not by accident. And with me in it. Almost to the bitter end.

"The hovel…" A flicker of light showed at the back of her eyes. "Appropriate." Then the light was gone and her next words were monotone. "Diana's a good person. Hard on her when she lost Gary with the kids so young."

Her silence held the thought that she had lost her husband, too. Certainly in one sense as his illness had progressed, then in another sense today, and possibly in the final sense tonight, depending on the result of this search. At least her kids weren't as young as Diana's had been.

"It was a terrible accident," I said, though I didn't know much about Gary Stendahl's death nearly a decade ago, only that it had been an accident on their ranch and Diana had lost the husband she loved and their kids had lost the father they loved, so by any definition it was terrible.

"Yes," she said woodenly. "An accident."

DAY TWO

TUESDAY

THERE WAS A stir.

Not the same as the one in the newsroom.

Then Tom had been a man on a mission and hadn't cared who knew. This stir rose from someone trying to not be noticed.

I saw Cas Newton return from the northeast. He reached the edge of the lighted area, and I caught a glint of light from his belt buckle. He skirted the light, making his way to Deputy Shelton.

There was no reaction from the deputy to whatever Cas said to him.

But after enough time for maybe three or four sentences, Shelton said something short to Deputy Sampson and then Shelton and Cas quietly started back the way Cas had come, around the edge of the light, then back to the northeast.

I stood. Belatedly, I gave the movement an excuse by asking Connie, "More coffee?"

She made a negative noise without looking up.

I ignored her refusal, but went the long way around for the coffee—stretching my legs, I'd say if anyone asked—but none of the few around appeared to notice.

Two steps into the dark, I knew I'd never find Cas and Shelton.

I stopped.

As much as I hated it, I was going to have to wait for the information to come to me.

Connie showed no sign of having noticed their departure or my detour.

Nothing happened during the next hour and three minutes. I refused to count how many times I checked my watch.

First, lights bobbed into sight, like fireflies stripped of their joy and pinned to the earth.

By the time flashlights became recognizable, there also was sound. Mostly footsteps. I also thought I caught Shelton's voice in full command mode, though words weren't distinguishable.

Shelton was the first into the light. He pocketed his phone and moved to the side, letting Tom Burrell step ahead, then fell in behind him as they came straight toward us. The others filing into the light held back.

Connie rose, and I realized I had, too.

Tom's granite-carved face gave little away, but his words were as direct and unwavering as his gaze on her face. "We found him, Connie. He's dead."

Chapter Four

THERE IS NO logic in grief. Anyone who thinks there is has not grieved.

At Tom's words, Connie's knees buckled and an anguished "Oh" streamed from her slack mouth.

It wasn't that she hadn't known the odds were against her husband, in his condition, out there. She clearly had known. On top of that she'd known—no one knew it better—that he would likely have died soon even if he'd been safely in his bed. I was certain she'd been grieving bit by bit for months.

Knowing and believing are two different things.

Now the worst had happened. Brian Walterston was dead.

She sagged. I reached for her. Tom was there first, and his hold didn't let her sink.

He said something to her. After a long moment she shook her head.

With his arm across her back and partially around her waist, he half-carried her up the porch steps and into the house. Shelton went ahead to hold the door.

Following, I could see around Tom to a tableau of women frozen into place by their first look at Connie.

I stepped to the side, letting others file in ahead of me. The dozen or more included Cas, Needham Bender, Rich Taylorman, and Drivers 2 and 3.

"You going in?" Shelton asked when he and I were the last ones on the porch.

"No."

He considered me an instant, then closed the door with himself outside, saying, "There's still work to do."

He started off the porch, heading toward his vehicle. Its radio was more reliable county-wide than cell service, though he'd clearly had service before.

None of those standing around the fires stopped him or asked any questions, though their eyes followed him.

I pulled out my phone and called the station, checking my watch. Not yet five a.m. No one would be there—unlike the places I'd worked where news was a twenty-four-hour operation—but I'd leave a message with the information I had so the earliest arrivals would have a head start. Also so they'd turn off the crawl requesting searchers who were no longer needed.

Official vehicles came up the drive. Shelton must have called them before returning. After consultation with Shelton, the lead one took on Sampson as a passenger, circled wider than the path the searchers had taken and led the others in close single-file. They were following good procedure to minimize the tracks left on the scene, even in a situation like this.

Search teams trickled in from many directions, looking haggard and sad as they blinked their way into the circle of light. Their voices were subdued. After signing out on the clip-boarded sheets some headed for their vehicles. Others got coffee and stood staring into the fires, not yet ready to leave.

First Diana's group, then Mike's came in. Each paused for a quiet word, then went inside. I remained where I was.

Deputy Richard Alvaro's group came in last. Utterly silent.

Brian's two sons took separate paths around the closest barrel fire, both heading for the house. Kade's jaw was clenched hard enough that I could see muscles throbbing as he passed. Behind him, Austin looked numb.

I watched them enter, then turned back in time to see Shelton take hold of Richard's arm and start him away from the fire. He talked rapidly, got one nod from Richard, then gave the younger man a slight push back out into the darkness, sending him in the direction taken by the team that had found Brian.

The radio in Shelton's vehicle squawked to life. I wasn't far away when he answered, but the incoming voice was too garbled to hear. Still, I heard Shelton say, "Found anything beyond the obvious?" Then, "No. Looked that way to me, too. But run it out all the way. Thorough never hurts."

The sound of the door opening behind me brought my head around. Diana stood in the doorway. She spotted me and tipped her head toward the inside.

It was a command. I obeyed.

There was no time to ask her "what?" because she backed away as soon as I had hold of the screen door.

Besides, by that time I could hear the "what."

"I want to see him." Connie's uninflected words had the stolidity of having been repeated several times.

Staring straight ahead, she said it to the room at large. Her sons looked at her. Everyone else looked at Tom.

Over a murmur of automatic protest from several women, I heard one voice say, "If she wants to see him..." I thought it was Loriana, the neighbor. Perhaps she, too, knew the illogic of grieving.

"That's not a good idea, Mom," said Kade.

She didn't look at him, but repeated in the same tone, "I want to see him."

"They'll bring him in, Connie. Wait and—"

"No. There. I want to see him where he is. Where he died. Now."

"Me, too."

It was the insurance man, Taylorman. No one paid him any attention.

Instead, all eyes went to the door. Deputy Shelton had come in behind me.

"Wayne," Connie said.

It sounded monotone to me, but maybe he heard more in it, because he shifted his gaze.

I followed the direction of his look to Tom, standing back from the center.

The worst had happened. I'd thought that just a few moments ago. Now, looking at Tom Burrell... Was there more? Was that what I'd seen in his eyes in Haeburn's office?

"I'm sorry, Connie, but proper procedure means—"

Shelton was cut off by the acting sheriff. "For God's sakes, Shelton, there's a time for procedure and a time for compassion."

Yes, it was the acting sheriff speaking to a subordinate, yet it wasn't an order. That was the power of Wayne Shelton.

Shelton's gaze flicked to his superior, then back to Tom.

There was no nod or other gesture from either man, but apparently there was agreement, because Tom was the one who spoke. "You'll need a coat, Connie."

Austin got a coat from the closet. He had to circle around his immobile brother to get to his mother, holding it for her to put on.

She looked at it a long moment then said, "No. I want your dad's. The blue one."

Kade spun around, yanked a jacket free of its hanger and shoved it toward his younger brother. Still holding the first one, Austin scrambled to bundle it in his arms and against his chest to keep it from sliding to the floor.

It took him long, fumbling moments to get it right side up and straightened enough to hold it for his mother to rise and put on.

Then turn for the door.

WE MUST HAVE made a strange parade through the darkness.

But I couldn't spare any attention from concentrating on where I was putting my feet to observe the snaking line of flashlights.

Maybe a couple dozen of the searchers came, including Needham, Taylorman, and all three of those late-arriving drivers, though they stayed separated. The only women who made this trip were Connie, Diana, Loriana, the gray-haired woman someone had said was Brian's aunt, and me.

It would have been a much smaller group if Wayne Shelton had

had his way. At first the acting chief backed him. But when Loriana said that refusing Connie the support of her friends and neighbors would be cruel, he crumbled.

He shouldn't have. Connie wasn't aware of anyone except her sons and possibly Tom. And letting us all go up there was lousy procedure, even for an accident scene.

Sure, I could have declined to go, presenting a model of good sense and responsible citizenship. I might even have earned brownie points from Deputy Shelton.

Put potential brownie points on one side of the scale and the journalist's instinct to see what there was to see on the other, and it was no contest.

The journey was silent except for an occasional murmur of warning passed down the line about a particularly tricky patch of rocky, uneven ground.

There was a path to our right, but as the official vehicles had done, we paralleled it. It would require daylight and scientists to know if that was the route Brian had taken. Shelton was going to follow that precaution despite not being allowed to follow others.

The ground had been rising for a while when we took an abrupt dip, then climbed hard. Coming around an outcropping twice a tall as Mike, who was just in front of me, artificial lights suddenly blazed with a brightness I knew from too many police scenes to count. Also familiar was the precision of the experts assessing and documenting what was before them.

These suited-up experts toiled in a relatively flat area spread in front of us.

We couldn't get close because yellow police tape created a horseshoe around the flat area with the open end of the horseshoe to our right, where what looked like rock slanted up. I had the impression that the slanted area ended in an edge that likely indicated an abrupt drop, like many we'd see driving in, though beyond the central area dark reigned.

"We're north of the house?" I asked Mike quietly.

He nodded. "Pretty much. That—" he tipped his head toward the slanted area and the possible edge beyond it. "—is east."

Led by Shelton, we filed into a narrow gap between the crime scene tape and the red rocks of the outcropping now rising behind us. According to Mike's internal compass, we faced north. By silent accord, we sorted out so Connie and her sons were at the front and center. Mike tipped his head, I nodded, and we dropped even farther back, brushing against the rocks in order to move to the far eastern edge of the group. Diana joined us.

With no one between us and the fluttering tape, a wheelchair came into view first. It was tipped over on one side, and angled forward so the right handle rested on the ground and one of its oversized rear wheels was free to turn slowly when the wind got busy.

Past the chair we could see Brian Walterston's body.

He was on his side. That position can convey comfort, the cozy side-curl of a nap. Brian's body didn't.

Perhaps it was the rigidity. Or the incongruence of lying on hard and rocky ground. But he did not look comfortable or cozy or at peace or enjoying a final rest.

One arm reached out as if toward the darkened eastern edge of this stage where he'd made his last appearance on earth. His face was also tipped in that direction.

A shudder caught my shoulders before I could squelch it. I did my best to mask it by shifting from one foot to the other as I pulled my jacket tighter around me.

Tom, looking over heads from a position behind Connie, shot me a look from under the masking brim of his hat.

Shelton's attention never wavered from Connie and the boys.

"Ma'am? Connie? Will you make the formal identification?"

She licked her lips twice before any sound came from them. "It's Brian. But…"

That last word sent a crackle through those gathered.

"But what?" prodded Taylorman, his pork pie hat bobbing slightly in the breeze. "Is it him or not?"

Someone let out a hiss of disapproval, but Connie didn't seem to notice Taylorman's coldness or the others' response.

"He's gone." She sounded surprised. "I didn't know…"

"Oh, that."

Again, Connie didn't appear to hear Taylorman. She held onto her sons while she stared at her husband's crumpled form in the sharp light.

"He'd lost so much. I forgot how much more he still had to lose."

It felt as if all those gathered behind the tape sucked in a breath at the pain in those words.

No, not everyone. That became clear an instant later as a cell phone camera flashed.

A second simultaneous sucked-in breath had an entirely different feel.

"For God's sake," Loriana muttered.

"Get out of here, Taylorman," someone on the far side of the group shouted. I thought it was Driver 2, the older man.

"I got a right to be here. Doing my job. If the family tries to make a claim, I gotta have documentation."

A rumble of outrage was cut short by Deputy Shelton's authoritative tones. "You're all going to get out of here. It's time to—"

"No." Connie's voice cut across his. Or maybe he let her. "This is our property. Mine and my husband's. Ours and our sons."

The final words trembled.

The group near Connie closed in tighter, some of them elbowing Taylorman back. Amid the general murmur, I caught snatches of comfort, of support, of shared grief … and sharper phrases aimed at the insurance man.

Leaving way for those who wanted to move in, I stepped farther to the side, still behind the police tape but closer to where it gave way to the rising ground and the darkness beyond it.

It gave me a new angle on the scene in the center of the spotlight.

The chair was outfitted with holders and a carrier bag. The holders were empty, the bag flattened. The bright lights showed no items scattered around and I doubted the experts had picked up any items yet.

But that wasn't what bothered me the most.

"What is it, Elizabeth?" Mike asked quietly from beside me.

Not quietly enough, though, because I was aware of both Tom's and Shelton's attention tuning in, though neither looked at us.

"It's like he was reaching for something. Or someone. But all that's there is the edge," I said as quietly as I could.

Again, not quietly enough.

Tom's head jerked toward us, then to the body.

Shelton grabbed a flashlight from Alvaro, passed us, ducked under the crime tape and strode out of the primary light and into the darkness, the bobbing flashlight providing a guess where he was.

"Alvaro!"

Richard had followed him, so Shelton's next words were too low to hear. The flashlight bobbed farther away, angling away from us, then disappeared. But immediately after, those few of us who were listening heard the skitter and slide of earth under the boot heels of someone descending a sharp incline.

Mike, Diana, and I started forward as close to simultaneously as three people could. Shelton's voice snapped from the dark, "Stay where you are."

So he'd been smart enough to send the younger, more athletic man down with the flashlight. Darn it.

Then came Richard's voice from below. "There's ... something here. Someone."

Chapter Five

"**DON'T MOVE HIM,**" Shelton said immediately then came back into the light.

"I'm not. Just … checking to be sure … He's dead."

"Okay. Don't holler any more. We got big ears here." He didn't bother to look toward us as he shouted to Sampson, "Get these people back. And don't let anyone move or leave."

Shelton disappeared into the darkness, then similar sounds to those Alvaro had made indicated he was going down for a look.

Sampson strode to two other deputies and pointed toward where we all had entered the area. They looked unconvinced and didn't move. I thought I heard Sampson say "Wayne." The other two immediately moved.

All the people who'd been in our parade, along with the scientists who continued their work were between us and whatever the deputies were doing.

But Mike could see over and around enough people to tell us the deputies were stringing tape across the entrance where we'd come in.

The group around Connie stirred with a new uneasiness, recapturing my attention. For an instant I thought they'd caught on to what the deputies were doing, but, no, their focus was on the newly widowed woman.

The acting chief was clearly trying to soothe or dissuade Connie about something. She was having none of it.

"I want to stay here with him until they take him."

"Connie, please, let us have some folks take you back, stay with you. You've had a shock and the best thing would be to get some rest—"

"I'm staying here with him. It'll be daylight soon and—"

"You can't." Shelton strode in from the darkness, inside the tape. A few people shifted as if aware of a change in his attitude. I hadn't picked up any sound of his climbing back up from wherever Alvaro had found "something."

"Deputy Shelton, there's no reason not to let the widow stay here," started the acting chief, who clearly was not among those who'd started to recognize something else was going on.

Neither Shelton nor Connie looked at him.

"It's our property," she said, "so I have every right—"

"It's also a potential murder scene, Connie." He was even brusquer than usual. With another man I'd suspect stress. Considering it was Deputy Wayne Shelton, I guessed it was on purpose, probably with the intent of snapping Connie into reality.

Or possibly to snap his superior officer into attention.

At the moment, the acting chief stood stock still, looking confused. "What? Brian wasn't murdered."

"Not Brian. Don Hazen."

Connie gaped at him.

A cry rose and Loriana surged forward. "What? What did you say? Don? *Dead?*"

"Well, dead, anyway," Shelton conceded.

The woman cried again, and began to crumple. She was a slow crumpler, so Taylorman, Needham Bender, and Austin had time to grab various body parts to keep her from the rock underfoot.

Chapter Six

"**WHAT'S HAPPENED? OH,** ohhhhh…" Loriana moaned from Taylorman's shoulder. "Don… Don. Where is he? What happened? You said—No, no. *Murdered?*"

"Don't know what happened yet, but he's down the bottom of the cut."

"How did he get there? How could he have—? Was he—oh, God, was he…" She looked around at Brian's body. "Pushed?"

Rich Taylorman and Needham had relinquished their holds already. Now Austin released the arm he'd still held. The woman tottered.

But Connie acted this time.

She slapped Loriana across the face. Not lightly, either.

For an instant both women looked blank with shock. Then two very different reactions surfaced—satisfaction from Connie and fury from Loriana—before each reaction was quickly covered by a new, careful, blankness.

The slap stopped all other conversation and movement.

Shelton took advantage.

"Everybody stay right where you are," he ordered.

He got the other deputies—except Alvaro who apparently was still down below with the second body—busy beyond where we'd entered, creating a sort of chute between two more strings of tape. They started taking people through one at a time. One deputy getting name and address, another taking photos of clothes and shoes. Then they were passed on to more deputies who were writing down accounts of activities and movements.

Shelton sent his boss and Loriana through first. Then Cor
her sons, accompanied by Tom.

"I'll be right there," he said to Tom. Then gave a few more orders
to Sampson.

As they walked past us we heard Sampson say, "That guy with the
pork pie hat? He's raising a fuss."

"Too bad. All of them. And when we're done here, we're going to
have to look at every last one of the searchers—volunteer or official—
the family, the ladies back at the house. Everybody."

I could love Wayne Shelton.

Until I realized that his methodical arrangement meant that since
Mike, Diana, and I were the farthest from the entry, we were going to
be the last ones released.

✧ ✧ ✧ ✧

THE SKY HAD lightened considerably by the time we finished the
gantlet of Cottonwood County deputies. Nothing I would consider
daylight, but enough to make the return trip faster.

Almost all of the vehicles had left when we reached the home
ranch. Among those remaining, most were official, though I also
recognized Tom's truck. Only one barrel fire still showed light. The
tables remained, though they'd been cleared. The chair Connie had
been sitting on was still overturned. The house showed lights in every
window.

"They won't be sleeping," Diana said, then yawned.

She headed home to see her kids before they left for school. Mike
and I straggled into the station. He and Diana had been my primary
source of transportation since my car had been consumed in the fire
that destroyed the hovel.

Over copious amounts of coffee, we told Audrey Adams, today's
early producer, what we knew. One lost, found dead. A second found
dead nearby.

I was in that state I recognized from many stories I'd covered—
half exhausted and half adrenalized. Even as we filled in Audrey,

thoughts flowed, most quickly burning out, but a few leaving a streak of embers.

Two men dead, but how?

Brian Walterston could have died of exposure. Don Hazen went looking for Brian then met with an accident. That was the simplest explanation.

Something sizzled through my nervous system. Adrenaline? Exhaustion? Or something else?

Shelton had said potential murder for Hazen.

Did one kill the other? If so, which was the killer, which the victim?

Could someone else have killed them both?

Who?

And why?

KWMT-TV had given up morning and mid-day news long before I'd arrived last spring, so the first broadcast would be at five. Plenty of time to plan coverage to develop the story. As long as nothing went wrong.

And then something went wrong.

Thurston Fine walked in.

I can't say for sure our unesteemed anchor hadn't ever arrived earlier at the station, but it had to be a challenger for the record.

"Well, didn't expect to see anyone here at this hour," he said.

"Early shift's always here now," Audrey said.

He ignored that as he tugged at the bottom of his suit coat. "Had an important breakfast meeting. Very productive. Very productive."

I heard what he said, but I was focused on his wearing a suit. Most anchors dress for the camera from the waist up on set. But anchor desks are seldom fine furniture on the non-camera side, so once you've ruined decent clothes, you dress down. If you have good sense.

Fine did not dress down.

Still, he rarely dressed quite *this* up. I'd been told he went to Denver for haircuts. He'd probably gone at least that far for this suit. I was half tempted to send a picture to a sartorial splendor buddy in D.C. to find out how much it might have set Fine back.

"Big story afoot," he said.

"You heard about it?"

Mike's amazement wasn't flattering, but Thurston didn't seem to recognize that. "Heard about it? I have been at the epicenter."

We looked at him blankly.

"The breakfast meeting," he said impatiently.

"Breakfast?" Mike repeated.

"Of course. With the leaders of this county."

We still looked at him blankly.

His superior smile was undimmed as he gave us an airy wave and departed toward his office.

"What the hell was he talking about?" Mike asked.

Audrey shrugged. I would have, too, but I didn't have the energy.

"Let's get some sleep before we try to figure out Thurston."

IT WASN'T ENOUGH sleep—certainly nowhere near enough to tackle trying to figure out Thurston Fine—but it was some. Combined with a shower, I was functional when Diana gave me a ride back to the station in the early afternoon.

Inside, I discovered a clot of people near the bump in the hallway that served as a break room. Amid the chatter, I caught phrases about two deaths, lead story, and unanswered questions. I also heard anchor Thurston Fine's voice from the front of the group.

"What's going on?" I asked Leona D'Amato, who was at the back of the clot.

Leona had been at the station since it opened nearly fifty years ago. She covered the social happenings of Cottonwood County, which meant she worked part-time. She was also one of the few people Thurston allowed to fill the weekend anchor spot, presumably because she didn't threaten his job security.

She wasn't a bad reporter and she had good on-air presence. Plus, how could a woman of my age not love a woman of her age still being on the air, even part-time in Sherman, Wyoming.

The trouble was, she hated news—real news, hard news. It made for some fluffy weekends.

"Les isn't back from lunch yet, so we can't get in his office for the meeting."

Other newsrooms had conference rooms for the early afternoon meeting when stories were pitched and tribal warfare was waged for block placement and time allotment.

A block is a segment of the broadcast—A comes before the first commercials, B before the second commercials, etc. Some shops had imaginative names for specialized blocks. One of my alma maters referred to a short segment before the weather as the "Front block."

Nearly as important as the block was the time a story was allotted. I've seen men moved to tears of rage after losing five seconds to a rival. Or a best friend.

Overt jockeying for placement and time begins at the staff meeting. Covert jockeying goes on all the time. Rather like a pack of wild dogs sorting out who's in charge. I used to mix it up with the best of them—always because my stories deserved better placement and more time, not from mere ego, of course—but not so much here in Sherman. My "Helping Out" segment had a standing slot in theory. In practice it was bumped a lot. Yes, I fought for it, but KWMT-TV had never seen me in full form.

"Late, even for Les." I spotted a glint in Leona's eyes.

Not only was it late for Les Haeburn, a champion long-luncher, but it was highly unusual for him not to be accompanied by Thurston during one of his extended meals.

"What—?"

My question was drowned out by Thurston Fine's voice cutting through the chatter.

"It's not even really a story. It's perfectly obvious what happened."

On air, he kept just this side of sounding like an announcer in a Saturday Night Live skit. In person he frequently crossed to the wrong side of the line.

"Perfectly?" Mike asked from a spot by the break room.

Thurston smirked with pleasure. The man had a tin ear for sarcasm. "Indeed. The second dead guy went out to search for that first guy. Came upon him and was so startled that he stepped back as a natural instinct." He demonstrated with a move that looked more like bad pantomime than anything natural. He barely missed clocking Audrey in the face with a hand-raised-in-shock gesture. "Unfortunately, he was close to the edge and tumbled backward to his death in a tragic accident. One tragic accident compounded by another."

Faces turned toward me.

When had it become my duty to show Thurston the flaws in his thinking?

Okay, it was more a pleasure than a duty, but, still, they shouldn't expect it. Not every time.

Though maybe *this* time.

"A few problems with that supposition, Thurston," I said. "Don Hazen—that's the second dead guy to you—wasn't among the searchers who signed up. That was checked." True, Loriana had said he might have gone searching on his own, but that was unconfirmed. ... Besides, I wanted to test my theory that Thurston hadn't bothered to read the background Mike and I had provided this morning.

He flicked away my objection. "Not wanting to delay his search for his lost and helpless neighbor for one second longer than necessary, he bypassed all red tape and went out on his own, like a true westerner."

"Possible," I conceded, carefully avoiding looks from Mike, Audrey, and a handful of others, who clearly *had* read the material. "Not very bright, since a coordinated search is much more effective, as all those who did check in recognized. Still, it's possible. But why would he do that when even his wife says he wasn't on good terms with the Walterstons?"

"You haven't been in our fair state long, so you wouldn't know the character of Wyomingians." He got dangerously lost in the last two syllables. He should have played it safe with Wyomingites. "The frontier spirit where neighbor helped neighbor—"

"And sometimes neighbor whacked neighbor," Mike said. "Remind me to tell you some of the tales."

"—has not faded from our collective psyche the way it has elsewhere. Rivalries, disagreements, even deep divides are put aside in time of need. So it is perfectly clear to those of us who know the people of this fine state that he would rush out to help his neighbor."

I'd seen and been impressed by the concern and generosity of the Walterstons' neighbors. Yet Thurston's paean made me want to gag. Maybe because the people forming the search parties and supporting the family had appeared genuine.

"Why didn't he see the edge of the drop-off he fell over?"

"Too startled by the sight of his dead neighbor to notice. Now—" He brought his hands together in something between clapping and a brushing motion. He was on the cusp of making the smug-o-meter go ding, ding, ding. "—lots for this crew to get done to support me in another fine show. And here's Les to lead the way."

Show. A fingernails-on-a-blackboard shudder went through me. *Show* was entertainment. We did news. At least some of us did.

Okay, some of the shudder was also for the idea of being led by Les Haeburn.

"Unavoidably detained," the News Director said, not in apology, as he elbowed through the crowd.

"Wonder where Les has been," Leona murmured.

His tie was loosened halfway down his shirtfront and the collar was awry.

In the same low tone, I said, "Why, Leona, you can't possibly be imagining our esteemed leader took a long lunch for, ah, illicit activities, can you?"

"Please. I don't want to imagine any such thing or my lunch won't stay where I deposited it."

I chuckled and started to follow her in the flow toward Haeburn's now-open office. Mike's hand on my arm held me back momentarily.

"Diana says six-thirty's a good time. But she's got a full schedule today, so she asked if you'd pick up snacks and drinks."

"For what?"

His eyebrows shot up. "To meet at her house after the five—" He was referring to the five o'clock news broadcast. *Show* to Thurston Fine. "—to discuss ... you know." His voice dropped. "The case. Our investigation. I said she didn't need to feed me dinner, but she thinks we need snacks."

Since I'd arrived in Sherman, Mike and I, along with several other people, had been involved in digging into a few deaths and we'd gotten great stories for KWMT-TV. Deputy Shelton had even provided backhanded help on the most recent. But if he heard Mike referring to "the case" or "our investigation," I suspected Mike and I would find ourselves deposited on the other side of the county line quickly and permanently.

We'd have to make sure Shelton didn't hear.

"I'll pick up snacks and drinks." Diana was right. Every time we'd gotten together for such discussions or for anything else, copious amounts of empty calories were consumed. "But I don't know if I'll have enough brain power to discuss anything, much less a potential story." I emphasized the last word.

There wasn't an opportunity to say more, because we were in Haeburn's office now, which was crammed with staffers trying to find any halfway comfortable spot to park themselves for this episode of All-Thurston-Fine-All-Of-The-Time.

Haeburn and Fine took the most comfortable chairs, but I was glad to see someone had made sure Leona was seated—most likely Leona herself—as well as Jennifer, who was responsible for typing notes for Haeburn.

"I'll lead with the county attorney and sheriff jobs," Thurston said.

That got everyone's attention. Mike half-straightened away from the doorframe he was resting against.

"You've got the names of who they're going to appoint? Great," Audrey said. "We can—"

"Not who'll be appointed." Thurston waved that petty detail away.

"The three candidates for each job?"

"Not specific names."

"What's left?"

His confidence not even dented, Fine said, "I have a confidential source who says the search is going well and they hope to have it wrapped up in a few weeks."

Into the silence that followed came a whisper. "What was his confidential source? A news release?"

"Great," Haeburn said quickly, apparently to save Fine from trying to work out what that very audible whisperer might have meant. "That's the lead, then."

"Over two deaths?" I protested. "Even if 'going well' and 'a few weeks' weren't what they've been saying for months, it doesn't advance the story. And—"

"Does, too." Fine might, for once, have recognized the lameness in one of his responses, because he turned red and went on quickly. "Those deaths were merely accidents. Sad, I'm sure, but no more than ranch accidents that happen around here so often they don't warrant air time. Besides, that's the past. Old news." His broad gesture brushed away the past.

Uneasiness ruffled the room. Diana's husband Gary had died in an accident on their ranch. And this jackass had just dismissed his death along with the two recent ones as trivialities.

"We have to look ahead. My story is about the future of Cottonwood County and how some are working hard to rebuild it after *some* tore it apart—" He accompanied that with a pointed look at me.

"Why, Thurston, are you talking about the *past?*"

"—by bringing down our leading civic, uh, leaders with underhanded means."

"Our leading criminals you mean?" Mike asked.

"No one's been convicted," Fine said.

"Yeah. And why not would make a great story," Mike shot back. "Why don't you get *that* story? Or what about the two deaths discovered last night that—"

"Perfectly obvious what happened, as I said."

"—have not yet been ruled—"

"Accidents," they finished together.

"Enough of this," Haeburn said. "Thurston has the lead."

I swear KWMT-TV's anchor started to stick out his tongue at me, catching it in time to, instead, lick his lips.

All things considered, I'd rather he'd stuck out his tongue.

"Now—"

"Les," I said, "before we move on, I want to be sure I'm clear, here in front of everybody, so there are no misunderstandings later—" As there had been in other situations when Fine threw a hissy fit that someone else was chasing a good story. "—that Thurston has no interest in the coverage of the two deaths last night."

Thurston didn't give Haeburn the chance to respond. "If it turns out to be a story—a real story, which it won't, since they were accidents. Tragic, but accidents." He'd clearly lost the thread of his sentence. He coughed, holding up one hand as if apologizing for the delay to throngs eagerly awaiting his next words.

"How would you know it became a real story if you don't work it now?"

"The sheriff's department will announce it."

There was a low moan emanating from several directions. The whisperer gave it voice, "Waiting for a news release."

"If it turns out to be a real story, I get it, because I get lead story," Thurston insisted.

"But you've said the progress toward filling the sheriff and county attorney slots is the true lead story. And you're not interested in two accidental deaths ... oh, unless you're *not* sure they were accidental."

Everyone in the room except him knew his best move was to back off his adamant "accidents" stance.

"They were accidents," he said.

"Okay. So, you don't want the story, which means it's fair game for someone else."

"Well, if something changes..."

"How can it, when you're certain they were accidents?"

"Enough," Haeburn said. "Thurston has the lead. You can't go on the air anyway, Elizabeth, not looking like that." Such a considerate way to allude to the recent fire that in addition to consuming my rental house and everything I'd had with me in Wyoming had also put a dent in my eyebrows, eyelashes, and some hair. The hair loss wasn't very noticeable. The eyelashes and eyebrows were, especially since I hadn't resorted to fake eyelashes or eyebrow pencil. At least not yet. "Besides, you have your own beat. Stick to it. That goes for you, too, Paycik. Audrey, find someone to report on these deaths."

"Sure thing."

"It'll go third up in A Block. After the price of hay. Now, let's get on with the rest of it."

Haeburn clearly thought he'd closed the door on Mike and me, and Thurston certainly looked satisfied with that conclusion.

But neither of them could see Audrey's hand behind her back, giving Mike and me a thumbs-up.

Chapter Seven

MIKE HAD WORK to do for his sports reports at five and ten. He'd also be at the station for live reports on both broadcasts, especially after missing last night.

I was less encumbered.

Not only was I off the air in my current lash- and brow-less state, but I was chronically underemployed as the "Helping Out" reporter, a far cry from the top news stories I'd been covering in New York until the beginning of the year.

I certainly didn't have enough "Helping Out" work to keep myself awake this afternoon. Better to keep moving.

Checking out with Audrey as day producer, I provided a vague excuse of researching a local angle for an upcoming "Helping Out" segment on selecting a Halloween pumpkin. She noted it with a straight face, but a knowing look.

"Walt is doing the day story on those deaths. Okay if he calls you?"

By saying he had the "day story," she was tacitly accepting that I'd be working a longer-range angle on the story.

"Sure. Though, you know, Audrey, I might start something on insurance. Not sure yet. Have to do the background before I decide. Picking a pumpkin or insurance scams. One or the other."

"I can see where that would be a tough choice." She kept a perfectly straight face.

From there, I swung past the desk of newsroom aide Jennifer Lawton.

Jennifer-previously-known-as-Jenny had decided her name was the primary impediment to her achieving journalistic super-stardom. She didn't see having no background or training as a problem at all. As penance for any past journalist sins I'd unknowingly committed, I was periodically force-feeding her Journalism 101 along with a remedial course in journalist ethics.

The ethics instruction was essential because she was so good on computers she delighted in going where no one had gone before. Or should be going now.

As reward for all she'd done for the special stories we'd given KWMT, Les still had her pegged as a newsroom aide and sometimes-utility-infielder production assistant.

No one ever accused Les Haeburn of knowing how to develop resources.

"How about if we step outside?" I suggested.

"Outsid—? Oh, yeah. Sure." She looked around like Mata Hari with a crick in her neck. "Maybe we should go one at a time so we're not seen together."

"I think we can risk it." Anyone looking out the front door or window on that side of the squat building would see us.

Out the double set of doors to the parking lot, we walked to one side, so we weren't in the direct path of anyone entering or exiting.

Having others know that Jennifer and I were talking was one thing. Having them overhear what I was asking her to do was another.

The sun was bright and strong. But I quickly discovered there was little to block the wind streaming in from the west. I tightened my sweater around me, holding it in place by hugging myself.

"Would you have time to do a preliminary check on the two men who died, Jennifer?"

"Sure."

"On your own time?"

"Um."

That might be too strict. Besides, anything she found could contribute to a story for KWMT. No guarantees, but there never were on these sorts of stories.

I adjusted. "Without getting into trouble because Thurston or Les realizes what you're doing?"

"Sure."

"You know the names of—"

"Of course. I read the backgrounder."

"Great." This indicated promising interest and initiative—certainly more than Thurston had shown. "Basic background from public sources and the station's morgue—better add the *Independence*'s files, too. See if there are any red flags."

"That'll be easy. I can dig deeper—"

"No." Her deeper digging always left me with the concern that she'd hit buried power lines that could blow up in her face. But that same face now looked so woeful that I added, "Not yet anyway."

Jennifer cheered up immediately.

Another thought occurred to me. "Add Rich Taylorman."

"Who's that?"

"I was told he's an insurance broker. He seems to be involved with the Walterstons' insurance. There was some issue with their medical insurance this summer and maybe earlier, but I don't know if he was their agent then. See what you can get about that and then basic background on him."

"Got it."

DIANA WAS USING the Newsmobile for an assignment and had left me the keys to her pickup.

The Newsmobile was the best of a bad lot that made up KWMT's fleet of news vehicles. It did have four-wheel drive. Shock absorbers, however, appeared to be an accessory the station hadn't sprung for. Considering the way Diana drove, maybe it didn't matter. The first bump she hit—always at high speed—and she'd sail over the next dozen.

After driving to the sheriff's department office, which sat behind the Cottonwood County Courthouse in the center of Sherman, I hit an entirely too familiar bump in the road for every reporter.

The "he-or-she gave instructions not to be disturbed" obstacle.

When I saw the expression of a stern gray-haired veteran behind the front desk when he looked up and saw me, I didn't even ask. Instead, I started confidently toward the hallway that led to the interview rooms and offices.

"Deputy Shelton left orders not to be disturbed," Deputy Gray Hair informed me, simultaneously moving to intercept me.

"Oh, that's okay, I'm not here to see him."

"You can't go back there, Ms. Danniher." He clasped my arm.

Not a good sign that he knew who I was. It almost sounded as if Shelton had given orders to block me.

"I have to use the facilities, Deputy." I scanned his hand—yes, a wedding ring. "As I'm sure you know from your wife, there are times when it's essential."

He blanched, his grip loosening.

"Thank you." I put a lot of heart into that and hurried on.

The doors to both interview rooms were closed, but I heard voices behind the door to Interview Room 2.

I didn't try to go in. I didn't even slow down. Deputy Gray Hair was watching. So I went into the ladies room at the end of the hall.

With the Cottonwood County Sheriff's Department decidedly undiversified, I was confident I would not be disturbed. I stayed right by the door, listening.

This was a must-try-despite-the-odds effort. Law enforcement had a wealth of information I would love to have—preliminary reports from the scene, from witnesses, from the bodies. For the one time in a billion when that information might be shared with me, I put in the time and effort that resulted in being told no the other 999,999,999 times.

So, I waited.

The payoff came sixteen minutes later. Yes, Deputy Gray Hair had to be wondering if I'd passed out, but clearly he wasn't going to risk having to deal with the situation by checking on me.

The payoff came in the form of the creak of one of the interview room doors opening and Shelton's voice saying, "This time use the real stuff, not that white colored water."

This is what I'd counted on. Members of law enforcement, like journalists, need periodic infusions of coffee to keep operating. Actually, it was impressive Shelton had gone this long between doses.

After footsteps passed the door to the ladies' room, I slipped out silently and waited behind Deputy Richard Alvaro while he poured two cups of coffee. As he began turning with them, I said, "Hi, Richard."

He spun around, one cup sloshing over. "Arghh." I chose to believe the sound of pain was in response to the hot coffee, not to seeing me.

"Where the hell did you come from?"

"Now is that any way to—?"

"You're not supposed to be back here. You have to go."

"I have a few questions."

"*No.*"

Richard had once gone out on a limb to give us information that helped find a murderer. But he'd been much less cooperative since some bad apples had been cleared out of the sheriff's department. Also since he'd spent more time around Shelton. The man was a bad influence.

"Richard, you know we can keep a confidence—"

"Does he?" Shelton's voice came from behind me. So I hadn't been as silent as I'd hoped. Or Wayne Shelton was really, really worried about getting real cream in his coffee.

I looked over my shoulder, but didn't turn to him. "Yes, he does."

"Something to do with this department?"

"First, if it were, I wouldn't tell you." I could practically hear Richard's face losing color. "Second, I would have said he knew we protect our sources. But as long as you're here, Deputy Shelton, I do have questions about the deaths of Brian Walterston and Don Hazen."

Shelton stepped around me into the break room. I would have said that he'd lost the body language battle by being the one to move, but since he headed for the fridge and pulled out a container he might not have been aware the battle was going on.

"What direction is evidence at the scene pointing you in?" I asked.

He grunted. He took one cup from Richard and poured generously into it. "Did you send out that press release, Alvaro?"

"Yes, sir."

Shelton looked at me. "Then you've got your answer."

"You and Thurston, the happy pair. One sending, the other waiting for news releases."

He nearly winced at that. But not enough to weaken.

I tried another angle. "Pretend the news release went into a black hole and tell me what it said."

Shelton nodded to Richard, who said, "We're investigating them as unexpected deaths."

"Suspicious deaths?"

"Unexpected deaths," Shelton said.

"You said murder at the scene. Are you retracting that?"

"I'm retracting nothing. I said potential. We preserve the scene as if it's the worst possible scenario, but we don't assume it is."

"What was found at the scene?"

"Nothing we're going to share with the media."

"Have the preliminary examinations of the bodies provided likely cause of death for either man?"

"No comment."

"Have the preliminary examinations ruled out accident for either victim?"

"No comment."

"C'mon, Deputy. Haven't my colleagues and I helped you? You're the one who lured me in with Mildred."

"Don't need you this time."

A challenge if I ever heard one.

He might have recognized he'd gone too far, because, with a screamingly obvious change of subject, he said, "Why aren't you fighting Thurston for the big story—the one about who's going to be named county attorney and sheriff?"

I raised one eyebrow, fleetingly wondering if that expression had lost impact since the fire.

"Why, Deputy Shelton, how could I possibly hope to keep up with Thurston on a truly big story?"

He snorted then tried to mask he'd had any reaction by drinking from his cup of coffee-flavored cream. When he came up for air he said, "I heard a rumor they're bringing in outside candidates next week."

Did he think he could feed me garbage and make me forget the "unexpected" deaths he was working on?

"Nobody for sheriff, though," Richard said.

My quick calculation was that pushing to get back to what interested me would only erect a brick wall. Better to keep access to both of these men by humoring them now. "From what I hear they're not interviewing sheriff candidates because the top outside candidate for county attorney wants to bring in his own man. A two-fer."

Richard gave a short whistle. "Boy, you have good sources, Elizabeth. How'd you hear that?"

"From you," Shelton said, though his tone didn't rub Richard's nose in it. "She was fishing, and you took the bait."

I made a mental note to follow up on that.

"Damn." Richard grinned. "Not that you couldn't have gotten it from a dozen guys. Lots of speculation about who's thrown a hat in the ring. Got to watch everything you say, because you never know if you're talking to an interested party."

I turned to Shelton. "Are you an interested party?"

Richard stopped with his cup halfway to his mouth, but before he could feel the full potential, Shelton said, "Hell no."

Rallying, Richard said, "You'd be a great sheriff."

Shelton appeared to restrain himself from rolling his eyes. He was a pushover for the young deputy. If I'd said that, his eyes would have spun like a top.

"Know anything about anybody who does have a hat in the sheriff's ring?" I asked.

"Nothing I'm telling you."

"What about a new county attorney?"

"Nothing I'm telling you."

"So you know things, but you're not telling me? Or you don't know a thing because you're out of the loop?" Sometimes a little goading does wonders.

"Not telling you, one way or the other."

No wonder-working with Wayne Shelton. Not today, anyway.

On the other hand, a journalist who keeps a source from ending all communication lives to pump that source another day.

Chapter Eight

MY NEXT ERRAND was to pick up the snacks and drinks Diana had asked for. I'd also get personal items. Plus, I wanted to find out what was humming on the Cottonwood County grapevine.

For all this, the Sherman Supermarket was one-stop-shopping.

A burly man who looked familiar pushed out one side of the double doors as I pushed in the other side. That coincided with a not-so-playful gust of Wyoming wind creating a vortex, which ushered me into the Sherman Supermarket with a rush of air and a skittering of leaves up to my knees.

"Whoa. Where did that come from," I said to nobody in particular. If I kept pulling this sweater around me, it would be tent size.

"That's fall clearing its throat," Penny Czylinski called out from her position behind the register.

"I'd rather it didn't."

But Penny wasn't listening. A customer had entered her checkout lane. "Well, hello there."

The customer said something I missed as she began emptying an overflowing cart.

"…he was mistreating her," Penny said. "They got calls, but never could prove it. He definitely—"

"Heard he—" the shopper tried.

I stopped to listen.

"Hit her. Yup. Saw evidence with my own eyes. And I'm not the only one. Family," she said with significance.

"Justice," the customer said.

Keeping her comment telegraphic indicated familiarity with Penny's conversational style. But it barely gave me time to absorb that Penny had said Don had mistreated Loriana.

"They'll likely never know what happened," she continued. "But one way and another I'd say some don't think he got justice. Not by a long sight. Got off too easy. Falling," she said disparagingly. "A real man would've gotten up and dusted himself off."

That seemed a bit harsh. Bad enough to die, but then to have your method of death scored like a Russian gymnastics judge critiquing a U.S. competitor's routine? Definitely harsh.

I picked up the items on Diana's list first. I added food and treats for Shadow, the dog who'd started hanging around the hovel as a stray and moved with me to Diana's after the fire. Then I got a pre-made salad for my dinner. I also supplemented my supply of Pepperidge Farm double chocolate Milano cookies. Just in case.

Then I headed for Penny's lane.

Ideally, I'd be behind a shopper stockpiling supplies for a month, so I could catch the gossip Penny imparted to that customer even before my turn.

Luck was against me. The customer's collection of groceries was darned near pathetic.

"—and Connie stands up for what she believes in, for herself and for others. That can rile some folks. Like her and others wanting justice for Mindy for—"

"*Mindy?*" I blurted out. "I thought you meant Loriana."

I'd broken protocol. One could listen while Penny talked to another customer but one always pretended not to. And one certainly didn't interrupt that interaction.

The customer gawked at me.

To my relief, Penny snort-laughed. "What would *she* need justice for? Tongue that could etch a mountain, that one. Too smart to go toe-to-toe with him and get a wallop for her trouble. No, when Loriana went after him, he'd be like a bear swinging away at horde of stinging bees. Takes care of herself. Course everybody thought Mindy could, too. Her people've always thought he did her in and they didn't mind saying it. Said if you dug up all of his land you'd be sure to prove it. But what's the point of saying that when nobody's going to do such a thing. They keep on saying all they want is justice."

I've lost count of how many times I've heard people involved in a story say all they want is justice.

They don't.

People saying "we want justice for X, Y, or Z" have made up their mind what happened and see no reason to waste time and effort investigating. They think whoever they've decided is guilty should be summarily punished. Do not pass Go, do not investigate, do not bother with proof—they *know* what happened—just throw the "obviously guilty" in jail. But only if drawing and quartering isn't on the menu.

I blinked back, knowing I'd missed some while my thoughts had wandered to matters of justice.

"—and never will forget last time I saw him, a week ago or so. Passing the time. I asked after the ranch, Loriana, and all. And he said clear as day, 'I was too subtle the first time. Not going to make that mistake again.' "

"Subtle? He wasn't—"

"Never knew him to be subtle a day in his life, so made no sense." Penny spoke over the other woman, not about to let her take over. Or to participate. "Just saying what he said, the way reporter folks report what the president or those other politicians say without knowing least bit of what they actually meant. Leastwise that's the way it seems, 'cause if those reporter folks knew what they really meant, they'd put it into words that someone with a lick of common sense could understand instead of that gobbledygook."

In a few words, she'd indicted my profession and—less important and more understandable—politicians and she'd left me with questions about what Don Hazen had been thinking he'd been subtle about. It was the last one that bothered me.

"Bye now." Penny's farewell to the previous customer yanked my attention back to her. "Well, hi there, Elizabeth. Heard you were out to the Walterstons' last night. Just as a person, not a reporter, too. Sad business. Real sad. Lost a good man. Sad to see Brian dwindle away the way he was, but sadder still to have him gone for good. Connie and those boys will feel that blow a long, long time. And that's if those boneheads don't put one of those boys in jail, which is just what I told Wayne Shelton when he was in here earlier with his ears flapping. Those teenagers don't realize what they're saying. Think nobody around them hears or understands a thing. As if they're the first who ever did such a thing. Though it did surprise me they'd seen the movie. Would've thought it was way too long ago for them. Even—"

"One good man? What about—?"

"—knew the baseball song. No telling with most so when you get a man like Brian Walterston who's truly good, you sit up and take notice. I say if Brian wanted to be done with his suffering, whose business is that besides his? And if a boy helps his father, that's nobody's business either. That's my idea of justice. Not that you'll be worrying about that much longer. The one—"

"Justice?" I slipped in. Was she repeating what I'd missed earlier or was this a different justice-related topic?

"—thing I know Brian would want in this world or the one beyond is what's best for his boys. It's not right dealing a blow to a boy's life that way. Maybe we're more practical about these things. Justice is like meat. And we don't just buy our meat in the grocery store like you folks do back East."

That didn't seem fair, considering she was selling meat in a grocery store where people like me bought it. And that had nothing to do with East or West.

"We know where it comes from. We know how it got there. We know it's practical and nothing high-falutin' about it. And all that stuff about needing a village is foolish. Most often slows it down if it doesn't stop up the works completely."

I *thought* she'd shifted from meat back to justice.

"But you won't need to worry about that much longer, now will you? You've done some good here for people, but you'll be moving on, not tied here anymore, so no need to worry about the justice this time. End of this month, isn't it? Hah!"

Hah? "Penny, I—"

"Bye, now. Well, hi there, Karen."

Another customer had supplanted me, popping me out the end of the lane, bagged and dazed.

The stream of Penny's words often made me feel that way. But this flow had hit close to home.

She was right, of course. At the end of October I would complete the contract my network executive then-husband had urged me to sign. When he'd become my ex and tried to maneuver me out of network news completely, the thread I'd grasped was this job in Sherman, Wyoming.

But come November, I would no longer be tied to KWMT-TV.

Nor to the network.

Nor to my past career as a hotshot news reporter.

I wouldn't be tied to anything. Or anywhere.

Was that freedom? Or being cut loose?

Where was I going to go? What was I going to do?

Applying those questions to my job situation brought no answers.

Short-term, however, I *could* answer.

Where I was going was back to the station to meet up with Mike. What I was going to do was eat double chocolate Milano cookies.

Chapter Nine

I ATE THE salad while watching the five o'clock broadcast from the newsroom.

Thurston was as good—or as bad—as his word, leading with that we've-heard-this-before from the county leaders about filling the county attorney and sheriff posts. I wondered how close he came to precisely the same wording he'd used in previous broadcasts.

I might have explored that, but I was eating.

Walt did a solid job on the search and grim discoveries at Red Sail Ranch, including comments from several searchers. I recognized Driver 1, now identified as Terry Waymark, and Mike's former football opponent. Brian's aunt spoke for the family, thanking the searchers and all those who had sent their condolences.

As soon as Mike was done, he came out of the studio. He'd shed his jacket and tie—to keep them clean for use another day—and we were out the door before the broadcast ended.

Unlike every other station I could think of, KWMT-TV did not do a final shot with the on-air crew together. Thurston refused to have anyone else in the close shot.

As we exited Hamburger Heaven with takeout bags, I stopped and stared past Mike, looking at a horizon made up of endless peaks stretching beyond comprehension.

"Something looks different," I said.

He turned and looked, too. "What? Different perspective?"

"I don't think so." Surely I'd seen the mountains from this perspective before with the number of times we'd eaten here.

"Speaking of mountains, we should get you up to the Beartooth Highway to see them up close. Road follows a route explored by General Sheridan in the early 1870s. Great views. It runs mostly along the border with Montana, then leads into Yellowstone Park."

"That sounds great. I haven't been to Yellowstone yet." And now that I was in the final month of my contract, there wasn't much time left to get there. "I could drive this Beartooth Highway to get there instead of going through Cody."

He shook his head. "Beartooth's closed for the season. It'll have to be next year. Here, take the keys so I can eat."

"Closed for the season? What season? Summer? August just ended."

"It's Oct—

"Fine. I know. October. Barely."

"Happens sometimes," he said vaguely. "Oh, look, there's Sam McCracken."

I looked around at a medium-height guy in jeans, boots, and a cowboy hat. Yet he didn't look like a rancher. "Who's Sam McCracken?"

"I'll tell you while we eat. I'm starved."

✧   ✧   ✧   ✧

ON THE DRIVE to Diana's ranch, Mike told me about Sam and Serena McCracken and their family.

"McCrackens are neighbors of the Walterstons and Hazens. New folks. Bought out the Pecklies. Seem like pleasant enough people, but they're not ranching their land, so that's a barrier between them and a lot of folks around here. They leased out nearly all of the land at first."

"You mean like you do? Is that a barrier between you and other folks?"

He either didn't hear or ignored my dryness.

Possibly he was too occupied with eating and talking to bother with nuances. He didn't talk with his mouth full and didn't dribble down his front. Impressive.

"Now that the McCrackens' kids are getting bigger," he continued, "they started holding back a half-section to have more room for pleasure horses and such."

He darted a look at me, quite pleased with himself. "And this is why you'll be interested—I don't know all the ins and outs of it, but I hear Sam McCracken and Don Hazen had quite the feud. Could be worth looking into. Okay, I'm done. You can pull over and I'll drive."

By the time I'd finished a few comments about guys and their vehicles, control issues, and real men having no problem being driven by a woman, we'd arrived.

"HAND OVER THE goodies and have a seat." Diana invited us into her comfortable ranch house.

Mike deposited the bags he held on the counter, then retired to the couch by the fireplace. He extended his arms along the back and stretched out his legs, heaving a satisfied sigh. "I hope it's not too soon to speak ill of the dead, but this is a lot more comfortable than the hovel."

"Don't get a swelled head," I told Diana. "The hovel set a low bar."

"I'm darned proud nothing sticks permanently to my coffee table."

"We got that pad off the table eventually," I protested. By tearing vital pages off, then soaking the cardboard until it came loose.

They ignored me. "And the coffee table wasn't as bad as the one in the kitchen," Mike said.

"Really?" Diana, the showoff, delivered two napkin-lined baskets with chips to her pristine coffee table. What was the matter with bags? "I never saw the kitchen table uncovered."

"It looked like it had had every liquid known to humanity spilled on it at least once. What was that puke green stain, Elizabeth?"

"I refuse to guess." I'd covered the table with oil cloth and tried to avoid contemplating the possibilities. Now that cloth, table, and hovel were gone in the fire I saw no reason to revisit them.

It was bad enough rebuilding my wardrobe, records, contents of my purse, phone contacts, and other necessities. No sense dwelling on things I didn't miss.

"In fact," I added, "I gladly stipulate to this being much more comfortable."

Partway through my comment, a knock was followed immediately by Jennifer's entrance. "More comfortable than what?"

"The hovel," Mike said.

"At least it was convenient for you, Jennifer. Your folks practically live around the corner." I couldn't believe I was defending the place.

"I don't mind. This isn't much of a drive."

"Maybe not by Wyoming standards," I muttered.

"Sure. Because that's where we are. By the way, have you made a decision?"

There it was again: What would I do when my contract ran out.

Then I remembered the "by the way" context of Jennifer's question.

"Oh, you mean decided on a car—a vehicle?"

No great loss seemed to be the general attitude when the fire also consumed my previous one. But I missed having my own transportation.

"Of course." Jennifer's tone added, *What else could I mean, you crazy person?*

"Ordered one over the weekend. Should be here any day. Shall we get down to this before I curl up and fall asleep."

"It's early," protested Jennifer.

"Mike, Diana, and I got no sleep last night and about three and a half hours this morning."

"Not even a real all-nighter."

We three oldsters groaned. I was loudest, since I was oldest. "We'll ignore her youthful insouciance before—"

"My what?"

"—we kill her, and get started."

"Tell you later," Mike said to Jennifer. More generally he asked, "Where do we start? Brian or Don?"

"Both, until we know otherwise," I said.

"Boy, this is complicated," Diana said. "Somebody could have been after Brian and killed Don because he happened to be there. Or somebody could have been after Don and killed Brian because he happened to be there. Or one of them could have killed the other and then died accidentally. Or somebody could have meant to kill them both."

"And each of those somebodies could be a different person," I confirmed. "If we're going to figure this out, we have to keep our minds open to possibilities."

"Like the possibility that Don killed Brian. Then one or the other of the boys—or both—killed him in revenge," Mike said promptly.

"Or in an effort to protect their father, but they were too late and—"

I interrupted Diana. "Let's stick with main possibilities, because each could have a lot of variations."

I grabbed a legal pad and wrote: Don K Brian. Son K Don.

Jennifer frowned at the pad. "I can't read your writing. I'll take notes. I could set up a secure group and—"

The rest of us groaned.

"Fine. I'll email a copy to you. But someday you'll have to catch up with today's technology."

"We will," I promised, "though probably not until several years from now."

"By then it'll be out of date," Jennifer protested.

Mike sputtered.

Diana helped cover it by saying, "Next: One of the boys killed his father—perhaps at his father's request—to collect the insurance money. Or one boy took him out there and the other killed—"

"Main possibilities."

"Right. Okay. Boy killed Brian. Boy killed Don because he was a witness."

"It's not as likely," Mike said, "but Brian killed Don, then died with no one else involved."

Jennifer tapped away on a small keyboard. Just watching made my wrists hurt.

"Someone else killed Brian or Don and killed the other as a witness," Diana said.

"Like the insurance guy?" Jennifer's fingers paused. "I've started pulling information on him."

"What was it he was saying about accidental death coverage?" Diana asked.

I nodded. "Right. Jennifer, add that, will you? Find out what you can about accidental death coverage in general and anything on Brian's coverage without—"

"Sure."

"—hacking." Her expression could have been boiled down to *spoilsport*. "I don't want you arrested."

She brightened. "Oh, I wouldn't get caught."

"Jennifer. I mean it. No hacking."

Mike said, "What about the flipside? Where Don is killed first and Brian witnessed it. How about those motives?"

Before anyone could answer, we heard a car door—or, since this was Wyoming, probably a truck door—closing. My dog Shadow gave one, alert bark, then was quiet.

That was odd.

Actually, there were several odd things about it.

Thinking of the standoffish stray who'd lurked around the hovel for months with a look in his eyes that clearly said *I don't trust you. I don't trust you for a second* as "my dog Shadow" was definitely odd. At least it was new.

He'd taken to spending nights in the bunkhouse with me. But he was a far cry from a cuddly lap dog ... even if I had a lap that big.

It was also odd because he didn't bark much.

But the oddest part was his note of happy greeting.

At the sound of a knock Diana, Jennifer, and I looked at each other. Mike looked down at the table.

Ah.

Mystery solved.

Diana went and opened the door. "C'mon in, Tom."

"I thought you might all be here," came Thomas David Burrell's low voice.

It would have been surprising if we weren't. We couldn't all fit in the bunkhouse that served as my temporary residence, Jennifer lived at home with her parents, and Mike had yet to invite us to his "tidy spread," perhaps because it was farther out of town than Diana's, a fact I knew solely because I'd been trying out the navigation app Jennifer loaded on my new phone.

"Give it up," I said. "Mike called you, right?"

Tom pretended he couldn't answer while transporting a chair to join us around the coffee table.

"Yeah, I called him," Mike said. "He knows these people really well. If we're going to investigate—"

"Who says there's anything to investigate?" Tom asked.

At the same time, I said, "There's a good chance he knows them too well."

I stared at Tom and he returned it.

He looked tired. Heck, we all looked tired except for Jennifer. But his was deeper. And sadder.

"Why not wait until there's something official," he said. "Sheriff's department's looking into it. Wayne Shelton's looking into it."

"First, you should be horrified to know that you and Thurston Fine are in agreement."

Telltale lines at the corners of his eyes flickered to life—could have been amusement. Or annoyance.

"If we wait to see, the trail would be old and cold. I was wrong about a lot of what happened with Mildred." I was referring to an elderly neighbor who'd been involved in a mess we'd finished looking into a couple of weeks before. "But I was right about the rumors and questions and doubt hanging over everyone touched by a murder—or a questionable death," I added to stop the protest brewing in Tom's eyes. "It would follow them all forever."

After a couple beats, he removed his cowboy hat and hooked it on the arm of the sofa next to him. It wasn't exactly waving a white flag, but at least he was staying awhile.

Diana told him, "We've started listing the possibilities. How about a recap, Jennifer?"

"I added some and filled things in. Brian went out on his own and dumped himself out to be sure he died. Kade took Brian out there and left him, helped him kill himself, or killed him."

The lines at either side of Tom's mouth deepened but Jennifer wasn't looking at him and he didn't try to stop her.

"Austin took Brian out there and left him, helped him kill himself, or killed him. With either son, Don saw them and had to be killed because he was a witness.

"Brian and Don had a confrontation and they killed each other. Or Brian killed Don or Don killed Brian, then the other one died by accident. Or someone else killed one and had to kill the other as a witness."

She looked up. "That's as far as we'd gotten, though Mike was starting on the angle of Don being the target."

Tom said, "Or both deaths were accidents."

"No."

"Is that based on anything other than you don't want Thurston Fine to be right, Elizabeth?"

Now, how did he know about that? The Cottonwood County grapevine clearly had offshoots in the KWMT-TV newsroom. "It's based on logic."

If some of the logic was that if Thurston believed it, it couldn't be true, there was no reason to blab that to Mr. Doubting Thomas Burrell.

"What logic?"

"First, it relies on Brian going out there for benign reasons. If there was only your reaction, Tom, how you responded to his being missing, that would have been plenty to know how unlikely that was.

"Second, have you ever been out with Brian when he was using that wheelchair, Tom?"

"Yes."

"What did he take with? Anything?"

No one ever said this man was stupid. He recognized where I was going. He was also honest. "Water, food, flashlight, phone, signal flare in case the phone didn't work."

"None of that was there when we saw the scene. When you found him...?"

"It was the way you saw it. Nobody touched anything."

"Don't you find that telling?" I didn't wait for his answer. "Next, the timing of when Brian went missing. If Connie had come back in the evening the way she'd planned, the search would have been delayed." *I thought he was with Mom,* Kade had said. "Even if it could have started in the middle of the night—"

Tom shook his head. "Wouldn't have had the numbers to cover the ground. Probably would have waited for daylight."

"So the timing raises the odds that Brian being out there was deliberate. We can't ignore the possibility that someone took him against his will. Neither can we ignore the more likely possibility that he went deliberately. And meant to die."

Grim silence stretched.

I picked up, "And then there's the question of Don's timing. If he's searching for Brian, as Loriana said he was, and he found him during daylight, what should he do?"

"Contact the base," Tom said.

"Would he?"

Tom and Diana exchanged a look. She was the one who said, "Probably. He wasn't that much of an ass."

"Unless Brian pushed him off the edge before he had a chance to," Mike said.

"Why couldn't an able-bodied man sidestep Brian? Besides, remember the position of Brian's body, well back from the edge."

"He stumbled back after pushing Don over," Mike proposed.

"In that case wouldn't he have fallen facing away from the edge instead of outstretched as if reaching toward it? Plus, the position of the wheelchair. Either he got up from the chair, then fell forward, scooting it back and turning it over on its side. Or—"

"Someone staged it to look like that," Diana said.

I nodded. "But without leaving any apparent footprints."

"How do you know that?" Jennifer asked.

"Very few of the crime scene guys' markers on the ground and none where you'd expect footprints. Daylight might have shown things we couldn't see last night, though." I wanted to see that scene in daylight.

"Unlikely up there. What dirt there is gets blown around a lot." Tom appeared to be counting rocks in Diana's fireplace.

"What if Don found him after dark? Don could have missed his footing, not knowing how close he was to the edge," Mike said. "Then Brian could have tried to get to him to help and couldn't make it."

"But Don would have had a light if he was searching after dark. Sheriff's department should know for sure if he did." Diana gave Mike a look.

He nodded. "I'll see what I can do." His Aunt Gee, Gisella Decker, was head dispatcher for the sheriff's department station in O'Hara Hill in the northwest part of the county. Whatever information she gave us was solid gold.

"Even in the dark, the presence of an able-bodied ally of Brian's would be the most reasonable explanation of Don going over—"

"You think it's a reasonable explanation that one of those boys took their father out to die, pushed Don into the cut, then left his father sprawled on the ground like that?"

Tom's effort to keep his words even deserved a similar response.

"If Brian asked for their help to die his way? Yeah, I do." Then I heard myself piling on reasons. "If it was dark, the kid might not have known how close Don was to the edge. With the emotional stress, that would certainly be an argument that—"

"No."

At his single word, we all looked at Mike. He leaned forward, hands on his knees, then looked at Tom. "Sorry. But if the boys were involved, together or one of them alone, it wasn't in the dark. Austin arrived at the house not long after Elizabeth and I did and Kade was already there. That was well before sunset."

Of course. I must be half asleep to have missed that.

"Can't they figure this out by looking for fibers, hairs—Why not?" Jennifer asked.

"What could be more normal than fibers and hairs from his family?

Besides that—" Mike bit it off.

Surprisingly, Tom was the one to pick it up. "They were all out at the scene. Got close. That could explain anything of them on Brian or anything of him on them. Some might even wonder if that's why Connie wanted to go out there. To make sure to account for any evidence. Against her or against the boys."

"Even before," I said. "When Connie said she wanted to go out there after Brian was found. That fumbling with their father's jacket. Both sons and Connie had it up against them. That could have been another way to explain any transference."

He twitched.

"That's the thought that went through my mind. And you can't tell me it wouldn't have gone through Wayne Shelton's, too. We have to look at everything—everything—under that same harsh light. We can't pick and choose or we'll miss things. Maybe those things will lead us to a conclusion that we don't like, but they'll lead us to the truth."

Tom didn't give in. "Two good kids supposedly wanting to help their father die to get insurance money by fraud and pushing another man to his death can't be the only explanation. Even if you won't consider it could have been an accident—"

"Accidents." I emphasized the plural.

"—what about other motives?" Tom asked.

"Like what?"

"Like the hare-brained motives you've pulled out of your hat other times," he said with more snap than I'd ever heard from him. "Like other people who—"

He thunked a fist on his knee, accompanying the chopping off of his own sentence.

"Other people who what?" I asked.

"I shouldn't have taken that swing at you." In a newsroom that would count as a love tap, not a swing. "But there are other explanations than Kade or Austin taking Brian out there to die then killing an accidental witness."

"Tom's got a point," Mike said. "We haven't looked at the normal kind of suspects. Who benefits? Who inherits?"

"The wife," Jennifer said wisely. She didn't appear to notice Tom's grimness. "Or maybe a girlfriend. Or ex."

"Don't know anything about a girlfriend, but Don has a wife." With that kind of redirect, Michael Paycik had a future in diplomacy. He'd deliberately pretended *wife* didn't apply to Connie. "An ex, too, right, Tom?"

"Yeah. But the ex has been gone for years. Before the current one showed up."

"Showed up?" I asked. "Loriana isn't from around here?"

"She grew up here, left, then came back a few years ago," Diana said. "But that was after Mindy took off."

"I nearly forgot." I filled them in on what Penny had said—at least the part of it that had to do with the two deaths. No need to mention her riff on my future.

Diana said, "What about that insurance guy Taylorman? Could he have a motive?"

"Definitely a suspect," Jennifer said.

"Why?" Diana asked before I could.

"He looks like a jackass." With the air of delivering the clincher, she added, "His website's a mess."

Nobody laughed, but Mike, Diana, and even Tom found the occasion to put their hands over their mouths. "It takes more than being a jackass," I said.

Jennifer nodded slowly. "Yeah. Or Fine would be the prime suspect every time."

This time the laughs were let loose.

"Why'd you bring up Taylorman, Diana?" I asked.

"He was like a buzzard circling around. It seemed ... weird. I don't have the experience you do, Elizabeth, but in the stories I've covered, insurance agents show up for natural disasters and such, but not for missing persons. He certainly wasn't searching."

"Interesting. Let's—"

"Oh, let me," Jennifer said. "I'll get everything on him. I know, I know. No hacking. I started the background sweeps you wanted, Elizabeth. So far no red flags for either man."

"What about the ditch, Tom?" Mike asked.

"Ditch?" I repeated.

"Red Sail Ditch Company," Mike said, as if that were a full and complete explanation. He turned back to Tom. "There's been trouble, hasn't there?"

Tom paused so long I thought he might not respond. "Bad feelings. Yeah."

"Between Brian and Don," I guessed, remembering Loriana's comments.

"And others."

"Were these others there last night?"

Tom's expression was bland. "A number of them."

Mike looked at his watch, muttered a mild curse, and stood. "Sorry to break this up, but I've got to get back to the station."

"But we've hardly started," Jennifer protested. "How're we going to tackle all these possibilities?"

"You could keep going without me," Mike offered morosely.

"No. I need to catch up on sleep after last night and I bet you two—" Diana tipped her head from me to Tom. "—do, too."

"Yes. As for the possibilities, Jennifer, we start whittling away. So, I'll keep on Penny and the sheriff's department. Jennifer, you check out Taylorman and gather backgrounds. Diana, how about you talk to Loriana about Don's movements yesterday and—"

"Have Mike do that," Tom interrupted. The twitch at one corner of his mouth was as good as a laugh. "That piece of advice will be my contribution to this effort."

"She's a brand new widow," I protested.

"Just saying she has a reputation for enjoying the sight of a man. One who's on TV can only help."

Mike groaned, but said, "Fine. I'll sacrifice myself for the sake of truth and justice. Let's meet tomorrow. Okay here, Diana?"

"Fine here, but Thursday night. Parent meetings at school tomorrow night. I've got a couple things I want to check," she said.

I nodded about the schedule, but asked, "What things?"

"I'm not saying more until I know more."

"Okay. Mike, also see if Aunt Gee has anything else for us. Considering the brick wall that is Wayne Shelton, we'll need it. Also, I'd like to see that scene in daylight."

Tom said, "Wayne told Connie it was off limits today. I'll check and let you know in the morning. Which reminds me, you're all invited to Red Sail Ranch tomorrow."

No one else looked surprised. Mike said, "See you then" and left. So I asked, "Tomorrow? Why?"

Diana told me, "Open house at Connie's. It's tradition to thank the searchers. And I'd imagine it will be an informal memorial."

Tom nodded. "Law enforcement's holding the body—bodies—so this will let everybody offer condolences. There'll be a private funeral later, when they can."

"You gotta go, Elizabeth," Jennifer said. "Well, not just you. All of us. But I know we will, so no point saying that. But we need you because you have experience with murderers and since they go back to the scene of the crime and funerals you need to see who's there. This isn't the funeral but pretty close."

"I'll go, but where'd you hear that, Jennifer? About murderers going back to the scene of the crime and to a victim's funeral?"

"Police shows on TV."

"In this instance, it wouldn't do us any good even if it were one hundred percent true," Diana said.

"Why?"

"You'll see," she promised.

Chapter Ten

AFTER HELPING WITH the minimal clean up and wishing Diana a good night, Jennifer, Tom, and I walked out.

Jennifer waved as she got in a small all-wheel drive she'd said was her mother's.

I said good night and started the three-minute commute to what Diana called the bunkhouse and would be a pricey studio apartment in Manhattan.

Tom walked beside me. Shadow fell in step beside him.

I slanted Tom a look.

"I'm walking you home," he said.

"You think something's going to happen to me between Diana's door and the bunkhouse?"

"No telling with you," he said dryly.

I considered asking him more questions about Brian, Connie, and their sons, but before I could frame the first one in a way I thought he might answer, he spoke again.

"So. Made up your mind?"

I looked up quickly.

The lines around his eyes deepened, but his mouth didn't budge. "I mean about a vehicle," he said levelly.

He did, but he meant other things, too.

I addressed Tom's out-loud question. It was the only one I could take on for now.

"You didn't expect me to be one of those people who walks into a dealership and falls for the first shiny thing that met my eye, did you?"

"No way in hell. But for the record, it's four dealerships. So far."

"I've had a lot of material to sort through," I said with dignity. "I researched gas mileage and durability. Then I researched the most frequently stolen vehicles in Wyoming. Don't raise your eyebrows like that. It's logical. I've had a car stolen and I don't want to go through that again."

"Any fireproof vehicles among your candidates? You've gone through that, too."

"I wish. But it's sensible to find out if there's a vehicle that's catnip to Wyoming thieves and to avoid it. And it turns out there is, though it doesn't really affect me."

"How's that?"

"White pickups dominate Wyoming's most-stolen list. No big surprise since they also dominate the most-popular list. But here was the surprise—most are five years old or older. So as long as I don't get a used pickup I should be fine."

He chuckled. "Law of averages. Bigger population of older trucks. So that's what thieves encounter, so that's what they steal."

We'd reached the bunkhouse porch. He stopped at the bottom, with a foot resting on the first step.

It was a nicely nuanced stance. Close enough to leap into action if danger burst out of the door at me, yet not inviting himself in. I appreciated the latter more than the former. Especially since Shadow, who'd taken up a mid-steps stance between us would sniff-test the bunkhouse thoroughly as he did each night.

"Darn. And here I thought I had the thieves outsmarted."

His face grooves deepened and so did the chuckle. "I'm not counting you out, Elizabeth. Never counting you out."

I leaned down to pat Shadow's head.

"So you got the pickup?" he asked.

"No. I like the way it handled and it actually gets a little better mileage. But I couldn't imagine trying to park it in New York or D.C."

"So you decided what to get based on what'll be better for when you leave."

"I..." I shut my mouth on the denial. "Just being practical."

He leaned down and patted Shadow's rear.

He kept his head down as he said, "What did you see out there, Elizabeth?"

"Out where?"

"Brian."

I'd been thinking I was glad of the change of subject. Now I wasn't so sure.

"What do you mean? I saw the same things you saw."

He shook his still-lowered head. "No. You saw something else. Or you put what you saw together different, like…" He let it fade out. I did not ask "like what?" "You knew Hazen was down there."

"No way. I had no idea." I laughed. "You're not trying to say I'm psychic are you?"

"No. But we all saw Brian and that setup. You were the one who sensed something more was wrong."

"No."

I hadn't responded fast enough. He looked up and repeated, "You sensed something more was wrong."

"Maybe I guessed there could be something. But I didn't know anything. It was lucky."

Despite the shadow of his hat brim, I knew he was looking at me with his deep-set Abraham Lincoln eyes. He gave a slow nod. "Okay, Elizabeth."

I didn't fool myself that that meant he'd accepted what I'd said. More like a promise to deal with this later.

He dropped his foot off the first step and started to turn.

"Tom?"

He looked back over his shoulder, waiting.

"Other people who what?" I asked.

"Good night, Elizabeth." He tipped his hat and was gone.

SHADOW HAD SCOPED out every corner of the bunkhouse, then curled up on the dog bed I'd placed where he always slept—midway between the door and my bed.

Making one last check of email on my new phone before I turned off the bedside lamp, I found Jennifer's notes.

Reading through them reinforced what I'd been thinking as I'd brushed my teeth. We'd barely scratched the surface.

DAY THREE
WEDNESDAY

OUR NEXT MEETING came earlier than expected.

My phone rang as Diana and I turned onto Highway 27, heading toward KWMT, east of Sherman.

Before I'd become homeless and carless she'd frequently gone straight to assignments, but insisted driving me to the station each morning was not an inconvenience. Another reason I hoped the SUV came soon.

"Elizabeth?" came Jennifer's voice through the phone. "We're in the parking lot at the station."

"Okay."

"We're waiting for you and Diana. How soon will you get here?"

"Five minutes, maybe."

"Less," Diana said, dropping her foot on the accelerator.

"Is this urgent?" I asked Jennifer. I've been a passenger a couple times when Diana decided to get somewhere in a hurry.

"Not really."

"Not urgent," I said to Diana. "Not an emergency. No need to speed."

I think my words were lost in the G-forces.

Maybe it's from having so many winding roads in the mountains and so many rough and rocky roads everywhere that when Wyoming drivers hit a nice, straight patch of paved highway, some drive with … let's call it gusto.

Diana took the turn into the KWMT-TV drive with enough of that gusto to spew a dust tail that any rooster would be proud of. She drew up to the edge of the lot closest to where Jennifer, Mike, and Tom stood by a scrubby natural area that passed for landscaping.

Mike whistled as we got out of the truck. "That was impressive, Diana. You must have something important to tell us."

"To tell *you*? Jennifer said you guys were meeting," I protested. Diana was too busy grinning to talk.

"I saw Mike and Tom out here, so I came out and called you on the way," Jennifer said.

"I just got here from seeing Loriana. I took breakfast burritos out there this morning, and she seemed glad to see them."

Was it unfair to think the new widow might have been glad to see Mike, too?

Didn't matter. None of my business. Absolutely none of my business.

"I pulled in right after Tom and was asking what brought him here when you came rushing out, Jenny—Jennifer."

She punished Mike's name slip with a short glare then turned to Tom. "What *are* you doing here?"

"I came to thank Les Haeburn for the station's help Monday. You all can roll your eyes, but it's better to keep those wheels greased. Let him think he did the right thing without needing a shove."

"So we're all here by happenstance and there's no news?" I didn't know if it was recovering from Diana's driving or the ebbing of the something's-up adrenaline, but I felt a definite dip in energy.

"I did have one thing," Jennifer said. "Not from research or anything like that, though. Something I sort of wondered. I wouldn't have gotten everybody together like this, but as long as we're here..."

She stopped.

At first I thought it was to take a breath. But, no, because she breathed several times. The others looked at me.

I looked back.

Diana tipped her head toward Jennifer, conveying I was to draw out of Jennifer what she'd "sort of wondered."

"It doesn't have to be research, Jennifer. We'd like to hear what you wondered—wouldn't we?"

Everyone else nodded. "We would," Diana added.

"If it was an accident ... How could you be sure?"

"We can't be sure, but the odds—"

"Not you *you*, Elizabeth. I mean you, the murderer. How could you—the murderer—be sure?"

"That he'd die," Mike said slowly.

"Right. Either of them."

Mike said, "Brian was pretty weak, so there was a good chance he wouldn't survive."

"Okay, but would that be good enough for somebody who wanted to murder him? And what about Don Hazen? I started looking up falls and these professional kayakers go over hundred-foot waterfalls all the time and—"

"Professional kayakers?" Diana muttered.

"—and they don't die."

"That's a trained athlete going into deep water, not somebody falling into a bed of boulders," I said.

Jennifer kept going. "A flight attendant survived a fall of ten thousand feet and pilots in World War II whose parachutes didn't open survived, and—"

"But those are anomalies," I said. "That's why people wrote about them."

"Still, Jennifer has a point," Mike said. "How could the murderer be sure Don would die from that fall? Yeah, it was *possible*. Maybe even likely, but would somebody be willing to settle for likely?"

"For that matter, how could a murderer be sure Brian would die," Diana added. "Isn't it possible he could have survived the night? Tom?"

"Possible, but never likely. His doctor said that flat-out," Tom said. "Another point. I know that stretch where Don was found. Haven't been there in a while but it's not what I'd call a bed of boulders. Say a thirty- to forty-foot fall onto hard, rocky ground." He shrugged. "Wouldn't surprise me if a man survived that. Wouldn't surprise me if he didn't."

"I definitely want to see that spot in daylight," I said. I put a hand on Jennifer's back. "That was good wondering. I'm glad you called us all together for this meeting."

She beamed, then said seriously, "I didn't really call you together for a meeting you know. It was an accident."

Chapter Eleven

THE OTHERS WENT inside. Tom for his diplomatic mission, the others to pursue their KWMT workdays.

I remained outside to call a certain number in the Washington, D.C., metropolitan area.

"Dex? It's Danny."

"Danny. What residual impairments are you experiencing from the smoke exposure? Your hoarseness has mitigated."

Most people would have said "How are you?"

He'd started calling me Danny years ago and I'd encouraged it, since that name was less likely to clue in someone he worked with in the FBI lab that he was communicating with a reporter. Last thing I would want would be to imperil his ability to continue doing great work on important cases.

Except then the nickname caught on with colleagues, friends, and family. So it probably didn't afford Dex much protection now.

On the other hand, it might not matter anymore. As far as most of the law enforcement world was concerned, I was no longer a vessel they needed to worry about catching stray leaks.

So maybe my exile to Wyoming had an upside.

"I'm fine, Dex. Thanks."

"No you're not. Without access to your records I couldn't provide a useful timeline for your impairment, but impaired you are."

"Nice to talk to you, too, Dex."

"It is nice to talk to you, Danny. Because you can talk."

That was Dex being as matter of fact as always, yet I swallowed and said in a small and slightly hoarse—not only from residual impairments—voice, "Thank you, Dex."

"I haven't done anything."

"You're glad to talk to me. Not everyone is."

"You ask a lot of questions. Not everyone likes answering questions. I do," he said simply.

I wished I could have hugged him at that moment. "And I love you for that, Dex. In fact," I added, knowing he wouldn't know how to respond, "I have a question for you right now."

"As long as it doesn't compromise—"

"—your professional ethics. I know. Would I ever ask you to do that?"

"Yes. But I'd say no."

I laughed. "Fair enough, Dex. But this one won't. Nothing touching on the FBI at all. Here's the situation. Say a man is pushed off a sort of cliff and drops thirty or forty feet to hard, rocky ground. How could the pusher know for sure that he would die?"

"It depends." Always his favorite answer.

"What does it depend on?"

"The force with which he was pushed. Whether anything broke his fall. What condition the victim was in. Kinetic energy produced from the fall converts to mechanical energy, producing fractures and ruptures in organs—"

"Could the pusher know that would kill the victim?"

"No. Realistically, the only way the pusher could know for sure that he would die would be to kill him first."

A zing up my back straightened my posture to the point that even my mother would approve. "To kill him first?"

"Yes, before pushing him off the cliff."

He and Jennifer would make a great pair—both so literal. Though I shuddered to think of how any potential offspring would make it through life.

"Alternatively, to kill him after he'd been pushed off the cliff," Dex added. "Specifically, after he'd landed." Responses like that were why Dex had not been called as an expert witness for a long, long time. The lawyers had learned their lesson.

"Okay, so how would someone kill this guy—before or after he landed—that would make officials think he died from the fall?"

"It depends on how thorough they were. Strangulation is unlikely to be missed in the autopsy. If they're not looking for it, a gunshot could be missed among other extreme injuries and if the shot did not kill him immediately, the injuries from the fall would be perimortem, so it would not be obvious that it wasn't the fall that killed him. A poison not included on a standard panel or that they didn't test for could work."

"To use poison," I said slowly, "the murderer would have to have known that an opportunity to mask it with the fall was going to happen. Or to be extremely lucky to have had the fall happen as the poison was taking effect."

"There are quick-acting agents."

"That doesn't feel right."

"Danny—"

"I know, I know. Feeling has nothing to do with it, but if I told you all the shreds of reasons that add up to my feeling I'd keep you on the phone so long the FBI lab would grind to a halt."

And that was if I could articulate all of them.

Something other than what the rest of us saw.

Tom's words popped into my head.

And then another voice. Another conversation.

You don't want people to know how easy things come for you. You want them to believe you work as hard as they do. Because that's what makes people respect you. You understand that, don't you?

Dex made a sound between a chuckle and a cluck, pulling me back.

"You're too flattering, Danny. The lab would continue to function effectively without me. However, I tentatively concede your point about the accumulation of small observations that could lead you to that hypothesis—not a feeling, a hypothesis. There are other possibilities, of course. Including a perpetrator using the tools at hand."

"What do you mean?" Though I had a guess.

"Bash him in the head with a rock," Dex said with relish.

"The blow could be mistaken for impact with a rock when he fell?"

"Perhaps in a cursory examination, but—"

I knew his view on what constituted a cursory examination. "Dex, think normal people, ordinary labs, real-life situations. In those circumstances, could a bash on the head with a rock pass for hitting his head when he fell?"

The silence meant he was considering it. "It depends."

That was the best I was going to get.

"**TOM TOLD ME** another way to get to Red Sail Rock so we wouldn't disturb Connie at the house," Mike said.

I hadn't even made it inside KWMT before Mike had emerged, saying Tom had called, saying we could revisit the scene this morning.

Mike passed the ranch road we'd taken Monday then turned off the highway on a track that angled north and east.

"There it is," he said with a nod across the mostly dun colored landscape to a gently snaking stripe of muted green that indicated a creek. "This track should meet up with the ditch and then follow along to Red Sail Rock."

Ah.

Not a creek, a ditch. A ditch by Red Sail Rock.

That answered one of my questions about "Red Sail Ditch."

I debated asking Mike more, but the driving was tough enough that I decided to wait rather than distract him.

We continued beside the water for a while, then had a choice of staying there, or following a track along rapidly rising ground, like a ramp in a parking garage. A ramp with more potholes than pavement.

We took the up-ramp, while the creek and a strip of ground beside it stayed level.

Yellow tape came into sight ahead, with the rocky rise that backed the scene to its south.

And now I understood the name Red Sail. We'd been too close to it in those early morning hours of Tuesday. Now, from a bit of distance the rocky rise we'd come around before seeing the police-tape-enclosed scene resembled a triangular red sail.

Mike stopped his four-wheel drive half a dozen yards from the tape. Wind tugged, but the tape remained intact for now. No humans were in sight. Clearly the scientists had finished their work here and it had not been considered necessary to set a guard.

Before approaching the taped-off area, I went to see how much above the water we were. I had to get nearly to the edge to see the creek—no, ditch—just to the north. This was more of a prominence than I'd thought.

"That's Don Hazen's land." Mike nodded toward the north. "And that must be where Richard and Shelton went down night before last." A very rough track showed signs of recent disturbance, with more police tape strung across it. "It would have been Don's most direct path up, too. If he'd come from his place."

"Up *that*? Nobody could get up that."

He grinned. "Wanna bet? We can put it to the test."

"Not unless we find out it matters how somebody got up here."

We approached the tape, working our way around the northern curve until we were opposite where we'd stood before, with the open portion of the horseshoe between the two positions.

In daylight, the slanted ground gave way to rock, which became a broken off edge that clearly overlooked a drop-off.

For once, I wished Thurston Fine was on hand.

He was even more wrong than I'd thought.

"Thurston's theory was Don didn't see the edge of the drop-off because he was too startled by coming across Brian," I said.

Mike huffed. "Only if he was blind."

"And stupid," I agreed. "He'd have had to circle around both wheelchair and corpse, and back up ten feet to stand with his back to the drop-off. Where, even if he then had a bizarrely delayed reaction of shock, he would have had to take a backward step *up* to that rock outcropping, then another step backward to go over the edge. Unless, at the sight of Brian's dead body, Don skirted both chair and corpse and then, apparently in utter despair, made a swan dive off the outcropping."

"Take that, Thurston," Mike muttered.

Not that logic would shut him up. I could hear his response as if he were here. *Despair can be a powerful and unpredictable source. No one knows the depths of darkness in another man's soul.*

On second thought, I was glad he wasn't here or the temptation to push him off would have been strong.

"Well, this ends any doubt I had about Hazen stumbling over the edge by accident," I said. "Even in the dark, if he were backing up, he'd have felt that incline. It's too sharp not to."

"And Don knew this land. Not as well as Brian, but he knew this spot. Heck, I knew Red Sail Rock and this cut growing up in another part of the county."

I shaded my eyes and slowly scanned the horizon. "It provides quite a view, doesn't it?"

"Yup. Red Sail Rock is a real landmark."

"What are they building over there?"

"Building? Where?"

"You can see construction machinery." I could identify it as one of those digging machines frequently used at ground-breaking ceremonies.

From this vantage, the line of greener vegetation looped south before resuming an eastern line. That's where I pointed.

"That's a track hoe. Don't see ones that size being used as much as—" Mike interrupted himself and pointed. "Tom and the Walterston boys. Must have been watching the track hoe working."

Three riders had come into sight by cresting a ridge of a buttress-like extension from a rise in the corner where the water turned east again.

"That track hoe's pretty big to be up here," Mike continued. "More often you'd see a backhoe doing that sort of work."

"So, what are they building?"

"They're not. They're cleaning the ditch. Usually only see track hoes if they're building a good-sized new ditch and not always then. Sure is easier than when they first built ditches a hundred years ago using mule teams and Fresnos."

"Think we have time to get down to the water—ditch—before they get here?"

I saw no reason to confide to Mike that I'd thought it was a creek.

"Get there and back without Tom knowing? No."

He picked up right where he'd left off with talk of excavators, track hoes, draglines, interrupted only when a shift in the breeze brought us spurts of clanging that I suspected emanated from the machinery.

The three riders, with Tom in the middle, picked up the pace. None appeared to be paying much attention to the fact that they were on thousand-plus-pound animals, though body language said the brothers were far from at ease.

One impression that kept resurfacing from Monday night and early Tuesday was the tension between Connie's sons. There'd been grief, yes. And worry for their mother. But this had been something different ... hadn't it?

I couldn't help comparing it to their slightly self-conscious delight in trying to out-eat each other at Aunt Gee's spread.

"Poor kids," I said.

Mike shot me a look. I suspected he was remembering our theories about one or both of them being involved in the deaths. Feeling sorry for them didn't mean I'd back off trying to find out what happened. It just meant I felt sorry for them.

They disappeared for a few moments then emerged from behind the rock rise. Both boys glanced toward the enclosed area then quickly away.

When they got near enough, Tom said, "Mike, Elizabeth. You know Kade and Austin."

We all nodded.

"How's your mom?" I asked.

"Okay," Kade mumbled.

Before the silence calcified, I asked, "Were you all by the, uh, track hoe? What's it doing?"

"Repairs." Tom made do with a single word to answer the second question and thus confirm the first. It seemed a bit short even for him.

"Today? Were they urgent?" I shaded my eyes with my hand to

look up at one brother then the other.

"Loriana ordered them up." Tom's voice was unnaturally neutral.

"Should've been done a long time ago," muttered Kade. "One more drop and Loop Field would've flooded. Never seen banks get that bad that fast."

"Never seen" would have had more impact from a wizened old-timer. This kid's frame of reference was pretty short.

"It's not her fault they got in bad shape," his brother said. "Not her fault repairs weren't done before. She's doing them now, isn't she? Soonest she could. *And* paying extra to have it done fast. You gonna blame her for that, too?"

"Should've started on the west side, because of the water flow, besides it's worse than the east."

"You heard her—she meant west, she just mixed it up. Now they've started, they'll continue. Give her a break. Her husband just died."

I noticed that Austin hadn't said murdered.

"It's waited this long, why'd it have to be today?" Kade demanded with a blinding pivot. "We shouldn't be out here having to check that stuff. We should be at the house with Mom and Jaden. Shouldn't we, Tom?"

Ah. I think I understood Tom's neutrality now. The brothers were rubbing raw against each other as they had during the search. They'd simply switched topics.

Sometimes people in a crisis lash out at those closest to them, perhaps with a hope or expectation that they'll be forgiven whatever is said. Often they are wrong.

Tom apparently was trying to dampen the discord with a strong dose of unemotional. I had a vision of him on a tightrope strung between the brothers, trying to keep his balance while avoiding stepping toward one side or the other.

"Your mother's got plenty of company at the house," he said, even and cool.

"It should be us, too. It's not right leaving it to Jaden."

Austin leaned forward with a creak of his saddle to fire at his brother. "You don't want to admit any Hazen could do what's right, and that's damned childish. Blaming her for what he did." He faced me now, apparently trying to recruit reinforcements. "She called early and said that in light of our mutual tragedy she wanted to show that bygones would be bygones now, so she was paying for the repairs all herself and they were going to start right off. Couldn't do better than that, could she?"

His brother turned away from us to spit on the ground.

Austin's hands tightened to fists on the reins.

Were they brothers who naturally took opposite opinions, as some siblings did? They hadn't given that impression at Aunt Gee's, but perhaps that day had been the aberration.

"Still a sight of work to be done," Tom said. "You asked if it was urgent, Elizabeth. Hard to say, but it's certainly needed. Don had let the banks in that section degrade."

"Degrade, my ass," Kade muttered.

"Kade," Tom said quietly.

"Well, it's true. He was a mean cuss who was doing it on purpose to agitate Dad."

Austin reentered the conversation. "That's another reason you should give Loriana credit for making things right as soon as possible. Most people would say she's being a good neighbor. Acting responsibly like Dad always said to do."

Now Kade leaned forward to connect in a glare with his brother. Color rose up the younger boy's throat into his cheeks, then disappeared into the shadow of his hat.

Since there didn't seem to be anything in Austin's comments for Kade to take exception to or for Austin to color up about, I figured both were based on general principal.

Kade broke the look and began to wheel his horse away. He jerked to a stop, looked back, tugged the brim of his hat sharply and said, "Ma'am. Tom. Mike."

Then he was gone, aiming toward the house, I guessed.

Austin waited only long enough to make it clear he hadn't wanted to leave at the same time as his brother, uttered the same terse good-bye and turned his horse back toward the repair work on the ditch.

They hadn't gone completely opposite directions. More like one o'clock and five o'clock.

I wondered if that was progress.

Tom crossed his arms on the horn, leaned forward, and sighed.

"Tough morning?"

He grunted confirmation, then changed the subject. "Find what you wanted to see here?"

"There wasn't anything in particu—"

Mike ruined my foray into reasonable. "Yeah, we did. Because there's no way Thurston's right. Don couldn't have just stumbled backward over the edge because he was shocked at finding Brian."

"That was his theory?" Tom asked with a spark of amusement.

"Yes." I pressed the point. "And that goes to show how unlikely it is that these deaths were accidental."

"There are other ways for an accident—accidents—to have happened."

"Meteors? Aliens? Ice knives?"

"Don't let Thurston hear any of those ideas," warned Mike.

I shaded my eyes to look up. "Tom, do you know about the insurance stuff Taylorman was talking about?" I'd realized belatedly I should have asked him last night. "If Brian wasn't covered for suicide—"

"He was."

"And that accidental death benefit Taylorman was talking about?"

He nodded. Tom started to swing out of his saddle. His horse shifted, which made me scoot out of the way. Tom adjusted in mid-air and came down smoothly instead of in the heap of broken bones I'd envisioned for a split second.

Mike took my elbow, possibly because he thought I intended to run. "Chico was shifting his weight."

Why didn't they outfit the creatures with beepers like they do for trucks backing up?

Tom looped the reins around one of the stakes holding up the police tape.

"Can't he pull free?" I asked, keeping an eye on the horse.

"Yeah. But he won't. Brian wanted to provide for Connie and the boys, but with his health, to get enough basic life insurance was out of reach. The accidental death benefit didn't cost much for a good payout." Tom shrugged. "He felt it was worth it."

"He talked to you about it?"

"Connie did. Have you seen what you want to see?"

Okay. That door was closed.

"Not yet. What about the path from the house here…?" I let it go when Tom shook his head once.

"Wayne says they couldn't get anything usable to know whether Brian's wheelchair did or didn't come up that way. No footprints, either. You can walk it if you want."

No point if there was nothing to see. "I want to go down and see where they found Don Hazen. When are they going to open that?"

He shrugged.

"Can we see anything from up here?" Mike asked.

"Don't know."

We all moved forward. Beside the last stake was enough ledge for one person at a time to stand.

I stepped forward, but each of them checked me with a hand.

"I'm probably heavier than you, Tom. I'll check it," Mike said.

Tom nodded, but also got behind him and grabbed the back of Mike's belt.

"If it's dangerous—"

"Just a precaution," Tom said.

Mike moved slowly, testing the ground under his feet with each step. Right out to the edge. "It's solid here. Can't see much, though. A bit of the police tape. You next, Tom?"

They swapped places. Tom looked but said nothing.

"Now that you two have weakened it, is it my turn?"

Mike grinned and gestured me forward. Then he grabbed the back waist of my slacks. "Just in case."

I made use of his hold to lean out farther.

"Hey," Mike protested.

He was right about seeing only a small segment of police tape and a patch of ground a good distance below. The ditch showed to our left and to the right, so presumably it ran below us, too, but the structure of this rock protuberance blocked sight of it from here.

As I came back upright, I tipped my head to the right. "Looks like some of this ledge crumbled in the middle. And it looks recent."

Both of them looked, but they hadn't had the angle I had to see the raw edges.

"Broke off under Don's feet?" Tom did not give up.

"Still have the problem of how he got out there," Mike said.

"Among other problems," I agreed.

Chapter Twelve

"I SEE WHAT Diana meant last night."

I made the acknowledgment as Mike and I entered the Walterston house shortly after eleven a.m.

I was referring to what she'd said last night in response to Jennifer's theory that the murderer might be here. Going by that, instead of narrowing our suspect pool, this gathering widened it to most of Cottonwood County and beyond.

We'd had a hint from the vehicles parked out front. But judging from the number of people, there'd been a lot of carpooling.

As if to prove that all the county's important people were on hand, I immediately spotted Leona D'Amato.

I turned to point her out to Mike, but he was gone. I spotted Diana hugging Connie, then her head bobbed in the direction of the kitchen, while I was carried away toward several long tables set end to end stretching through the heart of the house. They were jammed with food.

On my way, I saw many of the searchers, plus one special addition.

Tom's daughter Tamantha, a third-grader who would scare Vladimir Putin if he had any sense.

But in this moment she did not look scary. She stood in front of Connie, looking up at her, as the press of people opened a little to give them room.

Tamantha stepped forward and wrapped her arms around Connie in a grave hug. Connie brought the girl in close, with a lift of her lips, while her eyes teared.

The crowd couldn't be held back long and as my view of her closed off, I saw Connie's expression return to the sharp grooves of exhaustion and grief. The third Walterston son, the oldest, Jaden took her arm.

"So sad," Leona D'Amato said from beside me.

"It is. Amazing turnout. Can you help me with names?"

"Of course." You'd think I'd asked if she knew her ABCs.

She confirmed Hannah Chaney's name and Terry Waymark as Driver 1.

Driver 3, glowering from a corner, was Hannah's husband Paul Chaney.

Driver 2, she told me was Otto Chaney. "He's Paul's uncle on the paternal side."

"They're all on the Red Sail Ditch?"

She nodded. "All members of the company. Hazens and Walterstons, too."

"Also the McCrackens? The people who bought the Pecklies' place?"

"My, my, you are getting to know your way around Cottonwood County. Them, too." She reeled off another four family names. "Though they've stayed pretty much neutral in the problems. Did you know Paul Chaney and Don Hazen were cousins? On Paul's mother's side. Oh, I need to catch Gisella Decker. Excuse me."

Trying not to speculate what that conversation might be about, I turned away. And found the tables in front of me, loaded with potential distractions.

As I approached the table corner closest to the entry, I could look down the entire length. Since the culinary offerings were mostly low, I had a clear view of Kade beyond the buffet's opposite corner, as deep into the shadows as he could get and still be in attendance.

For most of the visitors, he'd be obscured by all the other people between them. Even those nearby would have to peer around to spot him because he stood in an office alcove set off by poles.

I could see that—and him—only because the tables opened a line of sight from my spot to his. If I hadn't looked up from the feast, I would have missed him, as everyone else seemed to.

No, not everyone.

Loriana appeared around a pole and approached him.

A small jolt hit me that she was here.

It took half a beat to realize I was reacting to the private hypothesizing Tuesday night at Diana's that one of the Walterston sons might have killed her husband. There was no reason to think she might share that suspicion.

She gave Kade a small, sad smile.

He didn't look like he welcomed her condolences, but that didn't stop her.

As she spoke, she ducked her head, apparently trying to catch his gaze. He dropped his head lower.

She stroked a hand up his arm. He stepped away.

No, that might be misleading, because it would be like saying someone stepped away from contact with a live electrical wire. He jolted away and turned his back on her.

A hint hard to ignore.

She paused a moment, then moved on with no sign of perturbance, while his face flamed red and his jaw tightened enough that I could see it from where I stood.

Interesting.

Then I saw Loriana making her way toward Mike. Saw him smile at her, and I wasn't quite as amused.

Not that Mike couldn't take care of himself.

No doubt their conversation now was part of his doing exactly what we'd talked about—feeling her out about Don's mood and doings in the days leading up to his death.

Though I wished the phrase *feeling her out* hadn't popped into my thoughts.

I turned away from the thought and the view of the two of them looking very chummy. That brought me back to Kade in time to see Austin walk past him and say something that didn't appear to be pleasant. Their postures were stiff with antagonism as they moved in different directions.

Stillness in the foreground of this scene caught my eye.

Cas Newton stood beside the table to my left, frozen in the act of spearing a piece of beef and with his gaze directed at the spot Connie's sons had just occupied.

Cas—full name Caswell after his mother's family—had figured in an inquiry around the Fourth of July. At that time, his aunt had said the high school rodeo star was one of the good guys.

I slid up next to him.

"Hi, Cas."

He gave me a look that did not indicate he thought I was one of the good guys.

It was a variant of the simple Oh-God-help-me-a-reporter look. It had that in it, but it added a thick layer of concern and, yes, fear.

I tipped my head toward where we'd both been looking. "Seems to be tension there."

"Their father just died." Interesting that a western drawl could have that much snap to it.

"Yes, he did. You were in the group that found Brian, weren't you. That must have been tough."

He jerked a shoulder. "He wanted to die. Everybody knew that. It was killi—It was real hard on him the way it was dragging on."

"Is this any easier?"

"They'll be all right. The Walterstons stick together. No matter what."

His voice had skidded up with tension. Or worry. Or both.

I decided to push him. "The question could be how strongly you think they might stick together. And to what lengths would that sticking together carry them?"

He turned to me, belligerent. But not belligerent enough not to keep his voice down so only I could hear him. "You trying to say if one of them did something wrong the other would cover for him?"

"Not trying to say anything. Though insurance fraud…" I figured my small chance of getting something out of him would go to zero if I brought up murder.

But then he opened the door by repeating in a mutter, "He wanted to die."

"But he wasn't dead yet. Not until he was left out there, unable to get back in his chair. Even if he wanted to die, he had no opportunity to change his mind. That was taken away from him. Without any water. Or a way to get help—"

"He did have—" He clamped his mouth shut, but couldn't stop the hard swallow that pulsed his Adam's apple.

I rocked back, considering him. "He had what, Cas?"

He gave me a look he probably thought was tough. "They didn't do anything wrong and I'm not talking to you."

"Okay. But you should talk to somebody. Soon."

He walked away.

A knot of people moved in on the tables. That left no opportunity to talk to anyone one-on-one but plenty for picking up general attitudes and interesting tidbits.

It's amazing the things people will say in situations like that, apparently thinking that no one can hear them if they lower their voice a bit. And some didn't even bother with the voice-lowering part.

Yes, I picked up some very interesting tidbits.

Chapter Thirteen

AFTER A MINISTER, Brian's aunt, and his lifelong best friend who'd driven up from Colorado made comments in the brief formal portion of the gathering, I saw Tom make a break for the front door and maneuvered around to exit the kitchen door.

Yes, I could have gone out the same door, but this way I caught pieces of different conversations.

Outside, I met up with him by the front of his truck, which was near the house as one of the early arrivals.

He gave me a wary look. "Elizabeth."

I opted for the direct approach. "Tom, what do you know about dissension in the Red Sail Ditch Company?"

I'd overheard that phrase "dissension in the Red Sail Ditch Company" and based on the conspiratorial tone, it was worth asking about.

"There's always dissension in a ditch company. I doubt there's a landowner in Wyoming who doesn't think he could do good things with more water."

"All nice and theoretical. But what about non-theoretical dissension and specifically in the Red Sail Ditch Company?"

He narrowed his eyes. That made the lines at their corners deeper. A lot of the times when those lines deepened it denoted amusement. Not this time.

It was the way he might squint at the sun that had given him those lines in the first place. Especially if he suspected the sun of trying to pull a fast one on him.

Me, innocent ol' me.

"Are you fishing for something specific?"

I raised my open hands, palms up, showing the utter lack of a dagger with which to stab him in the back. "Simply trying to find out about this group of people. Are these the other people you started to mention last night?"

He sidestepped the question. "Mostly hard-working, ordinary folks."

"So no squabbles?"

This time he didn't answer.

"I'll make this easier for you, Burrell. I've heard the Red Sail Ditch Company likened to a dysfunctional family." Overheard might be more accurate, but let's not get technical.

He breathed out short and irked. "*Talk*," he said disparagingly.

"Yes. Most people do. How about some from you?"

"About that tussle over the fence?"

What tussle over what fence? "Yes."

"They were wrong to start, Brian would've straightened it out, but Don bulled in and made a mess of it."

This was promising. Not just Brian, but Don also involved.

"Let's go back to 'They were wrong to start.' "

"The McCrackens should've put up a portable fence. But they didn't know. Moved in to the Pecklie place not long before Brian started getting real sick. Was in the hospital a couple weeks. When he came out, he was in the wheelchair. The boys tended the ditch some, but with school and the ranch and trying to be with their dad... Meantime, the McCrackens saw this moving water and with a couple kids of their own they were worried about it. Before anybody knew it, they had a fence up."

"On their own land?"

"Doesn't matter. Ditch has an easement. You can't build anything that interferes with maintaining the ditch."

"Like a fence?"

He nodded. "Like a fence. Fences gather trash, impede the flow. Worse, McCracken put the fence up at Don's property line. He tore the whole thing down."

"The McCrackens weren't happy?" I guessed.

He grimaced. "There was shouting and pushing, I hear. I tried to talk to them, but by then everybody had their heels pretty well dug in. Sheriff's department got called out a couple times over it."

"But nothing's come of it since?"

With clear reluctance, he said, "McCrackens filed a lawsuit."

"Against?"

"Word is they were going to sue both Don and the Red Sail Ditch Company. Brian talked them out of suing the company. First he got them to accept a donated portable fence. Don couldn't object to that, since it didn't come out of the treasury. As for the rest of what he'd destroyed, the ditch company compensated the McCrackens. Only it basically came out of Don's pocket, because Brian fined him for infractions, so nobody else had to pay for what Don did."

I would need a manual to work my way through all this stuff about a ditch company. But I wasn't stopping to ask about that now. I brought the focus back to the people. "So that set up bad blood between Don and Brian?"

"More like it turned up the heat under what had been a constant simmer."

"Was that when Don started his campaign to take over from Brian as ditch boss?" Another bit I'd picked up inside.

He eyed me. I knew he was trying to figure out how much I knew and he knew I knew that's what he was doing.

"Pretty much."

"You know, other people having disagreements with Don can't hurt the Walterstons and might help them."

He waited, expressionless.

"You hate talking about other people that much?"

He tipped his head forward, slid his hat off, drove his free hand through his hair, put the hat back on, then brought his head up to meet my eyes from under the brim. "Yup."

This time I did the waiting.

Finally, he said, "It's like a disease with some around here. I don't like having my business chewed over, so I don't do it to others."

"I get that. Sometimes, though, telling what you know about other people can help find the truth. You've seen that happen."

His gaze went to the horizon. I followed it and was struck again by a sense that something had changed. Could it be perspective?

Before I could sort that out, he spoke. "I grant that in your hands it's an effort to find the truth, not just jawing about people, Elizabeth. It still goes against the grain, but I'll keep that in mind."

I felt like I'd negotiated North Korea into opening its borders and emptying its political prisons.

"Thank you, Tom."

The sound of footsteps brought my head around quickly.

Loriana.

Her gaze went from me to Tom and back. I had a flash that the next time she sat next to a stranger by a coffee pot the topic might not be Hannah and her travails.

Tom stepped forward, putting a hand on her arm, saying he was sorry for her loss. Her hand came up to cover his, stroking it.

I followed, echoing his condolences. I didn't touch her and she didn't stroke me.

"Thank you. Thank you both. It... doesn't seem real. Any of it. Coming here today has helped. Being with my neighbors." She looked up into the bright sky and swallowed hard. "We had a partnership. A true partnership. Hard to believe I'm alone now." A sheen of tears covered her eyes when she dropped her head and looked at me. "You must know what I mean, since you're married, right?"

Sticking to facts, I said, "I was. However, my husband and I divorced."

"Oh, I'm sorry. I thought... I'm sorry. No, you're right. That is an entirely different matter." She shook her head. "I think it's time for me get home. This gathering *has* helped, but it's been tiring."

We made appropriate farewells. She headed down the line of vehicles, hips swaying.

It had to be unconscious.

"You okay?" Tom asked.

"Yes."

"Liar."

I turned away. "If you're so sure you knew the answer, why'd you ask?"

"She rattled the knob on your door with the Keep Out sign nailed to it." I hate it when people don't answer my questions, especially when they instead make a statement about me.

"You mean my divorce. Was that what you want? To see if I'd say the word again?"

"It's not a scarlet letter—or word—you know."

"It is in my family," I muttered. Maybe that wasn't fair, though. None of my family had said I was a failure because I'd divorced. None except me. "Even without the scarlet letter, it doesn't add to your confidence when you thought you knew someone well enough to pledge to spend the rest of your life with him—in fact, *did* spend a good chunk of a life with him—and then discovered you were entirely wrong."

Tom nodded slowly. "You're still a good judge of character, Elizabeth."

How did he know that was bothering me? How had I not known it until now?

"Sure doesn't seem like it lately," I grumbled.

"What happened with Mildred—"

"Is the latest in a trend that included my once-dear husband extending our divorce to my career."

"Everybody misses now and then," he said, deadpan. "Could be worse."

"Really? Because to my mind it says your judgment about people is crap when someone you thought you knew better than anybody else in the world did something you never saw coming. That you were—Oh." I regarded the glint in his eyes in an otherwise bland expression. "You mean..."

"That's right. You're talking minor league. To get to the majors you'd have to find out that the person you'd married was someone you couldn't be sure hadn't committed murder."

I nodded, then added, "Not to mention that she was perfectly willing to have you take the rap for the murder." In fact, his ex-wife's behavior made my complaint look almost petty.

"You don't need to sound so cheerful about it," he said.

"Why not? You've cheered me up no end. You're right. It could be a whole lot worse. Heck, compared to you, I'm a rare and fine judge of character."

The lines at the corners of his eyes deepened into a smile. Heat eased into it.

"What does it say about you, then, that I'm drawn to you, Elizabeth Margaret Danniher, and suspect you might be feeling the same?"

All joking vanished.

He stepped closer. I didn't move back.

"Definitely drawn to you," he said.

The front door opened with a squawk and the force of nature who was his daughter came out, trailed by a half dozen other kids. She gestured to them to stay on the porch the way I might gesture to Shadow if I thought he'd obey. They obeyed.

Tom turned back to me, his dark eyes and serious face giving away nothing now. "Time to get Tamantha to her next engagement."

"Got to take care of Roxanne," she said as she approached, apparently having heard her father's comment.

"That's nice of you to do," I ventured carefully.

"If you're going to have an animal you need to care for her," she said, clearly quoting her father. "Like you have to take care of Shadow. Roxanne needs to know she can count on me, then I can count on her. Needs regular exercise, so I'll ride out her fidgets this afternoon."

"Roxanne's a horse," I deduced.

"Of course. See you later, Elizabeth."

Tom swung the truck door open for her, grinning. As he rounded the front of the truck, I said, "Tom?"

He turned to me, waiting.

"Who donated that portable fence?"

He said nothing and his mouth didn't move, but there was a flicker around his eyes.

I nodded. "I thought so."

I RETURNED TO the house by way of the back door, stepping in to the crowded kitchen in time to hear Rich Taylorman say, "This was no accident."

Silence spread like a drop of black ink in water.

It was hard to tell who he was talking to unless it was Deputy Wayne Shelton, who stood some distance away. No one else looked at him.

"If you have evidence—" Shelton muttered.

"He went out there on purpose. Meant to die. Wanted to die. Clear as anything. Suicide.—"

"He's covered for suicide," a voice said.

"Basic, maybe, but suicide disqualifies accidental death benefit. Wipes it out. Not a penny."

Now the silence held disgust. Without being seen to move, the people nearest Taylorman shrank away, leaving him isolated. He didn't seem to notice.

"We're a long way from knowing the ins and outs of what happened," Shelton said brusquely.

"Stands out like a sore thumb," Taylorman declared. "Wanted to collect that ADB, so he went out there to let himself die of exposure. That's suicide and that disqualifies him from the ADB. And if one of his beneficiaries helped—"

Shelton took a step toward him. He retreated, but the stove prevented him from going any farther.

"Got that accidental death coverage yourself, Taylorman?" a low, unfriendly voice asked from somewhere beyond the front circle of observers. "You might need it."

A grumble of agreement went around.

"Best you'd get along, Taylorman," Shelton said. "There'll be time enough to deal with getting Connie what's rightfully owed to her by you."

Somehow, despite his even voice, that sounded like a threat to me.

Apparently to Taylorman, too. Keeping up a muttering with the terms "exposure," "suicide," and "fraud" recognizable, he went out the back door.

Shelton didn't say anything, but he made eye contact with several of the more vociferous grumblers. After a minute, people started turning away, heading toward the living room.

Next I knew, Jennifer was standing so close beside me that her mouth nearly touched my ear as she whispered, "There's more on him. Tell you later."

I turned to ask for details—like what on earth she was talking about—but she'd sped off toward the main part of the house.

When I turned back, Shelton had exited by the back door.

I went after him.

Taylorman's car was turning around in the one lane left free by vehicles lining the road.

Without turning or slowing, Shelton said, "I'm not telling you anything about this case."

Showoff. Trying to pretend he had eyes in the back of his head.

"It's not about this case."

He stopped, turned, and gave me a disbelieving look.

"Not directly," I added.

He started off again. I stayed beside him.

"Consider it background."

Silence.

"I've heard that some people—including her family—blame Don Hazen for his first wife's disappearance. That could be a motive in his death."

More silence.

To try to pierce it, I used the sharpest tool I had. "In fact, they think he murdered Mindy."

Without slowing, Shelton said, "His alibi was airtight."

"Few alibis are airtight."

"This one was."

"Why?"

He stopped again. "Because it was me."

Chapter Fourteen

"You?"

"I arrested him for a bar fight."

"That was the same time as his wife disappeared? What happened?"

"He was in a fight in bar. Sheriff's department got called. He went to jail. End of story."

"Beginning of story. Who started the fight?"

He grimaced. "I should make you get this from your buddy Needham Bender." But then he answered. "Him."

"Was that usual?"

"Not that unusual."

"Was it usual for him to go to jail after he started one of these fights?"

"No. But it wasn't the first time, either."

"Why did he this time?

"He was wound up. Usually, he'd throw a few sucker punches, then be cool and collected when we got there. Doing his damnedest to have the other guy look like the hothead. Not that night. That night he got everybody stirred up like the Hatfields and McCoys. He kept jawing at one guy from across the parking lot. And when it looked like things had finally settled down, he broke free from a Sherman officer and charged over and swung wild. Had to arrest him then.

"So, what with transporting and processing and waiting for his hearing and all, there was no way he could have done anything to Mindy between the time she left the movies with her girlfriend

Saturday night and the time her mother went by Sunday afternoon like she always did, except this time she found Mindy's suitcases, clothes, and other things gone, along with her car. And Mindy, too, of course."

"He got someone else to do it for him. An alibi like that? He had to."

He squinted up at me. "You've got a suspicious mind, Elizabeth Margaret Danniher. It's your one redeeming quality. But got to prove it for an arrest. And his two best cronies were in jail with him, even if I could imagine either of them having the brains to pull off such a thing."

"Loriana. The replacement wife. She's got brains. And if they were having an affair—"

"She didn't move back here until almost six months after Mindy disappeared. They did take up together fast, but they had history, so that's not strange. There's nothing anyone's been able to find that ties them together before Mindy went missing. And they tried."

I raised one eyebrow. "Who tried?"

"Mindy's family hired some folks."

"And found?"

"Nothing."

"How about you?" I didn't wait for his "what about me?" but added, "Did you check?"

"As much as Sheriff Widcuff allowed."

Which wouldn't have been much. Would that have stopped Shelton? I opened my mouth.

He interrupted, "Nothing. I found nothing, either."

Without a farewell he turned and continued to his car.

I watched him pull out, replaying the conversation in my head. Was I constructing a new peak in the Rockies from a gopher hill, all based on the fact that he hadn't said something along the lines of "I didn't find anything, because there was nothing to find."

Maybe.

Still, I made a mental note to have Jennifer check this when she'd worked through the rest of the massive to-do list I was accumulating for her.

But first I had another potential source to pump.

AS DIANA AND I left Connie's ranch house, we saw a burly man ahead of us, walking down the line of vehicles.

"Who's that?" I asked.

It was the familiar-looking burly man I'd seen exiting the Sherman Supermarket on Tuesday. Now that I saw him again, I realized he'd been familiar because I'd seen him at Red Sail Ranch, heading out with one of the early search groups as Mike and I arrived.

"Not your type. Though he was a star pitcher for the baseball team. You've already got Cottonwood County's best-ever football and basketball players, so baseball—"

"Diana," I said dangerously.

She chuckled. "His name's Greg Niland. Manager at a tire place in town. Why?"

"I saw him at the search and then at the supermarket."

"Most of the county was at the search and all of the county eats, so I don't get your interest."

"Putting names with faces."

"Actually, he's Mindy's brother."

"One of the members of Mindy's family who thought Don Hazen had something to do with Mindy's disappearance?"

"That's him."

I'D SEEN *INDEPENDENCE* editor/publisher Needham Bender and his wife at Connie's, but only for a brief hello. Now I had Diana drop me off at the *Independence* offices to combine business and pleasure.

The business was to widen my circle of information about the characters and conflicts in the Red Sail Ditch Company. KWTM-TV's library had file copies, but that dusty, windowless, crowded storage room wasn't my favorite place. It also lacked the heady smell of newsprint.

That was part of the pleasure, to visit both Needham and the newspaper offices. The building dated from the 1890s and had been home to the *Independence* ever since. Certainly there'd been improvements and remodeling but none of the changes had eroded the character.

I'd yet to work for a TV station or network that came close to matching it. Maybe in a hundred years.

Needham greeted me with a smile and said, "You've come to ask me questions."

"Also to take you out for a cup of coffee." He raised his cup, reminding me of the *Independence*'s lobby coffee pot. I adjusted my plan. "Or I could ask you the questions outright, then take you and Thelma to dinner."

He unabashedly studied my expression.

Couldn't blame him, since the last time he'd invited me to have dinner with him and Thelma I'd stiff-armed him. But I'd reassessed some things since.

Nearly dying can do that to you.

"Maybe you could come to dinner at our place. More privacy."

"Thank you, I'd like that. And not only for the privacy."

"I'll check with Thelma and get back to you."

"Perfect."

"But I won't make you wait that long to ask your questions— although I am going to make you wait some because I've got a column to finish. Tell you what. I'll meet you over at the museum in half an hour."

"The museum?"

"Sure. It's a good place for perspective."

"I've been there."

"Time you go again."

Chapter Fifteen

AFTER PAYING THE entry fee for the Sherman Western Frontier Life Museum, I started toward the gift shop.

I'd volunteered to wait at the *Independence* office, but Needham hustled me out. I understood. There's nothing harder than writing with someone looking over your shoulder—literally or only in your head.

The reason I headed for the museum shop was that these days, with so much destroyed in the fire, I shopped about every chance I got, trying to fill in gaps.

Sherman is not a Mecca for shopping unless you go in for the Western Utilitarian look. I'd picked up basics, added more from online, but some things you didn't want to buy without trying on, like sunglasses. I'd spotted a rack in the gift shop.

Then I recognized the woman behind the counter. Vicky Upton. Not one of my fans. Even though I hadn't gotten her arrested for murder.

I veered away and was nearly to an exhibit entitled "Cottonwood County's Evolving Settlement," when I heard a woman's voice say, "What are you doing here?"

Not the woman behind the gift shop counter. It was Clara Atwood, the curator. I make friends everywhere I go.

"Hi, Clara. How are you?" My bright smile didn't lift her frown.

"We'll have no comment until there's a decision," she informed me. "I told Thurston that."

"He called you?"

She grimaced slightly and for that instant we were united by our opinion of Thurston Fine.

Her expression changed, probably remembering the historical booty found a few weeks ago, which was already tangled in legal claims and counter-claims, including one by the museum saying it should get everything.

"There will be no comment until there's a decision," she repeated firmly.

"Guess I'll have to accept that for now." That was easier than trying to persuade her I wasn't here to extract a comment. "As long as I'm here, I'll view a couple exhibits."

From the look she gave me, you'd think viewing exhibits confirmed her deepest suspicions about me.

But at least she didn't trail me into the "Evolving Settlement" section.

Sure I could have told her I was meeting someone, but then it would have been natural for her to want to know who and what we were going to talk about, so she might try to overhear us.

At least that would have been natural for me.

The first display reproduced the inside of a cabin from—according to the sign—fur trapper days. Against log walls, the furnishings were sparse and rough-hewn: a table, two stools. An iron pot hung in the fireplace. Our fur trapper had the minimalist lifestyle pegged.

I moved on to see the same basic room, now as an early ranch's bunkhouse. Bunkbeds, of course. Chairs around the table. A hat, shirt, and work pants hung on pegs. Boots tucked under one bed. The sign said a painting visible through a new window depicted a cookhouse, kept in a separate building in case of fire.

I'd reached the third incarnation of that log room—a single bedstead, a cradle, and a few pieces of china now in the mix—when Needham's voice came from behind me. "Irrigation is the reason this region ever reached the homesteading stage. Over here. This is what I want you to see."

An old black and white picture showed a man sitting on the bank of what I now knew was a ditch. Water showed in the foreground. Beside him and behind him was dirt.

That's all. Dirt.

Oh, a handful of one-story frame buildings lined what might have been a street—dirt, of course—but they were nearly lost in the expanse of dirt.

"That's 1910. That part of Cottonwood County would still look like this if not for irrigation."

He moved down three photos. Stalwart two-story buildings had replaced or filled in around the earlier ones. Sidewalks had appeared. Wagons marched down what could now be recognized as a street, though still dirt. "This is taken from the same spot in 1917. Water's the miracle-worker."

"Water in ditches, I know."

"Ditches are the branches and twigs. First you need a tree. You need water to supply the irrigation districts, which supply the canals, which supply the ditches." He turned and gestured toward the three log rooms. "The fur trappers, then the cattlemen, and a little later the sheep men came to Wyoming for the easy-to-see resources—the low hanging fruit. But irrigation took human ingenuity to collect and redistribute a resource. And they had to fight the Easterners to do it."

I exhaled an exaggerated sigh. "Of course the Easterners were the bad guys."

"I'll give them the benefit of the doubt and call them dumb as rocks."

I laughed. "Okay, what did they do this time?"

"They didn't have the imagination to recognize that the arid West couldn't be handled the way Pennsylvania or Ohio or Wisconsin could be. They tried to divide it up into little plots that might sustain someone where the land was good, but not out here. You need a lot more space to sustain a living here, especially if you're the unlucky homesteader who got a patch nowhere near water."

"The Easterners finally saw the light?"

"More like after several decades, big shots in Washington got softened up enough that they'd wheel and deal. Good thing, because private irrigation schemes fell apart. Buffalo Bill and other promoters couldn't get enough investors with the low payout." He grinned. "Need the government for that. Also for dams and reservoirs to hold the water. You know where the water comes from? Snowmelt. Wyoming has ice running through its veins."

"Who said that?"

"I did."

"That's good. You should use it."

He snorted. "Don't think I won't. Without irrigation systems, snowmelt would flood in spring and be gone. Instead, it's directed to reservoirs, held until there's need, and delivered through canals to the ditches. That's not the half of it, but I won't hit you with more, especially considering this isn't what you want to talk to me about. Since I doubt you want to be overheard—"

I looked around. Clara Atwood was nowhere in sight.

"—let's pick up brownies from the gift shop and go sit in the square."

My acquaintance behind the gift shop counter limited herself to glaring at me. I should have tried on sunglasses when I'd had the chance. After all, I was already dealing with the glare—*ta-dum-dum.*

The courthouse had been built in the middle of the square block early in the 20th century. The portion behind the courthouse now held the Sherman police department and the Cottonwood County sheriff's department, plus parking areas.

But in front of the courthouse was landscaped and sported scattered benches. The one we selected sat in splendid isolation, making our conversation private.

The brownies were delicious. I received a bit of a jolt when Needham's exchange with my non-friend behind the counter indicated Vicky Upton had made them. But reason reminded me she wouldn't have had any expectation I'd be eating one while she was making them or time to slip something in once she knew.

Okay, maybe I was being a bit paranoid, but having someone try to turn you into a melted marshmallow in the bonfire of your house can do that to you.

Despite reason, I felt a little chill at the idea of eating something she'd baked. But I didn't let that keep me from the chocolate. There are limits to paranoia.

Instead, I shifted to sit more squarely in the sunlight.

Needham watched my move with an indulgent smile. "It's not really cool. It's our atavistic instinct that the cold days are coming. Rather like those days in January when something in the air suddenly gives you a whiff of spring."

"I wasn't here in January, but I don't recall a whole lot of whiffs of spring when I arrived in April." I considered that. "Or in May for that matter."

He chuckled. As if I'd been kidding.

Abruptly, he said, "I called Thelma. How'd you like to come for supper tonight. Nothing fancy."

"I—" I stopped my automatic response. "I'd like that. I'd have to call Diana, because she was going to pick me up and I know she has something at school for the kids tonight—"

"We'll drive you out to her place after supper. Happy to."

After a quick phone call to Diana that was settled.

"Now," he invited, settling back, "ask."

"The Red Sail Ditch. Shorn of the gossip."

He laughed. "You shear off the gossip and you have no sheep left at all. I can tell you Sam McCracken called the sheriff's department out a couple times on Don. First time when Don tore down a fence McCracken put up. If he'd had anybody around here build it, they'd have told him not to."

"Because of the easement for the ditch."

He cocked a surprised eyebrow. I saw no reason to confide that my limited knowledge of easements was newly minted.

He said, "Second time was a he-said-he-said assault situation, each of them saying the other one attacked and each of them saying he was defending. They both had shiners and bruises, so hard to tell.

McCracken changed strategy and pursued it in court."

"That can't have made Brian happy as ditch boss."

"It didn't. The law's clear that the ditch boss has the right to have access and room to maintain the ditch. There's plenty of precedent with folks like the McCrackens moving in and making changes— improvements, to their mind—that end up getting pulled down. Not long ago some folks had to take out an indoor swimming pool down near the Colorado border. But McCracken might have spotted a way around it, because Don was not the ditch boss."

"Ahhh. Smart. And I can't imagine Don was acting at the ditch boss' behest."

"Nope. And Brian said so in a deposition. Which made Don see red—or redder than usual."

"When was the deposition?"

"A week ago Monday."

In other words, a week before Brian and Don went missing. "So what happens now?"

He shrugged. "Don't know yet if it will be dropped or if McCracken's thinking he can go after the estate."

If Sam McCracken had been angry enough at Don Hazen and had thought his case wasn't going well, might he have decided to pursue a more permanent judgment? Brian could have gotten in the way. Or McCracken's anger could have included him.

"How'd McCracken get along with Brian? He didn't join the search."

He slanted me a look. "No, he didn't." He removed his cowboy hat, vigorously rubbed at his short hair. "That didn't do him any good around here. When somebody's in trouble, everybody rallies 'round. There aren't enough people here to let personal grudges stand in the way. Everybody's got to have everybody else's back. Look at the way even Les Haeburn pitched in with that crawl—what? You telling me it wasn't Les' idea?"

By his expression of totally unconvincing innocence, he knew it wasn't.

"Back to McCracken," I said.

"Yeah, there's plenty of grumbling about his not being there. Amid a lot of other grumbling."

"About?"

"The lawsuit."

"The people of Cottonwood County don't back McCracken turning to the legal system to solve the dispute?"

"Most folks in ditch companies believe in keeping it inside the company." He huffed out a breath. "No telling what'll happen with the lawsuit now. And these two deaths could mean nobody does much about the ditch for some time to come."

"Work has started on the repairs Brian had been on Don about."

"Loriana? Well, that's good to hear. She didn't show much interest when she came to live with her aunt and uncle—."

"It wasn't her parents' place?"

"Nope. They died when she was a kid and she came here. Can't say it was a bed of roses. Uncle ended up in jail and died there. The aunt up and left. Loriana graduated high school, sold to Don and blew out of town."

My mind had gone to another point. "You know, with McCracken not being involved with the search, if they find trace evidence…"

"It could prove he was there." He gave me a sharp look. "And so many others being there makes trace evidence tying them to the site much less informative."

"Yes, it does."

"You find that suspicious?"

"I don't know about suspicious. It's certainly convenient."

"It's also Wyoming. It would have been remarkable if those people hadn't been there."

"Including Rich Taylorman?"

"Hard to say with him. He's only been around a few years, so—" He bit it off and more color came into his already ruddy face.

"So he's an outsider. And since I've only been here since April that makes me a super-outsider. That's okay, Needham. That truth won't hurt my feelings."

"Thing is, I wouldn't have started to say that if I didn't keep forgetting that you *are* a—let's say a newcomer."

"Good recovery. Would you have expected another insurance broker to be there?"

"As a participant in the search, sure. As an observer, no."

"He did bestir himself to make the trek to the site after Brian's body was found."

"Yes, he did."

He didn't need to say what we were both thinking—another person who could conveniently explain away trace evidence.

"Have you talked to McCracken?" I asked abruptly.

"You keep coming back to him, don't you?"

"A fellow outsider." I grinned. "Are you avoiding answering for some reason, Mr. Bender?"

"Oh-ho, going to try to use that one on me, are you? No, Ms. Danniher, I am not avoiding answering. Though it would serve you right if I clammed up after that. I've talked with him a bit. Never interviewed him. Haven't written about the lawsuit, either. James Longbough asked me to give it time to see if he could negotiate something without court time."

"James Longbough? Boy, he gets around. I knew he did criminal law and wills, now ditch disputes, too? Which party does he represent?"

"In a county with such a high percentage of law-abiding citizens, he's got to do a little of everything to have a thriving practice. Besides, his great-grandfather James drew up the original agreements for most of the ditches in this county, including Red Sail. Now the current James represents the company. McCracken has some fella from Cheyenne and Don hired a guy from Cody."

"How about Brian, since he was ditch boss?"

"I haven't heard that he had any representation. I suppose unless the interests of the ditch and Brian's conflicted, James might have kept an eye out for him at the deposition and such. I know he was there."

"Has he told you anything about it?"

"Nah. He's one of those ethical close-mouthed attorneys," he said with so much disgust I had to laugh.

DAY FOUR

THURSDAY

Chapter Sixteen

THE SUN WAS shining as I pulled into a development of spread-out lots the next morning.

Dinner last night with Needham and Thelma had been delicious and relaxed. I'd been an idiot to ever delay it. I was determined to repay their hospitality soon.

A good night's sleep hadn't hurt, either.

The brown frame house nearly blended into the background, but a clean white pickup out front caught my eye, so I saw the address before I missed the turn.

The woman who came to the door had a phone to her ear. She stared at me a moment, either listening to or ignoring a muffled voice coming from the phone.

"I gotta go," she said into the phone. "There's somebody at the door. It's about damned time."

I blinked at that last sentence, clearly directed at me. But years of professional training kicked in, along with a suspicion that she thought I was somebody else.

"Hi, I'm E.M. Danniher from KWMT-TV. I do the 'Helping Out' segment that runs…"

Two reasons I let that die out. First, the segment doesn't run with much regularity and I hate to build up someone's hopes that are destined to be crushed when Haeburn bumps it. Second, she wasn't listening.

She'd turned back inside. "Greg! Get out here."

When she came out on the small front porch, I nearly shivered. She was wearing shorts and flip-flops.

Her hair was the kind of blonde that I thought of as Barbie doll blonde. Not that my solitary Barbie had been a blonde. She was a brunette, who mostly wore a trench coat as she traveled the world in search of truth and justice. But a neighbor girl had a new blonde Barbie every few months.

Each of those dolls had the same improbable color as this woman—well, except the dolls' had no dark roots. What shine the hair had—dolls' and woman's—looked like a plastic coating that would come off, leaving the hair snarled and dull, the first time the hair happened to be subjected to a maximum strength garden hose spray to represent getting caught in a rain forest thunderstorm during an adventure while traveling the world in search of truth and justice.

Just for an example.

"What do you want?" demanded a male voice from inside. Wasn't sure if it was meant for me or the lady of the house.

"It's somebody from TV to talk to you, so get out here," the woman said. Then to me, she continued, "I saw you at Connie's on Monday. We got there among the first. I was in the house helping with things there and Greg went searching. Brought back memories, I'll tell you. It was just like for Mindy. Now, finally, somebody's going to look into her death."

"She's not here for that." The burly man pushed open the screened door.

"Greg Niland, Mindy Niland Hazen's brother?" I asked.

"That's him," the woman said before he could respond. "And I'm his wife Krystal, Mindy's sister-in-law. And her friend."

He wore clean jeans and a blue oxford shirt with the insignia of a local tire company on its pocket.

Still without looking at me, Greg said to her, "They're only interested now because someone did this world a favor and got rid of Don Hazen. Garbage."

He spat. He missed my shoe by a good three inches. I didn't know if that was on purpose or if he'd been aiming for the shoe and missed. I wasn't going to ask. Not about that and not about whether he was indicating Hazen or me as garbage.

I turned an earnest face to his wife. "I am interested in Mindy's disappearance."

"Shit," he said this time.

"Disappearance my ass," the woman elaborated on his statement. "He killed her."

"What makes you think that?"

"She's gone, isn't she?" Perhaps my expression told her that wasn't enough. "She didn't tell a soul about going anywhere, which she would've. She had about ten of us she called every day, but she hasn't been in contact with a single one and that's not like her. Like we told the sheriff, she was leaving *him*, she wasn't leaving here. And," she concluded triumphantly, "she always said if something happened to her it was him that did it."

She said it as if she were the first person to deliver that line to a journalist. She wasn't. According to their surviving relatives and friends, at least ninety percent of the women who disappeared or were murdered knew who was going to do the deed and talked about it.

It always made me wonder why, if somebody was so sure they were going to be done in that they predicted it and gave the survivors a name, didn't they get away beforehand?

It also makes me wonder how many are still walking around who've said the same thing to somebody and have never been—will never be—proven true?

Neither is a question to ask someone's surviving relatives and friends. Not only because of their grief, but because those repeating the line seem to feel it's proof positive of the guilt of the named party.

"What made her believe Don Hazen would harm her?" I asked instead.

"He hit her," her sister-in-law said.

I was too subtle the first time. Not going to make that mistake again. That's what Penny had told that other customer Don had said. Had he considered Mindy's disappearance subtle? Had he intended more for

Loriana? Could self-preservation have given her a motive to kill him? Or could someone else out to protect her have a motive?

I made a mental note to raise those points with the group.

"Did she report it to the police—to the sheriff's department?"

"No. But she was going to. Was going to leave him, was going to divorce him, and was going to get everything in the divorce."

"Bull," her husband scoffed. "He was the one with the land and money. That's why she stayed. Stayed too long like an idiot, like I told her last time I saw her. It wasn't the backhands across her face. She could take that." His mouth shifted. He might have been expressing amusement, but it wasn't particularly appealing. "Take it and give back as good as she got most times."

"If it wasn't the beatings why was she getting out, if you're so smart?" Krystal demanded. "And she did so say she'd get everything in a divorce."

"Hold your horses. I'm telling you."

Well, no. He wasn't telling us. He was making us wait. But clearly there was more. His mouth worked as if it needed to form the words before they could be released.

"It was the way he held the reins so tight. Sawing at her mouth when there was no need. Even with a headstrong mare there's no need for that."

"Nobody can ride like him," his wife said with pride.

He accepted that as his due. "But some riders want the horse afraid of them. They want that more than they want to get where they're going. Think it gives them control."

He spit again. Six inches from my shoe. Either he was warming up to me or his aim was getting worse.

"Can you tell me about when Mindy disappeared?" I wasn't particularly interested, but getting people talking is the first objective.

Krystal jumped at the question. "It was a Sunday. She'd called me first thing like always. She was telling me she had it all planned to leave Don by the end of the week. Wanted to pack a few more things in the attic where she was putting everything together so she could load up her car fast—and that's another reason I know she didn't just take off, because all those boxes and such were still there. Why wouldn't she take them with when they were all ready?"

Not a bad question.

"There was no indication that she was upset—more upset than usual or more frightened of Don or anything like that?" I asked her.

She shook her head. Even that didn't do anything to enliven her hair.

"So your conversation was normal?"

"Entirely normal. Well, a little shorter than usual."

Greg snorted. "Anything less than all day's shorter than usual for you."

"Ha. Ha. Ha."

I hurried up my next question. "Was there a reason it was shorter? Did you cut it short or—"

"I don't remem—Oh, wait. Yes, I do. Now that's funny."

She stopped dead.

"What's funny, Krystal?" her husband demanded.

"Oh, she said the same thing I just said—There's somebody at the door."

I perked up. "Like Don?"

She shrugged elaborately. "Don't know. That's all she said. Somebody's at the door."

"Wouldn't matter if Attila the Hun was at the door, Don killed her. There was always something wrong with him. Look at the way he went all moony about Loriana in high school."

"Yeah," Krystal said. "Mindy never liked living there. Wanted to move back into town. She was always after Don to sell the place. He got such a good deal on it, they'd have turned a good profit and could have been real comfortable."

"A deal? He practically stole it. That's one thing for sure, he wouldn't have gotten that price from old Earl or Ellen. So maybe Loriana was a little soft on him, too. Or she just wanted to get out of here."

"Were you surprised when she came back?" I asked.

Krystal nodded vigorously. "Could have knocked me over with a feather. Last person on earth I'd have expected back here. As I said to my sister—"

"No." Greg's single word cut across his wife's voice. "Wasn't surprised at all."

"No?" she repeated. "When all she'd ever talked about was getting away?"

"She got away. But where else are you going to go but home when you get hard knocks?"

I rather liked Greg Niland at that moment.

"What kind of hard knocks?" I asked.

Krystal said, "If there were hard knocks, I'd sooner believe she was giving them. The way she went after people who said the least little thing about him, you'd think Don Hazen was the love of her life when everybody knew she'd walked away from him without a backward look. Hard. That's what she is. Her marriage broke up before she came back and she won't talk about him. Not a word."

Before I could speak, her husband said, "Could be *she* likes to mind her own business."

Krystal huffed in indignation.

Before this could descend into what sounded like a well-worn track of marital discord, I thanked them and started to leave, but turned back quickly. "One thing I forgot to ask—have you had any trouble with insurance?"

"Huh?"

"Insurance. Crop, life, medical. Any issues you might need help with?"

"Why? You selling insurance?" Greg conveyed both suspicion and snideness. So much for liking him.

"No, no. I'm doing a piece on insurance scams for the TV station."

"I thought you were looking into Mindy being killed by that asshole."

I'd never said that. Krystal had said it and he'd eventually bought into the idea, too. But accuracy wasn't the point right now. "Both. I'm looking into both." Along with a lot of other things. "So, any issues with insurance?"

"No."

"Okay. Thanks."

Too bad. No progress at all on that piece for "Helping Out."

But sometimes that was a reporter's lot, as I would be sure to tell Haeburn if he asked about my work today.

Chapter Seventeen

RETURNING TO THE station, I made phone calls before lunch.

For background, I called the Wyoming Insurance Department and two of the top insurance brokers in the area.

I left the Walterstons' insurance situation to Jennifer. Instead, I was asking about potential insurance scams and frauds affecting consumers.

I might need to have something to tell Haeburn if he suddenly became curious.

I received two surprises.

First, when I think "insurance scam," I think of an individual trying to rip off an insurance company. Fake injuries after a car accident, listing items as stolen that are actually in a box in the attic, that sort of thing.

But the consumer is also vulnerable. Very vulnerable. Halfway through the first phone call, the outlines of a "Helping Out" piece began to take shape in my head.

The first area broker delicately introduced the topic of the difficulty for established, long-time members of the insurance community when they saw red flags concerning a newcomer to the area. In other words, Rich Taylorman, without ever mentioning the name.

The second broker was more emphatic. "Pond scum" was one of the nicer things she called Taylorman, and she did use the name. I scheduled time to do an on-camera interview with her, planning longer than usual because I figured we'd need to do a lot of editing to keep the woman from saying something that could get her—or KWMT-

TV—sued.

She also gave me the name of the Walterstons' previous broker.

I debated calling him, but decided his conflict of interest could skew the story. He could well tell the truth yet be dismissed as sour grapes. Too much downside with no apparent upside.

Better to keep this "Helping Out" piece separate.

✧ ✧ ✧ ✧

DIANA GAVE A wolf whistle as we each exited a vehicle in the KWMT parking lot shortly after one o'clock.

I had wheels.

I suppose a lot of people would have been enthusiastic about all the comforts and conveniences above the wheels, but after these weeks without them, the wheels thrilled me.

Okay, I liked the color, too. Red.

"Thanks for the endorsement."

"Going to test it out?"

"As a matter of fact, I thought I would. Since I see that Haeburn's not here, I thought I'd go talk to some people."

"Mike's not going along?"

"He's on assignment. He dropped me at the dealership on his way."

" 'Helping Out' people or Red Sail Ditch people?"

"The latter."

"Want some company?"

"Really? I thought you were going to be shooting all day today."

"I'm supposed to pick up signs of the changing season. I can do that riding along with you as well as on my own. Better, since I can catch some things out of the window, as long as you cooperate. I can navigate for you. Besides, I'm the one who knows the Red Sail Ditch gossip. I can spot if someone's trimming the truth."

"Great point. Let me make a pit stop and we'll be on our way."

✧ ✧ ✧ ✧

DIANA NOT ONLY navigated, she selected the order of our visits, once I said I wanted to talk to Hannah Chaney and Terry Waymark, Paul Chaney, and Otto Chaney.

When I commented about taking a different road from the one Mike had taken to Red Sail Ranch, she said, "They're all on the north side of the ditch. You can see Red Sail Rock from here, though."

She pointed and I caught glimpses of it under a glowering sky until the glimpses went from the windshield to the side window, then behind us.

"Why do you want to talk to these people?"

"Things I've heard about the ditch company, like that Don was campaigning to take over from Brian."

She acknowledged that with a one-shoulder shrug. "There's more going on than Don campaigning to take over. Though that's no small thing."

"Meaning?"

"Don was stirring up civil war. With Don, you either backed everything he wanted or you were totally against him."

"Just like—"

"Middle school, I know."

"I was going to say like Thurston."

"Same difference." We grinned at each other before she continued. "Early on Brian kept him in check. But with Brian sicker and not as active, some of the weaker characters have drifted into Don's camp. And on the other side, Otto Chaney called his water."

"Wow."

She grinned. "Calling water is a big deal. In theory, the person with the most senior rights gets all his water before the second most senior. Second most senior gets all his before third most senior, and on down to the last person. Properties along the ditch seldom match the order of rights seniority, so it would mean a lot of opening and closing of gates to let the water flow in that precise order.

"Most times, people get all their water, so they don't insist on getting it in order. Sometimes in a drought there's an issue. Or when members of the ditch company get into a snit."

"Ah."

"Otto Chaney's grandfather bought the land from the first one to settle on that water. Water rights go with the land. So he had senior rights and he demanded all his water before anybody else got theirs. That was in reaction to Don using more than his share, starting last month. It's a good thing most irrigating is over. If it had been peak season, even with the Walterstons giving up some...." She shook her head. "Still, it's a headache for the ditch boss. With Brian so ill and Connie taking care of him, Kade was out there a lot, checking flow, opening and closing gates.

"Turn left at that mailbox. Follow the road around and we're at our first stop. The Waymark Ranch."

Where Paul Chaney's young wife was living with another man.

The drive to the house was rutted and dusty.

The signs of neglect I'd spotted at Red Sail Ranch had appeared recent. Not here. The house almost appeared to sink into the ground as if its bones were giving way. A branch rested across the hood of a blue truck with rust spreading from it like leaves. It was hard to tell with the white truck close to the house if the red marks were rust or dirt. Long grass peeked out from the wheel compartment of a tractor. Nature was doing its best to hide irregular heaps of machinery.

Even the bark of the dog who wandered out in response to my tap on the horn to announce our arrival seemed lackluster and uninterested.

The back door opened and we saw Hannah Chaney standing there.

"This could be good," I said to Diana. "We might get more from her if Terry's out working—"

"He won't be."

He wasn't.

Hannah ushered us in with what appeared to be a variety pack of emotions. Tiredness, wariness, but also pleasure and ... was that relief?

Terry Waymark was sitting at a scarred and cluttered kitchen table, reading the sports section from Sunday's paper. Agreeably, he dropped the paper on the table and greeted us as we sat at Hannah's invitation.

"We'd like to ask you some questions about what's been going on with the Red Sail Ditch," I said directly.

"Sure, sure," he said.

Hannah didn't look up from making a fresh pot of coffee, but her shoulders appeared to tighten.

"We understand there's been dissension in the company."

He chuckled. "Sure to be when Hannah came to me when she got fed up with Paul. You'd think the guy thought every day was a funeral the way he acts."

Color rose up the side of Hannah's neck, which was all her hair and the angle she was standing at let me see.

"What about other members of the company?"

"Why would they care?"

"I mean dissension among other members, not necessarily with you. Or Hannah."

"Oh." He sounded less interested.

As Hannah turned with the first two cups of coffee, Diana and I stood to take them from her. Terry didn't move.

"You sit down," Diana instructed. "We'll get those."

I did my part toting the cups, pot, and a plate of sad cookies with not a bit of chocolate on them. But my mind was occupied in revamping the angle I was about to take.

When we were all sitting and sipping, I turned to Terry and said, "I understand you're Don Hazen's close friend."

"Yeah."

"As his friend and his ally in the Red Sail Ditch Company—that's right, isn't it? Good," I said after his nod. "You'd have insights into the activities and actions that I couldn't get anywhere else."

"Yeah."

It didn't take much more coaxing to get him to tell his version of the ditch company's disputes. Most of what he said rehashed what we'd already learned.

Satisfied he'd wound down, I hoped he'd be receptive to specific questions, laced with a good dose of butter.

"What was Don's relationship with Sam McCracken—from what he confided to you and what you observed as his close friend?"

"They had a fight."

"Not right off," Hannah said softly.

"Huh." He considered. "You know, that's right. They were real friendly to start. Thing is, Don expected loyalty of his friends. He knew he could count on me because that's the kind of guy I am. But McCracken's a city guy. He doesn't know about loyalty. When Don saw that, he wanted nothing to do with him."

"That's when they had a fight?"

"Yeah." Terry nodded.

"It was later. After…" Hannah's voice faded away.

"After what?"

"I don't know. Really, I don't," she insisted, even though no one had indicated they thought otherwise. Terry looked at her, but he seemed no more than mildly surprised. "I, uh… Something happened at the supermarket."

"At the Sherman Supermarket?"

"Yeah."

"With Penny?"

"Oh, no." Her eyes and mouth formed appalled circles. "It was his wife. That Mrs. McCracken."

"Mrs. McCracken and Don?"

Terry laughed. "Those two? Thought Loriana had him too whipped. That *dog*."

"Not like that." She blushed.

"Like what then?" I asked.

She hitched a shoulder, looking down. "I dunno."

I turned back to Terry. "What about you?"

He shrugged. "I don't go to the supermarket much now Hannah is here." He smiled at her.

She smiled back, but it trembled before disappearing quickly and I saw tears in her eyes. Over the Sherman Supermarket? I found that hard to believe.

Unless it ran out of double chocolate Milano cookies, of course.

Terry leaned back in the chair. "I can tell you the real trouble started when McCracken put that big ol' fence up right along the ditch like a total greenhorn. Don wasn't going to put up with that sort of crap from anybody."

"But he wasn't ditch boss, was he?"

"As good as. Not to speak ill of the dead, but Brian was ditch boss by default, because his father had been. What kind of way is that to run a ditch company nowadays? Modern times call for modern thinking." I had the impression we were hearing quotes from a dead man. "Don should have been ditch boss. He sure as hell was the only one doing anything, trying to keep the company going."

Hannah's thin shoulders tightened again.

He seemed to sense the silent disagreement and made his argument. "All he wanted was what's good for the company. Sometimes you've got to tear down an old place before you can build a new one. That's what Don was doing. And if people with sticks up their asses like Paul can't see that, can't move with the times they should get out of the way. Don told him that, too."

"Was that when the sheriff's department came out because of a confrontation?"

"Yeah. Paul and Don mixed it up. Hey, you think—?"

"Paul wouldn't—Paul didn't. You can't think he—He'd never." Despite the incoherence, Hannah's intended point was clear.

I pushed, keeping an eye on her. "They came to blows, didn't they?"

"Yeah," Terry said.

"Don was pushing him. Pushing and pushing. Paul hit him just to make him stop. That's all. If he'd wanted to really hurt him—"

Hannah broke that off with a slight, frightened sob and tears welled in her eyes as she stared at me.

"The dispute was all about the ditch company?"

"Sure," Terry said.

After a moment's hesitation, as if she were weighing the impact of her response, Hannah slowly nodded.

He wasn't watching, apparently still chewing over my question. "Ditch company's a mess. It was clear to everybody Brian was past it. And if they think that kid's going to take over, they're nuts. Got to consider that this is people's livelihoods. Can't have a kid running the ditch."

"Have you ever been left short of water for your ranch?"

His face darkened. "Not yet. But next year, when I get some help so I can use more of my land, I could be, what with the way things are going."

"The way things are going?"

"The way the ditch is being mismanaged. Don said it's only a matter of time before those of us with newer rights get shorted."

"Especially with Don using more water than he was supposed to?"

"He wouldn't do that."

"He was."

He looked at Diana for confirmation. She nodded. "Otto's calling his water, too."

"Now? That's crazy." He looked genuinely perplexed.

"Why do you think Don let the banks in that section of the ditch—by Loop Field—fall into disrepair? Or even possibly actively damaged them."

He scoffed, "No way he'd do that."

"But Loriana's paid someone to come out to repair them, so..."

"Well, maybe he was showing how bad the ditch boss situation had got. He was a smart one. Real shame what happened to him. It's a loss. A true loss. Shame about Brian, too, I guess, though it was gonna happen soon anyway. But not Don." He shook his head. "And I was supposed to be there. Gotta wonder if that would have changed things."

"What?"

"Yeah, I was supposed to pick him up out by the ditch because his truck wasn't working and we were supposed to go into Cody together that night. When word came about Brian going missing, I called him and said I'd come early and help him look around over there. But he didn't call back. Called a few more times and he still didn't answer and didn't call back and what with Hannah getting all antsy about not being there to help, we went to Red Sail Ranch to sign up for the search."

Chapter Eighteen

"**DO YOU THINK** Shelton knows Terry was supposed to have been with Hazen?" Diana asked once we were back in my SUV.

"Probably. He certainly has Hazen's cell phone, so he'd have heard those messages. Better question is if anyone else knew Terry was supposed to have been with Don."

"And if he could have been an intended victim," Diana added. "That would probably make Paul Chaney the murderer, because I don't see anyone else going after Terry. Actually, I don't see Paul doing it, either. Not really. He so down-to-earth."

My SUV handled the bumps of this untended drive a whole lot better than my incinerated car would have. "Down-to-earth doesn't mean he's not a murderer, but more convincingly, I don't know how a murderer could have known ahead of time that Terry was going to be at Red Sail Rock. Or Don for that matter. No, that murder had to be spur of the moment."

"As opposed to Brian's you mean? But how could anyone have known Brian was going to be there? Turn left out of here."

"If someone brought Brian out there or even helped him, they'd know."

"Back to the boys, then."

We were both quiet as we returned to the highway and went further east.

When she had me leave the highway again we began a zig-zag southeast route.

"Now, straight ahead. This road ends at Otto's front door." Diana said, then seemed to brighten. "Did you notice Hannah sticking up for Paul? Maybe that marriage isn't doomed."

"Yes, I noticed, but considering the situation, I don't know—

We hit a bump that jolted the SUV. I might have groaned.

"Any buyer's remorse?" Diana asked.

"No remorse."

"Regrets then? You sure liked that pickup at Rondello's."

"What's there to regret?"

I'd selected a middle-of-the-road all-wheel drive. Not too large for city driving. Not too much of a gas-guzzler for distances. Not too Spartan for passengers. Not too swanky for me.

It left all my options open.

"Besides, I'd have to have waited weeks for the pickup. And— Hey, what was that?"

"What?"

"That—there. There's another one." I pointed at the windshield.

"Oh, that. That's a heavy raindrop."

"That was *not* a raindrop. Heavy or otherwise."

"Of course it—"

"That is snow. *Snow.* Heavy raindrop my—" I shook my head. "I'm from Illinois. I know snow when I see it."

I suddenly remembered the discussion with Mike about Beartooth Highway closing, and some research I'd intended to do.

"Sometimes that works on the tourists," she said complacently. "They can get worked up about snow. If they think it's a heavy raindrop, they relax. Ah, there's Otto."

There was no need to honk since the man I remembered as Driver 2 at the search stood on the small porch of a dull green square house, with his arms folded across his chest. I saw no sign of a dog, which made this an unusual ranch.

"Hi, Otto," Diana said. "This is Elizabeth Margaret Danniher from KWMT-TV. Do you have some time to talk?"

He snorted. "He said you were coming. Wasn't sure to believe that guy. Loco enough to smoke ditch weed."

"Hello, Mr. Chaney."

He waved away my outstretched hand. "Otto. What do you want?"

"We'd like to ask you some questions."

"Like you were asking Greg Niland?"

That surprised me. Since he'd clearly had a call from Terry Waymark, that was the direction I'd expected him to take.

My surprise appeared to please him.

"You know Greg and Krystal Niland?"

"Course I know 'em. We're family."

"So you and Mindy—"

"Her, too. Greg's all right. That Krystal talks way too much. Like most women. Why I didn't marry. Can't take all that talk."

I wondered if he was also related to Tom Burrell.

"Probably gave you that line about the dozen people Mindy called every day, huh?"

"She said ten," I said.

He snorted again. "Should have said five or six because Mindy was always feuding with half of them—different five or six each day."

"Was Mindy the reason you and Don Hazen didn't get along?"

This snort was scornful. "We didn't 'get along' because he was a weaselly asshole and he knew I knew it."

"What was he being weaselly about?"

"What do you think? The ditch. Wanted to run the whole thing and wasn't going to go at it straight. Splittin' everybody up, making everybody spit and snarl."

"And calling your water? How do you see that helping matters?"

"Shakin' things up. Especially shakin' Hazen up. Couldn't use up all that water if I called mine."

"Did you know what he was using the water for?"

"Wasn't using it for anything. Lettin' it run over the banks and goin' to waste."

"You know where Loop Field is?"

"Yeah." The subtext on that "yeah" was "you daft woman."

I shifted. "What does Paul think of your tactic?"

He shot me a look. Not friendly. "We don't always agree, but we're family. And we're not like those delicate ones that give up ranchin' and run south as soon as the first bone aches."

That sounded like a reasonable reaction to me, but saying that wasn't likely to win me points with this interview subject.

"Time I get back to work. You gotta leave," Otto said.

So much for winning points with him.

"Otto, why were you late getting to the search?"

His eyes went sharp and wary. "Working. Didn't know Brian had gone missing until then."

"THAT WAS INTERESTING," Diana said.

"Uh-huh."

"Why did you ask him about being late to the search?"

"Terry's explanation of why he was late made me realize it was interesting that those three were all late and all arrived at the same time. That made me curious."

Diana nodded. "Okay. I get that. And I know I'm not as good at this as you are, but may I say Otto was lying about why he was late getting to the search. I wonder why."

"Good question, and one it will be good to try to answer. But I have another one in the meantime. What's ditch weed and why would Terry Waymark be smoking it?"

"Well, he is known to smoke a lot of things. To give him credit, I'd heard he's not doing it around Hannah and the house doesn't smell like it. But he gets together with some cronies in his barn every night from what I hear."

"And ditch weed?"

"Pretty much what it sounds like—a weed that grows in ditches. It's from hemp plants, so it's a cannabis plant, but not *the* cannabis plant. All smoking it will do is give you a headache."

"So that was a put-down by Otto."

She chuckled. "He was probably sparing your urban sensibilities by not saying Terry was the kind of calf who'd suck all day on a dry teat."

THIS WAS A shorter drive before Diana directed me to turn into a ranch road.

"Leona told me Paul and Don were cousins. How'd they get along?" I asked her.

"Don was older, so I doubt they did much together growing up. They definitely didn't get along once Paul let it be known he thought Mindy's disappearance was fishy. Here we are."

There was no need to honk here, either.

Driver Number 3—a k a Paul Chaney—was working on the engine of a truck.

"Oh, my," Diana said under her breath. "And I remember him as a kid."

I had to admit, the male hind end sticking out from the side of this hood-up white pickup was worth looking at.

As we started to exit our respective doors, Diana sighed. "I need to start getting out and dating."

It was the first time I'd heard her say something like that. But this was no time to follow up.

Paul straightened, watching us.

He made a hand gesture to an alert rusty-red dog that must blend in with a lot of the nearby rocks and cuts. The dog instantly sat.

The house and yard were neat and organized—apparently as well-trained as the dog.

He wiped his hands on a ripped towel, said "Hey" to Diana, then listened to my introductory spiel about seeking background information.

He shot Diana a look, then came back to me.

"I don't know anything."

"Of course you do. You're a member of the ditch company. You know the people. And you were there for the search."

"Yeah. So what? Most people were there."

"That indicates concern. Did you participate in searches for Mindy?"

"Yeah." In a delayed reaction, he said, "Mindy? Why are you asking about Mindy?"

"A disappearance, Don Hazen's first wife, now Don dies in unusual circumstances…"

"Not unusual. This is rough country. Can be dangerous."

"You don't think two men dying like that, one at the top, one at the bottom of the cut? Two men who were at odds."

He hitched an uninterested shoulder.

"Do you agree they were at odds?"

"I suppose."

"What do you think of the McCrackens?"

I'd surprised him again. "They're okay."

"Have you had any trouble with them as neighbors?"

"Their land doesn't touch mine."

"Still, they're in the area and part of the ditch. And there's the lawsuit."

"No business of mine."

"It would have been if the ditch company was drawn into the lawsuit."

"Brian made sure it wasn't. Despite Hazen's troublemaking."

"Like his campaigning for ditch boss?"

"He wasn't just campaigning. The son of a badger was damaging banks in his own section."

"Why would he do that?"

"To cut our water in an effort to blackmail us into backing him. To make it harder on Brian to maintain the ditch. To do what he did best—be an asshole. Take your pick."

"What's your pick?"

He shrugged. "All the above."

He didn't sound like he cared much. But something was biting him.

"Paul, why did you get to the search so much later than most people?"

"Didn't know Brian had gone missing until I came in from working."

He'd bungled it. He said it too fast, too rote, too flat. Paul Chaney was either a lousy liar—which meant his other statements could be given more weight—or he'd flubbed this particular lie.

His tight jaw said he also was determined not to let me behind the wall of that lie.

"Well, thanks for your time. I might be back with more questions later as pieces start to come together. That would be okay with you, wouldn't it?"

"Suit yourself." He wasn't thrilled, but he wasn't quaking, either.

We said good-bye and started off.

"Diana," he said when we were a few yards away. We both turned back. "Heard you were at the Waymark place earlier. Asking the same questions as here?"

"Pretty much."

He nodded slowly. "Both of them there?"

"Yes."

His head came up. I saw longing for a flash, then he looked away. His voice rasped as he asked, "She was okay?"

Diana said, "Yes. Seemed tired, being that far along, but okay."

He jerked a nod of thanks or acknowledgment or dismissal, and turned back to his truck.

Chapter Nineteen

"YOU WORE A blanket over your clothes from the bunkhouse?" Diana asked as I deposited it on her coatrack that night. She looked as if she wanted to laugh.

"I haven't had a chance to get a winter coat yet and it was snowing today. Snowing." I pitched my voice to the two men sitting by the coffee table.

Their heads came up, looking at me as if awaiting a punchline, when I'd already delivered it. "Snow. White, flaky things falling from the sky."

"We see that now and then here," drawled Tom.

"In early October, barely past September," I said, hammering home the point. "That is not natural."

"If you can't take a little winter…"

"You go cover a pileup on Lakeshore Drive during a blizzard and talk to me about someone who can't take a little winter."

"That's true," Mike said. "Not that I covered a pileup on Lakeshore Drive, but I spent time offseason in Chicago, not to mention playing in December and January at Soldier Field—" A shadow crossed his face. "And in Green Bay." He seemed to shake off a bad memory. "Those winters aren't for wimps. Not as long as here, but wind coming off Lake Michigan will make you take notice.

"Now if you want weather wimps, try Washington. D.C., I mean. One flake and the place acts like the sky is falling."

They looked at me. I raised my hands. "No argument. They *are* weather wimps in D.C. I'm not. But that doesn't mean I want snow in

September. Or October. And that reminds me—" I rounded on Mike. "I looked up that Beartooth Highway you said I should see. You said it closed for the fall—it's closed for the *winter,* as of the end of September. Winter. *September.*"

"Actually, I think I said closed for the *season.*"

"It did close for fall—snowfall," Tom said.

I ignored that. "And do you know when it reopens, which presumably would be the *end* of winter? Memorial Day. Memorial Day. End of May. That's the end of *winter?*"

"Mostly."

"*Mostly?*"

"Besides," Mike went on as if I hadn't spoken, "you know what they say about the weather in Wyoming. There're two seasons: Winter and the Fourth of July."

Tom added, "Winter and getting ready for winter."

"And if you don't like it," Diana said, "open your coat and the wind'll blow you east to Nebraska."

They all chuckled.

Jennifer knocked and came in, wearing only a light sweater.

Diana waved her over as she said to me, "You're not living in the hovel anymore. You'll be fine."

Yeah," Mike said, "and you've got all-wheel drive now."

"I'm not worried about needing all-wheel drive. I'm worried—"

"You got your vehicle?" Tom asked.

A legit question or a ploy to stop me?

"I did. And Diana and I used it to go see Terry Waymark, Otto Chaney, and Paul Chaney today."

Diana and I filled in the other three.

"Why'd you pick them to go see?" Tom asked at the end.

"They were late to the search. In other words unusual behavior."

Mike nodded. "Follow unusual behavior. Okay, so Terry Waymark had a reason to be late—"

"Might have had a reason. If he's telling the truth."

Diana's brows rose. "Hannah didn't dispute what he said."

Next, I told them about my conversation with Krystal and Greg

Niland.

Including what they'd said that had reminded me of Penny's quote of Don: *I was too subtle the first time. Not going to make that mistake again.*

"The first time. Could that have been referring to the unrest within the ditch company? His dispute with Brian about the property? That would fit with Penny saying they'd been talking about his ranch," Diana said. "Oh, or you said Penny said he'd mentioned Loriana, so first time might have meant his first wife—Mindy. Why are you frowning?"

"There was something else Krystal said…"

"What?"

"If I knew what I wouldn't be frowning."

"Something about the ditch?"

"I don't think so. Maybe. Do not grin at me that way—any of you."

"Have another cookie," Diana suggested. "I hear they're brain food."

I followed her advice. Twice. But the elusive memory remained elusive.

Jennifer spoke up next, "At the Walterstons', Elizabeth and I heard Rich Taylorman take off on how Brian died. Tell them, Elizabeth."

I did.

"Did Connie hear—?"

Jennifer interrupted Tom's concern. "Not then, but she probably knows. He's been saying that all over the county. And that's not all. He has a great motive for murdering Brian—revenge."

"Revenge for what," Mike asked obligingly.

"He got in all sorts of trouble over the Walterstons' insurance and he blames them. Fraud and—"

Tom interrupted. "He was not charged with fraud. You can't go around saying that, Jennifer. It'll get you in trouble."

For once, she directed that "Spoilsport" accusatory look at someone other than me.

"He kept denying and stalling—he *was* trying to screw them out of their insurance," Jennifer said. "There was an investigation."

"There was. And the Wyoming Department of Insurance found in favor of the Walterstons."

"Impeding—they said he was impeding access to medical help for Brian."

"No. They said his actions could be viewed as contributing to impeding their access to insurance."

Jennifer huffed, but didn't dispute Tom.

"That's why Connie needed insurance through your road construction company?" I asked.

He nodded. "But they were still using up all their reserves, when the insurance Taylorman sold them should have covered a lot more."

Jennifer sat up. "And that's what the Department of Insurance ruled. It said the insurance company had to pay."

"So is the insurance company responsible or Rich Taylorman?"

"That's not clear." Jennifer shot Tom a look before adding. "The Department of Insurance was real careful, but it sounds like they were blaming him. That had to piss him off and he lost all sorts of money when the insurance company took back his bonuses." She was building up a head of steam again. "After the Department of Insurance's findings, he lost a bunch of clients."

"Did he?" I tapped my chin. "But that was medical insurance, this is life insurance. Different policies, different companies, right?"

Tom nodded.

"Same broker," Diana said. "Was Brian covered for suicide? If the policy's less than two years old, there's usually a contestability clause…"

"The two-year date was three weeks ago," Jennifer said.

Before Tom could ask how she knew that, I asked, "So how'd your session with Loriana go, Mike?"

"Sessions. It's been hard for her to talk about Don. I've had to dig at it a little bit at a time. But I did get a rundown of how Don spent his last two days."

He pulled out a reporter's notebook. "Monday before word came about Brian was normal, according to Loriana. Don ran an errand in town, then was putting the part he'd picked up into their ranch truck.

She said he'd finished that when word came about Brian. She said he drove off to search from their side, while she went to the Red Sail home ranch.

"What might be more interesting is he'd spent both Saturday and Sunday evenings at the Kicking Cowboy. I talked to Badger, the bartender, who said Don had a scuffle there with Otto Chaney on Sunday. But Badger didn't consider it anything out of the ordinary for Don."

"What was it about?"

He grinned and nodded. "About the ditch. About Don taking too much water. Also Otto was fuming that Don had threatened Paul Chaney that afternoon about something to do with the ditch. And Badger gathered that Don had threatened Otto, too. Plus, there was another fight Saturday night out in the parking lot. Badger knew less about that, but it involved Sam McCracken and Don. Broke up before the deputies arrived. Possibility that Otto was a witness to that."

"In other words, he spent the forty-eight hours before his death drinking, fighting, and threatening at least two people."

"Pretty much."

"And that was according to his wife," Diana said. "Wonder what his enemies would say. The man was not popular."

"Definitely not popular," I agreed. "So, as Jennifer pointed out, if somebody wanted to kill him, they'd probably want to make sure of it."

I recapped what Dex had told me, being careful not to give any hints about his identity.

"You could have told me—us—that yesterday," Mike said. "At Red Sail Rock."

"I wanted to tell everybody at the same time so I didn't have to keep repeating. That's why we have these gatherings. So everybody knows what everybody else knows."

Mike didn't look satisfied, but said nothing more.

"So, the murderer could have killed Don before or after the fall, not just relied on the fall doing the job," Diana said. "Does that help us? Could someone have shot him from a distance?"

"From where?" Tom asked. "Red Sail Rock blocks any shooter from the south. He'd see them coming from the west. They'd have to shoot from below him from the north or east, so Hazen would have to be standing right on the edge and why would he do that?"

"If the cause of death is something that happened after the fall, the field's as open as ever. Anybody who could have given him a good push, then climbed down and finished him off with a rock to the head," Mike said.

Tom shook his head. "*If* there's a murderer involved, the person still would have to get close enough to Don to push."

Ignoring the caveat at the beginning of that, I picked up, "But would he be on guard against somebody doing that? Also, it doesn't necessarily need to be a rock to the head. There could be other ways."

Mike groaned. "That opens the field even more. Not to mention that Don might not have been the main target. This thing is giving me a headache."

"Giving the Walterstons a hell of a lot worse."

Mike and I nodded at Tom's comment.

If journalists—good journalists—think of the tragedy behind a story every second, there will be nothing left of them in no time. But forgetting completely risks hollowing out the journalist's humanity. So you end up slipping toward one end of the spectrum or the other, then getting tugged back by circumstances, professionalism, colleagues.

What it most resembles is sleep deprivation torture, where the victim is pulled back to wakefulness each time he—or she—is about to fall asleep.

But it's the way to do a story justice.

I looked around. "What else have folks picked up?"

"Kade and Austin don't seem to be getting along," Diana said.

That reminded me we hadn't filled her or Jennifer in about the visit to Red Sail Rock yesterday morning. I did quickly.

At the end, Diana said, "The brothers didn't get any happier with each other at the lunch, though I only caught a few words—'Leave her alone' from Austin. Not in a friendly tone."

I added my inconclusive conversation with Cas Newton.

"There's another rumor floating around—that Don was hitting on other women."

Tom objected, "But he was always crazy about Loriana."

" 'Crazy about' doesn't always last," I said. "And it could explain a few things she said the night of the search."

I told them about that conversation. Loriana looking for Don's arrival. Her unconvincing certainty that he was out searching for Brian and that betraying "Unless…"

"You mean she was thinking 'unless he was out with some other woman?' " Jennifer asked.

"It's a possibility."

I remembered more: Loriana's distaste for Hannah Chaney's tears, her obvious desire to be away from the younger woman, a woman reputedly pregnant by a man not her husband. Could there be more behind that?

Before I could raise that oh-so-tentative possibility, however, Tom cleared his throat.

"They found something."

We all stilled, waiting. But he appeared stuck.

"Who found something?" I asked.

"Sheriff's department. They searched the family's computers, phones. There wasn't anything on the boys', but on Brian's… Searches about dying from exposure."

That wasn't shocking, at least to me. Though it might be what Rich Taylorman had hoped for to prove this hadn't been an accidental death.

I had a feeling there was more.

Tom looked down at his hands, his fingers loosely interwoven. "And a lot about transference of trace evidence. Fibers, hairs, skin cells. Somebody's principle—"

"Locard," I murmured.

"—primary and secondary transfers."

"Who do they think…?" Mike asked.

Tom nodded. "That's the question, isn't it? It's Brian's computer. If he did plan it, if he did want to die, the exposure research makes sense. Maybe he worried about somebody getting blamed and that could explain the other. But the boys had access to it. That's—" He flexed his hands, then sat up and looked at me, his mind made up. "— the part that will haunt the both of them the rest of their lives unless you find out who did this."

He was sure they hadn't acted together, but he wasn't sure one of them hadn't acted alone. If one was guilty, he wasn't willing to have the innocent suffer for that.

"Unless *we* find out who did this," he added.

Slowly, I nodded.

"There's another area to look into." Tom took a swipe at his hat hooked on the sofa arm, as if to remove a smudge. "The one you asked about yesterday. There's been a lot of talk about Red Sail Ditch."

Thomas David Burrell voluntarily raising the topic of *talk*.

Holy moly, I *had* negotiated the opening of North Korea's borders and the release of all political prisoners.

Or maybe he had learned how to move the focus away from the Walterston brothers.

"Of course," Diana said.

"Good point," Mike said.

Jennifer nodded knowingly.

While I'd been celebrating my negotiating prowess I'd missed a turn into unfamiliar territory. Sure, I'd picked up tidbits yesterday about Red Sail Ditch, but tidbits seldom come with explanatory footnotes.

I had to say something. "Because of the ditch boss situation."

The lines around Tom's eyes deepened. "Don't really know what a ditch boss is, do you, Elizabeth?"

"The person in charge of a ditch."

Mike said, "But do you know what a ditch means in Wyoming."

"I know what it means in the rest of the world—a sunken area to hold water or pipes, or the act of skipping school, or getting rid of something. If it's different in Wyoming..."

"That part's the same. But here it's also a lifeline. An enterprise. A covenant. A community. A family—"

"Sometimes dysfunctional," I slid in.

"Frequently dysfunctional," Mike said.

Diana added thoughtfully, "And possibly a cause of death."

Chapter Twenty

I LEANED FORWARD. "How can it be a cause of death?"

"That might be overly dramatic, but there've been rumbles that several people on Red Sail Ditch have been ripe for killing." Diana added, "You must know more than any of us, Tom."

"First, you have to understand how a ditch works, Elizabeth."

I sat back. "Needham told me all about irrigation in Wyoming."

"All about?" Tom asked with a slight smile. "You know what a head gate is?"

"Yes." I hadn't been in Wyoming for six months without learning a thing or two. "It's that frame that holds a cow's head still while the rancher does stuff to it that the cow would rather skip."

His mouth twitched. "True. In irrigation, though, it's what separates a ditch from its next bigger supplier of water. It can be closed to prevent water coming in or it can be graduated to adjust the flow."

"Lots use a Parshall flume to measure flow," Mike said. At least he was speaking half English.

"The ditch company's responsible for maintaining the ditch," Tom said. "Members share the expense in proportion to the number of shares they hold. Shares usually comes with the property."

"So if you buy property and it has a ditch on it—"

"Might not be your ditch. Ditches can run through property that doesn't carry a share. Usually by easement. Those folks can't take water from the ditch, have no say in its running, but don't pay maintenance, either."

"What if it's a dry year and there's not enough water for everybody? The ones at the end of the line lose out?"

"It's not based on geography. It's based on seniority of shares in the ditch. The rule is 'First in time, first in right.'."

"Okay, I now know about ditches, but what does this have to do with the deaths of Brian and Don?"

"Brian's family's been ditch boss since the Red Sail Ditch Company started more than a hundred years ago. But Don was mounting a campaign to take over. Feelings were divided and strong."

Remembering the encounter with Tom and the Walterston boys Wednesday, I asked, "What about the section he let degrade? Does that play into this?"

Tom tipped his chin in a who-knows gesture. "Seemed to be part of his campaign. Though I don't know what he thought he'd get out of it."

"How bad was it?"

"It wasn't so bad that water didn't get distributed, but it needs a lot more attention than it's been getting or there could be trouble come spring."

I hadn't meant the overall functioning of the ditch, though his answer was interesting. "That section Loriana's having fixed now? How bad was that?"

"Bad. The banks had eroded enough that they were letting in water to a low area. Fool was wearing away his own soil."

"In other words, Austin was right that Loriana did good in getting it fixed right away? In that case, what was Kade's problem?"

"Loriana just seems to rub him the wrong way."

That moment yesterday at the house between the new widow and the young man replayed in my head.

Loriana just seems to rub him the wrong way.

I wondered if Tom knew how right he was.

"So, the ditch is vital to many of the ditch company's members. All this discord has made the ditch less functional—at best—than it should be. The center of the discord was Don and at least to some extent Brian as ditch boss. Seems to me that could give Brian or Don motive."

"Or make either one the intended target," Mike said. "So we're back to all those scenarios."

DIANA AND I cleaned up, with her washing and me drying the few items that didn't go in the dishwasher.

"What was that look you gave Tom when we were discussing Don letting the banks of his section of the ditch erode?"

"I don't know what you're—" She met my gaze and gave up.

Her voice deepened. "Word is that Don might have messed with the gates himself."

"That's bad, huh?"

"Very bad."

"Rustling bad?"

"I wouldn't go as far as *rustling* bad. But it's something you don't do. Could make other folks pretty darned cranky."

"Boy, all this was going on and Tom still hesitated about using it to distract from the boys' motives."

She sobered. "I can't imagine how hard it is for him. He's like an uncle to those boys. And to watch Connie go through all this on top of Brian getting sicker and sicker... It's eating him up. When he was accused of murder and the highway construction business stalled, he kept Connie—Oh." She eyed me. "That's right. You knew that. Tom told you—?"

I cut it off with a laugh and focused on drying a nonstick frying pan she'd had soaking from dinner. "Tom Burrell tell me anything he didn't have to? No. Connie told me."

"It's Tom's way. It's nothing to do with you."

"I know it's nothing to do with me. Though it makes it difficult to have him be part of these, uh, inquiries."

"Is that all it makes difficult?"

"Yes."

She snorted. Not sharply enough that I felt obligated to dispute anything, but with enough emphasis that I couldn't mistake her disbelief. It was a finely calibrated snort, darn her.

"Diana, there's something else." It wasn't subtle but sometimes subtlety was overrated when redirecting a conversation. "The authorities don't seem to be considering it and I would fear for my life bringing it up in front of Tom, but we have to consider Connie's alibi. At least to be sure that she can be eliminated."

"*Connie?* You suspect Connie?"

"Suspect is too strong. But she needs to be eliminated. I wondered if you could check out her timeline."

"I'm not comfortable asking people if Connie was where she said she was at the time her husband was dying."

"How about saying that you understood they were with Connie a short time before she heard Brian was missing and you hope she was having some pleasure then, because the poor woman certainly deserved it?"

She tipped her head and looked at me. "You're good. Scary, but good."

"Does that mean you'll—?"

"Yes, fine. I'll see what I can worm out of people."

"That's all I ever ask."

She threw a dishtowel at me, apparently not buying the meekness.

I caught it on the fly, then held on.

"Diana, this talk of accidents and dangers on a ranch..." I kept my voice low. "If you don't want to answer I understand, but, how did Gary die?"

Her hands stilled an instant, then resumed wiping out the sink. "He was haying. The baler broke. He was trying to fix it. The jack he had it on failed. By the time I found him it was too late."

"That must have been ... beyond horrible."

"It was. But you go on. You don't think you'll be able to, but you do."

"Is that what you said to Connie when she hugged you yesterday?"

"Something like that." She pointed to a lower cabinet as the home of the now-dry pan. I complied. With an abrupt shift of tone, she said, "You know, water isn't the only bone of contention with the Red Sail Ditch."

"Oh?"

"People on a ditch are like any other group. Same issues arise."

"You mean the universals—money, power, revenge, sex—*sex? Really?*"

Her face had changed when I said "sex," so I knew I was right. I just couldn't believe it.

Then I remembered interactions at the search, not to mention Penny's reports and I could.

"There are rumors."

"About Hannah Chaney," I said. "Like I heard from Loriana and Penny."

She groaned. "With all the trimmings, no doubt. Hannah and Paul Chaney were high school sweethearts. There were rumors about fights—arguments—nothing physical. Still, there were a lot of dropped jaws when she moved in to Terry's place. He's been Don's biggest backer and Paul definitely wasn't. Anyway, that's when the speculation started about who's the father."

" 'Peyton Place' of the Rockies."

"Dating yourself," she muttered. "At least make it 'Scandal' in Wyoming."

"Fine. Though 'Peyton Place' is a classic. No—don't say it. I give."

"Interesting what you said about Loriana, the possibility that she was thinking Don and Hannah might be involved," Diana said. "Very interesting, since there's also a rumor that Loriana's having an affair."

"Loriana?"

Okay, yes, my mind flashed immediately to Mike. I tried to stop it, but it was too quick for me.

Next up were the "He wouldn't, he couldn't" tropes.

It wasn't my business if he did.

"I know. I was surprised, too. Most of what I heard was about Don running around, but there *were* a couple hints about Loriana. All very vague."

"Any idea who the other party might be in her case?"

"Nobody seems to have any idea. And considering how bad those folks are at keeping a secret, that's surprising. So maybe it's not true."

DAY FIVE

FRIDAY

Chapter Twenty-One

I CALLED A source in Seattle for what might be a future "Helping Out" segment on student loans. Or the piece might be broadened and deepened ... wherever I ended up after this month ended.

As if I'd conjured him up with those thoughts, I saw a message from Mel Welch coming in as I wrapped up with the Seattle source.

Mel was acting as my agent in the search for my post-Halloween employment, as he had last winter after my ex maneuvered me out of my job in New York.

After the divorce, our mutual long-time agent had stuck with my ex. Mel, bless him, had stepped in. He was a well-regarded lawyer in Chicago, though he had no previous experience agenting a broadcast journalist. On the other hand he'd married into my extended family around the time I hit the age of reason, and his loyalty was unquestionable. Unlike a certain former agent.

Or a certain ex, for that matter.

I should call Mel back. It might be about an offer. As Penny had pointed out, my term here was running out.

But I also saw a previous message. From my long-time friend, Matt Lester, a reporter for the *Philadelphia Inquirer.*

It was only polite to answer the first call first.

Matt said he needed details on my recovery from the effects of the fire—because he would be expected to fill in Bonnie, his wife and my friend, when he got off the phone and there was no tougher audience for a reporter.

I answered as many health questions as I could stand, segued to replacing my car, then eased him into what he'd called about.

He wondered if I had a contact who could help with background for a story on a former Congressman from Pennsylvania. I did. But I'd have to dig for the phone number, since it had burned along with my previous phone.

As I promised to call him back as soon as I tracked it down, Jennifer said I had a call on one of the station lines.

I'd talk to Mel later.

"**WHAT DO YOU** think you're doing?"

"Who is this?" I'd recognized Rich Taylorman's belligerent voice, but I wanted him to identify himself.

"Trying to dig up dirt. Talking to people. Breaking into my website. You've been digging into my business. And I won't put up with that. I'll—"

"What—?"

"Don't pretend ignorance. I know you broke into my website. I know it. Took information and—"

"I have no idea—"

"You don't need any ideas. Just stay the hell out of my business. Or else."

Taylorman disconnected.

A definite anticlimax to his would-be threatening finale.

That was the problem with mobile phones. Can't slam them down.

Broke into his website? What did that even mean?

Still, better to check...

I went to Jennifer's desk and invited her to join me in a spot where we could be assured privacy—the ladies' room. With only two cubicles it was easy to be sure we were alone.

"Did you want that number saved?" she asked.

"Yes, but that—"

"The name was blocked. So, who—"

"Taylorman. It was Rich Taylorman. But that's not why—"

"What did *he* call you about?"

"That's what I'm telling you, Jennifer. He was complaining about my asking questions about him and—"

"Really? I bet that means we're on the right track—"

"*And*," I repeated more strongly, "about someone taking information off his website. He said he knew we 'broke into' his website. You didn't hack it or disable it or crash it or remove—?"

"No way. I saved everything to my server so I can look at it at home, not on KWMT time," she said virtuously. "It was all right out there in the open. Well, most of it. He offers about every kind of insurance. Couldn't find anybody else that spreads that thin. He's been here four years. Previously was in Iowa and before that in Kentucky and before that in Pennsylvania. He makes it sound like he went from one state to the next. But there are gaps."

I was still focused on her hacking tendencies. "Could he have known what you were looking at somehow? Known it was copied and who did it?"

She snorted in disdain. "Him? No way. I've heard there's some software that—But him? I told you, his site's a mess. He doesn't even secure it. He was trying to scare us off. Besides, you guys go around asking people about their love lives, so why shouldn't I copy a public site?"

She had a point. Maybe several points.

"I found this picture." Jennifer handed me a color printout.

It was the photo Taylorman had taken at Red Sail Rock.

People were recognizable as people. Brian's body and the wheelchair were also recognizable. But detail was washed out by the flash and, possibly, movement. "Interesting."

"I've sent copies to everybody, but it's awful. I'm asking a friend about cleaning it up—You aren't saying you want me to stop looking into him, are you?"

"No way. Rich Taylorman just convinced me there's something to find. But be more careful."

Chapter Twenty-Two

THE MCCRACKENS' HOUSE might have fit in a suburban subdivision—as long as the subdivision was western themed.

It was a new L-shaped log structure with a green metal roof and green accents. The inside of the L framed a planted area that led to the front door. A split rail fence kept separated a parking area that held a dark SUV and a white pickup that seemed lopsided with its oversized passenger compartment.

Driving in I'd spotted a deck that appeared to wrap around the outside of the L, which must offer nice views of the buttes and the mountains in the distance behind the house.

No sign of a ranch dog, but as soon as I was out of the SUV, here came the medium-height man I'd seen before. Hatless now, he displayed a mop of dark hair.

"Mr. McCracken?"

"Who are you?" His body language wasn't any friendlier than his greeting. He stood at the end of the walkway, arms crossed over his chest, blocking me from advancing toward the front door.

"My name is E.M. Danniher—Elizabeth." I extended a hand. He was reluctant, but he met it. "I'm with KWMT-TV. I'm doing background for a potential piece on newcomers in Cottonwood County. Since I am one myself—" I added my most winning smile to that you-and-me-against-the-world effort at bonding. "—I have a strong interest in how the new and old come together here. I was told you and—"

"You're from back East."

His tone left no doubt of what he thought of *that*. He might be from the city, but at least he wasn't from—gasp, horrors—the East.

"Illinois, actually." His distrust didn't waver.

How could that be when Illinois was the Land of Lincoln. Okay, also a disgraced and jailed governor or three or four, but still. Honest Abe shone down on me from every classroom wall from my first day of school to my last. That had to count for something.

I kept going. "I was told you and your family would be good people to talk to. Part of the influx of new residents in Cottonwood County, who bring fresh eyes, yet appreciate it for what it is."

"Influx? Part of the reason we came here is there isn't an influx. We want peace and quiet and stability."

"There. That's exactly the kind of insight I'm hoping to get about your experience and—"

"My wife doesn't find that the convenience store tucked into a corner of the closest gas station carries much of what she likes."

Oh-kay. That was certainly a change of topic. But I would follow the trail.

"That would be another area to talk about. Adjusting to the differences living here, such as—"

"She goes into Sherman. To the supermarket there. There's some checker who talks a mile a minute."

Uh-oh.

"She says you're looking into the deaths of Brian and Don Hazen as a double homicide."

I couldn't imagine Penny saying it that succinctly.

"Only law enforcement has the authority to declare a death a homicide, Mr. McCracken. Also, while I work multiple stories at a time, looking into those two deaths is not among my assignments." Just ask Les Haeburn.

"But that's what you want to ask me about."

Honesty wasn't always the best policy for a reporter, but sometimes it was the only one left. "Yes. For background, so I underst—"

"I have nothing to say about—"

"Why? You have nothing to worry about. You weren't there and—

"

I stopped because he'd flinched.

"Don't think I haven't heard about not being there. And they're right. I should have been there to search for Brian."

"Why weren't you?"

He uncrossed his arms and let them drop. He stepped away from blocking the entryway, but instead of inviting me in, he jerked his head toward the other side of the parking area where a substantial outbuilding stood.

On the butte side of the building there was an old table with a couple of chairs. He gestured to one and took the other. That left my back to the domestic scene I'd glimpsed on the house's deck of a woman in jeans watching over a boy and girl playing with a dog about the size and color of a pillow.

It also put the light on his face and I decided that at least one of the reasons he didn't look like a rancher or a cowboy was that his skin wasn't weathered enough.

"I didn't join the search for Brian because I was still angry at him." He tapped the edge of his fisted left hand on the table twice. "Man dies, and pretty damned fast it all seems petty. I knew he was sick, but at the deposition, he seemed stronger. I thought…"

Before resuming, he glanced at me, then away. "Connie's been good to my wife. She and Kade have had the kids over to ride a couple times."

"Which means you're now getting a horse for your kids."

He smiled for the first time. "Not getting. Got. And not *a* horse. Four. One for each of us."

I chuckled.

He grew serious again. "Look, I'm sorry about Brian's death. Very sorry. I've said he should have given up the ditch boss job to somebody who could handle it, and I stick by that. But he was a good man."

"Why were you angry at him?"

"The deposition. He stayed neutral. Kept the ditch right out of it, when if the ditch company would have come together—at least the sane ones—and told Don Hazen they wouldn't put up with…" He opened his fisted hands. "Guess I'm still angry."

"No change of heart about Don now that he's dead?"

"No." For a beat I thought that was going to be it. But then he added, "He was a manipulative, scheming sociopath."

Nope. He definitely wasn't a believer in speak no ill of the dead.

I poked a bit. "Others have said he was a great guy."

"He could be charming enough, but only if he thought that was the way to have what he wanted. When he saw he couldn't order me around the way he did Terry Waymark, he did a one-eighty. I was no longer an ally. I was an enemy. And he showed that pretty damn quick."

"I heard there was some sort of incident..."

Muscles along his jaw pulsed. With his mouth clamped closed that hard I doubted he'd volunteer more. So I nudged.

"About the fence?"

Still silent, his jaw-pulsing eased a bit. So maybe he would say something.

I tried priming the pump. "Don Hazen tore it down?"

"No warning, no discussion, he just comes along with that old beater truck of his and plows into that fence. My kids could have been on the other side and that maniac wouldn't have cared.

"As it was, do you know what he did? Nearly killed our dog. Was driving straight for him. If I hadn't gotten there and whistled for Snowman, he'd have been under the tires of that truck of Hazen's."

I **DIDN'T GET** any more useful information from Sam McCracken.

And wasn't sure how useful what I had gotten was.

Would I be that angry if someone drove straight at Shadow?

Okay, yes, I would.

That still didn't stop me from thinking there was something else going on.

That odd spell of silence when he'd otherwise been willing to talk...

I ran the conversation back through my head.

"I heard there was some sort of incident…"

That's when he'd clammed up.

What was it Hannah had said about a fight…?

Something happened at the supermarket. …It was his wife. That Mrs. McCracken.

I needed to find out more about that.

Chapter Twenty-Three

"CAN WE USE your living room again to meet this evening?" I asked Diana on the phone as I headed toward her ranch.

"Sure. Who are you going to meet with?"

"The regular group. I'll call them as soon as—"

She laughed. "Not in my living room you're not. Everybody'll be at the football game. It's homecoming and we all went to Cottonwood County High."

"But—"

"Give it up, Elizabeth. If there were a meteor hurtling toward us everybody would still go to this game. You might as well come, too. Believe me, there's nothing else to do in Cottonwood County tonight."

MY PHONE RANG as Diana pulled into a packed parking lot between the high school building and the football field.

It was Mel. Again.

"I better answer this," I said to Diana. Her kids had exited the truck practically before it came to a stop. "I'll catch up with you in a minute."

She said she'd save me a seat.

"There's interest," Mel announced. "Do you want to know details?"

"No."

Wes, my ex, had always handled this part of the business. I'd never been good at waiting to hear, at not thinking too far ahead, at telling the difference between simple feelers and serious interest, at the whole dance.

"Okay. Danny, you know that demo, uh, what do you call it?"

"Resumé reel."

"Right. The resumé reel you gave me doesn't include Sherman. I want to send them some of your work from there."

I laughed. " 'Helping Out' isn't going to get me back to a network or a top market, Mel."

"I was thinking of the specials you've done. Those investigations." He lowered his voice. "The ones we're not mentioning to your parents because of, you know, the *murders*."

Judging by the near-whisper, he also wasn't mentioning it to his wife, Peg, whose mother was my mother's cousin.

I had never thought of adding the KWMT specials.

They were good. Damned good. But I'd thought of them mostly as examples of my colleagues stretching their skills. But I had stretched, too, by putting the specials together.

"I'll look at them, Mel, and let you know."

"Soon. Don't want to let this interest cool. By the end of the weekend?"

"I'll try, but—Uh, how's Peg? The kids? How are you doing, Mel?"

Mel Welch was no match for my mother, but that didn't mean he was stupid.

"But what, Danny? What aren't you telling me? Oh." His voice shifted from concern to sotto voce intrigue. "Another *murder?*"

"Possibly," I admitted.

He whistled softly. "What is it out there, something in the water?"

"You could say that."

"Well, don't wait until you solve this one and do a special on it to send me your resumé. Your reel, I mean. Because I promised some people I'd get back to them next week. Of course, one contact doesn't need to be told about what you've been doing these past months."

"Right. About that…"

A couple weeks ago, he'd asked if I wanted him to approach KWMT-TV about staying and I'd said okay. More in a what-the-hell attitude than any expectation that they'd want me or that I'd want to stay.

What had I been thinking, to give Haeburn the chance to turn me down?

"Yes, what about it, Danny?"

"I'm not sure it's a good idea for you to talk to Haeburn."

"Who's that?"

"The News Director. Les Haeburn."

"Oh, I'm not talking to him."

That left only the general manager or the owners. Owners who were so hands-off that I'd yet to see any of them. Including matriarch Val Heatherton's son-in-law, Craig Morningside, who was the only general manager I knew of who didn't come to the station, instead keeping an office in his home.

Mel talking to the ownership had to tie in with my ending up in Sherman, Wyoming of all places when my ex had tried to boot me out of news.

"Mel, what did you do? How did I end up here?"

"The same way anyone ends up anywhere. Serendipity and odd circumstances and chance and luck."

I let my silence stretch after that bit of chirpiness. "You know the owners, don't you? You pulled strings. Mel, tell me."

"You needed a place to go. I had tried a couple—but I didn't have the contacts," he added hurriedly.

Ah. He'd approached people and they'd turned him down, refusing to hire me. That didn't do the ego much good. At some level I'd known that. Was I starting to care about it now?

"I understand. And thank you, Mel. I hope you didn't use up too many credits in getting me a job."

"Not at all. They owe *me*."

✧   ✧   ✧   ✧

I HESITATED ONLY an instant before checking my reconstructed contacts for Wardell Yardley's number.

Anyone who watches news knows Wardell Yardley is a network

White House correspondent with a prodigious knack for getting into the shot of every news outlet's coverage of White House press conferences. It's known as "Where's Wardell?" among the White House press corps.

He answered on the first ring.

"I need a number for Sanderford Jenkins, Dell."

"Why? You got a story?"

"No. It's for a friend and the story wouldn't interest you. If my phone hadn't been ruined in the fire, I wouldn't be bothering you."

"Way to use the sympathy card," he said admiringly. Then he rattled off the number. Probably from memory. "Okay, why did you really call?"

"I promised I'd get the number and—"

"Tell Uncle Dell, Elizabeth Margaret."

I hesitated.

Stupid, stupid, stupid.

"Ah-*hah*. I knew there was something. Knew it from the sound of the phone ringing."

"You can't possibly—"

"I did. Now, tell."

I told him what Mel had admitted. "...So I wasn't supposed to be here. If—"

"Of course you weren't supposed to be *there*. You're supposed to be *here*."

"No, I meant if Mel hadn't interceded as some sort of balding, rounded guardian angel, I would have been completely out of news."

"If he's a guardian angel, that makes Little Lord Fauntleroy the devil who manipulated your downfall. That works."

If I let him get started on the topic of my ex, we'd never get off it.

"I feel like that character Joe Pendleton in *Here Comes Mr. Jordan,* the one Warren Beatty played in the remake, *Heaven Can Wait.*" Dell might love old movies even more than he hated Wes. "I wasn't supposed to have been dead, but I also wasn't supposed to be in this current limbo life. But the longer I stay in the limbo life, the more tendrils attach me to it. So where am I supposed to be? And how do I get there?"

"You're supposed to be here," he said again.

"Freelance? You know—"

"Okay, you don't want freelance? Let me put out feelers."

"But Mel—"

"Is the official voice, sure. But you know he's not going to get the attention a hot agent would. And you're not going to get a hot agent out there in Hooterville. I have—"

"Hooterville's in Illinois."

"No it's not. It's somewhere southern."

"Hooterville in *Green Acres* is in Illinois."

"Who cares about *Green Acres*? I was thinking of *Petticoat Junction* with the hot girls."

Dell was comfortable enough with many women that certain men speculated he had to be gay. I had it on good authority—but not personal experience, contrary to rumors—that he was not.

But, as Dell said to me when we'd discussed the topic once over way too much wine in a country far, far away, why disabuse the speculators of their comforting fairy tale. He'd winked when he called it a fairy tale before adding, "Besides, it's so much fun watching them be so smugly wrong."

I snorted now. "*Petticoat Junction*? Hot girls? Really, Dell?"

"They were to me. Innocent that I was. Anyway, as I was saying before I was interrupted, I have influence. I'll drop a word with a few of the right people and—"

"The BBs?" As a testament to his friendship it didn't get much higher than Dell being willing to talk to the "Big Bosses."

"No. I'll talk to the people who really make decisions."

"Oh, Dell, I do miss you."

"Of course you do. And before you know it, we'll be scrapping and snarling over stories again, here in Dysfunctional City." That's what he insisted D.C. stood for. "I'll set it up so all you have to do is make a phone call to the right person."

He dangled it, the sparkling bauble of returning to my former life, possibly in triumph, almost certainly in vindication. And it would be sweet. So sweet.

But...

Well, I didn't know "but" what. Why shouldn't I go back? Why shouldn't I return to the career I'd known?

"Okay."

"Great. Gotta go now. Got stories to cover, deals to broker."

As we said good-bye, I chuckled at how Dell would delight in everyone saying he was crazy for helping a professional rival.

He not only marched to his own drum, he had his own damned band.

I thoroughly enjoyed and admired the beat of his band, though I wasn't sure I wanted to keep up with its rhythm.

And I'd let him loose.

Chapter Twenty-Four

THE GAME WAS in the middle of the second quarter when I joined the crowd after calling to give Matt the phone number.

As I searched the stands for Diana, I spotted Mike up in a press box that seemed to sway with the wind. I had to look away before it gave me motion sickness.

Ah, there was Diana, waving to me. I climbed the bleachers to her. On my way, I spotted Jennifer in the next set of seats over. Needham Bender was here, too, with his wife Thelma. And not far away I saw Driver 2 and Driver 3, who I now knew as Otto Chaney and Paul Chaney, but neither of the occupants from the first pickup, Paul's wife Hannah and her companion, Terry Waymark.

The odd couple of substantial Aunt Gee and tiny Mrs. Parens sat side by side, both bolt upright.

They were next-door neighbors in the town of O'Hara Hill northwest of Sherman. Perhaps having their focus concentrated on the same small area—a continent might be too small—was the source of the deep-seated rivalry that largely played out in undercurrents and peculiar things like presenting me with hideously clashing afghans when I was hospitalized after the fire.

In their hands afghans were scarier than nukes.

But just as strong as the rivalry was a solidarity between them.

"Good phone call?" Diana asked as I took the seat she'd saved.

I grunted noncommittally. "Quite the crowd."

She let her question go, though I saw curiosity in her eyes. "You obviously haven't seen all of it."

I raised my eyebrows.

"Six rows below us, exactly at the fifty yard line," she said.

It took a moment. "Oh, my."

Thurston Fine. Looking uncomfortable in jeans so new they apparently didn't allow him to bend his knees and a matching denim jacket. Thank heavens he hadn't tried for a cowboy hat. The two couples he was with looked prosperous, a bit self-important, yet part of the native fauna.

"Talking county attorney and sheriff?" I asked.

"Probably. The woman on his left and the man on his right are county commissioners."

"Why do I have the feeling we're in for another lead story taken directly from a news release?"

"Not until Monday. He made it very clear he has plans this weekend and shouldn't be bothered."

"Ah, a true news hound."

"Yup. That's halftime. Let's go get some food."

Halftime. I hadn't watched a single play. And I like football. "What about our seats? Shouldn't one of us stay here to save them?"

"Why? They're our seats."

Sometimes I forget I'm in Wyoming.

As we followed the crowd down the bleacher steps, I noted Cottonwood County was leading 14-7. Go team.

We didn't get far because the concession line stretched nearly as long as the women's restroom line.

"You guys are standing in line for concessions way back here?" Mike asked from behind us.

"Yup. Want something?"

"Nah. They bring food to the press box."

Diana glared at him. "Don't you have somewhere else to be?"

"Nope. Ted is getting cheerleader and crowd shots. I'm free for now."

I tried to make Diana feel better. "Bet the press box food's not anything like what he was used to in the NFL."

"Never got anywhere near press box fare because I was playing."

He grinned. "Besides, I'd stack Mrs. Baranski's pigs-in-a-blanket up against anything—"

He was swamped by a torrent of words. "Did you know falling into water can be worse than falling to the ground? If you—"

"Jennifer?" Diana identified the torrent's source before she closed in as a fourth side to our conversation.

"—fall into water, you better do it from less than a hundred eighty-six feet. They call it the upper limits of survivability." We edged forward. "And then there's being trapped in a falling elevator. That's worse. Because—"

I interrupted. "What do elevators have to do—"

"—there's no good option. In six stories, you're going about fifty miles an hour."

"Tallest building in Wyoming is only twelve stories," Mike said.

Diana groaned. "Don't encourage her."

"How do you know that?" I asked him.

"Don't encourage him, either."

"Mrs. Parens."

Of course.

"In twelve stories you'd be going even *faster*." Jennifer was undistracted by our detours. "So your options are even worse. Forget about jumping up, that only cuts your speed a few miles per hour and you'll probably hit your head if you don't time it perfectly and who knows how to time it perfectly? And bending your knees to absorb the impact won't do much, either, so you have to get on the floor—only that's hard, because you're not feeling any gravity—then lie stretched out—"

"Jennifer," I tried.

"—on your back and try to stay there without bouncing up and of course your head's exposed, so that's not good, and the rebound could—"

"Jennifer."

"—be like a car crash, except—"

"Jennifer. No elevators."

"—there's not even a headrest, so—"

"Enough Jennifer," Diana said in her mother voice. "No more

research on falls for you. That's it."

"Besides," Mike said, "most people who get killed in elevators are maintenance workers. Not many passengers at all. What they have to worry are about escalators. Those things are—"

"Michael Paycik."

"—vicious." He looked at Diana, then at Jennifer, whose eyes had popped wide open. "Oh. Uh. Don't worry, there are only two escalators in Wyoming. In Casper. Stay away from those and you're fine."

"Michael," Diana repeated with more emphasis.

"They're not super dangerous, not if you pay attention. Really, Jenny. I've been on lots in Chicago and all over and never had a problem."

Jennifer began to regain her color. She'd been so preoccupied she hadn't even noticed Mike had called her Jenny.

"Just don't wear long scarves," Mike added under his breath.

WE'D REACHED WHAT looked like a cattle chute to funnel the line neatly to the concession windows. Diana took Jennifer's arm and said, "C'mon, we'll get the stuff and bring it out. Elizabeth and Mike, go wait over there instead of all of us clogging up the line."

I barely waited to get out of earshot. "How do you know there are only two escalators in Wyoming?" Mrs. P would never highlight something Wyoming lacked.

"College football. Everybody gets a research question. Like cooking Rocky Mountain oysters for a guy from back East. Way back some player from a small town freaked first time he got on an escalator, so ever since, a player from a rural area gets picked to research them. It's not like I avoid them or let them freak me out." He gave me a lopsided grin. "But I don't wear long scarves."

I heard a familiar voice over the loudspeaker and turned toward the press box.

"He's on the field," Mike said. "In charge of the homecoming ceremonies."

Of course, Thomas David Burrell was in charge.

"Why aren't you out there, Mike?"

"I begged off since I'm working. I did it last year."

The festivities had started when Diana and Jennifer returned. They had barely sorted out our orders before Jennifer said, "I'm still working on that photo," then sped off with a wave.

Diana, Mike, and I started back toward the stands, not trying to talk over the loudspeaker.

I could only catch glimpses of Tom, along with one of the couples from Thurston's group, and a string of other dignitaries lined up along the sideline.

Abruptly even my glimpses of the field were cut off by a large hand followed by a large arm coming over my shoulder to dip into my popcorn.

"Hey!" I tried to keep it low, but a couple heads turned.

"I better get back to the press box," the thief said.

"Darned right, before I chop off your hand."

Mike grinned and departed.

I started to turn toward the steps we'd come down, but Diana jerked her head to keep walking, so I followed.

She led us up the next set of steps and slid into a row on the right. With a gesture, she indicated for me to take a seat on the far side of Gisella Decker, sitting alone now since Mrs. Parens was on the field.

Aunt Gee nodded regal thanks when Diana handed her one of the popcorns, then we sat watching the ceremonies and munching.

I'll admit my mind wandered.

Ask the Heathertons. Or I'll talk to them.

Tom knew the owners of KWMT-TV. How well? Would he know the connection with Mel, or why this out-of-sight ownership had accepted me earlier this year, or what their thoughts might be now?

We all applauded when the ceremonies wrapped up.

"How are you feeling, Elizabeth?" Aunt Gee asked me. "You should rest after the ordeal of that fire."

"That was weeks ago."

"It's very soon to dive headlong into the exertions involved in one of your, ah, endeavors." Her pointed look translated that oblique reference. She knew what we were digging into.

That meant there was no downside to being direct. "I was wondering—"

"I am not going to reveal facts of the investigation to you or anyone, including whether Don Hazen had a light or not. Deputy Shelton is conducting a thorough and professional inquiry."

In other words, she'd only helped us on previous occasions because the investigation had been shoddy. The second part was true. I hoped the first part wasn't. At least not completely. But her statement meant direct was out.

"I would *never* ask you to do anything against your conscience, Gisella, because I know you'd refuse."

Another regal nod.

"But you can tell Diana and me—" By drawing Diana in, I hoped for a dose of innocence by association. "—what's already public record, especially if the sheriff's department had interactions with either of the victims. It would be so helpful and save us working through public records. You have such a grasp—"

"Brian never. Deputies have been to the HY Ranch on numerous occasions over the years."

"Don Hazen's ranch?"

She nodded. "As a young man he was frequently cited and several times spent nights in jail, which you could find in the *Independence*. Most recently he was kept overnight because he refused to pay the fine after an altercation."

"Right around the time Mindy disappeared?" The alibi Shelton had talked about.

"Yes. Most of Don's issues involved public intoxication and public fighting."

"Deputies wouldn't go to the ranch for that," Diana said.

This version of the regal nod added a hint of approval for spotting that discrepancy. "The instances when deputies were called to the HY don't hark back to the beginning of Cottonwood County." That was a mild dig at her nemesis and friend, who specialized in county history—

and safe since Mrs. P was out of earshot. "But they did happen before Don bought the place from Loriana. Loriana's uncle Earl could be a hard man and he took out his frustrations on whoever was around. But I don't know of a single call there for that. However, there *were* trips to question him about rustling well before he was arrested on that charge."

Rustling? Needham Bender had skipped that fact.

Diana opened her mouth. I gave her a look and small head shake. One reporter skill I'd worked hard on was knowing when someone had more to say. Aunt Gee wasn't done.

"More often than not, deputies were called because Loriana and Ellen were at each other's throats. Earl was no fine example of an honest citizen, but he kept the peace. He mostly let Loriana do as she pleased, then bought off his wife with fancy things. Some say that being arrested and put in jail was the first peace he'd had in years. Then, he upped and died in jail."

Aunt Gee shifted on the bleacher seat. Following the direction of her gaze I saw Mrs. Parens beginning her return journey to this seat.

"Soon as he's in the ground, Ellen takes off. Don't suppose she could stand the thought of being there alone with Loriana. Not that they'd've needed to get along for long, since Loriana left immediately after graduation."

"Yet she came back."

"Many do. Suppose she didn't have the easiest time. Heard she'd married, but it didn't work out."

"So she returns and marries a hometown guy. But he wasn't a gem, either, was he?"

"You must be referring to the calls about him hitting Mindy. There's never been a call about his hitting Loriana. So maybe he learned his lesson." She considered that. "He always had a fascination with her. Half the reason he bought that place, I always thought."

What was the other half? Before I could explore that, Mrs. Parens arrived.

"Very impressive," Gisella said to her. Mrs. P nodded her acceptance of the tribute.

Diana and I added suitable congratulations while we vacated the seats and Mrs. Parens settled in.

With that accomplished, she looked up and asked, "You're coming tomorrow night, of course?"

Something in her tone made it feel like a homework assignment I'd totally forgotten. Before I could say "Huh?" or "What?" or "Tomorrow?" in utter ignorance, Diana said, "She's coming."

"Excellent," Aunt Gee said. "Nearly kickoff."

We'd been dismissed.

Mrs. Parens delayed our departure slightly by patting my arm and saying, "It's good that you're coming."

AS WE RESUMED our seats—as open as when we'd left them, just as Diana had expected—I kept my focus on the important element by repeating, "I'm not going to Cottonwood County High School's homecoming dance."

She'd informed me on the trip back to our seats that Mrs. P had been referring to Homecoming festivities Saturday evening.

"It's not like you're thinking. The kids have a dance. This is more like a big open house with all the alums mingling."

"You might have noticed I'm not an alum."

"We'll let you in anyway." She gave me a teasing look. "Lots of gossip."

Then she screamed.

Touchdown, Cottonwood County.

DAY SIX

SATURDAY

Chapter Twenty-Five

MIKE PICKED ME up after calling to say Tom would meet us at Red Rock Sail. Shelton was no longer blocking access to where Don Hazen had landed.

I might not have been coherent, because it was quite early when he called.

He brought coffee.

He probably thought he needed to do that to bribe me to let him drive. As if I wanted to drive my brand new SUV on that rough track. Much less at this hour of the morning.

Taking the up-ramp again, we found Tom already there, this time leaning against his truck with the sun barely risen behind him. And I'm not exaggerating. Much.

"No Chico today?" Mike sounded disappointed.

"Only needed him to get down to the repairs on the ditch. Can't get there by truck from this side and with Loop Field so boggy, shouldn't get there from Don's side at all. C'mon, I'll show you where they found Don. You can assess the fall he took yourself. Putting aside the feats of pro kayakers," he added dryly.

Then he gave my shoes a disapproving look. "You should've worn boots."

He led the way to the rough track Mike had pointed out on our previous visit.

"No way we're going down here. That's—"

Tom overrode me. "Here."

He took a couple choppy strides, then started skidding down the embankment toward water level. The sound effects reinforced that this was the route Richard and Shelton had taken in the early morning hours of Tuesday.

Mike beside me and Tom at the bottom focused on me. They expected me to follow suit.

Oh, *hell*.

I imitated Tom's short choppy strides. At least I tried to, but I quickly realized that while his boot heels had bitten into the earth, giving him purchase most of the way down, my flats moved like a pair of skateboards operated by two different people.

A quarter of the way down, I landed on my butt and stayed there for the rest of the descent. My right hand glanced off a rock when I instinctively reached out to steady myself. After that I curled my hands into each other to protect them.

It might have looked like I was praying.

Tom hauled me up before I could do it myself. His crow's feet were dancing, but he didn't make a sound, unlike Mike, who was chuckling as he started down—heels digging in like crazy.

Tom removed his hat and I realized—almost too late—why. He was going to whap at the seat of my pants with it.

"Don't you dare."

I pivoted away, using my unhurt hand to swat at my own backside. He raised both of his. "Just trying to help."

"Don't," I repeated, using both hands now, but not with the vigor required to remove all the accumulated dust, dirt, and grime, because the flesh beneath the seat of my pants was decidedly tender. Not to mention my right hand hurting.

"Are you okay?" Mike arrived on his feet with an impressive plume of dust behind him.

"Peachy."

"C'mon." Tom, his hat back on his head, had gone ahead. With that one word, he moved out of sight, around a jagged corner of rock.

When we followed—with me trying not to move as gingerly as my body wanted me to—I saw that the creek—*ditch*—swung well away from the base of the rock here.

There was a circle of police tape held up by stakes, two of them in the water. The ditch bank enclosed by the police tape was broken and matted down.

The water was about three feet wide, with low vegetation growing alongside it. The banks were regular enough that if I'd seen it up close like this earlier I wouldn't have thought it was a creek. Probably.

Downstream, a branch of the ditch split off north, where I spotted a metal contraption with a wheel atop it.

"That's a head gate?" I asked.

They both nodded.

Turning my back to the water, I looked up to the ledge above, then to tape-enclosed area. Rocks littered most of the area around the base of the cut-away cliff, blending in with the dirt. But in a patch halfway between the base and the water, the rocks gave the impression of being recent arrivals, judging by raw, lighter-colored edges on some of their uneven surfaces.

This must be the rock fall from the broken off ledge above.

Tom said, "Not ice knives, aliens, or a meteor, but falling rock. Rocks loosened by his fall could have hit him in the head. Fits your source's ideas."

I looked from the edge of the cliff above, to the patch of newer rock fall, to the matted vegetation on the bank and the police tape in the water.

I frowned. "I wouldn't expect him to fall straight down, but it doesn't seem likely he'd fall *that* far out. It looks like he was actually in the water."

Both men looked at me sharply, then turned to study the configuration.

"If he wasn't badly hurt, could he have moved toward the ditch on his own?" Mike asked.

All three of us moved around, leaning over, trying—without crossing the police tape—to get an angle that might show marks in the dust and dirt between the cliff's base and the ditch bank.

"Huh," Mike said. "Looks almost like someone scuffed up the area."

"Some of it could have been Alvaro and Shelton coming down here in the dark," I said. "But there's an awful lot."

"Wayne would have heads taken off if his men messed it up this much." Tom straightened. "I think you're right, Mike. Someone scuffed up that area."

"To hide drag marks?"

He shrugged. "Don't see how we could know that."

I was looking at the bank of the ditch again. "From the way the tape is... If he wasn't all in the water, it looks like at least his head was."

The edges of the bank were far from a bog, but mix water and earth and there was bound to be some mud. Surely someone who dragged Don to this spot would have shown evidence of it.

On the other hand, nearly every person in Wyoming could probably explain having mud on his or her clothes. Unless this particular mud had Sherlock Holmes-special qualities to it—

"I think you're right, Elizabeth." Mike's words ended my less than fruitful train of thought. "Especially if he was dragged. Why else would anybody drag him other than to get him into the ditch?"

"I sure would love to know for sure if his head had been in the water."

"No way for us to know one way or the other. And no use speculating," said Mr. Buzz Kill Burrell. "If you two are done, I should be getting to the home ranch."

I gave the area another survey, but saw nothing more worth checking out.

I led the way back around the curve, but stopped in front of the mini-landslide site where we'd come down.

"There is no way on earth I'm going to get up that thing without a rope or—"

"No need," Tom interrupted, walking past me and continuing on.

I fell into line with Mike behind. If we had to go all the way to where the up-ramp started, this could take a while.

But a hundred feet farther on and around another curve in the ditch, I spotted a path zig-zagging up the slope at a reasonable incline.

A path. At a civilized angle. Not far from where we'd wanted to go. We could have come down this way, too.

I glared at Tom, then Mike, then back to Tom.

Mike looked away. Tom shrugged. "It was faster. And you need to get boots."

"Not where I'm going," I grumbled.

"Besides," he added as if I hadn't spoken, "even if you'd known about this, you'd have insisted on going that way when you thought about it."

"I would not—"

"If somebody did push Don off, it's the way he'd most likely have gone to be sure Don was dead or to finish him off."

That stopped me.

Anyone who'd just pushed Don off the edge would have wanted to know his condition immediately. Even if it was by some outlandish chance an accident, the pusher would have wanted to know fast. Or, if Dex's possibilities came into play—because the pusher wanted Don dead and made sure of it by following up on any injuries from the fall—the pusher would have wanted to act quickly, in case Don could get away.

"Fine." That was the most I'd concede.

I started up the path.

At Mike's vehicle, Tom gave us a "See ya," and kept going toward his truck.

I headed for the SUV's passenger door.

"Hold up a minute," Mike said.

"It's okay. I can get in by myself." Though I figured I was going to feel the motion in my newly tender derriere.

"It's not that. I want to put a towel on the seat. I don't want the dirt skid marks on the seat of your pants to get on the leather." He came around the back of the vehicle with the towel in hand and saw my face. "Uh, of course, I'd be happy to help you. If you—"

Way too late. And way too little.

I snatched the towel, placed it on the seat, climbed in, and sat.

Way too hard.

If he'd laughed, he'd have died.

Chapter Twenty-Six

MIKE SAID HE didn't have time to get me back to Diana's but could drop me off at the sheriff's department in Sherman on his way to covering an afternoon high school football game.

Now, I regretted not driving myself. Especially since I had to call Diana and ask if there was any way she could pick me up in Sherman.

I had my own vehicle and here I was still begging for rides.

But I looked at the dust and grime covering Mike's SUV and regret slid away. Plus, it so happened that Diana was going to be in town anyway on errands. We set a time to meet.

Then, as we arrived at the sheriff's department, Mike announced he had time to come inside with me for a bit.

"You could have taken me back to Diana's."

He didn't even flinch at my steely glare. "Nope. Game's in the opposite direction."

The same gray-haired deputy was at the front desk. His nametag said Ferrante. His face said he'd be no help. Shelton wasn't there, he said. The acting chief wasn't there, he said. There was no news, he said.

My frustration level got relief when Mike nudged me and I saw Deputy Richard Alvaro coming down the hallway toward us. He had his head down, apparently thinking hard.

We shifted over so we stood between him and freedom.

"Hi, Richard," Mike said when it was too late for Richard to do anything but stop in front of us.

I felt a teacher's pride in an apt student. He was learning fast.

"Oh, no," Richard groaned.

While Mike got on the other side of him, I slipped a hand around his arm and said over my shoulder to the deputy at the desk, "You've been so helpful, Deputy, we really appreciate it. In fact, you've told us so much we won't have to ask our friend Deputy Alvaro here any questions at all."

I added a wave and a quick smile at the clearly puzzled man.

"I'm leaving," Richard said.

"Us, too, now that Deputy Ferrante's been so helpful," I assured him.

Mike held the door open. I kept a hold on Richard's arm as we exited then used that hold to slow him down outside. He was far too polite to shake me off.

"Ferrante didn't tell you anything, did he?"

"Of course he did. Not as much as we'd like to know, though, and certainly not as much as you could tell us, since you're in the thick of the investigation. Why, you're the one who found the body."

"Thanks to you," he muttered.

"You're welcome," I said, though his tone hadn't held gratitude. "All we want now is a little reciprocation. For example the cause of death for both men."

"No. I—"

"If they're not finalized, the preliminary—"

"No."

"Or if the medical examiner has found anything that contradicts Brian dying of exposure. Ah, I see he hasn't."

He jerked. "I didn't say a word. Not a word. You can't possibly know—" He bit it off, realizing what he'd been about to say.

"It's the way you didn't say a word, Richard. So there's no point in not telling us, say, when Hazen died."

"Medical examiner set the time of death at two-oh-two a.m."

Mike lit up. "Great. Amazing he could pin it down so precisely. Now if we could get a firm time on Brian's death, we could really get a handle on this."

An apt student, but still so much to learn.

"I think Deputy Alvaro is pulling our legs, Mike."

He looked around at the younger man. I couldn't see Mike's expression from this angle, but I knew his knack for inducing guilt without looking so hangdog that you lost all patience with him. It was a talent, a true talent. And right now he was practicing it to good effect, based on Alvaro's face.

"Sorry, Mike," he mumbled. "I was being a smart-ass. Wasn't directed at you at all." He darted me a look. "Or even completely at you."

Hometown hero got full dispensation. Me only partial. But I could take it. All part of the job.

"Frustrated, I guess," Alvaro continued. "Especially when the medical folks wouldn't commit to anything closer than the guy died sometime after he was born and before we found him."

Mike groaned.

"I know," Alvaro said, the two of them apparently back in accord. "Said the stomach contents might, maybe, possibly, could give more information, but that's only if all the planets align right and we find out precisely when and where he last ate and what utensils he used, and if he held out his pinky finger when he drank his coffee."

Such bitterness in one so young was hard to witness. So I pretended I was digging something out of my purse to hide my grin.

"Gave some mealy-mouthed lines about variations in temperature and a lot of other stuff. Best he'd do was to say Don died around the same time as Brian. Within an hour or two, anyway."

Ah-hah.

Alvaro realized immediately what he'd said. Looking up, I could see him stepping back behind his uniform's armor ... then he did a double take at me.

He whistled, as he looked me up and down, focusing on my jeans. "What did you do, Elizabeth?"

"My job as a journalist. It's not all bright lights and glamour, you know."

In fact, my current state wasn't a bad metaphor for my journalism career. Going after a story by the seat of my pants and holding on to dignity by a thread.

Mike checked his watch. "Sorry, Elizabeth, I've got to go. You want me to drop you at KWMT—"

"That's okay. You go ahead. I'll be fine." No way was I leaving, because I'd spotted Wayne Shelton walking toward us, accompanied by the sandy-haired deputy named Lloyd Sampson.

Mike started away, saw Shelton and Sampson, turned back to me and mouthed, "Tell me later."

The deputies gave him a pleasant hello as they passed him.

Sampson's smile for me was just as pleasant as they neared. Shelton's expression not so much.

"Deputies," I said cordially.

Shelton said, "I've heard what you've been up to."

"Oh?"

"Yes, and you mind if I ask you a question?"

"My life's an open book to you, Deputy Shelton."

"Why'd you get that SUV?"

I'd braced for him commenting on the state of my clothing or more directly on my revisiting the scene. And he knew it.

I covered pretty well. "I suppose you knew what I was looking at before I left the first dealership."

"As you pulled in," he corrected. "A young lady like you doesn't want a big vehicle like that. Shoulda got something fun."

If I hadn't been put on alert, I was now. Not only had he said I was a *young lady*, but he was advocating I have *fun*.

"Okay." I drew out the syllables. "Like what?"

"One of those foreign sports cars. Real low to the ground. Kind of racy. A convertible."

Richard tried to smother a snort.

Lloyd frowned. "Not one of those, Deputy Shelton. Rough country around here'd rip out the undercarriage first time she tried to go off the highway. Remember that guy from Toronto we came across a few weeks back? He wasn't more than thirty yards off the pavement. Nobody around here would touch the repairs."

Shelton scowled. Richard tried to stop a grin by biting the inside of his cheeks, which made him look like a fish.

I turned to Lloyd.

"Thank you, Deputy Sampson. As tempting as the kind of car Deputy Shelton describes would be, your points reinforce my decision to get something practical for Wyoming. For as long as I'm here. Especially for outings like we took earlier today to the Walterstons' ranch to look around the scene in daylight."

Shelton was watching me with that unnerving stare of law enforcement wearing mirrored sunglasses. He didn't need the sunglasses to pull off the look.

"Appears you looked around on the seat of your pants," Shelton said.

I ramped up my smile. "The cost of doing my job well. Needed to get down to where Hazen was found to get a sense of what happened."

"Yeah? Any flashes of brilliance?"

"No. Simply observations."

"Like what?"

"Like the body must have been wet when Richard checked to see if he was dead."

Alvaro darted a glance toward Shelton, but neither said anything.

"Like there were plenty of rocks in the vicinity to help Hazen along toward dying if the fall didn't do the trick."

I kept my eyes on Shelton, who didn't show anything. At the same time my peripheral vision picked up Lloyd's twitch and the more subtle, but possibly more telling, fact that Richard held his breath.

"Of course the autopsy will tell you—if it hasn't already—if he died of a blow to the head and whether that blow came during his fall. Oh. Brian, too."

"What about him?" Shelton asked as if only mildly interested. "He didn't fall far enough to kill him."

"Perhaps not, but you're no doubt waiting to hear if he died of exposure or if he might have been helped along. There could be a rock—or rocks—with either or both men's blood on it. Surely an attacker wouldn't take it away with him—or her. Far easier to hide it in plain sight. Maybe not right where it was used, but somewhere along the ditch. Or maybe *in* the ditch. That would be even better from the attacker's standpoint, because he'd think the water would wash off all the blood. But there should be microscopic evidence."

Shelton tilted his head back. "So all we have to do is find every rock up and down that ditch—in or along it—that this hypothetical attacker might or might not have used on one or the other of them. Or both. Or neither, when it comes to that. Then test each and every rock for microscopic evidence of blood. We'd about finish that task when hell froze over ... if we were stupid enough to start."

So they were thinking something other than the fall killed Hazen, but they weren't focusing on rocks... Unless Shelton was leaving me a false trail.

I dropped the rock angle and kept going. "You know what we found most interesting at the scene was the police tape extending into the ditch. Almost—if I'm not being too fanciful—as if the body had been draped over the bank with the top part in the water."

Shelton's jaw tightened infinitesimally, but he might have spared himself the will-power to limit his response, because Sampson's gaze shot from me to Shelton, with how-can-she-possibly-know? shock radiating from it.

Half the job of finding something out is knowing there *is* something to find out. I'd just completed half my job.

"Don't worry, Deputy Shelton, we did not disturb or go inside the police tape. As I said, we simply observed ... and, of course, drew our own conclusions."

He swallowed what sounded like the beginning of a growl. "Anywhere else you planning on going to ask questions?"

"Lots of places. Oh, you mean right now? I had hoped to go to the Sherman Supermarket. But I don't happen to have my new vehicle in town right now."

"Lost it already?"

I ignored that. "So I have to rely on the kindness of other people. Or stick around wherever I happen to be, asking all my questions in that one spot. Of course, if Richard could give me a ride, since he was heading out..."

"I need Deputy Alvaro."

I nodded understandingly. "So I'll stay around here, asking every-one questions for another hour or two."

I couldn't swear I heard Shelton's teeth grinding, but the noise I heard was certainly similar.

"Sampson. Take Ms. Danniher to the supermarket on your way to that errand we were discussing."

"Oh, you mean going to the—"

"Yes. That. No need to broadcast it," he barked.

"Broadcasting's my job," I said with a smile at Sampson.

He was divided between smiling back at me and giving Shelton a wary look.

Chapter Twenty-Seven

PERHAPS I COULD have foregone asking Lloyd Sampson questions.

But, really, if Shelton hadn't wanted me to find out anything, he could have driven me himself.

Besides, there'd been Tom Burrell saying there was no way for us to know one way or the other about Hazen being in the water. Clearly a challenge.

"Such an interesting scene." Not much of an opener, but it let me add, "By the ditch at the Walterstons' ranch."

He flashed me a look that showed the whites of his eyes, saying nothing.

"How far into the water was Don Hazen's body?"

His hands tightened on the steering wheel. "I can't tell you anything."

"Of course not. I totally understand. It's fascinating, isn't it, that a man who fell from a cliff actually died of drowning."

"How'd you know—" He broke it off. Swallowed it with a working of his throat almost painful to watch. Searched around for what could replace the *about that* he'd just swallowed, also a painful process to watch, and came up with "—all those questions to ask?"

Outside, I hoped I was convincingly calm.

Inside, I was dancing. Heck, I was doing cartwheels. My Hail Mary shot had connected for a touchdown.

Since he'd already given me more than I could have dreamed of, I played along. "Lots of experience, I guess."

He bobbed his head quickly in relief. "But I can't tell you details of the investigation. Could jeopardize the entire case." That sounded like a quote.

I couldn't give up too easily or surely even Lloyd Sampson would smell a rat. "The public has a right to know…"

He shook his head emphatically. "Not during an active investigation."

I tried to look crestfallen. I was either a better actor than I thought or Sampson was a very easy audience. Your pick.

If Don Hazen drowned, and if he was conscious, that could limit the suspects to someone strong enough to hold him under water for sufficient time. Not to mention someone who had spare clothes to change into to replace an outfit that surely would have been soaked.

I had a vision of Austin Walterston arriving in those clearly fresh clothes. Creased and clean as if he'd just put them on.

Lloyd Sampson interrupted those thoughts.

"But let me say this, ma'am, when it comes to a vehicle, you should've bought a pickup."

I WATCHED SAMPSON'S cruiser depart, then found an isolated spot beside the Sherman Supermarket parking lot to call Dex.

"Dex, how long does it take someone to drown?"

"It dep—"

"Depends," I finished ahead of him.

"—ends. For example water temperature. Frigid water can induce cold shock, which will kill someone before they can drown."

"Good to know. What about in Wyoming in October?"

"It can get pretty cold there in the autumn."

"But it's barely October and this wasn't in the mountains. Nighttime chilly, but not icy."

"Under those circumstances, cold shock would be unlikely."

"So back to drowning."

"Is the victim conscious or unconscious to start?"

Remembering the litter of rocks in Don's likely landing area, I said, "Start with unconscious."

"Actually, even someone conscious will become unconscious in the process of drowning. Is this the same person you hit in the head with a rock?"

"I didn't..." With Dex it was easier to go along. "Possibly. Or he might have been stunned from a fall. Or both."

"There are a considerable number of other variables..."

"Give me a ballpark, a range."

"Four to eight minutes. Ten to be certain."

"*Ten.* So someone would have to hold the victim's head under water—"

"Oh, no. Once they're unconscious the dying process will proceed without assistance."

Of course. Like the tragic stories of a baby left in a bathtub. "An unconscious person left submerged in water would drown on his own."

That would open up the field. Once Don was rendered unconscious there'd be no need for strength to hold him down, no struggle, and no telltale splattering.

"No one can predict with one hundred percent accuracy—"

"Okay, okay. Is likely to drown?"

"That would be an acceptable assessment."

"Certainly the autopsy would show drowning?"

"Certainty is—"

"Likely. Is it *likely* that drowning would be apparent? And would the autopsy show if the person was conscious or unconscious?"

"It depends."

I dropped my head into my hand. "Wouldn't there be water in the lungs?"

"Water in the lungs or the stomach would be consistent statistically with the victim having been alive at the time of submersion. Froth might be found if water is not."

I was not going to be detoured by froth. "And no water in the lungs means the person was dead before going in the water."

"Not necessarily. It could be a dry drowning."

"*Dry* drowning?"

"The larynx constricts, preventing water from entering the lungs. In the majority of cases, that releases with unconsciousness and water then enters the lungs. However, in some instances, cardiac arrest occurs before the release, hence a dry drowning."

I asked a few more questions, received no answers worth repeating, thanked Dex, and hung up.

Dry drowning. And I'd thought the strangest things I'd encountered as a reporter were in politics.

"PENNY, DO YOU know Rich Taylorman?"

Yes, I was buying more cookies and dog treats. I had to have something to put on the conveyor belt. And I wanted to check in with Penny before her days off Sunday and Monday. "He's an insurance—"

"Him. Some people don't need knowing. Because nobody worth knowing ever had an ill thought about the Walterstons. Not like Don Hazen. Plenty had ill thoughts about him. Thoughts and words. Oh, yes, and not afraid to say it. Sheriff Widcuff told her daddy and momma and the boy's wife that they better stop saying such things when there was no proof at all. Didn't stop them.

"She said she told her she was sure she was dead at his hands even if she couldn't prove it, which I told her would get her in a heap of trouble and it did, only not from him, like you'd've thought, but from her."

"Who?" I asked desperately, trying to get at least one name among all those unattached pronouns.

"Why, Greg's wife. Mindy's sister-in-law. Talking to the new woman about what they thought he'd done to the old one. Though of course the new one was really the first old one. Now, I can't say for certain it wasn't to try to do a good thing, thinking she might be warning someone in danger, you know. But I'd wager money she also wouldn't have minded stirring up trouble. Some folks can't keep their tongue between their teeth."

I was working too hard to follow what she was saying to choke over that.

"Loriana put a stop to that. Mind your own business was the nicest she said. And it worked. They haven't been talking quite so much about what Don did to Mindy. Not until this happened, anyway.

"Yep, like I said, etch a mountain with her tongue. That's her. Heard she let it loose Wednesday night on Hannah Chaney. Comes in by herself—"

I jumped on that. "Hannah said she saw an incident with Serena McCracken and Don."

"—like a lost puppy now. Paul used to come with her. He took care of her. Other way around now. Reads her poetry and such, but she's tending to him. And doing most of the providing." She snorted. "Acts like ranching's a pastime when it needs to be a passion. Even then it can break—"

"Serena McCracken. Don."

"—a rancher's heart, man or woman. She was going out the door, he was coming in all roostered up. Like—"

"Roostered up?" Were we still on Terry Waymark? Or someone else?

"—he'd been doing more and more these past weeks. Like a switch got flipped on him. Like he was back when Loriana left after high school."

Ah. Don Hazen.

"But here she was, still here, yet he was falling apart. Could smell him from here. Never bothered with the good stuff, either so when he got soaked—"

"Drunk?"

Her quick nod didn't slow her hands or her words. "—you could smell him coming. But Serena McCracken didn't have a chance to sidestep him, because he was right there and before you know it, he slammed himself up against her, had a big hand on her butt and kind of pushed against her like in those dirty dancing movies, only he was no movie star, that's for sure. Thought she'd go for waterworks. But no such thing. Kept her head turned aside so he couldn't do what he wanted. And then she took care of him all right. Had a ham in a plastic bag on top of her cart, picked it up, swung around and got him good in the side of the head. He let go fast enough then. Started to have a couple nasty things to say, but I called out I was videoing the whole thing and held up my phone. Wasn't doing any such thing, because the battery was down to a nub, but he didn't know. When he stumbled on toward the back, I told the boy—"

That was Penny's term of something less than affection for the forty-something store manager. I wonder if I could get away with calling Les Haeburn *the boy*?

"—to go help Mrs. McCracken load up her vehicle and make sure she was all right. He said she was and she hasn't spoken a word about it since. Though—"

How could she speak a word about it, with Penny around?

"—she's a sight friendlier now. Funny how—"

"Hannah—

"—that works. Now there're waterworks. First I've seen radishes and peanut butter, but that's what that girl's been craving. That's how I knew. Silly thing marrying Paul Chaney, then thinking he'd change into a romantic fool. Works hard, Paul, but he doesn't have the time or money for messing with a romantic girl. Though things might be better for him now. Still, might rub her feet, but won't bring her flowers. She told Hannah her only hope was that she has twins and can give one to each man. Some are saying it's that Terry who's the father, but—"

"What about Don?"

"—I'm not. With little Hannah?" Her laugh was short. "He couldn't see past Loriana. Was always real rough on Mindy and I swear it was because she wasn't Loriana. Simple as that. He gave her a dose of that right here in front of me when—Oh, good, you're buying steaks again. Which one is it? Mike or—?"

"When?" I interrupted loudly. "Rough on Mindy."

Penny's hands paused for a microsecond before work and words resumed. "Not long before Mindy left. They'd been spatting like always. She had a tongue, too, no denying that. Few words from her and you'd feel like you'd been in a windstorm with sandpaper—stinging and raw. Then again he hit her. Chicken and egg. Egg and chicken. One day, she up and left."

A woman with a forceful enough personality that her words made Penny feel a sting—heck, that she'd gotten in any words with Penny— yet who'd stayed with a man who hit her.

Until she didn't.

"Right after buying all those Polish sausages, too, when Don couldn't stand them, but no telling when a woman will get in her right mind and leave a man who uses his hands. Though maybe he learned his lesson, since I hear he's never laid a finger on Loriana. Then again, there are other things a man can do to a woman and vice versa when they're living together. Bye, now, Elizabeth. Well, hello, there—"

Getting the bum's rush from Penny the second she'd finished my order or the next customer arrived in her lane was nothing new. This time I didn't feel as frustrated by it as other instances.

Mindy's family thought Don Hazen had killed her. Greg Niland definitely had a motive. But he'd been with his fellow searchers.

Mindy's sister-in-law had tried to warn Loriana about Don. Loriana had defended Don. That might explain Krystal being critical of Loriana.

As a minor point, Loriana had had only herself to blame for the waterworks that drove her out of the house the night of the search.

And I'd gotten nothing from Penny on Rich Taylorman.

Still, she'd given me a lot to think about. And to report to the group.

I ROUGHED OUT what I would add to my resumé reel using my laptop. Mel was right. There was some good stuff from the specials.

I would have worked on it more, perhaps have gone in to do the final edit in the booth at the station, but Diana had made it clear attending tonight's Cottonwood County High School homecoming festivities was not optional.

We drove separately at my insistence so I could leave when I wanted to without cutting her fun short. But we left her ranch at the same time and I arrived at the high school only a few minutes later, having failed to break the sound barrier.

She had waited for me in the parking lot.

"Don't worry, you'll be welcomed."

"Diana, there's something I learned this afternoon I should tell you about."

"Later."

Chapter Twenty-Eight

DIANA HAD PROMISED I would be welcomed and she was right.

So welcomed that I ended up in the girls' restroom running cold water over my hand.

I could have used a few more wimpy handshakes among the alums of Cottonwood County High School for my raw right hand.

She was also right about talking later about Don Hazen having apparently died of drowning.

Not that I gave up immediately. I tried to mention it to Mike and Tom, too, when we crossed paths. But all three of them were in such demand that they were quickly swept away.

In the end I not only accepted the inevitable, I decided it was better. I'd tell them all at once when we'd all be able to think it through.

So that left me to observe. One of my favorite occupations. I decided that if there were a king and queen of this homecoming celebration Tom and Mike would tie for king and Diana and Mrs. P would tie for queen. What do you know? I was finally friends with the cool kids.

And they took turns introducing me to every single person in attendance, which is why I was running cold water over my hand in the girls' restroom when the door opened just enough to let Hannah Chaney in, which, considering the dimensions of her belly was about as wide as it could go.

She saw me, gulped, and stayed where she was.

I tried a reassuring smile. "Hi, Hannah. You might not remember me. I'm Elizabeth Marg—"

"I remember. At—" This sounded less gulp-like and more sob-like. "—Terry's."

"Yes. I was hoping to talk to you again." I kept it brisk but friendly. "You mentioned an argument between McCracken and Don Hazen."

"She didn't argue. It was all him."

"At the Sherman Supermarket?" She nodded. Had she only seen that confrontation? But I thought... "You were there when Sam McCracken saw Don Hazen, too. You were at the Kicking Cowboy Saturday night?"

"Terry wanted to go." Her smooth young face winced. "That Mr. McCracken was so mad. He said if he ever touched his wife again he'd kill him."

Good heavens. She'd caught the unattached pronoun disease from Penny.

"Sam McCracken said that?"

She nodded, almost absently. "Don laughed—that nasty laugh that always makes Paul so angry, too, and then Mr. McCracken put his hands around his throat and started squeezing. Oh! This song."

Tears slid down her cheeks. I could just hear the beat of a forgettable, cacophonous number from six or seven years ago.

"He started squeezing and what happened?"

"He stopped," she said absently. "The first time we ever kissed was to this song. At Homecoming Dance my sophomore year."

It would have been like kissing to a dentist's drill, but I'd obviously lost her to a remembrance of young love.

"I dreamed and dreamed and dreamed. And it all came true. Everything I dreamed." She spread her hands over her pregnant belly, turning the wedding ring with her thumb. "And now..."

Tears spattered on the bodice of her dress.

"If you're so unhappy away from him, why don't you talk to him?"

Oh, God, what was I doing giving marital advice? Had I lost my mind?

She shook her head, flinging more droplets.

"I can't. Not now. Not with—" She sucked in a sob. "—the way things are. I've ruined everything. I don't know how I could have messed it up so bad."

Youth. Hormones. Swollen ankles.

But I guessed she wouldn't want to hear that.

The door opened again.

"Jennifer." I greeted her as a savior.

"What did you do to Hannah?"

"I didn't do anything. But she, uh, she needs somebody she knows."

I transferred the sobbing girl to Jennifer's shoulder and fled.

Shadow growled.

I twisted around on the desk chair where I'd been working on the laptop. And froze.

He stayed on alert but didn't make another sound.

A light knock sounded.

"Elizabeth?"

It was Diana.

I started breathing again.

"It's okay, Shadow," I said to him as I went to the door.

He looked totally relaxed, while my hands were shaking as I let her in. Which was stupid. How many people trying to burn down the building you're in knock first?

"I was checking one of the horses and saw your light still on," she started.

I invited her in. She'd exchanged her skirt for jeans and put on boots, but still had her party top on. She accepted my offer of wine. We sat on the loveseat and put our feet up on the wide ottoman.

She wanted to talk about the evening.

I think mostly she was feeling the absence of Gary. The man who should have been with her tonight, who would have shared all her memories and understood all her observations.

The best I could do was listen and sip along with her.

When she stood to leave, she announced that I was expected in her kitchen at ten in the morning for Sunday brunch.

"Diana, there's no need for you to feed me—"

"Not me. Mrs. P. and Aunt Gee. They called and said they want to check on how you're doing."

"I saw them tonight, not to mention at Connie's Wednesday and at last night's football game. What more—?"

Her laughter stopped my words. "That was hello. This is going to be the *real* inspection."

DAY SEVEN

SUNDAY

Chapter Twenty-Nine

I SHOULD BE getting used to Mrs. Parens and Mike's Aunt Gee showing up together.

"We came to check on your progress, Elizabeth," Mrs. Parens said.

They alternated firing questions at me that would have done the surgeon general proud—both for the medical expertise and for the military command.

"Eyebrows and eyelashes haven't started growing back yet," Aunt Gee noted, peering at me.

I needed no reminder. "Not since last night," I muttered.

"As long as the follicles have not been damaged, they should grow back in approximately sixty days, though perhaps longer at your age."

I didn't need a reminder of that, either.

"How's your vehicle choice coming?" Aunt Gee asked.

"All done. Did you see it parked out in front of the bunkhouse?"

"Ah. Then you didn't purchase a pickup truck," Mrs. P said.

From her twin sweater set to her sensible shoes, you might think Emmaline Parens was the prototype for the little-old-lady-who-only-drove-the-car-to-church-on-Sundays cliché that used car salesmen once trotted out. But I would not put it past Mrs. Parens to be an expert at doing wheelies in a pickup.

"No. I would have had to custom order the pickup I liked and it would have taken too long." Now, why on earth did I say that?

Her expression shifted and I swear there was some satisfaction in it

I didn't understand as she said, again, "Ah."

"Are you sure you're ready to start driving again?" Aunt Gee asked. "I'm sure Michael doesn't mind the opportunity to spend more time in your company."

"A woman needs her independence, Gisella," Mrs. P said. Gee opened her mouth, but Mrs. P was too fast for her. "I understand you have expressed an interest in how irrigation has influenced the development of Cottonwood County, Elizabeth. That is commendable."

As I swallowed a groan—I enjoy history, but a double dose of the history of ditches was pushing it—my phone rang.

I glanced at it sitting on the coffee table, saw who was calling, turned off the volume—I'd long ago learned it was not a good policy to reject these calls—and said, "Needham filled me in on the history. Now I'm hoping for information on more recent events concerning Red Sail Ditch specifically."

"I believe that phone call is from you parents." If her tone hadn't conveyed it, her pursed lips broadcast that she disapproved of my not answering.

"I'll call them back later. I don't want to interrupt our conversation."

"While that does you credit in most circumstances, one's parents must be an exception. I insist."

Mrs. P insisting was not to be trifled with.

I grabbed the phone, stood, hit the button, said hello, and moved away, intending to go out on the porch.

My mother's first words stopped me.

"Elizabeth Margaret, I'm so sorry to tell you this."

My heart clenched. "Mom—?"

"Especially when we have all our plans set to visit you."

That relieved my immediate concern. If something had happened to Dad or another family member, she'd have said that right out. Plus, she wouldn't be talking about visiting—

Visiting…

"*Visit?* Me? *Here?*"

"Yes. Drive out and—"

"There's nowhere for you to stay. Remember? Dad said he wouldn't stay in either of Sherman's motels and you didn't think Haber House's linens were fresh and—"

"I have a spare room," Mrs. Parens proclaimed. "Your parents will stay with me, Elizabeth."

"Nonsense," Aunt Gee said. "I have a guest room with its own bath, and no one would ever say *my* linens aren't fresh."

Since I suspected the woman ironed paper napkins, I wasn't going to argue with her. Or with Mrs. Parens, so I had to find another way to stop this train from gathering speed as it rolled straight at me.

"They're staying here," Diana said. "It's all arranged."

"What?" I said to something Mom had said that I didn't catch. Then Diana's words sank in and from beneath the wheels of the train I got out, "*What?*"

"It's only natural your parents want to see you," Diana said, as calm as ever. "And of course they'd want to be where they can spend the most time with you."

"Oh, that Diana is so sweet. I wonder if we could introduce her to Steve..." My mother's speculations trailed off into what I knew from long experience included more grandchildren for her and a move to Illinois for all. But since Steve was the one of my siblings who did his best to distance himself from the clan, the chances of that were slim. Not to mention Diana had a ranch and a job in Wyoming. "Tell Diana how much we appreciate all she's done and her generosity in inviting us to stay there. But that's why I'm calling."

Her dramatic pause drew a "Just tell the girl, Cat," from my father in the background, easing any lingering concern in that quarter.

"We can't come. Your father fell off the roof—"

"Off the *roof?* How is he? Is he hurt? What was he doing on the roof?"

"If you'll listen a moment, I'm telling you. Always so impatient, Elizabeth Margaret." She added a tut, which prevented her from hearing my "Am not," a knee-jerk reversion to a long-outgrown habit. "Your father was on the roof because the gutters were going to clog."

"Tell her who predicted that," came from Dad, so I was on speakerphone.

Unperturbed, Mom said, "Well, they were. The maples have dropped more whirlybirds than ever—" I had a flash of homesickness for the seeds that spun through the air attached to paper-like wings. "—and if they weren't out of the gutters before the leaves really start to fall, we'd have a mess."

I said, "I thought you got those gutter cap things so you didn't have to worry about that."

"Hah!" Dad said from across the room.

"I'm not at all sure they're to be trusted," my mother said. "I wanted to hire someone to go up and look. If he said everything was okay, then if there was any problem, he'd have to come back and fix it. But *Your Father*—" When she said it like each word was capitalized it was never good. "—insisted on going up, which wouldn't have done any good even if he hadn't—"

Dad's protest stopped her. "It did plenty of good if you *believed* me that the gutters are fine. If you believed the men who installed it. If you believed anybody about anything anytime."

It struck me for the first time that I might have gotten my journalistic skepticism from Mom. I knew the curiosity came from Dad, but hadn't considered this aspect before.

"You hardly had time to be sure before you fell off the roof," she pointed out.

I think Dad growled.

"Anyway," Mom said speaking directly into the speaker again, "the reason I'm calling is to tell you we won't be coming. You know how your father is about flying—" He's not afraid of flying. He hates waiting in airports. "—and with him not being able to drive, he doesn't think I can handle the trip on my own. Also, there are doctor appointments your father needs to keep, no matter what he says."

"What kind of doctor's appointments? How is he hurt? When did he fall?—I know, I know," I said at my mother's tutting noise. I was about to get another lecture on patience. "But I've waited long enough."

"The doctors say it's a broken ankle with minimal ligament damage." Her emphasis on *say* indicated her MMD—Mom Medical Degree—wasn't ready to sign off on that diagnosis yet.

"It *is* a broken ankle and there *was* minimal ligament damage. Cat, bring that da—darned phone over here and let me talk to her."

There was a pause in which I knew they were looking at each other. Messages zipping back and forth with silent shorthand developed from decades together and the need to communicate without the enemy (their children) intercepting messages.

There was a muffled rustle before I heard Dad's voice. "I'm fine, Maggie Liz." The inversion of my names had been his childhood pet name for me. "The doctors say as long as I keep weight off the break for ten weeks, I should heal up fine."

"It's a miracle you didn't break your neck." I recognized the fear behind Mom's background scolding.

Dad kept talking. "We've got things all set up for me in the family room. Everybody's been over, bringing two wheelchairs and this scooter gadget and meals so Mom doesn't have to cook for a month. Bill took pictures on the roof to prove to your mother everything's fine. Hey, and Robbie said he can set it up on the computer so we can talk and see each other."

"That sounds great, Dad. He can tell me how to set it up, too." I knew how. But I figured needing instructions from my nephew would delay this enough that my eyebrows and eyelashes might have grown back to a parent-acceptable level. "You sound a little tired, Dad, so…"

"He is exhausted," Mom said. "Please tell Diana how much we appreciate everything."

I promised. The call ended and the explanations began.

There was much sympathy for my distant father, much retelling of stories of other people who had taken similar falls. Some had been hurt just like Dad, some had died, and some had miraculously escaped injury. I figured the "just like Dad" stories were so he wouldn't feel alone or foolish in absentia. The "died" stories were to say how lucky he—and by extension, I—had been. The "miraculously escaped any injury" tales were to say that he hadn't, however, been as lucky as he could have been.

I listened, I commented, I thanked.

But when Diana got up to refill glasses, I insisted she needed help.

"You weren't going to tell me?" I would have hissed it, but the question had no sibilants so, instead, I said it in a low, accusatory tone.

"Oh, I would have told you before they got here." With a head tip she seemed to consider her words before adding, "A few hours before, anyway."

"Gee thanks. Now, you're conspiring with my parents?"

"Conspiring? They just want to visit, to see their daughter." She'd spoken at normal volume, which meant Mrs. Parens and Aunt Gee could hear her.

Did hear her, I confirmed when I looked over my shoulder and saw them watching us.

I smiled brightly at the two older women and raised the two glasses of iced tea I took from the counter. "Here we go. All set."

"I haven't refilled those yet, Elizabeth," Diana said.

I pivoted, returning the glasses to the counter to let Diana pour, then tried again with far less fanfare and a determination to change the subject as I joined them by the fireplace.

"Aunt Gee, you mentioned past calls to the sheriff's department, at HY Ranch and involving Don Hazen, but what about more recent ones concerning Red Sail Ditch. Those are public record, too."

She squared her shoulders, looking more stalwart than ever. For an instant, her response could go either way.

"There have been three calls for disturbances that involved Paul Chaney and Terry Waymark." As I'd hoped, rivalry won out as Aunt Gee saw the opportunity to take the floor. Though disturbances involving the love triangle weren't exactly news. "Don was a party to two of them. He also was a participant in confrontations with Sam McCracken."

Don being on hand twice was interesting. "I get the impression this rash of recent calls involving him was unusual?"

"In the past few years, yes, but during his time with Mindy... No."

That was delicate way of saying it. I didn't want delicate. "I hear he was hitting her. So Mindy reported—?"

"Not Mindy. She never called. Not her family, either, even with all their talk after she left. Connie was one who called in reports that Don was beating on Mindy."

"Connie?"

Mrs. Parens made a delicate throat-clearing sound.

Aunt Gee stiffened and nodded defiantly.

"Did he know?"

She nodded again, less defiantly. "Word shouldn't have gotten out about who called in, but it did. Wouldn't surprise me if Sheriff Widcuff told Don himself." Unlike Thurston, Gisella Decker did not lament the departure of the former sheriff.

"There are any number of people who could tell you that Don was fit to be tied. Went to Red Sail Ranch. Connie got her rifle and told him to get off their property. You can believe he didn't like that. Never did like being told to do things by anybody, much less a female.

"Wayne Shelton wrote him up, but the county attorney wouldn't prosecute. Speaking of which, have you heard that they're talking to an outsider about the county attorney job?"

I didn't need to be hit in the head to know that was the end of discussion on my preferred topic.

Chapter Thirty

WITHOUT BLINKING AT Mike's presence at her door instead of me alone, Emmaline Parens welcomed us later that afternoon and led us into the front room of her small frame house in O'Hara Hill.

As she and Aunt Gee left Diana's shortly before noon, she'd said they had two more stops to make but would be in O'Hara Hill in time for Gisella to attend a church committee meeting at four o'clock. Then she'd patted my arm and said, "Shall you come to see me then?"

An invitation, yet not a commitment.

Was I being cynical to think she was eager for equal time after Aunt Gee dominated the brunch?

When I'd prepared to leave Diana's, Mike, who'd shown up unexpectedly, asked if he could come along. I suspected he hoped to worm out of me what I'd mentioned Saturday night. Besides, he and Diana's son Gary had finished all the brunch leftovers by then.

"We hope you'll give us additional background on some of the people, uh, touched by these two deaths." I thought "touched by" was a smarter choice than "involved in."

Wasting no time, Mrs. Parens led the way to her front room, which was a museum of the county, with an emphasis on the schools. A wall sported framed class photos from the turn of the 20th century to the turn of the 21st and onward.

She retrieved a pointer from its place by the doorframe.

Mike's reaction to that simple implement never got old. Have you ever seen a grown man, a former pro football player, a professional with prospects for a great broadcasting career abruptly retrogress to about eight years old? It was actually quite endearing.

I will never tell him that.

"Brian was a steady, reliable student who worked for solid, though not remarkable grades." Mrs. P directed her pointer to a square-faced smiling young face.

A face I'd seen only in death, after a ravaging disease, yet I easily recognized him.

"Academic knowledge was not his greatest strength. That was leadership. He attracted good people to him. He gave loyalty and honesty. He worked hard for his community." Mrs. Parens' brisk tone slowed and deepened with sorrow. "He has died far too young. He is a loss to all of Cottonwood County."

"That's Connie, isn't it? In the next class photo?" Mike asked.

"Yes, Connie Chatham at that time."

The strength of character was there, much softened by youth. The Walterston sons had features from both of their parents, each representing a different mix.

"Brian's death must be a huge loss to his family. And his illness before that. Did you see signs in his sons, Mrs. Parens?"

"The boys resemble both their parents in parts," she said, echoing my thoughts, yet referring to character more than looks, I thought. And not answering my question.

"I understand Austin was hit particularly hard by his father's illness," I pursued. Another tidbit from Wednesday's buffet.

She sidestepped again. "The deterioration of Brian's health has been difficult on the entire family, naturally."

It's Murphy's Law for reporters—the source with the best information is invariably the most close-mouthed.

"But Austin most of all?"

"I don't know how one might quantify such a thing."

"Perhaps his grades have suffered?"

"I am retired. I would not have access to his grades."

That was baloney. But calling her on it wouldn't get an answer.

"I bet you hear everything that's going on in every school in the county." That was underselling it. Between her and Aunt Gee they probably heard everything that went on in the county. Period.

Her mouth pursed.

I shifted my approach. "It wouldn't be remarkable if a son's grades did slip under the circumstances, of course."

"No, it wouldn't be," she agreed. "He and his father appeared to share an affinity that was touching, particularly as it endured into these difficult adolescent years. However, I have no direct knowledge that I can share."

"You can share your expertise, Mrs. Parens. How would you assess Austin's and Kade's personalities?"

"I would not venture to comment." Her arched brows, however, did comment—by naming the two younger boys I'd made it too clear what my interest was.

I'd lost this battle, but figured it wouldn't hurt to fire off another missile. "Which would be more likely to assist their father in killing himself?"

The steel glinting in her eyes would have set me in a quake as a student, but I was a hardened journalist, who'd lobbed questions at some of the meanest, toughest, most ruthless people on this planet. So I only quivered a little.

"Were Connie and Brian high school sweethearts?" Mike asked hurriedly. "I never heard how they met."

After a final knife-edged look of admonishment at me, she said, "They had known each other from elementary school through high school, of course. However, I believe—" In other words it was information you could take to the bank. "—their romantic paths did not cross until they were at the University of Wyoming. They married immediately following Connie's graduation, one year after Brian's."

I'd spotted another class photo, eight or ten years later than Connie and Brian's. "Is that Loriana? She grew up here, but left right after graduation, right? When did she come back?"

Mrs. P's pointer rose, paused a moment, then zeroed in. "This is Loriana Sarano. She returned not quite three years ago after an absence of some ten years."

"What was she like in class?"

"If she had devoted her impressive ability to focus on her studies, she could have been a fine student."

"What did she devote her focus to?" I saw her about to object and quickly added, "From your observations on school grounds, during the school day."

"She was a couple years behind me and I'd say sex," Mike said.

"Michael."

He stood up straight, but looked stubborn. "It's true, Mrs. Parens."

"It can be true without being accurate. You must not confuse cause with result, Michael. Loriana was not backward in expressing her sensuality. However, that was not her focus. Rather she employed it as a means to an end."

"What end?" I asked, riding on the coattails of her instinct to educate Mike. If I rode them long enough I might be able to get more on the Walterston sons.

"Too many of our young people believe ease and fortune will find them, with no effort on their part, immediately upon departing the county. There are, of course, some who do succeed in a wider arena. However, they do it by diligent application of ability as Michael has."

He blushed. Grown man, former pro football player, professional broadcast journalist with prospects for a great career, and he blushed.

Endearing. It's the only word for it.

No, seriously, I will never tell him.

"And there are others who have no desire for acclaim or monetary reward beyond what is possible here in their home county. Those such as Connie and Brian."

"What about Don?" I asked.

"He showed no desire to leave Cottonwood County."

Ah, Mrs. P was being careful.

"What did he show a desire for?"

"Loriana," Mike said. He added with a mixture of defensiveness and resolution, "It's true. If she was using her sensuality as a means to an end, Don was first in line saying he'd get her whatever she wanted."

Mrs. P tipped her head to the left, but said nothing.

"Do you agree, Mrs. Parens?" I asked.

"It is not for me to agree or disagree."

"Is it both true and accurate?"

Simultaneously her mouth tightened and her eyes gleamed. I took that as a yes.

"Which one is Don?" I asked.

The pointer was on the move again, to the class before. It tapped a portrait.

He wasn't bad looking, but gave an impression of almost delicacy. Still, he'd had youth going for him in this photo. Regular features. Good teeth. He wore his hair back from his forehead. It waved slightly before showing behind his ears and at his collar.

"Did he lose his hair?"

"Yup," Mike said, with only a minimal amount of satisfaction from a male who had his full quota.

It was hard to tell in this photo, but ... "Was he tall or short?"

"Tall," Mrs. Parens said.

"Short," Mike said.

I grinned, looking from her barely five-feet to his comfortably over six-feet.

"A telling example of perspective," Mrs. P murmured.

I returned to the photo. This time I took in the whole, rather than looking at the parts.

His smile slid toward a smirk with a self-satisfaction that wasn't appealing at any age.

"What about his first wife?" I asked abruptly.

"Mindy Niland." The pointer came into play again, indicating a square-faced girl with round cheeks and a stubborn chin.

She didn't resemble her brother much, yet looked slightly familiar, but that might have been because she was young, moderately attractive, and unremarkable.

"Loriana wanted the big pond, Don wanted to be the big fish, what did Mindy want?"

"She wanted to be a wife and mother. She would have preferred town to a ranch, but that was less important to her than her other goals."

"But they never had kids?"

"They did not have children in the time before she disappeared."

I turned to her quickly. "Do you have reason to think she might have been pregnant when she disappeared?"

"I do not. My aim was to be precise."

Mike gazed from photo to photo. "He and Loriana didn't have kids, either. I wonder if Don was shooting bla—" He caught Mrs. Parens' look and stopped.

I bailed him out. "Did Mindy and Don get married right after Loriana left town?"

"Mindy and Don were married five years after their graduation, which was four years after Loriana had sold the ranch to Don."

"I remember hearing about that sale. There was some reason she sold low." Judging from his creased forehead Mike was pursuing his memories. "Some scandal. Was Loriana arrested?"

Mrs. Parens tsked. "That was not Loriana, but rather her uncle."

"*That's* it—her uncle was that rustler. He'd gotten a couple months in jail after being convicted earlier of rustling in Colorado—"

"The charge is theft of an agricultural animal in Colorado," interposed Mrs. Parens.

"—so he was suspected right away." He frowned. "I don't remember a trial."

"He died from an allergic reaction to peanuts while in jail shortly after his arrest. It was never determined how he ingested the peanuts."

"Did he? Wow. I don't remember that at all. But then something happened with her aunt, too."

"She left the area."

"Ashamed of the scandal or afraid she'd be arrested as an accomplice?" I asked.

"That has not been determined to my knowledge."

"Tough on a kid to have her uncle arrested, die in jail, and then her aunt desert her. How did that affect Loriana?"

"Loriana Salarno left Cottonwood County before any effects could be observed."

"But the Walterston boys are still here, and I'm sure those effects have been showing since their dad became ill, so—"

Mrs. Parens' raised eyebrows stopped that sentence.

Oh, I kept trying, but rivalry would go only so far with either of these neighbors.

Chapter Thirty-One

MIKE SUGGESTED AN early dinner at Ernie's in O'Hara Hill, which would get us to Diana's in good time for the next gathering, and I agreed.

When we passed along the counter to get to a table, Mike got nods and "heys" from every occupied stool, but I got a couple myself.

The décor and the burgers were authentic. The space between tables was minimal. All of which made it a great place to eat but not such a great place to talk about anything you didn't want immediately fed to the Cottonwood County grapevine.

That and the burgers kept our conversation sparse. We focused on how we would have handled past stories at KWMT-TV if we'd had decent equipment. That could have filled a month's worth of conversation.

We'd paid the bill—split, despite Mike's efforts—and were waiting for change when a man entered whom I recognized as the foreman from the ranch Mike had worked on summers while he was in school.

He started toward the counter, spotted us, and came our way "to say hello."

Mike stood and they shook hands strongly. Mike offered him a seat and he accepted.

"Jack, this is Elizabeth Margaret Danniher, she's a top-notch reporter who's working now at KWMT-TV. Elizabeth, this is Jack Delahunt."

We shook hands briefly. I was grateful it was brief, because Jack had quite the grip, especially for my still-sore hand. Below the level of the table, I used my left hand to support my right in a cupped position that was more comfortable.

"I remember you," he said to me.

I smiled. "From the search for Brian Walterston."

"Before that. From in here, when you were proving Tom Burrell wasn't a yellow murderer. Good job."

I could have said my efforts had been to find the truth not to clear a specific person. I said, "Thank you."

"But saw you at the search, too." He shook his head. "That was something, wasn't it?"

"Yeah," Mike said. "Guess we were all prepared that it might not be a good result with Brian, but who could have predicted Don Hazen?"

"Even before that it was strange. Heard a couple folks went AWOL from their groups. Deputy from another county was saying so. Harrison or something like that. One of the early groups, I think. And ol' Hiram Poppinger was in here in his cups last night saying he'd seen some things."

Hiram Poppinger was one of the people I'd recognized at the search, an elderly rancher who'd wanted to take out a group of thieves on his own and nearly caused the shedding of a lot of blood, potentially including mine.

Poppinger's lack of credibility didn't stop me from asking, "What things?"

Jack shrugged. "No telling with Hiram. Could've been owls, could've been aliens. You'd get about the same reaction from that old coot."

The server returned with our change, and we all rose—Jack going to a stool and Mike and I leaving.

On the return trip to Diana's, he wanted to discuss "the case," but I pointed out we'd have to repeat everything to the others in a short time.

Instead, I asked questions about when he'd worked under Jack Delahunt.

And didn't ask questions about the ranch his father had lost when

Mike was young or the one he owned now, but never invited people to.

A KNOCK ON the bunkhouse door came as I finished typing a to-dig-into list for Jennifer.

It was Mike.

On our return, we'd split up because I'd said I needed some work time.

"Ready?" he asked now. "Diana sent me to get you. And I thought if you want to do a dry-run on what you're going to tell us—"

"Good try. No. And you do know Diana was trying to get rid of you because you were eating all the snacks, don't you?"

"I was merely sampling."

I snorted, but put my laptop, phone, and other necessities in a bag and joined him at the door.

But he didn't open it.

"Have you been avoiding me, Elizabeth?"

"What? No. Of course not."

"Seems like I don't see you anymore."

"We spent all morning yesterday together and I saw you at the party and we were together for hours today."

"We hardly talked. Not about real stuff."

"That's because it was *morning,* then you were the belle of the ball last night. Today we were talking to Mrs. P and at Ernie's."

"You didn't tell me about what your source said about other ways Hazen could have died and there's something you weren't telling me tonight."

"Just so I can tell everybody at once. You didn't tell me what you learned from Loriana before you told the group, either. Maybe we're not as together as much these past few days because I'm not begging you for rides all the time now that I can drive myself again."

"You had your own vehicle other times we were looking into murders and we usually went together. But you went to see Greg and Krystal Niland alone and Sam McCracken alone. And you took Diana to see all those other folks.'"

"She asked."

He studied me a moment. "It's like we've gone back to the beginning when you didn't trust me."

I put a hand on his chest. "No. Really, Mike…"

I didn't finish because he was kissing me.

Really kissing me.

I was holding on. And kissing back.

But as much as I wanted to keep kissing back, lungs demand oxygen. And that can let the brain function again.

"This isn't—We shouldn't."

He pulled back to look down at me. "Are you with Tom?"

"What? *What?*" The first was kiss-dazed. The second was emphatic. "No. What are you talking about?" I didn't want him to answer that, so I quickly added, "I don't know where you would get such an idea. I wouldn't be kissing you if—" Nope, didn't want to go there, either. "This isn't—"

"I wouldn't ever try to move in on another man's woman."

"Oh, for heaven's sake."

"Especially not Tom Burrell's."

"It has nothing to do with Tom Burrell."

"Then what does it have to do with? Because that, in case you didn't notice, had some fireworks going off."

"I don't want—" No, I wasn't going to say that, either. I needed to think. To get my head straight. To figure out why I was saying—trying to say—no to these fireworks. To the lovely feel of his arms around my back and of my front snuggled against his—"I don't think—"

Or maybe I wasn't saying no…

Noise outside drew that same odd bark from Shadow.

Saved by the thud of truck doors closing.

"Oh. They're here. We have to go."

Saved or foiled?

"This isn't over," he grumbled, but he didn't argue.

Shadow appeared as we crossed the threshold, giving Mike a close look, appearing to remember him favorably, then passing close enough to let me pat him on the head.

I stopped on the top step to look at the peaks to the west, dark ghosts against the last of dusk. Maybe to give myself a bit more time.

"What are you staring at?" Mike asked. He and Shadow had stopped beside me.

"The mountains."

He looked, too. "Why?"

"It's *not* perspective."

"What isn't?"

"The proportions on those mountains has changed. It's not because I'm looking at them from different perspectives, they've definitely changed."

A sound brought my gaze to him. He was trying to swallow a grin. Some of it lingered around his lips, like chocolate on a toddler.

"What?"

"You're right. It's not perspective. It's snow."

"Snow," I repeated like a not-too-bright parrot.

"Snow. Snowcap's building, dropping lower down the sides."

"Snow." The parrot had not gotten any smarter since the first time I'd repeated the word.

"You coming?" Jennifer called from Diana's front door.

Chapter Thirty-Two

"ELIZABETH NOTICED THE snowpack's changed," Mike announced, holding the door open for me. The others were already seated around the coffee table. "That's impressive."

I had the feeling it was a distraction, though whether a distraction for our sometimes-too-observant friends, for himself, or for me I didn't know. Didn't matter, I was glad to contribute.

"*And* I know the significance of the snowpack is that it melts and is caught in reservoirs to feed the ditches during the next growing season," I bragged.

"That *is* impressive," Diana said. "We'll make a Wyomingite out of you yet, Elizabeth."

"On the flip side, she's been holding out on all of us about a development," Mike said.

"Hey, I wanted to tell everybody at one time," I protested.

Diana said, "So, here we are. Tell."

"Okay, okay. Remember how you said the ditch might be the cause of death, Diana? I think it truly was. I think Don Hazen drowned."

"*Drowned?*"

I had to backtrack to get Diana and Jennifer caught up with the trip to Red Sail Rock on Saturday morning, then tell them all about the exchange with Shelton and Sampson's giveaway, before ending with Dex's information.

No one lost interest.

"If he did drown," I added, "the killer wouldn't have had to hold him under if he was unconscious but would have to be strong enough to drag him from where he fell to the edge of the bank to get his unconscious head in the water. Possibly whacking him with a rock to make sure he stayed unconscious long enough to drown."

Jennifer made a disparaging sound. "Anybody could do that. He was scrawny."

I remembered his high school portrait and wasn't surprised.

An equal opportunity murder. Great.

"Scrawny, but with a nasty temper," Diana said. "He did not like being crossed."

She relayed what Aunt Gee had said earlier today about Connie calling in reports about Don hitting Mindy and Don's response.

Tom grunted. "That might give Don a motive to go after Connie back then but you can't be thinking it gives Connie a motive to go after Don now. There's no sign of him hitting Loriana."

"Maybe not. But it could have been a motive for Brian."

"How?"

"If he was going out there to die so the accidental death benefit kicked in so Connie and the kids would be better taken care of, he could have thought he needed to get rid of Don to make sure Connie was safe from him."

"Wrapping things up so his family would be okay," Mike murmured.

"Speaking of making sure things were okay for the family…" Diana seemed careful not to look at me. "Connie interviewed two of those hospice groups she had appointments with on Monday, but she cut the third one short."

Without looking at Tom I was aware of the thunderclouds gathering. If lightning was going to strike, might as well strike me.

"Could that have gotten her home earlier than three-thirty?" I asked.

"Yes, if she didn't stop to pick up a sandwich in Cody like she said she did."

"Any confirmation about the sandwich? Credit card? Security cameras?"

"Cash for the sandwich. Girl behind the counter doesn't remember any of her customers that day except a cute boy and this isn't Manhattan, so security cameras aren't—"

"This is—"

"Routine." I cut across Tom's words, then I continued briskly, "Okay, time for the rest of the updates. Jennifer next, since I can see she's pregnant with news."

"*Pregnant?*" She sat up straight so fast she bounced on the sofa cushion. "I am *not* pregnant. Is somebody saying I'm pregnant? Who?"

"Nobody. Nobody told me—

"It's a lie. Who said it? Who?"

"—anything about you. Pregnant with news doesn't mean—"

"Then why do you think I'm pregnant?"

"I don't. It's an expression. Just an expression."

Mike decided this was a good moment to sweep the crumbs in front of him on the coffee table into a neat pile. Tom slid back and put his hat over his face like he was turning in for a siesta, though whether in reaction to Jennifer or the news about Connie's timeline was unclear. And Diana picked up a half-full basket of chips and headed for the kitchen.

I focused on Jennifer. "It means it's obvious you have news to share. Like when someone's really, really pregnant, so it's obvious they're about to have a baby."

"Because I look fat? My clothes—"

"No, no. It has nothing to do with your looking fat. I mean you don't look fat," I said quickly. "You look like you always do. Which is wonderful and fit and cheerful and ready to help." Now I'd made her sound like a Girl Scout. Or possibly several of the seven dwarfs.

"Then why would you think—?"

"I don't. Truly. I was simply using an expression."

She scowled. "That's a stupid expression."

I didn't used to think so, but now...

With firm cheer, I said, "Tell us what you found out, Jennifer."

Her scowl disappeared and was replaced by the expression that had started all this. Briefly I considered saying she looked like the cat that ate the canary.

Better not.

"I've been doing those boring background checks you wanted, and it's pretty much only what's been said about Don Hazen's fights and stuff. Except Rich Taylorman. Like I told you—" She looked at me. "—there are these gaps between times when he was working. He's been barred from selling insurance in at least one state and I'm hoping to have word on two more tomorrow when their offices open up."

"Good."

"In the meantime I found some other interesting stuff. Like, guess what else he's insuring besides Brian?" She didn't wait for an answer. "Red Sail Ditch."

"Ditches need insurance?"

Tom lifted his hat. "The company does. Also licenses and such to stay on the right side of the regulators."

"Does he insure your ditch?"

"No."

I eyed him. "There's more to that no than just no."

"He tried to get our business. Underbid our regular insurer and a few members thought it might be worth trying him. The rest of us persuaded them continuity was worth a few more dollars."

He dropped the hat back down.

Jennifer fidgeted. As soon as I looked at her, she spoke. "So, from Rich Taylorman's website, I clicked over to the Red Sail Ditch website, and that idiot has it linked right into the members area. With his password. Can you believe it? That's not hacking," she said quickly as I opened my mouth. "All I did was click on a link on a public website. It's not my fault it took me to their member area. And there's no reason I shouldn't read what Taylorman shoved under my nose."

"Sounds reasonable," Mike said. "What did you find out?"

The Cheshire Cat could have learned grinning from Jennifer. "The one who was calling his water was Otto Chaney."

"We knew that."

"But we didn't know he'd called all of it—all the water in the whole ditch. Every drop."

Mike whistled.

"How can he do that?" I asked. "How can he have the rights to all the water when there are other members in the ditch company?"

"Must be based on the original claim," Diana said.

"I don't understand."

Tom's voice came from under his hat. "The virtue of self-denial had not been conspicuous."

I eyed him—at least his hat. "That sounds like a quote." And one that didn't clarify matters.

"It is." After two more beats, he removed his hat, straightened and said, "Elwood Mead."

Mike brightened. "Of course. Elwood Mead."

"Oh." Diana said with sage comprehension. "Elwood Mead."

"He's that guy Mrs. Parens always talked about, right?" Jennifer asked.

"I swear she taught toddlers to say Elwood Mead instead of Mamma and Dadda. He oversaw construction of the Hoover Dam and died right after it was finished." Mike grinned. "Who'd've thought I'd remember that?"

"Mrs. Parens would have thought it. Would have expected it." Tom turned to me. "He brought order out of chaos. Her kind of guy."

"Fine, he built the Hoover Dam. I'll—"

"And Lake Mead is named after him.

"Fine. That, too. What does he have to do with Red Sail Ditch?"

"What he has to do with Red Sail Ditch is he got provisions put in the state constitution for—"

"I don't care about—"

Mike interrupted my interruption of Tom to instruct him, "Tell Elizabeth about before Elwood Mead."

"Wyoming territory followed a first come, first served policy on water rights. In fact, first come, first take as much as they wanted. All they had to do was post a sign declaring a claim and how much. More than a few enterprising souls claimed more water than was in the stream. At least one claimed—"

"Oh, I remember this," Jennifer said triumphantly.

"—more water than was in all of Wyoming. Officials decided the sign on the tree system wasn't working, so they required claims be filed at the county courthouse." Tom reached for his glass of water.

"Couple problems, though," Mike picked up. "The county seat could be a long way away, so most didn't bother, so there were still on-site disputes, shall we say. Also, there was no requirement that claims be reality-based. Go ahead, Tom."

"After Elwood Mead was named territorial engineer, he started looking at courthouse filings and that's where his quote about lack of self-denial comes in. He put teeth into the concept that the state owns all the water because no one could use water without a permit. Plus, he took water out of the courts and put it in the hands of a Board of Control, to be run by experts. Rights to water lapse unless they're used. That keeps speculators from tying up a precious resource."

Mike sat up. "So how could Otto Chaney call that much water? Even if he's going back to original rights, his place never used that much water."

"I wouldn't be surprised if the call was to get Don's goat," Tom said. "Otto has been complaining for more a month that Don was taking more water than his share."

"*Was* Don doing that?"

Tom began, "I have no proof—"

"C'mon, here among friends, live dangerously."

His mouth twitched. "In my opinion, yes, he was taking a considerable amount more, probably to annoy people. No other reason makes sense. The ditch will close for the season in a few weeks."

"I bet that's what the fight between Don and Otto at the Kicking Cowboy was about," Mike said.

I looked around. "Okay, Don wanted to annoy people, but he had to be doing *something* with the water, right? Where's it going?"

There was a beat of silence.

"Damn." Tom straightened. "Diana, do you have a map…?"

She went to a drop-front desk between bookcases, sifted through folders, selected one, returned, and spread out a detailed map on the coffee table. "That section of the county."

It was so detailed I had trouble sorting out what was what.

Tom touched one finger to a spot. "Red Sail Rock. The cut."

He traced a line I guessed was the ditch as it dipped south, then almost immediately headed back north. His finger stopped where the line resumed its relatively straight march east. "This is where Loriana has started repairs."

"Didn't they say there were two spots? When Kade and Austin were, uh, discussing the repairs they said that. Where's the other spot?"

Tom's finger came back to its starting point.

Diana pulled in a breath.

"What?" I asked.

Then Mike muttered a curse.

"What?" Jennifer echoed.

"See where Tom's pointing for the second repair?"

"Yeah."

Mike plunked his fingertip on the map. "And this is where the first repair is. What do you see?"

"Uh, those points are fairly close together?"

"And?"

"And there's a parcel of land nearly enclosed by the loop of the ditch?"

"Exactly. Loop Field. It's part of what Don bought from Loriana." Mike seemed to think that clarified the situation.

"I don't get it," Jennifer said. Bless her.

"He was letting the ditch banks erode or degrading them on purpose," Mike said. "And water was flowing into that closed off bit of land."

"It makes no sense." Tom closed his eyes a moment. He opened them. "But it sure looks like Don was aiming to flood Loop Field."

Diana turned to Tom. "Could he have wanted to flood irrigate that field?"

"I don't know why. A field that has been dry most of the season, yeah. Get some moisture in it now, plow it up, then plant in the spring. But that field *always* has enough moisture. Driest season we've had in decades—eight, nine years ago—and that field was like it had been rained on every couple of days. It doesn't go dry like most because it's practically surrounded by water and there's a spring at the top. Flooding Loop Field makes no sense."

We all looked at the map.

"Could you be sure the damage to the ditch banks that was letting water into the field was done deliberately?"

He shook his head. "Not unless somebody saw him out there doing something. Even then... On the other hand, it would be damned clumsy to have that kind of damage in those two spots and damned irresponsible not to fix it right off."

Diana, Mike, and Tom all looked distressed. To them, we'd hit on strange goings-on, which went completely against good stewardship of the land.

To me, we'd hit on strange goings-on, which usually meant a promising area for asking questions.

"So, if he *was* doing this on purpose and legitimate ranching reasons don't apply, what else could he have been trying to achieve?"

"To cover the ground," literal Jennifer said.

Mike went more general: "To hide something."

Diana was next in the circle. "To deny other people water they need, to—"

"Wait," I protested. "But Tom said it was only to annoy people."

"I said Don probably did it to annoy other folks on the ditch, but there are some trying to do fall flood irrigating on fields that don't hold moisture like Loop Field does, so, yes, lack of water could hurt them."

"Who?"

He paused, but then he came out with the names. "Otto Chaney, the people leasing land from Sam McCracken, and Paul Chaney."

Chapter Thirty-Three

"**SOUNDS LIKE SAM** McCracken wins the motive lottery so far. Including the water, I count three reasons he'd want Don Hazen gone," I said.

I reported my Friday meeting with Sam McCracken.

"Doesn't sound like he would have meant Brian any harm, even if he was angry at him at the time," Diana said.

"Because he said so?"

"Well, yeah, I guess I am taking his word for it. But why would he lie about feeling bad about Brian, then say he didn't feel the same about Don?"

"Could be smart. Who'd believe a sudden reversal on both of the dead men. But admit he was angry at one of them, and that lends credence to *not* being angry at the other, and suddenly he doesn't appear to have motives for both deaths."

Mike whistled through his teeth. "You don't believe a word he said?"

"I'd rather have two sources. Always want two sources."

"You said three motives," Jennifer pointed out. "The ditch is one, the trouble with the fence is two. But what's three?"

"Ah. This one's more personal." I repeated the story of Serena McCracken's encounter with Don Hazen at the supermarket and Sam McCracken's assault on Hazen at the Kicking Cowboy. "Two sources for the cause of that trouble between him and Don. Hannah's source one and Penny's source two."

I repeated what I'd learned from Penny and Hannah.

"Nasty," Diana said. "Hope Serena McCracken had a bottle of disinfectant to use afterward."

"Oh, yeah, Diana," Jennifer said, "you don't have to ask Hannah again about what happened Monday. She says that what Terry told you about him planning to meet Don and all was true. I asked her about it Saturday night."

"In the bathroom? When she was crying?"

"Yeah. It was quieter in there. Besides, she was too busy crying to lie."

It looked like we might make a journalist of her yet.

Diana drew in an audible breath and let it out slowly. "This isn't getting any clearer."

We all agreed.

"Playing any FreeCell yet?" Tom asked.

I was known to play a game or two of the computer solitaire when I was trying to stop my brain from running in circles, which is why I didn't want to answer his question. "Why?"

"Might be time."

"We have way too much information to gather to—"

"Like what?" Jennifer asked me.

"Why?" Diana asked Tom.

I answered Jennifer. "Uh, you could add Loriana to your background checks. And—"

"Because it's good to watch Elizabeth figure out how the game's won long before it's over."

"I don't—Not any different from anyone else."

"No?" Tom asked mildly.

I didn't like the way he was looking at me. "I'd like to read that deposition Brian did," I said abruptly.

"Good Lord, why?" Mike asked.

"Partly because it would be such a nice change from all the gossip we've been swimming in. Something concrete and real."

"What's the other part?"

"It should shed more light on what was going on in the three-way tussle among McCracken, Don, and the rest of the ditch company, with Brian as their embodiment."

"Could we get it at the courthouse?" Diana asked.

I shook my head. "Unless it's on file with the court it's not public record. Law enforcement could subpoena it. I wonder if Wayne Shelton...?"

"You might persuade him to subpoena, but he'd never let you read a copy in this lifetime," Mike said.

Jennifer said, "If it's in some lawyer's computer—"

"No hacking," Tom and I said simultaneously. Her father was one of his best friends since childhood. He didn't want to see her go to jail, either.

"Besides," I added. "I have another route in mind."

"I'm not asking James Longbaugh," Tom said firmly.

Which was unreasonable of him. In the previous murder we'd looked into, Tom had asked his lawyer friend to tell him about a conversation with a client. Longbaugh had said he wouldn't— couldn't—tell him. But he'd also mentioned that segments of the conversation were likely overheard by a waitress, who happened to be Penny's niece, who talked nearly as readily as her aunt.

Longbaugh had helped the course of justice without breaking his code of ethics, so there was no reason he'd be reluctant to get another question from Tom.

But I'd save that argument until I needed it.

Right now, I said, "I don't want you to ask Longbaugh. I want you to ask Connie."

He looked at me steadily. I half expected him to say something about having Connie's alibi checked. Instead, he said, "Connie wasn't there."

"No. But as Brian's beneficiary she has every right to have a copy of the deposition."

"Do you know that for a fact?"

"That she's beneficiary—?"

"That she has the right to have a copy."

"The deponent has a right to a copy. If Brian didn't get one yet, which I doubt, then it makes sense that his widow would have the right to it. And if she's acting as ditch boss, that should clinch it. It's a legal document pertaining to a case that involved two men who have died in—to say the least—suspicious circumstances. We need to know what's in there. And that means I'd like you to read it, too, Tom, since you're the one most likely to spot something off-kilter pertaining to the ditch company."

If I'd hoped saying he should read it, would convert him to an enthusiast, I was wrong. He half-closed his eyes. It didn't make him look sleepy.

"I'll see about getting her a copy," he said after a silent spell. "She should have it. As for sharing it with you—"

"Fine. I'll ask her myself."

My words came out quickly—I wouldn't say snapped, but definitely quickly. So I was done when Tom's drawl was getting wound up.

"—I'll ask, but that's all."

"You'll ask her?" I repeated.

"I'll ask. But as I said I'm not going to pressure her or try to spin her."

I wanted to ask indignantly if he was implying that I would put pressure on her or try to spin her. But that would have been an indulgence. I wasn't the issue. Even if I was being so falsely and baselessly accused.

Keeping my eye on the goal, I said, "Great. Let us know what she says."

"What about what Jack Delahunt said? We saw Jack earlier at Ernie's," Mike explained, repeating what had been said. At the end he asked Tom, "Was there a Deputy Harrison?"

"No. But Matt Harston, a deputy from the next county over, led a group. One of the early ones to go out."

"Were any of the people from Red Sail Ditch in the group?"

"No."

His jaw had gone tight. "But?" I prodded.

"Greg Niland. He was in that group."

"He certainly had a grudge against Don Hazen," I said. "Let's check—"

Tom sighed. "I'll call Matt and check that Greg was there the whole time."

I ignored the sigh and said, "Good. Thanks." I remembered something else Jack Delahunt had said. "Was Hiram Poppinger in that group, too?" Could those have been the strange goings on?

He thought a moment. "No."

Damn. That meant I'd have to talk to Hiram Poppinger about what he'd seen.

DAY EIGHT
MONDAY

Chapter Thirty-Four

"EVERYTHING OKAY?" ON her way back to the house from the barn, Diana detoured to the bunkhouse porch where I was sitting with Shadow.

"Why wouldn't it be?" I asked, a blanket wrapped around me and my hands around a cup of coffee.

"You're up awfully early for you. What's wrong?"

"Everything. I'm making no sense of this."

"You will."

I ignored that. "I don't know what I've been thinking I'm accomplishing. I'm doing no good here."

"Aren't you?"

"No."

"Sounds to me like you're accomplishing feeling sorry for yourself."

I looked up at her. "Ouch."

She shrugged. "You already knew it. I got to get the kids breakfast. See you later."

"MORNING, DANNY," MATT Lester said when I answered my phone on the way to the station.

It wasn't that I didn't want to talk to him, but I'd already encountered one friend this morning who might know me better than was comfortable.

With minimal hellos, he launched into what he'd called to say. "You know rumors are flying about you returning to D.C.?"

"Dell," I said.

"I wouldn't be surprised. But even if he started the rumors, they've taken on a life of their own and they're spreading well beyond the Beltway."

I groaned.

"Is that a groan of Elizabeth Margaret Danniher not wanting other people to know her business? Or is that a groan of being pushed in a direction you don't want to go?"

"A direction I don't want to go? What do you mean? I'd understand it if we were talking Chicago, with my mother pushing me like a track hoe, but—"

"A track hoe? Since when do you know about track hoes?"

"—why wouldn't I want to go back to D.C.?"

"I don't know. But I get the feeling you're enjoying learning about things like track hoes."

DON'T MISUNDERSTAND ABOUT Sunday's phone call with my parents. I am not against seeing them. I love them. And I know they love me.

But lifelong experience told me that seeing them now was not a good idea. Not while my eyelashes and eyebrows were recovering from the arson that had landed me in Diana's bunkhouse.

So, the 'when' of the averted get-together had all sorts of bad mojo connected to it. So did the "where."

I was thinking about that as I finalized the resumé reel in the editing booth, with Dell's voice in my head. *Of course you weren't supposed to be* there. *You're supposed to be* here.

My parents had accompanied me when I moved to Sherman, Wyoming, and had not been impressed. From the moment I'd discovered that ending my marriage had put a noose around my career, they had wanted one thing—me back close to them.

No, make that two things, the second being smearing my ex in honey and dropping him into the bear cage at Lincoln Park Zoo.

Okay, maybe that was my vision, but theirs would be similar.

Mom had been turning the thumbscrews on Mel to get me an offer from a Chicago station. Although there was a chance Mom was losing her touch, in light of Mel asking me if I wanted him to explore the possibility of remaining in Sherman.

And with that thought, the question of how Mel Welch, sweetly henpecked lawyer from Chicago, could influence hiring practices at KWMT-TV in Sherman, Wyoming resurfaced.

On my way back to the newsroom I spotted Jennifer, camping out in a desk close to the main corridor.

"Jennifer, I'm going to send Mel Welch a new version of my reel. Will you talk him through accessing it again?"

"Sure. He's a nice guy. He even sent me gift cards just for helping him with some basic tech stuff."

"He is a nice guy. There was something else I wanted to ask you about."

"Sure."

"Can you tell me about Craig Morningside and the Heathertons? What's Les' relationship with them like?"

The voice that came from behind me was probably meant to crack like a whip, but mostly it just cracked. "Elizabeth."

Les Haeburn.

I had broken a golden rule of journalism.

Know who's in listening distance before you speak.

"Hi, Les." I smiled, though I doubted it was my best.

"My relationship with this station's ownership is none of your business."

Not only did he have a valid point, but his tone was the most impressive I'd heard since I'd arrived here the first day of April.

That didn't mean I was going to cave.

"You know reporters, Les," I tried in a let's-be-buddies tone. "What's none of our business *is* our business. Can't stop a reporter from being curious. When you said you had an important meeting, the family that owns the station seemed likely candidates."

Interesting. He still eyed me distrustfully, but somewhere in my innocuous little speech he'd become even more pasty-faced than usual. Catching me asking Jennifer about his relationship should have put him in a position of power. Somehow that had flipped. I was glad of that, but sure wished I knew how it had happened.

"Don't you have work to do?" he demanded petulantly.

"I do. In fact, I was getting ready to leave for an interview."

"Then go do it."

Chapter Thirty-Five

LES HAEBURN HAD given the order, so of course I obeyed.

In the parking lot, though, I reconsidered going alone and called Mike, who was inside.

"Give me fifteen minutes," he said.

I turned the heat on in the SUV, then called Dex.

"Do you have any voodoo tricks for figuring out what order these two people died in?"

"I don't practice voodoo," he said solemnly. "There is ongoing research into microbes that is promising for providing us with more accurate information on time of death."

"That is not going to help with these deaths."

"No," he said matter-of-factly. "Nor any of the deaths that went before. That's the way of it with science."

"Tell me about it." Something caught my eye. That moving line of white on the mountains. It was like the Red Light, Green Light game we used to play as kids, where "it" said "green light" and turned away from the other players. They moved as fast as they could before "it" yells "Red Light" and turns back. If "it" sees anyone moving, they have to go back to the start. I never saw anything change when I was looking at those mountains, but when I looked away, then back things had changed. "Did you know—? No, never mind."

"Did I know what?"

Dex on the hunt for a fact he didn't know was relentless. Better to give in fast. "The snowpack is already building up on the mountains here, which means the snow line is visibly lower."

"Yes." He didn't exactly lose all interest, but the thrill was gone.

"Of course you did. Okay, back to the situation I called about."

When Dex spoke, he had perked up. "Is the snowpack related to time of death? Was one of the bodies—?"

"Packed in snow? Left up above the snow line? No."

"Oh."

"Sorry to disappoint you, Dex."

"I'm not disappointed." He sounded puzzled, and I realized I'd snapped at him.

"I'm sorry, Dex. I'm on edge about finding a new job at the end of this month. And I'm spinning my wheels with this situation I've talked to you about. With two people dead we don't know which was the main target and there are probably a dozen suspects."

"Are you asking them questions? You ask good questions."

I chuckled a little. "Thank you. I'm asking and they're answering. Mostly. But...

"There's what a suspect says and there's what a suspect does. That's what science is for. It proves what a suspect has done no matter what he or she says. If you bring me facts, I can help you."

"I know you can, Dex. I just wish we had more facts."

But I felt better for having talked to Dex.

✧   ✧   ✧   ✧

AFTER A SHORT tussle about who'd drive, I let Mike win. I did not want to take my new SUV to Hiram Poppinger's ranch.

Yes, the roads were bad. But also he was known to greet callers with a gun. I wasn't going to expose my new vehicle to that.

Mike and I were getting nowhere discussing the murders—or deaths—even before the road became too rough to do more than hold on.

Hiram had no gun this time, but no friendliness, either.

"What do you want?"

"Hello, Mr. Poppinger. I'm Elizabeth Marga—"

"I know who you are. What I want to know is what you want. Hi, Mike."

"Hi, Hiram. How're you doing?"

"Not bad, not bad. Well, speak up, girlie. What do you want?"

Like I could have while he and Mike were playing Old Home Week. I'd forgotten Hiram had gone all fanboy over Mike when we were here previously.

Until now.

"It's actually Mike who wants something, Mr. Poppinger."

Mike shot me a look that wasn't particularly friendly but picked it up right away.

"Yeah, Hiram. We—um, I heard you might know something that could help on a story we're working on. About what happened at Red Sail Ranch."

"Don't know anything about bringing people back from the dead, so I don't know how I could help you." He made a sound after that statement. His version of a chuckle.

Mike "ha-ha'd" back. "No, no, nothing like that. But as I said, we—I heard you said you'd seen some strange goings on at the search."

"Strange? No, nothing strange. Just the usual ass-backward fool-ishness of people who don't know what they're doing. Puttin' me in a group led by a *deputy*. Some kid who wouldn't know how to bull moose if it was right in front of him. *Especially* being a deputy. And you can tell Wayne Shelton I said that."

He shot the last sentence at me, as if I were best buddies with the deputy. But he was right about one thing—I would report what he'd said to Shelton. With the greatest pleasure.

"Did you notice anybody leave your group?"

"Would've been better if they all had."

"But did any?" Mike pursued.

"Didn't see."

Mike kept at it, but Hiram Poppinger wasn't playing. In fact, Mike kept at it several questions after I would have bopped the guy on the head and gotten out of here.

Finally, Mike said, "Well, okay. Thank you, Hiram. And if you think of anything…"

"Yeah, yeah."

We started to turn away and there was something in the man's face...

"Mr. Poppinger, is there something we haven't asked you about that we should have?" It's one of my favorite questions. It gives the interviewee the chance to fill in gaps, to take the discussion in a different direction, and it plugs up the hole of "I didn't tell you because you never asked."

"Yup."

I don't recall ever being more surprised at that question bearing fruit. "What?"

He looked from me to Mike, who seemed to groan under his breath.

"What should I have asked you about that I haven't yet, Hiram?"

"About the truck."

"What truck?"

Hiram nodded. "Now, you're asking. I was past there earlier that day. Well before they called a search. And there was a truck pulled in on that road runs along the ditch, right near Red Sail Rock."

"A truck?"

He nodded. "White truck. Not many would've seen it, but I got eyes like an eagle. Always have. Weak-willed people these days wearing those glasses and bits of plastic in their eye—ruining their eyes. If they'd put their mind to it—"

"White truck, huh? That's interesting. You're sure it was white?"

"Of course I'm sure," he snapped. "You know how they get dirt on 'em and blend in. Most wouldn't have seen it, but I did. And it was white."

From researching before I bought I knew white was the most popular color for trucks. Of course.

"Any idea whose truck?"

"I wasn't on top of the thing. Just saw it tucked in there along the ditch like it didn't want to get seen. Wasn't counting on Hiram Poppinger," he boasted.

"The brand—"

"Could've been an Edsel for all I know. I keep telling you, it was a second, passed in a flash."

"Of course, of course, and we really appreciate it."

Back in his SUV after he thanked Hiram and I remained silent, Mike said, "Sorry about that, Elizabeth."

"No problem. You're a hometown hero."

"He shouldn't have been so rude to you."

"Mike, truly, it's not a problem. And you should never apologize for it. Or for people talking to you because you were in the NFL. As a reporter you use every tool to get people to talk to you. That's another tool you have—one you worked hard for. Use it."

He stared straight ahead a couple more beats, then gave a lopsided grin. "Thanks. You're right. I did work hard for it. Thanks a lot. I'll miss your words of wisdom if you leave."

He cut a look at me.

When I didn't respond, he added, "I know your resumé reel's out and it's amazing."

"Jennifer."

"Actually, no. I have a connection in Chicago who asked about you. You're going to get a million offers."

I laughed shortly. "That would be a million more than I had at the start of the year. Listen, let's drop hypothetical offers and get back to what Hiram said. I can think of a few folks with white trucks. Saw one at Greg and Krystal Niland's house. Paul Chaney was working on one. There was another ... Terry Waymark. He arrived at the search in a white truck. All smeared with red dirt, exactly as Hiram described."

"Interesting he said that about an Edsel."

"Why?"

Instead of answering, he asked, "You know who else drives a white truck?"

"No. Who?"

"Kade. An old white truck. Not as old as an Edsel. But old."

Chapter Thirty-Six

THAT WASN'T THE end of our list of white trucks.

After a call to Jennifer, we knew that the white truck I'd seen at McCrackens' was registered to Serena McCracken.

Would a newcomer have known her way around well enough to track down Don Hazen at Red Sail Rock?

Or his way, since spousal borrowing of vehicles couldn't be ruled out.

Could there have been a meeting set of McCracken, Hazen, and Brian? A meeting that went very wrong? But wouldn't someone else have heard the meeting was planned? And why at Red Sail Rock?

"I also did that background on Loriana," Jennifer told us both, since I had her on speaker. "Pretty much what we already knew, except her previous husband was killed."

That got my attention.

"They lived in Las Vegas—not together. They'd separated according to the news stories. He was on a business trip to Denver and he was shot there. She was in Las Vegas at the time. Every story mentioned that."

"Darn," Mike said.

That raised my eyebrows. "Isn't the widow treating you right?"

"She never gives a straight answer. Keeps giving me bits and pieces so I have to keep going back and going back. Gets old."

I was smiling when I disconnected from that call after thanking Jennifer and asking her to keep digging on all fronts.

The phone rang again immediately.

"Damned if you weren't right," Tom said by way of greeting.

"You're just realizing that? Kind of slow, aren't you, Burrell?"

"You have no idea what I'm talking about, do you?"

"No, because there are so many things I could be—I am—right about."

"I talked to Matt Harston. It was Mindy's brother. Greg Niland."

I looked up and made eye contact with Mike. "Greg Niland? He didn't stay with the search group?"

"About forty minutes out, Matt noticed he was gone. Greg had been assigned one end of the sweep. They spread a bit wider to cover the territory and didn't think any more about it, especially not when Brian was found well away from where they'd searched. I told him he should tell Wayne Shelton, too."

"Spoilsport. Tom, who do you know who has a white truck?"

"Why?" he was instantly suspicious.

I told him Hiram's account. "We already know about Kade's white truck And Greg's, Terry's, and Serena McCracken's. Paul Chaney has one, too. Anybody else?"

There was a moment's pause. "That ranch truck that Loriana told Mike that Don was working on that day—that's white."

"Is that so?"

Mike raised his eyebrows. I mouthed, *Tell you later.*

"One more thing, Elizabeth. Connie said yes."

"Oh?"

"To you reading her copy of the depositions."

"*Oh.*"

"That's more like it." That tone told me his crow's feet were crinkling while the rest of his face remained passive. "Can you meet me at James' office at three?"

"Absolutely."

✧   ✧   ✧   ✧

MIKE HAD ALREADY made a turn from our direct route back to the station. "Figured you'd want to see Greg Niland."

"Yes, but he won't be at home now, will he?"

"His work's not far from his house, which do you want to check first?"

Krystal might talk more, but she also might keep him from talking. "Work."

"Want to pick up lunch on the way?"

We ate in his SUV in the parking lot of Hamburger Heaven so we could talk in privacy.

We reminded each other that the white truck might not be connected to the deaths. If it existed at all, since it was Hiram Poppinger reporting.

Neither of us truly believed those cautions.

Hiram might not share his white-truck spotting with Shelton, but after talking with Tom, Deputy Harston would report Greg Niland's leaving the search. We didn't have much of a head-start. We ate fast.

We pulled into Roundup Tires and spotted the white pickup I'd seen at the Niland house. It was parked well off to the side in a spot inconvenient enough to be employee parking.

He was in an office that rivaled the KWMT-TV's ladies' room for compactness.

"Greg, do you remember me? I'm Elizabeth Marga—"

"I remember. And you're Mike Paycik." He came out of his chair to shake hands, smiling.

"We'd like to talk to you," I said.

"Sure. Have a seat."

I looked at the poorly fitted glass walls of his cubicle, the shop visible on one side and the front desk on the other. "It might be better if we go outside."

"Is this about—? Okay. Yeah."

He led us past the parking area with his truck, to a concrete table and bench under a tree. None of us sat on the bench but he propped himself on the edge of the tabletop.

"You found out something about Mindy?"

"Not directly." I moved past that quickly. "We understand that you left the search party you were assigned to a week ago today. Where did you go?"

"What?" His color rose quickly. Hard to tell if it was anger or fear. "Who says—"

"Leader of the group," Mike said calmly. "Deputy by the name of Harston. He remembers it clearly. Other people in the group remarked on it, too."

I added, "It's well-established that you left the search."

"Yeah, I left. So what? I wasn't feeling real good so I left. I'm not a kid. I didn't have to go to the nurse to report a tummy-ache. I just left."

"What we want to know is where you went."

"Well, I'm not telling you. It's none of your damned business."

"The sheriff's department will be asking you soon and they won't accept that answer, Greg." His body language and expression were settling into stubborn. I decided to hit him hard now in hopes the stubbornness wouldn't become an impenetrable shell. "Your truck was seen."

His color formed blotches on his face, redder in some spots, paler in others. "I don't believe you."

"It's not hard to recognize." I gestured to it. "People familiar with it, familiar with you, saw it parked and knew it was yours."

"No way." But he was having trouble swallowing and he had to lick his lips to get those two words out.

"I can't imagine the sheriff's office accepting your denial over the testimony of disinterested parties. Especially not when it involves murder."

"Murder? What the hell? My truck was nowhere near—"

"It was seen," Mike said in his best voice-of-authority broadcasting mode. "Close to where Brian Walterston and Don Hazen's bodies were found and at the right time to have—"

"By Red Sail Rock? Are you crazy? Where anybody could see it and tell Krystal? No way in hell."

It was like that moment when you're looking at an image of a young woman in a plumed hat and someone points out it's also the image of a crone if you focus on different elements and suddenly there she is. Same marks on the piece of paper, but your mind puts them together for a different image.

"But you were on the HY Ranch," I said.

"Maybe," he mumbled.

"Maybe isn't going to cut it, Greg. This is murder. You think you could have trouble with Krystal? Wait until people really start to come after you about murder."

Mike shot me a look. He must still be looking at the young woman in the plumed hat.

"I don't know anything about murder. I swear."

"You can't know that, because you don't know how what you know fits in with everything else. Tell us where you were."

"You can't tell Krystal."

"Only if we have to. And only if it fits in with murder." I knew by now. I imagined Mike did, too, but it would be so much better if Greg Niland came out with it.

"I was looking for Loriana."

"Because you've been having an affair with her." It fit those rumors Diana had heard. And the fact that Greg wasn't part of the Red Sail Ditch Company might explain why no one knew.

He gave a harsh bray of laughter. "We're screwing around. Not damned often enough to call it an affair. I wish. Between work and Krystal being on my tail and Don tracking her all the time we could hardly ever get together. That's why I thought... Hell, we were out there walking at a snail's pace, finding nothing, and here was this nice block of time when nobody'd check up on me. It seemed perfect."

"So you and Loriana..."

"Nah, I never could get a hold of her. Her phone stops working sometimes and she doesn't get calls, and damned if this wasn't one of those times. I worked my way back to my truck at Red Sail Ranch, kept trying to call, but never did get her."

"But you had to check back in with the search," Mike said. "Or they'd have known you were gone."

"My buddy was in the same group. He called me when Brian was found. By that time, I'd holed up in one of the places we meet and was getting some sleep. Went back, parked, then circled round to come in from the dark. Checked my name off the sheet and left again. Nobody paid any attention."

"So no one can vouch for your whereabouts," Mike said.

"No. But I didn't—I had nothing to do with what happened to Hazen. Not sorry he's dead, but I didn't do it."

Chapter Thirty-Seven

IN THE **KWMT-TV** parking lot, we sat in Mike's SUV for a few minutes, talking out whether we believed Greg Niland or not.

I believed.

Mike not.

Then I transferred to my SUV and headed into town to meet Tom at James Longbaugh's office.

I pulled into a spot in the abundant angled street parking that has to be one of the world's best inventions.

I was crossing toward the office when I saw a familiar figure turn the corner from Cottonwood Avenue.

Linda Caswell, the aunt of Cas Newton.

She ran a long-time family business and, as far as I could tell, two-thirds of the unofficial aspects of Cottonwood County.

I saw her temptation to cross toward the courthouse, pretending she hadn't seen me. I didn't take it personally. It was human nature to want to avoid a near-stranger who'd become acquainted with the secrets you'd most like to keep private.

It said something for her character that she didn't succumb to that easy out.

"Elizabeth," she said calmly as we neared.

"Linda." I slowed. "How are you?"

She stopped. "Very well, thank you."

Dorothy Parker and Oscar Wilde rapping out the *bon mots*, that was us.

"I understand you've been doing some traveling."

"Yes." She blushed.

So Penny was right. Linda had been following the rodeo circuit with a certain cowboy.

"I suppose Tom told you," she added.

I laughed. "Not in a million years. He either believes in taking discretion to the max or he doesn't trust me not to spill every syllable I hear on TV, because Thomas David Burrell doesn't tell me much of anything."

She tipped her head as she studied me, fully back in control. Now, like control was a zero-sum game, I felt mine ebbing.

"I better get going. Working." I gave a vague wave.

"Of course." She laid a hand on my arm. "But before you do…"

She looked away, but didn't remove her hand. Then she faced me again. "I think my nephew has something that it would do him good to tell you."

I felt my eyebrows hike.

Since she knew I'd suspected her nephew—along with several other people near and dear to him, including her, as a matter of fact—in a murder during the summer, I was surprised.

"Something that will do him good to tell me," I echoed. "But will he want to tell me?"

"Probably not. However, you can be quite persuasive. I'm sure you can persuade Cas."

It had to be about the Walterston boys, with the teenagers all being friends.

"Will *I* want to?" I asked. "Do *him* good, but will it do me any good?"

"It might." She pulled in a breath through her teeth. "I can only hope it brings the truth out. If I learned anything from that mess this summer it was that secrets shrivel up and die when they're brought out into the light of day."

Then she smiled—the smile that changed her from nearly homely to a stunner.

She chuckled. "Just don't let Stan know you're talking to his son." We had a mutual low opinion of her brother-in-law, Stan Newton. She lifted her hand from my arm, having accomplished what she meant to accomplish.

But then she surprised me a second time in this conversation.

"We should get together soon. Have lunch." She smiled, once again pulling off that transformation. "A real lunch."

Our previous lunch had been a tense affair, devoted to my trying to get answers to questions she didn't want to hear much less answer. All the while Tom—who'd arranged the little get-together—seethed at my asking his friend tough questions.

"I'd like that."

We said good-bye without setting a time and place, yet I thought this second lunch would happen.

Sometimes I forget how small Sherman is. I still reached Longbaugh's office ten minutes before three.

The law office was two doors down one of the side streets from the courthouse. It had been built as a combination residence and office by the current James Longbaugh's great-grandfather. His grandfather converted it to entirely office use. The current James Longbaugh had overseen a renovation to both upgrade for modern conveniences and restore as many historic features as possible. At least that's what the pictures and captions on one wall in the waiting room reported.

We had time to study them because James Longbaugh—the one currently practicing law—sent out a message that he was having a word with Connie before we all talked together. Lawyerly caution, no doubt.

At two minutes after three the twenty-something receptionist ushered us into a conference room in what must have started life as the family dining room.

After greetings, Longbaugh said, "I've told Connie I have reservations about this, both as her representative and the representative of the Red Sail Ditch Company. But there's no legal reason she can't allow you to read this deposition, Ms. Danniher, since that's her wish."

How was that for a ringing endorsement?

"However, it is to be understood that you will not report any of the material you learn from this document."

"I will not broadcast any of the material I learn from this document unless I obtain it from a separate source," I amended.

His eyes glinted. "If that source is one you would not have sought without having read—"

"Enough of this, James," Connie interrupted. "Elizabeth isn't going to make this into some tabloid report. Not that she could. It's pretty dry stuff." There was a glimmer of something that in a few more months might become her returning smile.

"James' job is to protect you. You should listen to him," Tom said to her.

"And it should be understood," I added, "that if we find anything in this deposition that law enforcement should know about, I'll tell them."

"You won't," Connie said at the same time Longbaugh said, "I would have informed them if there were."

"You might not have the context Elizabeth has, James." To my surprise, that came from Tom.

Longbaugh's grunt expressed skepticism too polite to be spoken.

Connie covered it by saying, "I just know the deposition took nearly the last bit of strength Brian had. For days, I thought… But he insisted. And he was satisfied after. He said the record had to be clear in case…"

She didn't cry or sob or tear up. I wish she had. It would have been easier to witness than the struggle not to.

Longbaugh stood.

"Connie and I have more to discuss. We'll leave you here to read the deposition. This is a loose copy from the court reporter, so you both can read it. You may take notes, but no photographing, videoing, or copying by any other means. Do I have your word on that? Both of you."

He did, and with utterly no reluctance on my part. If he thought I was all aflutter to video words on a piece of paper, he knew nothing about good visuals. Didn't get much more static than that.

Didn't get much more boring than this deposition, either. As I learned over the next hours. I read how the position of the Red Sail

Ditch Company and its ditch boss was that this lawsuit was strictly an individual affair between McCracken and Hazen and did not involve either said company nor its ditch boss. That was worked in to just about every response.

I would read a page, then hand it to Tom, who was a slower reader than me. So at the end I had the opportunity to observe him as he finished the last several pages.

When he turned the last face down on the neat stack, I immediately asked, "What's bothering you?"

"I don't know if it's something bothering me. In a way..."

"Let me rephrase. What's got you looking more like Abraham Lincoln's good-looking cousin than usual?"

"Abraham Lincoln's good-looking cousin?"

"Oh, c'mon, you must have heard that you resemble him before."

He nodded slowly. "It was the good-looking cousin part that caught my attention."

With that glint of humor in his eyes... I looked away to concentrate on tapping the piled pages. "Tell."

"First, tell me what struck you."

"Tom—"

"I'll tell you. First, let's hear your take."

"It's from that one time Brian went off his script about how neither the ditch nor the ditch boss was responsible for or involved in this mess. When he basically said Don and McCracken were both at fault and being childish to boot." I tapped my pencil on the table. "But he seems to blame Don more."

I found the number I'd noted and flipped back through pages to it. "First he talks about what McCracken did. 'The fence he built did impede maintenance and repair ability on the ditch. He should not have built it. If he'd consulted with me I could have told him how much more clearance he needed to leave.' So he's certainly not saying McCracken is blameless. But then he starts talking about Don. 'Mr. McCracken can plead ignorance. Don cannot. He's been part of the Red Sail Ditch Company since he bought that property and he was raised with irrigation. He knows that the degradation he's allowed—

no, not allowed, actively encouraged, because those walls were fine last spring—' "

I looked up, but Tom apparently wasn't going to explain the sound he'd made.

"Don's lawyer objected. When Brian resumes, he says, 'The result cannot be argued. This deteriorated section is capturing more water than he's entitled to because it's in addition to what's monitored at the head gate. And to his own detriment, since serious erosion has begun in the Loop Field. It makes no sense. And even if Don claims he didn't damage those walls himself, even if he claims he managed to never learn about the consequences of damaging ditch walls, I told him and you have official correspondence from the ditch company—' Then another objection from Don's lawyer saying this was not responsive, not germane to the lawsuit."

I put the pages back in the pile before adding, "So my takeaway is that Brian thought McCracken was technically wrong but thought what Don was doing was far worse. And the fact that the deposition didn't concern what Don was doing in Loop Field wasn't going to stop him from saying it. Now, what's your takeaway?"

"That last part of what you said, that's some of my takeaway. Brian was getting things on record he thought needed to be on record. Setting it out clear that the ditch wasn't party to the dispute between the two men. Also some of what you just talked about—stating for a record how Don was doing wrong."

He folded his hands on the table, rubbing the side of one thumb against the other.

There was more to his reaction to the deposition, more takeaway to be had. I knew it. The question was whether he would say it or not.

He stared at his hands as he started speaking.

"Brian was putting things in order, doing his best to make sure the ditch wasn't pulled in." He turned to me. "Brian was getting ready to die."

Chapter Thirty-Eight

WE CAME OUT to find Tamantha reading a book in James Long-baugh's waiting room.

While she packed up her backpack, we thanked James, then all went out on the sidewalk.

"We'll walk you to your vehicle."

"No need—I'm parked just over there."

Tamantha fell into step beside me. "We're walking you."

She knew her father well.

He said, "Think I'll take another trip out to that part of the ditch. Want to take another look after reading what Brian had to say."

"I'll go with you," I said immediately.

Something flickered across his eyes and was gone. "Better let Mike be the one to come with."

"He can come, too. But I'm going. I want to see the spot."

"You have."

"I don't mean where Brian and Don..." With a glance toward Tamantha, I let it go unsaid. "I want to see where Don was letting the ditch wall erode."

"If you're sure."

"I'm sure.

"Okay. I'll let you know when. I'll try for tomorrow."

That was too easy.

"So we'll drive out and—"

"Not drive. Can't get to it from Connie and Brian's land that way. And with the condition of Loop Field it would be criminal to drive across it."

"But if there's no way to get to it—?"

"There is. On horseback."

"No."

"Only way."

Tamantha had been listening to this exchange with a growing frown. "Elizabeth can borrow one of our horses, can't she, Daddy?"

"That could be arranged. Or one of the Walterstons'. But I don't think that's the problem."

She looked from him to me and back. "What's the problem?"

"I believe Elizabeth doesn't know how to ride a horse."

Her head whipped back around to me. "You can't *ride?*"

"I can ride," I started. But with those eyes on me, my ending joke came out lamely. "A bicycle. The subway. Those I can ride."

She absorbed that a second before asking, "Are you a city girl?"

I have been sworn at in more languages than I can remember, spat upon, threatened with weapons from firearms to a yard-long salami. I don't know that I've ever felt quite as defensive as I did in that moment.

I considered lying—fibbing, really—to spare myself the strafing of that look. But there was no lying to those eyes. If the Spanish Inquisition had had Tamantha Burrell, they wouldn't have needed the gadgets.

But before I had to face the ignominy of admitting to her that I was a city girl, a hole in my life skills occurred to me, and I slipped right into it, like someone near drowning who surfaced in the center of a life preserver. "Not a city girl. More of a suburban girl."

She tipped her head in skepticism. "Why?"

"Can't parallel park to save my soul," I admitted happily. "Too used to suburban parking lots."

Tom made a noise.

She turned to look at him, then back to me. "What's a parallel park?"

"It's something you do in cities with your car—or truck. Instead of pulling into a spot, straight on or at an angle like you do here, you have to get in parallel to the sidewalk, in a small space left between other cars."

She humphed disdain for such heathenish doings, and returned to her point. "Everybody knows how to ride, so I guess you'll have to learn. Though you are pretty old."

"Which is why I'm not going to try."

"You're not going to even *try*?" Tamantha demanded.

Oh, hell. I was going to try.

I HAD BACK-TO-BACK evening interviews scheduled with two local insurance agents, the one I'd already talked to on the phone and a second who was past-president of the Chamber of Commerce.

Most of both interviews focused on general consumer concerns about insurance. Off-camera each expressed carefully worded concerns about Rich Taylorman. "Came out of nowhere," the past-president said.

On the way back to the bunkhouse, I left a message for Jennifer asking for an update on her research on Taylorman.

I also listened to a message from Mel.

"Call me back. We have to talk. Lots of exciting things."

There was no reason for that message to make my stomach drop. No reason at all.

It wasn't quite ten o'clock in Chicago, but he and Peg might already be in bed. I didn't want to bother them. It could wait until business hours, surely.

I settled into bed, found the movies I wanted and streamed them. Repeatedly. Despite heavy sighs from the vicinity of the dog bed in the middle of the floor.

DAY NINE

TUESDAY

Chapter Thirty-Nine

I WAS STILL alternating *Here Comes Mr. Jordan* and *Heaven Can Wait* as daylight began to show, I gave up on sleep, got up, showered, and mostly dressed.

Even if he was dead—or at least sort of dead—I felt a lot of connection with the character Joe Pendleton.

Both Joe—a boxer in the original and an NFL quarterback in the remake—and I had thought our lives were heading the way we wanted them to go. We thought we were in charge and by hard work, talent, and some breaks we were coming up to the top of our games.

And then everything went to hell.

Well, in the movie character's case, actually he was snatched too early from his body and sent to heaven.

I was snatched from New York and sent to Sherman, Wyoming. The jury was out on whether that figured as hell or heaven in my story.

On second thought, how different were Joe Pendleton 1, Joe Pendleton 2, and I from anyone else?

Connie and her husband must have thought their lives were on a good track—until his illness, followed by all the many ways their lives went to hell, along with their boys' lives.

Maybe Brian had thought that ending his life would get theirs back on track. But that hadn't turned out, either.

Even Don Hazen. I'd bet when Loriana came back into his life he'd thought he finally had things going his way. Instead, he had all the conflicts in the ditch company and ended up dead. Not exactly what he'd hoped for.

Or Hannah and Paul Chaney, starting out on their married life together. Or the McCrackens, coming to Wyoming to raise their kids in the country.

Shadow stood and listened alertly.

A knock sounded.

"Come in."

Diana opened the door. "You should find out who it is. You seemed a little down yesterday. Thought I'd see if… What are you doing?"

"Watching an old movie."

"What movie? Is that…? Who is that?"

"Warren Beatty. *Heaven Can Wait*."

"Huh."

The movie went on. I finally broke the silence between the live people in the room by saying without looking at her, "I'm not crazy, Diana. I had a yen to see these old movies."

"I thought things were heating up and you'd be following up loose ends."

"Maybe I am." Though I was thinking of the E.M. Danniher Story, rather than the tangle of unrelated information we seemed to have amassed to this point concerning the deaths of Brian Walterston and Don Hazen. I sighed. Neither story appeared to have a tidy resolution in sight.

"You look awful and you're not out of bed," she said.

"Thanks and I'm dressed underneath. I just got back under the covers."

"If you were going to watch any movie, I'd think it would be the one Penny told you about."

"Couldn't if I wanted to. I never did figure out which movie she was talking about with a boy helping his father end his life."

"You think she was saying something that directly tied to the situation? That wouldn't be like her."

I stilled, hearing Penny's voice in my head … without me interrupting her this time.

Connie and those boys will feel that blow a long, long time. And that's if those boneheads don't put one of those boys in jail, which is just what I told Wayne Shelton when he was in here with his ears flapping. Those teenagers don't realize what they're saying. Think nobody around them hears or understands a thing. As if they're the first whoever did such a thing. Though it did surprise me they'd seen the movie. Would've thought it was way too long ago for them. Even knew the baseball song.

Diana was right. It wasn't like her to be direct.

So if it wasn't a movie about a boy helping a father commit suicide...

A fragment of song came into my head. Not a perfect match. But interesting ... very interesting.

Only one way to find out if I was right.

"Where are you going, Elizabeth?" Diana asked as I scrambled up.

"Chasing a movie. The way I should have done that first day, instead of getting distracted by meat and justice and East vs. West and whether I belong in this body or a new one."

"A new body?" She looked startled.

I spotted my shoes partly under the bed. "Never mind. I'll explain it all later if it turns out I'm right."

"About the movie?" She glanced toward the screen.

I finished wiggling my foot into the shoe and stabbed the button to stop the movie.

"Not this movie. The one I need to get from Penny. And if I do get it, I need to talk to a teenager. And I have to do it fast so I'm not late for my first horseback ride."

I headed for the Sherman Supermarket.

I WALKED STRAIGHT to Penny, going around to her side of the register and grasping her arms.

"Penny, you were talking about teenagers thinking they're the first to do something and your being surprised they'd seen a movie that had the same scenario—"

"Did I? Who'd believed you could worm such a thing out of me when I'm known for keeping a secret a secret."

I kept going. "You were surprised, because you thought the movie was too old for them to be familiar with, a movie with a 'baseball' song. Did you mean a song that mentions 'Joltin' Joe' DiMaggio?"

"Maybe. But I'm not going to let you worm any more out of me. Even if they didn't ask me to keep it a secret. Even if they thought I couldn't put two and two together. Even if—"

"Just give me the name of—"

"—they acted like I wasn't even here, much less having ears and—"

"—the movie. What was the name of the movie?"

"—a brain. Is that all you want to know? The movie? Nothing else about who was doing what?"

"The name of the movie," I repeated.

"*The Graduate.*"

Bingo. "Though if you want to tell me who was doing what with whom—"

Penny chuckled mightily as she turned to an arriving customer. "Well, hi there."

Chapter Forty

I STOPPED HUMMING Simon and Garfunkel's "Mrs. Robinson" when I saw Deputy Shelton leaning against the driver's side of my new SUV in the Sherman Supermarket parking lot.

I loved the red color of my new vehicle, but maybe I should have gotten a white pickup so it wouldn't be as recognizable.

"You're nosing around where you shouldn't be," was his greeting.

"You should go in and talk to Penny."

"Talk?"

"Okay, listen."

"Ask her about the movie 'The Graduate' and Mrs. Robinson."

He slowly nodded. "Doesn't surprise me much," he said with distaste.

"You just don't like Loriana because her uncle had the nerve to die on you before he was convicted."

His face tightened. "I didn't mind Earl dying. It was how it happened."

"How was that?"

He shot me a look. "You be careful, E.M. Danniher. There are powerful feelings you're messing with here. I don't want investigating your murder added to my workload."

✦ ✦ ✦ ✦

"HI, CAS."

Caswell Newton groaned as he got out of a dark green pickup at Cottonwood County High School. I'd heard that his father's financial woes had prompted him to trade his glossy new truck for something more economical.

I could pretend the groan was from whatever injury had his right arm in a sling. But I knew better.

"What do you want?"

I'd hoped I'd have a better chance of catching him here than trying to get to his father's ranch before he left for school. So far, so good. "What do I ever want?"

"To ask questions."

"And to get answers," I added.

"My father's still mighty peeved with you. From the rodeo, and from the house burning down." The change of angle—along with the fact that he hadn't walked away or shut up—was a hopeful sign.

"He's not on my Christmas card list, either."

He ducked his head to hide the flicker of a grin.

"So, with me not being favored by your father, are you going to talk to me or not, Cas?"

"Don't always walk in my father's footsteps. I saw for myself you got to the truth in the end. There's…" He paused. "Value in that."

He must have gotten that moral compass from his mother's side of the family. It certainly hadn't come from Stan Newton.

Yeah, this kid was shaping up well.

"That's what I'm after this time, too. The truth. About the deaths of Brian Walterston and Don Hazen."

"I don't know anything about that. I wasn't there until the search and you know about that."

"What I'm hoping for is background. I understand Loriana was having an affair with someone."

"Gossip isn't—"

"But you've heard more than gossip, haven't you? Heard about it directly and maybe saw some things that—"

"Who told—" He bit it off, but then had the maturity to not pretend it had been in time.

I said, "I bet you also know which of the Walterston boys."

He said nothing.

"I know you're friends with them."

"Yeah, I am," he said with emphasis.

"It's like you said, Cas. It's getting to the truth."

He muttered a curse under his breath.

I backed up. Sometimes damn the torpedoes, full speed ahead is not the best approach to an interview subject.

"I get the feeling you and other friends didn't approve."

"What makes you say that?"

"Likening Loriana to Mrs. Robinson from *The Graduate*."

He was going to deny it. Had the words ready ... then didn't use them.

I still wasn't ready for torpedoes, but a nudge couldn't hurt. "That's not exactly a sympathetic role. She's a man-eater."

His mouth twisted.

So I nudged again. "Or perhaps kid-eater's more accurate, since Mrs. Robinson seduced someone her daughter's age."

His mouth twisted harder. This time he put his hand up, rubbed at his mouth. Too late.

"Austin," I said. Not a question.

His jaw tightened and the next word came out between clenched teeth "Gross."

I agreed. The kid was, what, fifteen? Sixteen at the most?

He loosened up a bit to add, "She tried it on with other guys—us older ones who knew better. But he'd never ... you know. He really wanted to know..."

Curiosity might or might not have killed the cat, but it has certainly seduced countless hormone-swamped wretches on both sides of the gender divide.

"But it doesn't have anything to do with what happened," he said. "It couldn't have. Don never knew. Not about him or her others. She had it all worked out."

My thoughts had also turned from Mrs. Robinson to the deaths.

"Cas, you said something at the Walterstons' last week. When I said Brian had no way to change his mind. You said yes he did. Or you started to. What did you mean?"

Silence.

"Did Austin or Kade tell you that they took Brian out there and he had his usual equipment when they left him?"

Silence.

"Did *someone* tell you that—no name attached?"

Still silence. Damn the kid's loyalty.

"Did you have reason to believe that Brian's chair was equipped the way it usually was? Listen, this could be important. It could make all the difference if there are charges brought. Do you understand that?"

He looked away. My heart thumped harder.

Without looking back, he said, "Yeah, I have reason to believe that. And I'm not telling you another damned thing."

"Okay, Cas. Okay."

Okay for now, I thought, but didn't say. It might or might not come to a point where he had to be pressed harder.

I touched his shoulder lightly. "Thank you. This might help…" His friends? I wouldn't make the false promise. "Find the truth."

I started away. His voice stopped me.

"Ms. Danniher, who told you to come talk to me?"

"Sorry. A journalist protects her sources."

He squinted at me. Not happy.

"That means I also won't reveal who told me about Austin and Loriana, Cas."

The squint eased.

Chapter Forty-One

I RODE.

A horse named Babe.

If a turtle could have been turned into a horse, it would have been Babe.

Some elements of his turtleness, I happily applauded.

He was built low to the ground. Yes, that did eventually leave my head an extra foot below Tom's and Mike's when we were all mounted at Red Sail Ranch, but the benefits outweighed that drawback.

He was slow. I considered that an unmixed benefit.

Babe never lifted his feet higher off the ground than absolutely necessary. This, too, was a pure positive in my eyes.

The aesthetics of the way his head jutted forward didn't ruffle me.

It was the broad back I wasn't fond of.

The very, very broad back. It was like trying to ride a stretch of floor.

If God had wanted me to do the splits, I would have been born a Romanian gymnast.

Muscles and joints I hadn't known I had were not amused. Not one little bit.

And that was just from getting on.

Tom and Mike had me climb on a stump in order to straddle Babe. That gave me enough height advantage to see over the other horses when Mike said something quickly to Tom, then both looked at me.

There was something in their look that made me wonder if they thought I'd survive this trip.

"He's awful," Tamantha declared.

I wasn't the least surprised that she was here. Tom had mumbled some things about her missing only lunch and PE, but that was cover-up.

"He's been retired a while and he's gotten fatter," Jaden Walterston said.

"You should exercise him more," Tamantha said sternly.

Jaden, a decade older than her and two and a half feet taller, bowed his head, accepting the reprimand. "Yeah."

"Even then, he'd be awful," she added.

"Elizabeth isn't an experienced rider like you are, Tamantha." Tom cupped his hands, his daughter stepped into them, then like a feather—if a feather had cast iron determination—she alighted on the back of a glossy auburn creature as unlike Babe as the sun was unlike a mud-encrusted flashlight.

"Why haven't you learned to ride?" she asked me, as if I'd missed a key developmental stage like getting past burping whenever I ate.

"No horses around when I was growing up."

"You've had lots of time since then." She needn't have emphasized "lots" quite so strongly.

"No horses around where I worked, either. Not until I came here. But I have driven a tank," I said in a pathetic attempt to recoup my coolness factor.

She humphed tanks into oblivion.

With the others now mounted, she satisfied herself as we set out by adding, "Even Elizabeth shouldn't have been stuck with Babe. And she needs a hat."

WHEN MIKE TRIED to hurry up Babe, I reminded him that the idea was to let me see the lay of the land close up and in detail, so the slower Babe went, the better. Mike argued that getting there didn't need to be slow, but I contended Babe was practicing.

Even with Babe slowing the pace it took less time than I expected to reach our destination.

We skirted the knobby hill I'd seen from Red Sail Rock, then followed single file between it and the ditch.

The machinery had swapped places with us from last week. Now it was close to Red Sail Rock, while we were at the eastern point of the ditch's path around Loop Field.

"Still working at it, huh?" Mike asked.

"That's the worst area," Tom said.

Right. The repairs not starting with the worst damage had been one of Kade's complaints.

I needed to let the others know what I'd found out about Austin and Loriana. It wasn't going to be easy for Tom to hear.

Or for me to tell him.

"They've done a good job," Tom said. "Banks look good and solid and they worked back a way to avoid it being undercut. See that dip in the ground? Before, you could see erosion slicing through that whole area."

He and Jaden talked technical aspects of the ditch with occasional contributions from Mike and Tamantha.

I was smart enough to remain silent.

I don't know what I'd expected to see or learn or sense out here. Other than this part of the ditch being in significantly better repair than the section near Red Sail Rock and confirming what Tom had said about the limited access, I was remarkably short of insights.

We continued alongside the ditch as it headed south. The path widened past the knobby hill and Tom, who'd been in the lead, drew up there.

"This is the southern tip of Loop Field." He glanced at me. "Want to follow along to where they're working on the western turn? Or head back?"

"Head back. Unless there's any chance of seeing something startling?"

He and Mike flickered grins at my morose tone. "Not likely," Tom said.

"I don't know about startling," Jaden said slowly, "but that's an interesting group."

I squinted in the direction his cowboy hat had tipped.

The machine—track hoe—had backed up more than usual on its latest pass and revealed three people on its far side.

Loriana. Terry Waymark. And "is that Taylorman?" It had to be. Pork pie hat and all.

"Yup," Mike confirmed. "And I think they were being real careful to stay behind the track hoe. If it hadn't swung wider this time we wouldn't have seen them."

"Well, in that case... Let's let them know we have seen them."

The others all stood in their stirrups and raised their hats. I elevated a good two inches and raised a hand.

As they waved back, Tom said, "That's Don Hazen's old white truck they're leaning against."

"**YOU'LL FEEL BOW-LEGGED** for a while," Mike said, his sympathy soured by his grin.

"To be bow-legged now, I would have had to have been able to actually bend my legs while I was on Babe. I will never walk again." Or do a lot of other things again.

The inside of my thighs and the outside of my hips practically screamed at the thought of stretching ever again.

"Well, you were already tender in, ah, certain areas." Tom looked meaningfully toward my backside.

"Thanks for the reminder, Burrell. I'm beginning to think you two have decided I should stay in Wyoming—six feet underground."

"Of course you're going to stay," Tamantha declared. "But not underground. That would be boring."

"Yes, it would."

Chapter Forty-Two

AFTER THE HORSES were cared for, Jaden said his mother had left iced tea and lemonade for us. As everyone else headed for the house, Tom stepped back into the barn, carrying a halter.

I went after him.

My comment about staying in Wyoming had reminded me of something I wanted to ask him.

"You never mentioned you knew the Heathertons. Not until last week with Les Haeburn."

"Nope."

"You didn't think I'd be interested?"

He shifted to look at me squarely. "You're interested in everything, Elizabeth Margaret Danniher. Just like Tamantha. If I told you two everything you might be interested in I'd never stop talking."

"That would be a change. But you can't pass this off as my being interested in everything. The never-seen owners of the station where I work? When my rep is talking contract and—"

"You are?"

I hadn't meant to spill that. "*I'm* not."

"You're sending out your resumé."

Ah, had that been the exchange between Mike and him earlier?

I found occasion to look toward the horizon, where heavy clouds blotted the light, and gave an involuntary shudder. "I feel as if a cold wind passed over me."

"A cold wind *did* pass over you. A front's moving in from Canada. But you're trying to change the subject." He hung up the halter and faced me. "You planning to use an offer from the Heathertons to nudge other bidders higher?"

I laughed. A genuine laugh. "An offer from KWMT-TV would probably start an anti-bidding war, where anybody interested *lowered* their offers."

"Yet you're talking to them. So you're considering staying?"

"I'm keeping all my options open." I'd said it too fast, too pat.

Those Abraham Lincoln eyes studied me. "You don't know what you want to do." He stated it.

"There are a lot of factors to consider," I hedged. "Tom, please keep this confidential—"

"You were just complaining about me *not* talking. But being unsure about this decision is another angle of not having confidence in your judgment."

"Who says I'm unsure? I don't—"

"You've got to shake that, Elizabeth. You are a good judge of character. You make good decisions. Mostly. Tamantha will be real disappointed if you leave."

I tried a chuckle. "You mean because it would be the rare instance of someone defying one of her edicts?"

"She's taken to you."

"It's mutual. Even though she terrifies me."

More studying. I wasn't liking this conversation. "She's not like you in some ways—"

"She's not like *anyone*."

"—but you're both smart as a whip and some things come easy—"

"Easy? No way. I work hard to figure things out, to—"

"You're apologizing because you've got abilities and skills not everybody has?"

"I wasn't apologizing—"

"Call it defensive, then. Is this related—"

"I am not defensive," I said, and yes, I said it defensively.

"—to you getting squirmy about being so good at FreeCell?"

"I didn't get squirmy and I'm not all that good."

"What's the big deal about being better at something than other people? It's not like you're better at everything. I've seen you ride."

I huffed at that crack. "Thanks a lot. Just because you grew up in the saddle—"

"That's the point, Elizabeth, I did. I'm a good rider. Statement of fact. Like you being good at FreeCell. I'm a good rider from experience and because there's something in me that clicks with what's needed to ride. There's something in you that clicks with seeing things faster than other people. Faster in FreeCell. Faster in other puzzles. You know it. The rest of us who've watched these past months know it. Why pretend you're not?"

"I'm not pretending—"

"Elizabeth. You've got enough of your light hidden under a basket to qualify as an eclipse of the sun." A mixed metaphor, but vivid.

"I don't hear you bragging about your riding, so why you should expect—"

"No bragging. But no—" He added emphasis to the word this time. "—pretending." He took his hat off, whapped it against his thigh, setting up a mini-cloud of dust. "For a smart woman— Somebody's got you all tied up, twisted around. Somebody probably looking out for his own ego."

A click of recognition sounded in my head. I was back in time, back in geography.

St. Louis. Not long married. I was crowing to Wes because I'd put together a piece in record time, allowing us to skid into the theater before curtain. Wes had given me the tickets for my birthday. Then an area police chief's arrest for DUI in another jurisdiction had led to two days of non-stop reporting. I'd thought I'd finished with half an hour to spare when the demand came to do an additional remix for the network overnight news. I'd still pulled it off.

"Don't tell people that," Wes had said. "That you could just *see* how it should go together."

My giddiness had slid several notches. "I would only tell you. I'm sorry. I didn't think you—"

He'd talked over my apology. "No, you don't think."

I'd recoiled. He reached out so quickly I hadn't completed my withdrawal before he captured my hand. "That's what *other* people will think—that's what I meant, Lizzie. That you don't think. You don't want people to know how easy things come for you. You want them to believe you work as hard as they do. Because that's what makes people respect you. You understand that, don't you?"

I suppressed a tart response that I worked plenty hard, which anyone who cared to notice would see. He was under a lot of pressure—he was trying to find his footing at this station, while I'd had an easy transition. I needed to cut him some slack.

"I understand," I'd said, confident this was an aberration.

It was not.

I blinked. Tom Burrell was still studying me.

"We've wasted enough time on this." I started to step around him.

"It was your ex," he said flatly. "So, screw him. Him and anyone else who can't appreciate you. It's like I tell Tamantha—"

"I am not your daughter."

"No, you're not." The significance of his look and tone threw me off, giving him the chance to keep on talking. "But you and Tamantha have things in common. Like getting messages about what it means to be smart. Some of 'em good, some of 'em not. Somebody sure as hell fed you a load. You do pretty good, but something will trigger it and you scrunch up. Like that." He rested one large palm where my right shoulder met my neck. I felt tension in the muscles under his warm touch.

"I can talk to the Heathertons—"

"No. I mean it, Tom. Don't."

He stepped in closer. I had to tip my head back. "I'm not your ex. I'll do what you ask. But…"

He took my face in his big hands and kissed me.

Under the brim of his hat was a private universe. Hot and spinning. His tongue touched my lips and they opened. So easily. So, so easily.

I backed away, his hands still on my face.

"The boys have been lying, Tom. You don't know everything yet, but they are. It's for sure. I need to talk to them. To ask questions."

I watched his eyes change as I talked. From melted heat. To recognition. To wariness.

I kept going. Knowing I was pushing him.

"Both of them. Austin and Kade. They know a lot more about what happened. It's past time to find out what they've been hiding. You had to see it the day of the search and ever since. They—"

"What are you saying?" We both turned at Connie's voice, coming from the brightness beyond the barn door. "Tom? What is this about?"

I expected Tom to soothe her. To put her off. "Elizabeth thinks the boys might be involved."

"That's not—" I started.

Connie, continuing to come toward us, cut across my words. "With Don's murder?"

"With their father being out there," Tom said curtly.

"Oh."

The syllable was so flat it silenced me completely. It also told me that Tom had known, which frightened her more.

Then she knocked me sideways with two words: "Which one?"

Chapter Forty-Three

"YOU'VE SUSPECTED?" I demanded.

Tom snapped, "You can't ask a mother if she suspects—"

Connie silenced Tom as I so rarely succeeded in doing. "I have wondered if one of them ... helped. But which? I don't know."

"Could both—?"

Her head shake stopped me. "No. Not both. Or they'd be united. There's been an argument between them and it's not done. It's there, under the surface. I suppose I should have—" Tom made a sound and Connie put her hand on his arm, almost consoling, stroking it slightly. "I know. There have been other things. And they'll work it through. Because it doesn't matter now."

"Yes, it does."

"Elizabeth, this isn't the time."

"You're wrong, Tom. We all wish Connie could take the time to grieve. But this isn't going to wait for her and the boys to heal. They have to deal with this now. For one thing, Rich Taylorman isn't going to sit back and let it be. Neither is law enforcement."

"Taylorman," she repeated with distaste. "He's the reason we couldn't even tell our friends and neighbors what was truly happening, because Taylorman might use honest mistakes as supposed proof that Brian didn't really have what we knew he had.

"Liver cancer as a result of untreated Hepatitis C. The doctors think he got Hepatitis C from a blood transfusion as a teenager. They didn't know to screen blood for Hepatitis C then. They never knew it was damaging his liver. Not until the cancer. If he'd known, there were things that might have helped. He'd given up smoking but he drank a little and the meds for aches and such he'd have gone without."

This sounded familiar ... yet Connie said they hadn't told their friends or neighbors.

Connie shook her head. "It was the perfect storm. A death sentence. All he could say was how grateful he was it wasn't genetic. And he hadn't transmitted it, not knowing."

The perfect storm. Loriana had used that phrase the night of the search. She'd also told me nearly the same story of how Brian had come to have terminal liver cancer.

The same story...

"What's the matter, Elizabeth?"

"I... I've heard this before. Even that phrase 'the perfect storm.' "

I had a vision of Austin arriving in those clearly fresh clothes. Creased and clean as if he'd just put them on. And Connie patting the jeans, stroking the sleeve...

"You couldn't have. Only the family—" Connie broke it off, staring at me.

Then I could see something else from that night and knew more than which son was Loriana's lover.

I saw Connie slapping Loriana across the face. And her satisfaction.

There are powerful feelings you're messing with here. Did Shelton know how right he was?

"Connie, you knew Austin was sleeping with Loriana, didn't you?"

"No," Tom said. "He's not—"

"Yes," Connie said.

Tom cursed, low and vehement. "You never said anything."

"No, I didn't. Not to anyone. Not even Brian."

"You never spoke to Austin about it?"

"Worst thing in the world would be to make him feel he needed to defend her. Bad enough his brother was on him about it. But I couldn't let Kade know I knew, either."

"That must have been hard."

"Yeah," she said in dry understatement. "Nothing ever felt so good as slapping her across the face. Others might have thought it was to snap her out of it, but she knew. Oh, yes, she knew."

Remembering Loriana's expression, I agreed.

"Connie, you've got to talk to Austin about this now. But first, get James Longbaugh—"

My phone rang, then announced it was the station calling.

I pushed on. "It gives Austin a motive for Don. If Shelton doesn't already know, he will soon. Better he hears it from—"

Audrey's voice came from the phone, leaving a message. "Elizabeth. You've got to get back here right away. You've got to be in the story conference. They're running a 'Helping Out' piece today and Les is on the warpath that you're not here. Get back *now*."

When the voice ended, the three of us looked at each other.

"Go," Tom said. "I'll get James."

"**THURSTON'S UPDATE ON** the county attorney and sheriff's jobs fell through," Jennifer said, greeting me at the door.

"So I hear. What? Someone couldn't write a news release?"

"Audrey said to get you in the meeting as soon as you came. Thurston was making noises about stepping in and doing an update on 'those deaths' if you don't have a 'Helping Out' to plug the hole."

"Plug a hole? I've got enough to build the whole dike."

A few noses wrinkled as I wormed my way into Les' office. Eau d' Babe lingered on my clothes.

"Nice of you to show up, Elizabeth," Haeburn said snidely.

"Thank you. I heard 'Helping Out' is on the budget today."

"Yes, whichever is up first in the queue. Next—"

"No. I'm swapping in the new piece on insurance scams."

Haeburn glowered. "If it's not ready—"

"It is." It would be.

He flipped his hand, a gesture that clearly said it made no difference to him.

"…and then Warren's piece on Wyoming Winter Weather Awareness Day. Followed by—"

"*What* day?" I demanded.

"Wyoming Winter Weather Awareness," Warren Fisk said. "The National Weather Service does it every year. Reminding people to get vehicles winterized, prepare their snowbound kits for house and car, things like that."

He sounded delighted. He rarely was allowed anything beyond the basics.

"Actually, we don't get all that much snow. It's the wind that makes it tough." He chuckled. "In fact, the Weather Service says it's hard to measure accumulations because the snow just doesn't stay put."

I did not share his amusement.

Chapter Forty-Four

POLISHING THE INSURANCE scam piece kept me occupied. Along with changing out of my Babe-infused clothes into a studio backup outfit I kept at the station.

Still, I took a moment for follow-up research.

Forget horror novels, I read the National Weather Service's synopsis of a Wyoming winter. Snow falls October to May—*May*—though it can start in September. That had to be in the mountains, right?

No, the Weather Service cheerfully reported, that was "across the lower elevations."

An average winter has five snowfalls of more than five inches. Snowfalls of ten to fifteen inches are "infrequent outside of the mountains." So if I stayed in Sherman, my first rule would be to not set foot in the mountains from September to May.

And then the National Weather Service landed its heaviest blow:

High winds, low temperatures, and moderate to heavy snow and or blowing snow cause blizzard or near blizzard conditions. These conditions sometimes last a day or two, but it is uncommon for a severe blizzard to last over three days.

Well, *that* was reassuring. Uncommon over three days. A walk in the park for anything short of that, apparently. That is if you took your emergency kit along for that walk in the park.

Oh, wait. No. Because the National Weather Service's first word of advice is to stay indoors and avoid "exposure." At that point I was thinking the best way to avoid exposure was to stay indoors in Florida.

I am not a weather wimp. I'm not. I grew up in northern Illinois. I know snow. I've lived in New York City. I know snow-snarled traffic. I've lived in Washington, D.C. I know panic over a flake.

What I don't know—but have seen plenty of here in Cottonwood County, Wyoming—are mountains, something Chicago, New York City, and D.C. don't have.

What had I been thinking to let Mel talk to KWMT-TV?

FROM THE ANCHOR desk, Thurston Fine said perkily, "When we come back, amazing video of a tornado that has devastated the small town of Orlington, Illinois, east of Chicago."

As soon as it went to commercial, I said, "West. West of Chicago."

I'd zipped in to the control room to be one hundred percent sure they had the right "Helping Out" piece ready.

Now, I looked at Bruce, Fine's favorite producer. "Tell him."

"I'm not telling him." He was Fine's favorite because he let Fine do whatever he wanted.

"It's your job." I glared.

"I'm not telling him."

I shouldn't have wasted my time. He put up with Thurston Fine, which meant he had no heart or soul left to be stirred by my glare.

I leaned in a whole lot closer than I'd ever wanted to be to Bruce, and said, "Thurston."

He looked up and around as if the voice had come from the heavens.

Bruce hastily put his hand over the microphone, clipping me in the jaw in the process, to smother a splutter of background laughter.

"Thurston," I repeated once the mic was open again, and needing to work my jaw a bit. "It's west. West of Chicago."

"What is?" He tried to scowl past the lights into the booth. Good luck with that.

"The town flattened by a tornado, the one you said was east of Chicago. Orlington, Illinois is west of Chicago. What's east of Chicago is a lot of water called—"

"Are you insane? Discussing geography now? I'm on the air."

"I know you're on the air, that's why I'm telling you—"

"Bruce," he shouted.

Bruce jerked away, getting the mic out of range. "Yes, Thurston... Yes... No. Absolutely. You're absolutely right." He turned to me and said ostentatiously. "You must leave the booth immediately."

"He's putting that town in the middle of Lake Michigan. He's making—"

"Leave now."

Every fiber in my journalistic soul wanted to correct the mistake. But Thurston and Bruce had made it clear that wasn't going to happen. So I could only take my consolation prize that he was making more of a fool of himself than usual and leave.

"THESE ARE REPORTS of people presenting themselves as bona fide insurance agents, who have been arrested in the past year for stealing their clients' money," I told "Helping Out" listeners. I riffled the stack of pages.

Riffling is an important ability for any TV journalist whose best video is a stack of paper. But you have to do it right.

Too fast and it's not impressive. Too slow and it's not eye-catching. Worst of all, if you get the angle wrong, the pages flop over like a dead fish.

I am a good riffler.

I should add that to my resumé.

"The most frequent scam is when a purported agent takes the client's money that is meant to be paying the premium and instead pockets the money, leaving the client completely uninsured.

"These thieves—" I tapped the stack of pages. "—frequently provide falsified proof of insurance to their victim clients. Sometimes developing elaborate schemes involving forgery and shell companies.

"How can you protect yourself against such schemes? Never write a check for insurance to the individual insurance agent or to his or her private company. Instead, write your check only to the insurance company who is named on the policy. Send it directly to the company without going through any middleman. And check directly with the company—not through the agent—that your policies are, indeed, paid up and in force."

"Experts say be especially wary of someone who inserts himself or herself into the situation for which you're making a claim. Insurance companies have experts to explore a claim with you."

Next, the interviews warned listeners about a scam in which thieves pretending to be agents called targets, saying their insurance was about to be canceled for lack of payment. They particularly targeted new widows. They would say the husband had taken out a life insurance policy he hadn't told his wife about. But it required one final payment—usually in a specific amount, say $3,892.48, to lend it authenticity. If they'd make that payment, everything would be fine.

Alternatively, the scammers would say all they needed was a little information to tie up the loose ends of a life insurance policy and send the widow the payout—little things like social security number, bank numbers, and passwords.

It never ended well for the widow.

I wrapped up and tossed back to Thurston.

With a big smile, he said, "Sure hope it turns out better for those widows than it did for the residents of Orlington, Illinois, that town east of Chicago that was hit by a tornado."

Chapter Forty-Five

DIANA HAD BEEN headed for the exit, but detoured to my desk.

I had my elbows on the desk, chin in my palms.

"Want me to get you some dinner and bring it back?"

"No. Thanks."

"Still in the I'm-not-accomplishing-anything-pit?"

"It's gotten deeper and wider." And I might have pulled a fifteen- or sixteen-year-old kid into it with me. True, he wouldn't stay in the pit if he hadn't done anything. I hoped. I prayed. "Did you hear Thurston?"

"You can't let him get you down. Only an idiot like Fine would confuse east and west."

"Not just confuse it. Repeat it."

"Elizabeth, I know what you do here aren't the big stories you covered back East, but they're important, too. Important on a person by person basis."

"Right. Mrs. Atcheson's toaster." Getting that repaired had been my first "Helping Out" achievement.

"Along with a few murderers brought to justice. Plus, look at Connie and her boys."

"I should have stuck with toasters."

"You helped them when you helped clear Tom's name. So Connie kept her job and they had insurance while that weasel Taylorman was trying to cheat them out of it."

"Yeah, and now I seem to be working toward putting one or more of them in jail. Not sure they'd consider that the positive outweighed the negative in that case."

"Elizabeth," Diana said.

I looked up.

"That jack that failed, dropping that baler onto Gary and killing him? It was brand new."

I had no idea how to respond. I waited.

"It never should have failed. It was defective."

"Did you go after—?"

But she was shaking her head. "No. No money for lawyers and no idea how to do it any other way."

She held my gaze.

"Because we didn't have somebody like you around here then. Somebody who knew how to find out things. Somebody who'd dig and dig. We didn't have you. You're doing a good thing, E.M. Danniher. Don't let anything make you think otherwise. Or anyone."

Someone was approaching my desk. Bruce.

Like the voice of doom, he announced, "Les wants to see you in his office. Right now."

"Diana—"

"We'll talk more later."

As I started toward the office, he added, part warning, part anticipation, "Thurston's in there."

My knock on Les Haeburn's door was perfunctory, since Thurston was yelling loudly enough that no one inside could have heard it.

He spun toward me as I entered.

"I will not have this—this *person* yammering in my ear during a show."

"That yammering was telling you that you were putting the town of Orlington, Illinois in Lake Michigan. Bad enough they got leveled with a tornado—which you were damned cheerful about—but you also drowned them."

"Because I prefer an upbeat tone, which, I will remind you has been found to be far more soothing to an audience—"

"For what? Sunday hymns? Not for news. Real news."

"That's—"

"Let's get back on track," Haeburn interrupted.

That pulled us both around to face him. For once, our reactions might have been in sync. Surprise on my part that he'd interrupted Fine, shock on Fine's part.

"I've got an important dinner meeting with…" He wiped a hand across his mouth, as if to wipe out what he might have almost said. "I have to leave in two minutes. Are you saying there was an inaccuracy during the five, Elizabeth?"

Not that Fine had screwed up, just a free-floating inaccuracy, unattached to any stupidity on his anchor's part. "Yes. Thurston placed the town of Orlington in Lake Michigan."

"Don't be ridiculous. I said nothing about Lake Michigan." His haughty triumph would have worked if he'd actually proved something.

"You said—and you can check to be sure I have it word-perfect— 'the small town of Orlington, Illinois, east of Chicago.' The town is *west* of Chicago. What's east of Chicago is Lake Michigan. You put the town in the lake."

Les looked at his watch again, stood, said, "Get it right at ten," and strode out.

Fine and I watched him go. Though this time I don't think our reactions were in sync. His was still stuck in jaw-dropped shock. Mine had shifted to curiosity.

Who was Haeburn going to an important dinner with?

An interesting question considering he usually dropped names as frequently as possible, but this time had kept it quiet.

I SAW A pork pie hat bobbing along the KWMT corridor that led from the main doors.

This day kept getting better and better.

He spotted me and lumbered between the mostly empty desks.

"You're trying to ruin me! I'll sue you. I'll sue this station. I'll sue the network. How can I keep clients with you spouting those lies about me all over the TV?"

"About you? I never mentioned your name."

"Everybody knows I've got the Walterstons' account."

"I never mentioned that name, either."

"Everybody knows—"

"I talked about fake insurance agents cold-calling to scam people. Including new widows. All honest agents should appreciate that being exposed, since it makes them look bad."

"You don't know what it's like," he whined. "This is a huge territory. I have to call people. And if I didn't cold-call, my business would shrink away to nothing."

"So your problem keeping clients predated my report." I looked around at my few colleagues still here. "Everybody hear that?"

"Got it, Elizabeth," one said. Others nodded.

"That's going to hurt your lawsuit, Taylorman. What's also going to hurt you is that I've already had five insurance agents call thanking me for warning people about these scams. I'm going to do a follow-up with them on other aspects of insurance."

Seeing the calculation going on in the moon beneath the pork pie hat was not a pretty sight.

"You could make it up to me with a follow-up," he said. "Might even keep me from suing. But just me, none of those other people."

"I'd have to ask you questions. Like what were you doing by Red Sail Rock today?"

"What does that have to do with—"

"Is insurance covering the repairs to the ditch?"

"Not a penny, not for damage like that. I told Loriana that. But that doesn't have anything to do with that story you had on tonight. The follow-up—"

"Let me think about how that might all work and get back to you."

"When? It's got to be soon to avoid further damage to my reputation. And I'd have to make time in my busy schedule, so—"

"Elizabeth. Phone call on line 8," Jennifer called out.

A couple heads came up, since the newsroom only had six lines total.

But I wasn't about to quibble. "Thanks, Jennifer. I have to take this call." I turned away from Taylorman.

"Call me soon," he said. "Gotta hear from you soon."

I picked up the phone on my desk and said my name. Behind me I heard him shuffle, then start away.

JENNIFER WAS A full-service newsroom aide.

Not only did she contribute to dispatching Taylorman, she went out and got dinner. And, while Mike and I ate before preparing for the ten o'clock, she filled us in on what she'd found out.

"Here's the article on Ernie Salarno's death. Like you heard, he died from a reaction to peanuts. He'd eaten a brownie with peanuts in it. Sheriff's department tried to say it must have been smuggled in."

I skimmed the *Independence* coverage. Needham had been very careful not to get himself sued while still making it clear that the jail—then-run by now-departed Sheriff Widcuff—had been beyond lax in screening visitors. Forget a file in a cake, it sounded like they could have brought in a bazooka in a cello case.

On the other hand, brownies were on that day's menu. Though everyone swore up and down they had no nuts in them.

"I emailed you background on the McCrackens. Nothing exciting."

I opened the email and skimmed, with Mike looking over my shoulder.

"Not a thing," he said.

"True, but we do have the accounts from Penny and Hannah about that encounter between Don and Serena McCracken. I think it's time to follow up on that. Want to go see the McCrackens with me in the morning?"

"You bet. I'll drive—"

"No, I will." The road there was paved and relatively smooth. "I'll meet you here."

"Wish I could go," Jennifer said.

That made me a bit guilty. I hadn't considered asking her.

"We'll have a get-together tomorrow night if everyone can make it. Get everybody caught up. Can you arrange that, Jennifer?"

She brightened. "Sure. Oh, yeah, and I found out Loriana's husband was declared dead last month."

"*Declared* dead? I thought he was shot."

"He was. They found bullets, but there was no body."

"Then doesn't it take seven years?" Mike asked.

"Not necessarily," I said. "If there's a lot of evidence the person is dead, a court—"

Jennifer nodded vigorously. "The reports said there was plenty of evidence. Like lots of his blood, his clothes, his ID, and—"

"That could be faked," Mike said.

"—DNA from brain matter," she finished.

"Not so easy to fake," he said. "But if that was just last month... Everybody thought Don and Loriana were married. So unless they got married in the past month, she doesn't automatically inherit. I thought that might be a motive." The bloom sure was off that rose if he was considering her potential motives for murder.

Then the other side of it hit me. "What a dope I am. I went right along with everybody thinking they were married, too, but they couldn't be because Mindy hasn't been declared dead. Has she?"

"I'll check," Jennifer said.

"Unless—could Don have divorced her since she went missing?"

"I'll check. But does it really matter these days?"

"It matters because of what Mike said. If they're not married, Loriana doesn't automatically inherit. So who does?"

"If he has a will—" Mike started.

"I'll find out if he has a will and who inherits if he doesn't," Jennifer said. Definitely full-service.

THIS PHONE MESSAGE from Mel said to call back no matter what the time.

I considered waiting until I was in bed in the bunkhouse, but why make Mel stay up? It wasn't his fault I didn't want to hear that I was likely to be unemployed at the end of the month.

So I called as I drove.

I listened and absorbed. But I waited to consider what he'd said for when I was snug under the covers against the front arriving from Canada and with Shadow on guard—or sound asleep, they looked suspiciously similar—in the bunkhouse.

FIVE GOOD OFFERS. Not bad for someone booted out of her career nine months ago.

Two in D.C., one in Philadelphia, one in Chicago, and one in Sherman, Wyoming.

That was in the first two paragraphs of Mel's email that had followed up his phone call. Then came the details.

On paper, the one in Philadelphia looked the best. Chicago was a bigger market, but that job would be a step back to beat reporting. Not a step back from what I was doing here, of course, but a step back from what I had been doing in New York. Same with one of the D.C. jobs. And not prime beats by any means. Both came with promises of being kept in mind for anchor spots, but I'd count on a surefire system for winning the lottery before I'd count on TV news promises.

Philly would be somewhere new for me. That could be interesting.

Or I could try the rather amorphous second offer from D.C. A temporary full-time position. A real gamble. At its best, it would be something I could mold into what I wanted it to be. At its worst it could be a disaster. Hard to tell.

The last paragraph outlined an offer from KWMT-TV. A surprising offer. Not much money, but some definite perks.

Five offers.

Not bad? Hell, Mel had worked a miracle.

That thought echoed in my head.

How had it gotten to the point that I'd needed a miracle?

It wasn't because Wes had carried me up the career ladder. He'd had nothing to do with the work I'd done here in Sherman. And the work was good. Damned good.

So how had things gotten into such a mess?

The answer must have been waiting in the back of my mind for me to ask the question, because out popped the answer: I hadn't done the things necessary to protect my career. I hadn't made the connections, kept the relationships, paid attention to the hirers and firers. I'd left all of that to Wes.

You insure the things you value. So what does that say about something you don't bother to insure? Or let someone else hold the policy on?

No answer to those questions.

And they didn't help any with what I faced right now.

I had to make a decision.

DAY TEN
WEDNESDAY

Chapter Forty-Six

WARDELL YARDLEY CALLED as I drove to the station to pick up Mike for our trip to the McCrackens.

I debated not answering.

But Dell's voice as he started to leave a message prompted me to grab the call.

Something was up.

"Have a job on the line?" he asked as soon as I answered. "Returning to the network? I heard a rumor about Chicago. Taking my excellent advice and setting up shop for yourself so you can tell the damned BBs—" Big Bosses in Dell speak. "—to do certain anatomically impossible acts? Tell Uncle Dell all and tell me now, so I have the scoop."

"You'd have the scoop on me, because I don't know."

"You better get cracking. You're down to weeks before you depart that backwater and return to our shark-infested pool. You should have your teeth sharpened and your fins in high gear."

"Is that how you see our business?"

"You bet. So do you." He was on edge, though I couldn't figure out why.

"What about justice, Dell?"

"The Department of? It's a mess. The latest screw-up is—"

"No. I mean justice with a lower j. Or maybe it should have the capital j and the department should have the lowercase. But either way,

I mean the concept."

"Don't get philosophical on me, Danny. We report the news, we don't make it. Including the occasional justice among the injustices."

"Too many injustices. What if there's a way to influence that?"

"Your next job is going to be caped crusader?" His chuckle was strained. "You're serious? Oh, God, you're *not* thinking about staying out there in Hicksville are you?"

"It's not Hicksville. It's—"

"I know, I know. Grant or Lee or—"

"—Sherman. And I don't know if I'm thinking about it. Exactly."

"You listen to me." The edge sharpened. "You got thrown on your head and it shook you up, but now it's time to get back on the horse—"

"A horse metaphor, Dell? Really?"

"—and get your ass back where you belong. You understand? The first second you're out of that contract, you get on a plane and get here to D.C. and I will guarantee you a good job in a week. Two max. Forget an agent. Wardell Yardley will take care of you."

"I'm touched, truly I am, Dell." I also was suspicious. "But why are you so invested in this?"

"Because you have too much talent, you're too good a reporter to languish out there."

"Doesn't KWMT-TV deserve good reporting?

"No."

"Dell, what's really got you in such a froth?"

There was a pause then, he said in a tight voice, "Dammit, Danny, I'm counting on you."

"What—? Is something seriously wrong?"

"Yes, something's seriously wrong. Because I asked around getting you background that ended up with the discovery of that gold a while back, this idiot baby BB with too much time on his buffed and polished little hands decided it would be 'synchronicity' for me—*me!*— to go out there and do a piece. Make me more relatable by having me rub elbows with the common people. I couldn't tell this half-brained BB who happens to be related to the top BB—how else would he get a job?—what I thought of his idea, so I said it would only work if the great E.M. Danniher was on the ground there. Never thinking you would be. But if you're still there, they'll actually send me. For a week—a *week*, Danny. And you would not believe the shark they want to put in for me. I've been delaying vacation waiting for this glossy cutout to reveal his feet of cardboard, because I do *not* want him in my spot until he does and—What? What are you laughing at?"

"You, Dell. I'm laughing at you. Oh, God, I might have to stay here no matter what, just to get you to Sherman, Wyoming to see how the two of you get along. Oh, and to have you meet Thurston Fine, because he has the exact same attitude. He also thinks I'm a shark."

"What is a Thurston Fine? No, don't tell me. I don't want to know. But this is no laughing matter, Elizabeth Margaret Danniher. You belong here, in the big-time. You're great at it. It's what you've always wanted to do. It's what you're meant to do."

"For now what I'm meant to do is keep working the best way I know how while I finish out this contract. Which is why I have something to ask you."

He groaned. "Oh, God, is this going to mean a second week in Hellhole, Wyoming for me?"

I DIDN'T KNOW what it might mean for Dell, but I was pleased that our call gave me a contact in the Denver police department's major crimes division.

I called as I reached the highway.

Dell's contact hadn't worked the case, but transferred me to the detective who had.

Detective Trudy Bellefleur and I were hedging around each other when Mike climbed in to my SUV in the KWMT-TV lot. She used the it's-an-open-case line a few times and I countered with the public-record argument an equal number of times.

She broke the logjam by suggesting I talk to the insurance company. It had balked at paying out on the policy, which had still listed Loriana as beneficiary, because of the lack of a body.

I said, "You're thinking the estranged wife had motive? Killing him off before he could change the policy?"

"Do you have any idea how many people are walking around with outdated policies? Plus, the wife wasn't here. Was. Not. Here. That's solid."

"Spouses outsource killi—"

"Pros do not take the body," she talked over me. "Especially not if you're thinking the wife wanted the insurance payout. She *still* doesn't have that money. She'd have to be a real screwup or one hell of a patient murderer."

She had a point. And I admitted it.

That didn't thaw her, but at least she didn't vow to block any future calls from me.

✧   ✧   ✧   ✧

THIS TIME MCCRACKEN came around the corner of the wraparound porch and waited for us as we got out of my SUV.

The man seemed determined that I would never cross his threshold.

"Now what?" he asked. He didn't even seem impressed by Mike's presence. Boy, he *was* an outsider in Cottonwood County.

No point in leading up to it gently with him taking that tone.

"We'd like to talk to your wife."

"You're not talking to my wife."

"We have accounts from witnesses to an incident with Don Hazen and we'd like to hear both sides."

"Both sides? There's only side—that son of a bitch touched my wife inappropriately. If I'd seen it—"

"What would you do, Mr. McCracken?"

He ground his jaw but said nothing.

"You know there were also witnesses to what you did to Hazen. How you put your hands around his throat and threatened him."

"He deserved worse than that." He cursed Hazen. "She said she'd handled it and I believe that. I do. But I had to let him know he'd deal with me if he ever touched her again."

That was Saturday night, Hazen was dead by Tuesday morning,

and McCracken still didn't seem to have cooled off much.

"Mr. McCracken, where were you last week from Monday afternoon to Tuesday morning?"

His anger didn't evaporate, yet his postured eased slightly.

"I was in Cheyenne on business. Left Sunday. Came back Tuesday afternoon."

I fought to keep my jaw from dropping. "But you said you regretted not going out on the search. If you weren't here—"

His mouth went grim. "I mouthed off to the first person who made a comment about me not searching for Brian and then it was too late to start making excuses about being out of town. But Shelton knows. He's confirmed I was where I said I was. Besides, I'm not the only one who was that angry at Hazen. *My* wife dealt with him. Doesn't sound like the same can be said for Hannah Chaney. So, what do you think Paul Chaney would do about that?"

Chapter Forty-Seven

I DIDN'T BUY it a hundred percent. After all, Hannah was living with Terry Waymark and Paul hadn't killed him. Not yet, anyway.

But further conversation with Paul made sense.

"You okay with going by Paul Chaney's?" I asked Mike.

"Yeah. I'll call Pauly to pick up an interview for me."

Before he made that call, he gave me directions for a "more direct" route no navigation system would ever consider. It got us there, but I was going to have to take the SUV to the car wash—or was it a vehicle wash in Wyoming?—first chance I got.

The white pickup and red dog were near the house. In fact, the red dog was in the back of the pickup. But Paul Chaney didn't appear in response to my toot on the horn.

The dog hopped out of the back of the truck quickly. "Think he's friendly?" I asked Mike.

"Probably. As long as we don't try to steal anything."

So we got out, made friends with the dog, then I headed toward the house. Simply to look in the windows, no more ... unless a door was open. But with my hand on the knob, I heard, "Elizabeth."

"I was just testing."

"Come look at this." The way he said it and the fact that he was looking into the bed of the white truck made me think he hadn't been aware of my door-testing.

I joined him and saw the bed was empty except for a medium-sized black garbage back tied at the top but with a gash in the side, allowing some of the contents to spill out. I strongly suspected the red dog of creating the spill.

"Water, an army knife, flashlight. But what's that?" I pointed to something poking out.

"Signal flare. And I'll bet there'll be food and a disposable phone and all the other things Brian Walterston would have had with his wheelchair."

WE DIDN'T TOUCH anything and got in my SUV. While I backed up—so if somebody happened to come home they would have no reason to think we had seen what was in the back of the pickup—Mike called the sheriff's department.

Shelton wasn't available. That seemed to be Deputy Ferrante's only line. Alvaro, either. But he got Lloyd Sampson. Mike explained succinctly, and Sampson said he'd come out right away, and we were not to move until he got here.

"Awfully damned convenient," Mike said when he hung up. "McCracken points us in this direction and, bang, all that stuff's right out there in the open?"

"Can't close your eyes to evidence."

"I didn't," he said grimly. "I saw it, but I don't believe it. I don't see Paul killing Brian. Or Don. On top of that, we still haven't talked to Serena McCracken, not with her husband sending us off on this— Are you listening?"

"No. I'm trying to find FreeCell on this damned phone."

"You told Jennifer not to put it on your phone."

I swore again.

"Listen," Mike said. "Let's talk this out, starting with Brian going missing."

What choice did I have? We went through the facts and were starting on the speculation when my phone rang.

Jennifer. Thank heavens. I hit speaker phone and answered with, "Can you load FreeCell on my phone remotely?"

"No. but—"

My *arrgh* drowned her out.

"Elizabeth's having FreeCell withdrawal," Mike said.

"We should be at the station soon, maybe then—?"

She shot down my hope. "I'm at home. Day off. You'll have to wait until I see you tonight at Diana's. I got that all set with Diana and Tom. Seven-thirty."

I sighed at the inevitable. "Okay. But if you could possibly put it on my phone without Tom knowing..."

"Why?"

"Never mind. It doesn't matter." He'd probably find out anyway. "Thanks for setting up tonight, Jennifer. Listen, there's one more thing to check."

I told her about the insurance policy on Loriana's husband and asked her to see what she could find. Yes, you're right. I had no compunction about asking her to tackle that bureaucracy.

"Sure. Do you still want to see that photo Taylorman took? I cleaned it up. Looks pretty good now."

"Great. Send it."

"Already did. Oh, I almost forgot to tell you why I called—who inherits from Don Hazen. I found this great info online and it goes through a sequence. If he doesn't have a wife or kids or parents or siblings, it goes to his cousins."

"Cousins." I heard Leona D'Amato's voice saying, *Did you know Paul Chaney and Don Hazen were cousins?* "I know about one cousin. I wonder how many he has."

"I wondered about that, too, so I called Mrs. P. He only has one cousin—Paul Chaney."

❖   ❖   ❖   ❖

NOT ONLY HAD Jennifer shown initiative by calling Mrs. Parens to check on Don Hazen's cousins, she had also done a remarkable job on the photo.

We could even make out expressions of the people on the right side of the shot now. Connie's grief, Austin's shock, Kade's horror. The dismay of those around them. Cas Newton was to one side, looking grim, perhaps because Loriana, cupping one of her hands with the other, stood next to him. Close. Taylorman also had caught the acting chief in profile, with his mouth open.

On the left was the body of Brian Walterston and the overturned wheelchair.

And open space, missing all those items that now sat in the bed of Paul Chaney's pickup truck.

✧   ✧   ✧   ✧

"THERE'S SAMPSON," MIKE said.

We'd been going round and round. The facts pointed toward Paul Chaney. And how many times had friends and neighbors said of a murderer "He was such a nice guy"?

But neither of us seemed able to say it was settled and done.

"About time—"

My phone interrupted my complaint. It also stopped me from opening my door to go try to wring information out of the deputy. It was a call coming in through my work line.

"KWMT-TV, E.M. Dann—"

"Elizabeth." It was Tom. "I'm not coming tonight to Diana's."

"Okay," I said slowly. There was a whole lot more in his tone than a-sorry-I-can't-make-it RSVP.

"Jennifer put me through to you. She said you'd want to hear it from me—I'm on my way to the sheriff's department. Connie's asked for me."

Had Shelton been out making an arrest when we called in? Could they already have Paul in custody? Or—

"Connie? They haven't—*She* hasn't been arrested?"

"No. The truck Hiram Poppinger spotted? It was Kade's. When they started to question him, Austin stepped in and swore he took it that day. They've arrested Austin. For murder."

Chapter Forty-Eight

SOMEONE HAD CALLED Thurston, so he had the front door to the sheriff's department office staked out with a camera crew and was waiting for the official announcement.

Austin Walterston was already inside the sheriff's department when Connie had called Tom, much less when Thurston arrived, so there'd been no perp walk.

Mike and I bypassed that scene. Partly because we didn't want to consort with Thurston, of course. Only a little bit because he would have gone apoplectic on us—actually that made going there tempting. But we withstood that temptation because we had our eye on the back parking lot used by deputies.

Thurston and the cameras had been gone about twenty minutes when I swatted Mike's arm, then opened my door.

"Something's happening out front. Let's go."

Actually several things were happening.

Connie Walterston was leaving the sheriff's department, accompanied by her two older sons, Tom, and James Longbaugh.

Paul Chaney, in handcuffs, was being accompanied up the front walk by Deputy Lloyd Sampson, and trailed by Otto Chaney.

And a small blue pickup was being abandoned a good five feet from the red zone curb in front of the sheriff's department.

Hannah Chaney came out of the blue pickup, gave a keening cry when she saw Paul, and hurried the best she could to intercept Paul and Sampson.

"*No, no, no.*"

"It's all right, Hannah. It's all right."

Paul tried to touch her but the handcuffs prevented it. He looked at Sampson.

Sampson unlocked one handcuff. "Only one," he said like that made a difference.

Paul put his arms around his wife and she sobbed into his chest.

"Don't cry, honey. It's okay, Hannah. It will all be okay."

"No. How… Nothing is…"

"You go on home now. It'll be okay."

"I can't go back to—"

His jaw went rigid. "Home. *Our* home."

She looked up at him, hope and fear in equal parts. "Oh, Paul…"

"Shouldn't be alone in her state," Sampson said. "You go on home with Otto, Hannah."

"Not me." Otto used the same tone Butterfly McQueen had in *Gone with the Wind* to cry, "I don't know nothin' 'bout birthin' babies." He recovered enough to say, "I'm staying here with Paul. Get him a lawyer or bail or whatever he needs."

James Longbaugh put a hand on Paul's shoulder. "I'll call somebody for you. I can't—"

"Doesn't matter about me. Hannah—"

"She's coming home with me." Connie's calm declaration quieted everyone.

Paul looked over Hannah's head at her. "Connie, you know they're saying—Brian. They think I might have—"

"They think Austin—" She swallowed, started again. "Whatever happens, you'll know Hannah will be fine with us. C'mon, honey. All this sobbing isn't good for you or the baby."

They sorted out, with Paul, Sampson, and Otto heading inside and the rest starting toward cars.

All except Tom, who looked from Connie to where Mike and I stood.

My phone rang. I almost dropped it. Recovering dragged one corner across my healing palm scrapes. This better be worth the sting.

"Hello?" I stopped.

Jennifer. "Stinking insurance company kept stalling for _years_, but they ran out of ways to block it now that he's been declared dead. You should do a story on that."

I'd heard what she said, but that wasn't where my mind was.

I was hearing all the voices saying how obsessed Don Hazen had been.

Click.

Then I was seeing the scene again—the scenes.

At the search center. Greg Niland who'd come to search, then went in search of Loriana. Connie. The boys. The people gathering. Search parties leaving. Loriana listening for pickups that went past, leaving Greg to stew. Then three pickups arriving late. Taylorman. Sam McCracken not there at all, but with an alibi ... but wasn't that suspicious when no one else had one?

Click.

There's what a suspect says and there's what a suspect does.

Dex had been talking about scientific results proving what a suspect does. But observation also counted when a suspect's actions ran contrary to what they said.

Click.

I was too subtle the first time. Not going to make that mistake again.

Click.

"Elizabeth? What would who do?" Mike asked.

I must have said something aloud.

I spotted movement from the building's back door to where deputies parked. Instead of answering, I jabbed Mike, and said, "C'mon."

We caught up with Wayne Shelton before he could reach his vehicle, standing between him and its door.

"There's been an official statement. You missed it."

"We don't want the official statement. We want your—"

"I have nothing to say to the media."

"Are you satisfied that this case is closed, Deputy Shelton?"

"The sheriff's department arrested Austin."

"For both deaths?" Mike asked.

"Yes. Now, go away and let—"

"What about Paul?" Mike interrupted like a pro. "You have him in custody, too."

"He's being questioned while evidence is processed."

"Are *you* satisfied that this case is closed?" I repeated.

He hesitated. Just enough. "I've told you what I'm going to tell you. Unless you have some great new evidence, go away."

At some level I was conscious of Tom coming up behind us, but it seemed as if that were at a distance and in slow motion.

"I do."

"You do what."

"Have some great new evidence—at least where to find it. Look for human remains in Loop Field."

Chapter Forty-Nine

"**WHAT THE *HELL*?**" Shelton muttered, then shot at me, "Who?"

"Mindy."

He glowered. "Why?"

"Because Mindy was sure she could take Don in the divorce, so he got rid of her."

"We've got two men dead last week and you're telling me one of them killed somebody years ago and you want me to go dig up a field on the off chance she's there? If that isn't—"

"Finding Mindy's body—"

"—the biggest mishmash of fact and leaps into the void—"

"—matters to her family."

"—I've ever heard of. Yeah, right, I'm going to take that to the acting chief, who's so scared of his shadow he—"

Tom cleared his throat.

Shelton snapped his mouth closed.

"Equipment's still out there, Wayne. Wouldn't take much."

Shelton looked at him, then at Mike, then up toward the courthouse tower for what seemed like forever. Finally he looked at me. "How strongly do you believe it?"

"What do you mean?"

"I'd be risking a good name for credibility I've built up over twenty-six years. What are you willing to risk?"

"You're *bargaining* with me, Deputy Shelton?"

"Yup."

"*My* credibility is on the line, too."

He made a noise that indicated what he thought of that. "I'll do it if you promise not to ask me another question if you're wrong."

"Do you know something that makes you sure I'm wrong?"

"No." And I believed him. "If I did, I sure as hell wouldn't consider this even to get you to stop asking me questions."

Then I recognized another angle. "You know my contract ends this month, so you're likely bargaining for a short period of time."

"Worth it to be free of your questions for as long as you stay here. If, of course, you're that sure you're right."

"Done."

We shook.

He went to his vehicle, pulling his phone. Then he turned back to us. "No cameras. And if a single one of you shows your nose out at Loop Field, the whole thing's off."

"Oh, come on—"

"I mean it. Stay away. That goes for you, too, Tom. You're getting as bad as the rest of them."

He left. And I began to hear a faint voice calling my name. Probably the worrier at the back of my head saying I should have told him everything.

No. It was Jennifer. I'd never clicked off the phone. And between calling my name, she kept repeating a phrase that paired "Holy" with something decidedly earthy.

As I PULLED into KWMT-TV's parking lot, I spotted Cas Newton's pickup tucked between bigger trucks.

"Mike, would you mind going inside for a minute?"

"I thought we were going to stay out here to talk with Tom when he comes, so we don't get overheard or roped in to something by Haeburn."

Something like our regular jobs.

"I need a few minutes. I'll call you to come out."

I went to the pickup.

I barely had the door closed before Cas accused me. "You told them. About Austin and her."

"I didn't."

"You had to. Otherwise, why did they arrest him?"

"He had Kade's truck and it might have been seen near where his father and Don died."

"So they don't know a motive. If they don't know to ask about it—"

I stopped that hope in its tracks. "Even if they don't—" Though Shelton surely had gotten the same lead from Penny I had. "—they'll ask something general, such as do you know anything else possibly pertinent to the case. You say no and you've lied. They'll get to you eventually, Cas."

Unless Loriana admitted it. Would she?

"It won't do them any good to ask Kade," he said, looking straight ahead. "He doesn't know." As an expression of loyalty, it was touching. It just wasn't believable.

"He knows. He and Austin have given it away dozens of times these past days. Deputy Shelton won't have missed that."

Cas swore. He stared at the tape-covered steering wheel. Swore again. "I'll have to go find Deputy Shelton and tell him."

"They'll still ask Kade."

"But he won't have to live with knowing he was the one who told first. He'll hate me." He shook his head once. "Doesn't matter. I can't let him carry that."

"Let it rest for now, Cas. It might not be necessary."

Still, I had to admire him.

"HOW ON EARTH did you start thinking there were human remains in Loop Field," Diana demanded.

She had accompanied Mike to the SUV when I called him to come back out. As they got in, Tom drove into the lot.

He sat in back, beside Mike, and distributed bags from Hamburger Heaven for our late lunch. Diana said she'd already eaten, but she'd nibbled here and there as we caught her up on what had happened.

Tom contributed details of Shelton's questioning of Kade about his truck, Austin saying he'd taken it that day, and Austin's arrest. Motive had not been mentioned. Yet.

"And why Mindy?" Mike now added to Diana's question.

"Loop Field because that's where Don Hazen was messing with the ditch banks. As for why Mindy? Because I didn't think Shelton would believe me if I said Loriana is a double, possibly triple, and potentially quadruple murderer. No, wait, the peanuts, too. So maybe quintuple."

That drew quite the response.

And since I knew Shelton's would not have been as mild, it made me feel better about my decision to ease Shelton in by looking for Mindy.

"Explain," Diana demanded.

"That photo Taylorman took started it."

"Because the boys looked so surprised," she said.

I turned to her. "They did, didn't they? That fits what's bothered me from the start—the position of Brian's body. As if he'd been dumped out or fell out, tried to reach toward something, and died in the effort."

Mike said, "If one or both of the sons struggles with Don and he goes over the edge, Brian automatically tries to stop it and falls out of the chair."

"Then what?"

"The son goes down to finish off Don."

"I could see either or both doing that—in anger, in fear, and especially in defense of Brian. Even in defense of his desire to die. But then what? Walk away? Without going back up to see if his father was dead or alive? That doesn't fit. And once they went up to check on him, could either son, loving his father as they so clearly did, have left him in that position?"

A low sound hissed out of Tom and he sat back, eyes closed. "Why didn't I see that?"

"You did."

Then left his father sprawled on the ground like that?

That's what he had said. That wrongness he'd pointed out had been scratching at me all along.

Combined with Dex's *There's what a suspect says and there's what a suspect does.* Leaving Brian in the position did not fit with loving sons.

"I didn't believe it enough," he said. "Not nearly enough."

"Neither of those boys has made it easy to believe. The lies, the animosity." Diana faced me. "But if it wasn't their surprise that caught you on the photo, what did?"

"Not anything the rest of you could have picked up. It started when Loriana came out of the house and talked to me. No. When she came out *to* talk to me. To set it up that Don was searching. She watched two pickups pass the road with great interest, saying she was on the lookout for him. But when trucks did pull in—two of them similar to his—she was uninterested."

Mike nodded. "Because she knew Don wasn't coming."

"But what about the photo?" Diana insisted.

"It was her hands. The night of the search, she did that three-finger barely-there handshake. It didn't match her attitude, her personality. But I forgot. Then I saw her holding her hand in that photo the same way I'd held mine after I'd hurt it going down that landslide. I guessed she'd done something similar. Most likely made worse when she dragged Don—'scrawny' Don to quote Jennifer—so his head was in the ditch."

Mike said, "Go back to the field. Explain."

"You all kept saying how strange Don's behavior was, letting the ditch go, potentially hurting his own land. There had to be a reason. And what was the first thing Loriana did after he was killed? Order repairs. Plus, there was what he'd said to Penny about being too subtle the first time."

"Mindy," Diana said.

"But that wasn't the first time he had trouble with a woman. What if Don thought he'd let Loriana get away the first time by not holding on tight enough? He didn't let Mindy get away, but having Loriana dead wouldn't give him what he wanted. So this time, he was going for a solution that kept her here and kept her alive. He was going for a way to control her."

"How was eroding Loop Field controlling her?" Mike said.

"Go back to Loriana as a teenager and how much she wanted to leave, but had no means. Her uncle is arrested. Lo and behold he dies in jail from a peanut in a brownie. People with a peanut allergy are usually very, very careful about what they eat. But would he suspect a brownie from someone who knew of his allergy? Loriana? The aunt? That got me thinking about how the aunt up and left, which was quite convenient for Loriana, since she then had the ranch to sell. But what if Loriana's aunt never left at all."

I heard a ragged chorus of sucked-in breaths as each got what I was saying.

Tom swore under his breath. "You're saying Loriana killed Ellen and buried her in Loop Field."

"Or Don killed her. Loriana practically gave the land to Don. Because she wanted to get away so badly or as payment? Murder for hire, with the payment made in bargain basement prices on ranch land."

"Don was letting water in to erode it, threatening Loriana that the murder would be revealed? That's crazy. He'd have given himself away, too."

"But he'd have kept control of her."

I saw recognition in their eyes as I looked from face to face.

We were still talking it over when Shelton called.

"This fast?" Tom said as I put the call on speaker phone.

Shelton must have heard. "We got there at the right time. Had them dig up instead of fill in. They just called. They found remains."

Chapter Fifty

I **HEARD THE** others releasing their breath, but mine was still held. There was something in his tone...

"Mindy?" I asked.

"No. Definitely not Mindy."

"Ellen?"

"*Ellen?* What the he—? No. They're male remains."

"Male?" I repeated. "How long—?"

"Clothes indicate a few years ago. But I shouldn't be answering your questions, since you were wrong and that was our deal."

My brain was too occupied to respond.

"She wasn't wrong about remains being there," Mike said.

"She said we'd find Mindy. We didn't."

Mike persisted. "You found somebody you'd never have known about if it weren't for Elizabeth putting the pieces together."

"She hasn't put pieces together. More like scattering some around and standing the rest on their heads. Last thing we need is another damned murder case to try to solve."

"He was murdered?" I asked.

"He was shot, anyway. I gotta go."

He hung up.

THOSE PIECES SHELTON had talked about were swirling in my head, rearranging, reconnecting.

Only an idiot like Fine would confuse east and west.

Not just confuse it. Repeat it.

Of course.

I was the idiot.

Because Loriana was *not* an idiot.

"We have to get Shelton." I tapped his number.

"Why?" Mike asked.

"To get him to go double or nothing."

His voicemail answered. I said he needed to call me back. Urgently. And if he refused to call me, he should talk to Detective Bellefleur in Denver. Immediately.

"Explain," Diana demanded.

"Repairs started on the eastern corner of Loop Field even though the western part, the part nearer Red Sail Rock was worse. Austin said Loriana made a mistake in giving the workers the instructions, mixing up east and west like Thurston did with the town hit by the tornado.

"But Loriana isn't Thurston. What if she had her priorities perfectly straight? What if she covered up *her* crime—or crimes—first? She let the other section be fixed later, because that's where Don's victim is. A death she has an airtight alibi for. Probably because Don killed him. Just like he had an airtight alibi for Mindy's disappearance, probably because Loriana killed *her.*

"We have to get Shelton to dig where it's been fixed. And fast. If she knows what they've found, she'll take off and we'll never find her. He's not answering. He's not calling back. We'll have to go out there—"

"No, wait." Diana stopped me from starting the engine. "He said they just called him. That must mean he's not at Red Sail Rock."

"Might be at Paul's looking for more evidence," Mike said.

"Or at Red Sail Ranch," Tom said. "He planned to get Kade's truck taken in to be examined."

"Or he could be anywhere in the county and not have service," Diana said.

"Okay, let's split up. I'll—"

"You and Diana go to the sheriff's department," Mike said firmly. "Get them to radio him. I'll go to Paul's and—"

"I'll swing by Red Sail Rock then check for him at the home

ranch," Tom picked up.

"But—"

"We'll find him. And we'll get him to go double or nothing."

Chapter Fifty-One

MY PHONE RANG as Diana and I jogged into the sheriff's department.

That was not a good start.

"You've got to turn that off in here," Deputy Ferrante ordered from behind the counter.

I hit the button blindly.

"We need to know where Deputy Shelton is."

"He's not here."

"Where is he?"

"I don't know."

Did the man ever share any good news? "Can you radio him? It's urgent. Please."

"He left word that he did not want to be disturbed by you, Ms. Danniher."

"Deputy Alvaro—"

"Him, either. Or Sampson. None of them want to be disturbed by you."

"Listen, Deputy—" Diana started.

But I was pulling on her arm, tugging her outside. Ferrante was not going to help.

As soon as we were on the other side of the door, I called Mike's Aunt Gee.

"We have to talk to Deputy Shelton. He left word not to be disturbed and Ferrante won't even try. Can you help us?"

She clucked. "Wayne went off radio. Said there was an emergency he had to deal with. But I'll try. I'll call around, see what I can find out."

"There's something else. The workers on Red Sail Ditch, are they still there?"

"The regular crew knocked off for the day." Her voice was more cautious. Either I'd ventured too close to what she considered official business or someone was listening to her. "They're going to get experts in to pick up on that."

Damn. It made sense, but it would delay things.

I thanked her only briefly, wanting to get off to let her get started finding Shelton.

Back in my SUV, I hit the button to get the message that had come in and listened.

"What is it?" Diana demanded.

I hit call back without answering.

"Loriana?" As I spoke, Diana jolted. "It's Elizabeth Margaret Danniher. You called me?"

"Yes, I did. Thank you so much for calling back. I've been in Cody all day. Just got back and now I'm hearing things… But I can't get any information. Deputy Shelton isn't returning my calls—" Join the club. "—and it's driving me crazy. With Don … and not knowing anything, I'm not sure anyone can understand what it's like."

"Connie—"

"Oh, of course, of course. That's one of the things I've heard, that she and all the boys were at the sheriff's department, but then there was something with Paul Chaney and—Oh, please. I know this is a lot to ask, but could we meet to talk? I have so many questions and you seem to know so much more than was just on the TV news."

For once I was thankful for Thurston's journalistic ineptitude.

"Meet?" My word widened Diana's eyes. "We can do that. If you come to the station—"

"Oh, I can't. But… Could you come to the ranch?"

I was thinking hard. "Your ranch? I get so lost in the county, I'd never get there." I sounded appropriately ditzy. "What about Red Sail Rock? I do know where that is."

Diana, who'd relaxed a bit when I mentioned the station, shook her head vehemently. But I was remembering two things:

Tom had said Red Sail Rock wouldn't leave someone vulnerable to attack—as long as she stayed away from the edge.

And the geography I'd lied about not knowing. Red Sail Rock was close to the Walterstons' house and not far from Paul Chaney's place, the two most likely locations for Deputy Shelton as well as the destinations for Tom and Mike.

✧   ✧   ✧   ✧

"MEETING LORIANA WOULD be crazy," Diana said as soon as I disconnected.

"We'll leave Shelton a message. He'll have to check in soon, wherever he is. We'll tell him what's happening and—"

"No way. It'll be close to sunset by the time—"

"If I can get her talking—and that is what I do, right? Get people talking—this might be our only chance. It can't hurt. If she's already suspicious, she's not going to get any *less* suspicious."

"You can't. She's killed—"

"That's why I have to try. We'll have Shelton and a hundred other deputies around—*Ah!*"

We'd screamed in unison and not like when Cottonwood County High scored a touchdown.

Someone had knocked on the driver's window beside my head.

With my heart hammering fast enough to close up my throat, I turned and saw Paul Chaney.

My fingers shook at I hit the button to lower the window.

"Sorry to startle you, ma'am, but I wondered if you could give me a ride, if you happen to be going out by Red Sail Ranch?"

I suspected we gaped at him stupidly, because he looked puzzled as he continued. "They just released me and I can't get a hold of Otto for a ride. But Hannah's with Connie there, so I hoped…"

"As it happens, we are going to Red Sail Ranch," I said. "Hop in."

"You can't," Diana said to me.

But I was already pulling away, barely giving Paul time to pull the back door closed.

"Keep calling Shelton. Mike and Tom, too. Paul, you wouldn't mind a little detour, would you?"

WHERE THE HELL was Shelton?

Diana, Paul, and I had pulled up behind Red Sail Rock with twelve minutes to go before Loriana's appointed time.

Diana had left messages while I drove like ... well, like Diana.

She'd not only called Shelton numerous times, she'd left messages for Tom, Mike, Deputy Alvaro, and Deputy Sampson. Even a message for Cas Newton on the wild chance that he'd ignored my advice and found Shelton, since Cas was more likely than Shelton to answer a call from someone associated with me. With all those SOSs out there, I'd hoped the cavalry would already be encamped at Red Sail Rock.

Not only was there no cavalry, but when we carefully checked on the other side of Red Sail Rock—in case Loriana was one of those early-arrivers—we'd confirmed that the machines were quiet and deserted, with a large area encircled by police tape.

That left Diana, me, and Paul.

He'd wanted to stop by the ranch house but I outvoted him by refusing to stop the SUV.

We hadn't taken the time to explain what was happening. And I don't know how much he heard of what Diana was saying because I was asking him questions.

"Paul, why were you late to the search?"

"I told you—"

"The real reason."

"I suppose it doesn't matter now. Might as well... I was following Waymark. In case—Anyway, I followed him."

"Where did you follow him to?"

"Why does that matter?"

"It doesn't. Unless it was to Red Sail Rock. Did you follow him there?"

"Red Sail? No. I followed him from the Kicking Cowboy where he'd had a liquid lunch, then back to his place. After a couple hours, I followed him to the search."

"And Otto was right behind you?"

He grimaced. "Yeah, the old fool. Like he thought I'd do something to Waymark."

"So, neither of your white trucks was parked by the ditch near Red Sail Rock?"

"No. Hey, you're not trying to say Otto or I—They released me."

"Yes, they did, and I'm not trying to say anything. I'm eliminating."

"Vehicle coming," Paul said now.

A vehicle approached from the direction of the Red Sail Ranch house.

So the good news was it wasn't Loriana. The bad news was it wasn't a sheriff's department vehicle.

Chapter Fifty-Two

IT WAS CAS Newton.

"What did you do, Cas?" Diana asked, gesturing to his sling.

He grimaced. "Got throwed over the weekend. Was having a real good ride and—"

I interrupted, "Where's Shelton?"

"He's at the house. Sent word that he'd be up here shortly."

"*Shortly?*" I repeated. "Did he get my messages?"

"Don't think so. He's been so busy we haven't had a chance to talk." He gave me a significant look. "He's been on the phone with somebody else. Somebody told him you'd been calling, but—"

"When is he coming?" Diana asked.

"I don't know, there's a lot—"

"Vehicle," Paul said. "Other direction."

He was right. A vehicle on the up-ramp along the ditch. "I'm going out there and—"

"Elizabeth. No—" Diana started.

"Stay here, behind this rock, all of you. Call Shelton back and tell him to get up here. Then keep *quiet*."

"I'm going with you," Paul said.

"No. None of you," I added as Diana and Cas opened their mouths. "She won't say anything unless it's just me."

"Ma'am, I don't think—" That was Cas.

"I need witnesses. When Shelton gets here, I want you all to be able to tell him every word that was said."

I strode around the rock, crossing the open area to see her climbing from her vehicle—yes, another white pickup—then retreated close to Red Sail Rock so my witnesses could hear.

"Thank you so much for meeting me, Elizabeth. Do you know what's going on? I'm so confused."

"About what, Loriana?"

"Well, like the repairs. They said they'd go late to finish today, but they're gone and there's *police* tape there."

"I bet that was a surprise when you came back from—where was it you said? Cody? All day? No time for a detour by Paul Chaney's place this morning? Nice friendly dog he has. His pickup out there in the open. Easy to put something in it."

"I don't understand, Elizabeth." Her wide dark eyes were puzzled and sincere.

"It'll save time if you accept that I know, Loriana. How's your hand?"

Automatically, she curled it at her side. But she didn't fold. "Know? There's nothing to know."

"Oh, there's quite a bit to know. I've wondered. How did you and Don get back together after all that time?"

She smiled pleasantly. "He had a knack for tracking me down. Out of the blue he'd call, telling me his troubles."

"He called saying Mindy was ready to leave him? Is that how it started?"

"You're confused, Elizabeth. I didn't come back into his life until Mindy had been gone for months and months."

"You didn't come back to Cottonwood County, true, but you already had a mutual secret, didn't you?"

"Mutual secret? We had no—"

"It was a good plan. Have Don drive to Denver and shoot your husband there before he changed his insurance beneficiary. You were separated, so it took a while for the inquiry to get to you. By that time you'd come up here and killed Mindy while Don was safely in jail."

"Kill Mindy? *No.* Why on earth would I kill Mindy?"

"I could say as an even exchange. But it was more—it was safety."

"Safety? Oh, God, *no.* I've been so afraid. It was all Don."

"He had an airtight alibi for Mindy's death. As you did for your husband's."

"He killed her later. He hid her away and killed her later. After he was out of jail. He was crazy. Always crazy. He wanted me and nothing—nothing—was going to stop him. He told me—Oh, God!" She was scarily convincing. "He'd killed my husband and he killed Mindy. He said so we'd be together. I had no idea—"

"And your aunt? She didn't get in Don's way, but she got in yours."

Her head came up slowly. With tears still slipping down her cheeks she said, "That bitch."

I don't know that I've ever been that chilled.

"Don buried her in Loop Field. Did Mindy know?" I shook my head. "More likely it was a straight up swap. His wife for your husband. But then Don brought the body back here. He had leverage to force you to come back here, to live together. Maybe you didn't even mind that much while you waited for the insurance benefit. But now it was going to be paid out. Don would have recognized your restlessness—he'd seen it before. So he started to let water into Loop Field. Letting you know that if you tried to leave he'd expose you. Expose himself at the same time, but he was willing to do that. So Don had to go. But how. Austin telling you Brian was here gave you the opportunity."

The breath she released was half exasperated, half self-satisfied. "He'd been crying to me for a week that his daddy wanted help dying. Kade wouldn't do it. Austin would say yes, then no, then yes. I was sick of it.

"That day he called and said Brian had begged him again and he'd brought him here. He was in the truck, crying. Couldn't decide whether to go back or to leave like his daddy had said.

"It came to me in a flash. Don would die trying to help the neighbor he'd been a bastard to. Had to work fast, but that was okay. I told Austin he had to do what his daddy wanted, to meet me at an old house we used—clear the other side of the ranch. Do you know, I almost sent him to the same place Greg ended up going? Luck was with me, though. Called Don and said I was going to Red Sail Rock to meet somebody and he couldn't stop me. He was half crazy when he got here. It was some scene. Him screaming, Brian begging us to leave. Some scene." She smiled.

Sam McCracken had called Don a scheming sociopath. He and Loriana had been well-matched.

"How did you get Don from up here—" I looked around, hoping to see Shelton's deputy hat peeking around Red Sail Rock. Nothing. "—to the ditch?"

"I walked to the edge and he followed me the way he always did. A good push and over he went." She looked me up and down. "Might be harder with you."

That was no surprise. Even before she'd stopped denying, it was clear what she had in mind. I wished Shelton would show up.

"And then you drowned him."

"Took hold of his belt, dragged, and it was done."

"That left Brian."

She sighed gently. "If there'd been time I could've let nature take its course, but I had to get to Austin before he melted down completely and came back here. Brian was out of the chair by then. Wasn't hard to smother him. Those things had spilled out of the wheelchair, so I took them. Thought they'd do more good than they did. Damned Shelton hardly held Paul for a minute and a half."

If she was thinking about Shelton, it was time—

"Now!" I hollered, and they all came around the corner. All three of them.

Still no cavalry.

Paul held a rolled-up floor mat, Cas carried a tire iron, and Diana had a safety flare.

Loriana smiled. "I'm leaving."

"No."

"What are you going to do? Shoot me?"

"Make a citizen's arrest." My phone rang. I ignored it.

She laughed. "Good-bye, Elizabeth. You do have some intelligence, after all."

Paul stepped up, blocking her.

My phone's audio caller ID announced: "You have a call from Cottonwood County Sheriff."

I grabbed the phone and answered. "Where the hell are you?"

I'd accidentally hit speakerphone. Not that it mattered at this point.

"Uh, beg your pardon, Ma'am." It was not Shelton. Or Alvaro for that matter. Lloyd Sampson.

"Where is Shelton? He knows—"

"He's been unavoidably detained here at the Walterstons'. "

"*Unavoidably detained?* What could be more important than capturing a multiple murderer?"

"He's delivering a baby. Hannah Chaney's in labor and—"

I lost some of what Sampson said because I was holding on to Paul's arm.

"—asks if you'd bring her—"

"I'm going," Paul said.

"You can't. We can't *leave* her. She'll be gone for good. She's killed all these people."

"—here to the house—"

He growled, "I'm taking the kid's truck. You want to come, get in and we'll take her, too."

"You can't drive, Paul. You and Cas are the ones who can control her."

"—before saying anything to her that might—"

"My SUV. I'll drive. Get her in back between you."

I hung up on Sampson still giving instructions as we all ran to it with Paul and Cas propelling Loriana.

"Go faster, dammit," Paul roared from the back seat, where he and Cas had Loriana wedged between them.

"This is a very bad road."

"I should've driven," Diana said.

"Not if I want this SUV to stay in one piece."

Diana, apparently the only one to hear my comment, glared.

From the back seat came, "Paul, this is silly. You know me." I was betting Loriana had a hand on his arm and was stroking.

"Get your hands off me. I'm a married man."

So maybe not his arm.

"You don't even know if it's your baby," she said mildly.

He growled.

"Could be Terry's. Or Don's."

I projected to the back seat, while keeping my eyes on the dusty track ahead. "That's unlikely, since you made up the stories about Don having affairs. He only wanted you."

"My wife. My baby," Paul declared.

"Cas—it is Cas, right?"

There was a shifting of bodies in the back seat. "For God's sake," Cas said with such disgust it must have penetrated even Loriana's armor.

We came over the last rise and down to the house. I pulled up behind two sheriff's department all-wheel-drive vehicles and Tom's pickup.

"Stay here. I'll go get—" Diana was already out of the front passenger seat, jogging toward the front steps.

"The hell with this."

"No, Paul, wait—"

Before I could turn, Paul jerked open the back door and was gone.

I heard a grunt behind me, and as I completed my turn I saw Loriana had something stuck into Cas' ribs.

"Leave the engine running and get out, Elizabeth," she ordered. "Now."

It might not be a gun. She might be faking.

I couldn't risk it.

I did what she said.

She held on to him as they got out of the back seat, using him as a shield. But she didn't need one because nobody was in sight except me.

She maneuvered behind the wheel, gave Cas a hard shove and took off with the door not yet closed.

She'd shoved Cas right into me. In trying to avoid hitting me hard, he went down heavily on the arm in a sling. I went down, too, but with a glancing blow. I popped back up and started after the SUV, turning fast in the circular area.

As I did, I saw Tom bang out of the back door and angle in from the right. But no way would he be able to outrun it. And if he did—

"Gun! She has a gun!" I screamed.

Another SUV was coming up the road, but without the driver knowing what was happening, Loriana in my vehicle would pass it by and be gone.

I heard footsteps on the porch behind me. Richard Alvaro passed, with Lloyd Sampson a little distance behind. I kept running.

Mike. It was Mike's SUV coming up the drive. Only a vehicle-length away. In seconds, they'd pass and he'd be a few feet from her—

"She has a gun!" I shouted again.

As if he could hear me.

In that instant, Mike's SUV made a wrenching left-hand turn right into Loriana's path.

Loriana must have wrenched the wheel, because my SUV also made a sharp left-hand turn. She was trying to evade him, accelerating. If she cleared the end of his SUV—

The crash stopped me in my tracks.

But Tom must have picked up speed, because he was there, yanking the door open, dragging Loriana out.

"Gun!" I shouted. It was lost in shouts from Alvaro to "Get on the ground! Get on the ground!"

He'd closed in, and he and Tom had her down. At least he had a gun, too.

Mike ran around the back of his vehicle, looking excited, but all in one piece.

Everyone was in one piece.

I looked back as Diana caught up and grabbed my arm. Cas was on his feet.

I slowed.

Deputies Alvaro and Sampson hustled Loriana, now in handcuffs, toward an official vehicle.

"We'll get your account in a minute. Stay here," Richard commanded me.

Mike, Tom, Diana, and I met halfway. Grinning and panting.

"Great move, Mike," Tom clapped him on the back.

"You, too," Mike said.

"Did you hear Elizabeth shouting she had a gun?" Diana asked.

"I heard," Tom said. "Thanks for the warning, Elizabeth."

"The warning was meant for you to get *away* from her. Not keep running *toward* her."

Delayed adrenaline and fear jangled through me.

"Mike," Diana said, "how did you know to stop the SUV? You couldn't hear the shouts, could you?"

"Nope. But Elizabeth running after her new vehicle hollering, with another woman driving it? I knew it wouldn't be good if it got past me. Besides, even if I hadn't seen Elizabeth waving her arms and shouting, I'd've known it wasn't her driving. That thing was *moving*."

I glared at him, but he missed it. He was looking at my brand new SUV, now with a crumpled right front corner and a spray of red dust all over its hood and up both sides.

"Now it looks like a real Wyoming vehicle."

And then we heard a baby's first cry from the house.

Epilogue

IT WAS A fine, warm day—probably the last one in Wyoming until July—if you wore enough layers.

Tom had invited a number of people to his ranch for a post-church lunchtime cookout.

Mike had driven Diana, her kids, me, and a triple batch of brownies—without peanuts—while my new SUV was in the shop. His had been fixed in record time. The Hometown Hero Factor at work.

As we stepped out the house's back door onto the deck, I spotted Aunt Gee giving Mrs. Parens a triumphant look. What were those two rivaling over now?

Before I could begin to guess, Connie Walterston engulfed me in a hug.

"I haven't had a chance to properly thank you for all you did, Elizabeth. You'll never know much it means to me, to us."

I hugged back, but didn't mind obeying Aunt Gee's peremptory, "Elizabeth."

Diana was already there and I joined her in sitting on the edge of the deck practically at Aunt Gee and Mrs. P's feet. Mike, they said, had been sent off for drinks.

"I do believe your eyebrows have improved," Mrs. Parens said.

"Definitely," concurred Aunt Gee. "A shame your new vehicle sustained damage."

"A pickup truck would not have been so easily damaged," Mrs. Parens said.

Aunt Gee ignored that. "It's fortunate that Michael's connection was able to take it so quickly for repairs."

"Yes."

"You're sighing again," Diana said to me, then added bracingly, "that's why you have insurance."

"Never brings it back to new." Then my mood improved. "Speaking of insurance, did you hear about the Walterstons'?"

"There will be a payout on the accidental death benefit," said Mrs. Parens.

What was I thinking? Of course they'd heard. But I refused to let that dim my pleasure.

"Yup. Murder qualifies under the policy Taylorman sold them. He was so busy worrying about proving that Brian's death wasn't an accident that he failed to notice murder was included."

"Justice," Diana said with a satisfied breath. And the rest of us nodded.

✧ ✧ ✧ ✧

DEPUTIES SHELTON AND Alvaro arrived just in time for two events.

The first was Tamantha presenting me with a cowboy hat. She had picked it out herself, she told me proudly. It was brown and it fit pretty well, which was as much as I knew about cowboy hats.

I hugged her. Hard.

The second event was lunch.

Richard let it slip that they were late because they'd stopped by to see Hannah, Paul, and little Shelly. Yes, they'd named the girl after Shelton.

We'd already had a rather heated conversation about his ignoring my messages. He had claimed—with some backing from Tom—that he'd been too busy with the mother-to-be to receive a complete picture of what was going on.

I'm not entirely convinced.

When I found myself next to him beside the condiments, I took the opportunity to say, "Don't think I don't know that you played me, Deputy Shelton."

"No idea what you're talking about, Ms. Danniher."

"You suspected Loriana all along, didn't you?"

"What would make you say that?"

"There was no reason not to tell me that Earl died from eating a brownie with peanuts in it. But you wanted me to dig up that information myself. So that while I was digging I'd also pick up other pieces."

"A happy accident. Just a happy accident."

AFTER EATING, I wandered out to a bench beside a fence. Three horses grazed on the other side of the fence and not too close. My side of the fence gave a nice view of the back of the house and all the people gathered.

It was also as far away as I could get from the temptation of a third brownie.

Before long, all four of the Walterstons assembled near the horses.

Their body language and voices said they were discussing something more emotional than Tom Burrell's stable.

The horses munched their way closer to me and the family followed, cutting the distance in half.

"I'll be ditch boss," Jaden said, loud enough for me to hear.

"You can't be. You're in Laramie," Kade scoffed.

"I'll quit UW. Come back here, take over the ranch, and be ditch boss."

"You don't want to run the ranch," Austin said.

"*It's a Wonderful Life.*" Only when they turned to look at me did I realize I'd said that out loud.

None of them appeared to get the connection that was so clear in my head. "The movie. You know, Jimmy Stewart, Donna Reed, Ward Bond, and a slew of other great character actors."

"We know the movie," Austin said. "It's like on all the time at Christmas. It doesn't have anything to do with the ditch."

"Yes, it does. You have a young man who loves and respects his father but doesn't want to pursue the same goals. He's going off to the wide world. Only his father is suddenly struck down. The young man takes over his father's business. Setting aside what he thought he wanted—"

"No," Connie said decisively. "You are not going to do that, Jaden. You're not. We'll figure out a way…"

"Like what?" Jaden said, half challenging, half hopeful.

"I don't know, but—"

"He was only supposed to stay a year, right? The guy in the movie," Kade said.

I nodded. "But he ends up staying for good because—"

"Of World War I, and his brother's a war hero while he can't go in the Army because he has a bad leg."

"Not World War I—" I said.

Kade talked over me. "But there's no world war going on and Jaden's leg is fine. So a year should do it."

"You're saying Jaden quits UW and comes back to be ditch boss for a year, and then what?" Austin demanded.

I tried again. "He didn't stay on because of World War I or II—"

"A year wouldn't do it," Jaden said.

"Boys, let Elizabeth finish—"

"If you give the year at the end, it would."

"—it was because—"

"The end of what?"

"After you graduate, you dope."

"But what about now?" Austin demanded.

"—what she's trying to say."

"—the brother got married and the father-in-law offered him a great job," I finally got out loud enough to be heard.

Jaden gave me a you're-crazy-lady look. "I haven't been offered a job."

"Even if you are," I said, "you'd have to put it off a couple years. But that's not so bad. It would all work. Have Kade be ditch boss now and next year, putting off starting college one year. Austin takes over his senior year and does another year, just like Kade. Then Jaden comes back—"

"Jaden comes back for two years, runs the ranch and is ditch boss, until I finish up," Kade said.

"Then you'd run the ranch like you want to do and I can take off," Jaden said.

Kade nodded. "And a Walterston would always be ditch boss. The way it's supposed to be."

The three of them looked at each other, each slowly giving a nod of commitment. They turned and looked at their mother, who had tears in her eyes.

She opened her arms and they all came together.

FROM THE BENCH, I watched Tom Burrell and Mike Paycik. Both such good men.

For no reason I could think of, a conversation with Dell slid into my thoughts.

You're great at it. It's what you've always wanted to do. It's what you're meant to do.

A year ago I was in the top tier of my profession. I had a rhythm, a stride that was working great and advancing my career beyond what I'd dreamed when I started.

I'd also had a hole in my gut—and my heart—from the recognition of what my marriage wasn't.

Then I thought of seven months ago when I'd arrived in Cottonwood County, Wyoming. My career shredded to a stick figure that might blow away at any moment. My marriage gone—no, worse than gone, far worse. A ghost still in need of exorcism.

My gut—and my heart—shaky at best.

I stopped, considering the metaphorical state of those organs now.

Healing. Definitely healing.

"Elizabeth, c'mon!" Mike called from over by the house. "Tom, you're closest—go get her and bring her back, so she stops brooding over there alone."

Obediently, Tom came across the opening to me. As he neared, he studied my face. I took great satisfaction in tipping my chin down so the brim of my new hat shadowed my expression, as he'd done so many times to me.

"Is that what you're doing—brooding?" he asked.

"Thinking."

"Deciding," he amended.

I flicked him a look.

"I mean about your job."

He did, but he meant other things, too.

Life in rural Wyoming could get complicated.

Yes, he had kissed me and Mike had kissed me...

Okay, in the name of journalistic accuracy: Yes, we had kissed each other.

Each seemed to know the other had an interest in me. So shouldn't they be at each other's throats like ordinary men? Instead, I had a pair of brothers-in-arms, all full of mutual respect and friendship.

So in some ways the complications had more to do with Tom and Mike than with me.

Didn't they?

Tom studied me a moment longer, peering into the hat shadow like a fortune teller assessing tea leaves. "You're staying."

Okay, so set up a fortune-telling tent for Abraham Lincoln's good-looking cousin at the next carnival. "I'm not going," I said. "Not yet."

He nodded slowly. "That's a big difference."

"Long-term, I don't know where I want to..." I almost said go, but that precluded one possibility I wasn't ready to preclude. "Be."

Slowly, he looked around at the scene here, then seemed to focus more distantly on the dramatic backdrop of snow-topped peaks. "Worse places to be while you figure it out."

I mimicked him, looking at the people gathered, laughing and talking, then at the majesty that surrounded us. Slowly, I smiled. "True."

"And it's a great afternoon for a ride." Tom flicked the brim of my hat lightly. "After all, you don't want to be accused of being all hat and no cattle—or in your case no horse. After the crowd thins out, Tamantha's going to exercise Roxanne and she's made a special request that you join us."

"If you think I'm getting back on Babe—"

"No, no. I have another horse in mind for you today." His eyes glinted. "Maybe a cutter. We could move some cattle and—"

"Very funny, Burrell. And then I'll join the rodeo and become a trick rider."

"If you wanted to do that, I wouldn't count you out, Elizabeth Margaret Danniher. Wouldn't count you out at all."

I was touched.

And, I realized, I wouldn't count myself out, either.

~ THE END ~

If you enjoyed Last Ditch, I hope you'll consider leaving a review, to let your fellow readers know about your experience.

For news about upcoming books, subscribe to Patricia McLinn's free newsletter.

www.PatriciaMclinn.com/newsletter

Caught Dead in Wyoming series

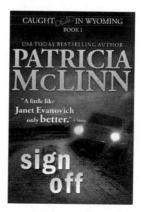

SIGN OFF

With her marriage over and her career derailed by her ex, top-flight reporter Elizabeth "E.M." Danniher lands in tiny Sherman. But the case of a missing deputy and a determined little girl drag her out of her fog.

Get SIGN OFF now!

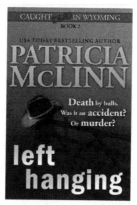

LEFT HANGING

From the deadly tip of the rodeo queen's tiara to toxic "agricultural byproducts" ground into the arena dust, TV reporter Elizabeth "E.M." Danniher receives a murderous introduction to the world of rodeo.

Get LEFT HANGING now!

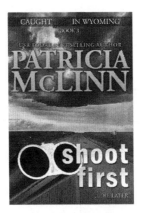

SHOOT FIRST

Death hits close to home for Elizabeth "E.M." Danniher – or, rather, close to Hovel, as she's dubbed her decrepit rental house in rustic Sherman, Wyoming.

Get SHOOT FIRST now!

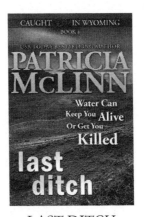

LAST DITCH

A man in a wheelchair goes missing in rough country in the Big Horn Basin of Wyoming. Elizabeth "E.M." Danniher and KWMT-TV colleague Mike Paycik immediately join the search. But soon they're on a search of a different kind – a search for the truth.

Get LAST DITCH now!

What people are saying about the
CAUGHT DEAD IN WYOMING series

"While the mystery itself is twisty-turny and thoroughly engaging, it's the smart and witty writing that I loved the best."
                              —Diane Chamberlain, bestselling author

"She writes a little like Janet Evanovich only better."

"E.M.'s internal monologues are sharp, snappy and often hilarious."

"McLinn has created in E.M. a female protagonist who is flawed but likable, never silly or cartoonish, and definitely not made of cardboard."

If you particularly enjoy connected books—as I do!—try these:
A Place Called Home series
Wyoming Wildflowers series
The Bardville, Wyoming series
The Wedding Series

Explore a complete list of all Patricia's books
patriciamclinn.com/patricias-books

About the author

USA Today bestselling author Patricia McLinn's novels—cited by reviewers for warmth, wit and vivid characterization – have won numerous regional and national awards and been on national bestseller lists.

In addition to her romance and women's fiction books, Patricia is the author of the Caught Dead in Wyoming mystery series, which adds a touch of humor and romance to figuring out whodunit.

Patricia received BA and MSJ degrees from Northwestern University. She was a sports writer (Rockford, Ill.), assistant sports editor (Charlotte, N.C.) and—for 20-plus years—an editor at The Washington Post. She has spoken about writing from Melbourne, Australia to Washington, D.C., including being a guest speaker at the Smithsonian Institution.

She is now living in Northern Kentucky, and writing full-time. Patricia loves to hear from readers through her website, Facebook and Twitter.

Visit with Patricia:
Website: patriciamclinn.com
Facebook: facebook.com/PatriciaMcLinn
Twitter: @PatriciaMcLinn
Pinterest: pinterest.com/patriciamclinn

ISBN: 978-1-939215-62-8

83092884R00210

Made in the USA
San Bernardino, CA
21 July 2018